NETI, NETI

NOT THIS, NOT THIS

Anjum Hasan is the author of two novels, *The Cosmopolitans* and *Lunatic in my Head* (shortlisted for the Crossword Book Award), a collection of short stories, *Difficult Pleasures* (shortlisted for the Hindu Literary Prize and the Crossword Book Award), and a book of poetry, *Street on the Hill*. She lives in Bangalore.

NETI, NETI

NOT THIS, NOT THIS

ANJUM HASAN

ROLI

First published in India in 2009
This edition, 2016

Roli Books Pvt. Ltd.
M-75, Greater Kailash II Market, New Delhi 110 048
Phone: +91 (011) 40682000
E-mail: info@rolibooks.com
Website: www.rolibooks.com
Also at Chennai & Mumbai

ISBN: 9788186939512

Typeset in Guardi by Roli Books Pvt. Ltd.
Printed in New Delhi, India

Contents

Hot Winter Day

First, the few birds remaining on earth calling urgently through the open window. Then the landlord, arguing with any one of the three nodal visitors of his morning – the jasmine-seller, the greens-seller, the milkman. Finally, the phone shrieking with all the insistence of the person calling. Sophie Das crawled out of bed, held the phone a few inches away from her ear and went to stand by the living room window. She liked to, as she talked to Swami, watch out for her landlord's two-year-old grandson who sometimes strayed out to play in the little mound of sand by the roadside, or climbed his grandfather's scooter, or just stood there, arrested by a mysterious thought, till his grandparents decided he'd had enough freedom for the morning and dragged him back, bolting the gate behind him.

'Sophie, I've got the loan,' announced Swami. 'I asked my dad for some dough to make the down payment but he won't hear of it. In fact, he could buy me a car off the shelf if he wanted to. But no one encourages that – not the car companies, not the retailers, not the banks. Anyway, I had to take another loan to make the down payment.'

'What did he say?'

'I didn't want a lecture on the meaning of life etcetera so I've kept this whole car plan to myself. But last week I just said to him straight – Appa, can you give me a bit of cash for this loan I'm taking, and instead of being curious he just quoted the Upanishads or something at me.'

'I don't like loans either,' said Sophie.

'What do you mean you don't like loans?'

'Just the thought of being caught in the web of them.'

'It's not about liking loans, it's about liking the things you can buy with them,' explained Swami patiently. 'Just last week you said you liked the Chevy Tavera.'

Sophie was actually car-blind. Swami was always pointing out different makes to her, but where he saw individuality and beauty, she saw something on four wheels that moved. The gleaming black and white Tavera had looked impressive in the showroom window – that was all, whereas Swami's longing for a car was a capacious thing that could suck him in, make him a shadow that would acquire features and personality only when he became the owner of a car. All Sophie had heard her boyfriend discuss during the last few months was the car dream ('I'm not saying I can afford a luxury sedan but there's still no harm drooling over an Audi … I hate small cars, I hate small cars, they're so nineties … Did you see that? Brilliant piece of work – sporty style, great safety features, high torque which ensures smoothness in stop-start traffic …'). Sophie so badly wanted Swami to shut up. The thought made her guilty and she tried to take some interest.

'So what happens if you can't repay the loan?' she asked.

'They'll take back the car, naturally.'

'I'll go out in it when it's actually your car,' she said, knowing she always spoilt it just when she decided to be good, as if there was a part of her that resisted the idea of being nice to Swami whenever another part of her made a conscious effort to.

'It *will* be my car the day I buy it. Sophie, loans make the world go round. People are even doling out easy monthly instalments for their cheap little cellphones and feeling proud about it. Soon you'll be able to buy a pair of jeans on EMIs.'

'But I don't want to have anything to do with this. I'm going to stay out of it.'

'Just because some lady in a book went bankrupt and died?'

Stop, that's Madame Bovary, thought Sophie. Most of the garbage Sophie had read in her twenty-five years had faded against the light of three major works – *Madame Bovary, Vivekananda: Awakener of Modern India* and *Swami and Friends.* She wanted to explain to Swami that Madame Bovary was no loan junkie. It was just that her longing for love and adventure often took the form of buying things she didn't need with money she didn't have. Instead of living one takes loans, Sophie thought grandly, then yawned noiselessly and wished she could crawl back into the wide camera angles of her dream. Once she woke up, everything narrowed down. Everything was degrees of pettiness.

Swami tried again. 'What I need to decide is whether to get a SUV, which is the sturdiest, or a three-box sedan simply because they're the best looking. Sophie? Say something!'

Mani, the toddler, emerged from the opposite house and sat down in the middle of the lane; his grandmother followed with his breakfast in a small steel bowl. Sophie tried to wave to him.

'Sophie, I just called to figure out which type to go with and instead you're being a pig about this.'

'*I'm* being a pig? *I* want to drive a car so big it'll swallow people if they so much as try to press their horns?'

'Fine then, I'll decide myself.'

Mani squatted on the ground with his mouth clamped shut, deaf to his long-suffering grandmother's entreaties.

'Of course you'll decide yourself,' said Sophie. 'You always do.' But Swami had already hung up.

Whatever, whispered Sophie, as she went into the kitchen and toasted a slice of dry bread over the gas. She then put four small blobs of butter on four corners of the toast and waited for them to melt. In the morning, everything felt *heavy*. A knife had the weight of an axe. Even from its distance, Swami's voice pressed so hard against her ear, she would do anything to cut it off.

After a few minutes he called back as Sophie knew he would.

'We need to feel happy about it two years from now, five years from now. It's a long-term thing,' he said, while Sophie said nothing – a blank space where the enthusiastic girlfriend should have been.

Sophie sat crosslegged and barefoot on the balcony behind the house from where she could see the two-storied choultry that stood at the far end of a balding field in which cars were parked and a cow nosed about in some dried bushes. The screeching of nadeswarams and the laughter of women in saris embroidered with flashing golden blossoms signalled a wedding reaching its climax. All weddings in the choultry were alike – a faded purple, green and red canvas shamiana with scalloped edges went up, the drums and pipes rang out all evening and a video camera (with a boy on the cameraman's side, beaming a blinding white floodlight into people's faces) followed the ascent of the bridegroom to the first floor where his bride awaited him. Wedding guests would spill into the lanes around Sophie's house – women wobbling in their uncomfortable-looking heels, thin boys shouting out urgent-sounding messages to each other, sticky babies enjoying screaming competitions. In the mornings the ceremonies that had abated in the night would reach their logical and satisfying conclusion. Sophie was a hidden spectator to these weddings and she liked it that they were so predictable. There was something about this human love of custom that appealed to her. Her own customs were much more modest: for instance, because it was January, she sat outdoors for a while every morning, soaking in the Bangalore sun before it got too hot – a throwback to all the winter mornings she had spent turning brown in the gentler sun of her hometown, Shillong.

She lit her cigarette and tossed the burnt match into a flowerpot. Then, recalling her landlord's response to seeing junk thrown in flowerpots, she went on her knees and buried the match deep into the soil supporting the rubber plant. It's not a very healthy plant anyway, she thought. The six pots, neatly arrayed on her balcony, had been handed over to her by the landlord and his wife soon after she'd moved in. Getting Sophie to garden was one of Mr Bhatt's ways of trying to civilize her.

'Give them water yeveryday,' Mr Bhatt had said as he and his wife and their maid came up one morning, each carrying a pot and forming a little procession. They laid them out in a row. Then they came back with three more.

'This tulsi here, you can eat the leaves. It's very good for stomach-aches,' Mrs Bhatt said, as she heaved the pot over the last of the steps. She was a shorter, plumper, kinder version of her husband.

Sophie had tried to create another small custom out of nurturing the plants. She watered them as often as she remembered to, picked black ants off the geranium, tore out weeds once in a while, but they refused to respond to her. She'd given up on them now that they'd been on her balcony for almost a year and showed no signs of improving.

A whole year, she thought. But what did the fragile habits built over a year count for when for decades her parents had lived in the same small town, bought their vegetables from the same vendor, got their shoes fixed by the same cobbler, bought the same brand of biscuits to go with their tea, known about the family affairs of their tailor, become close friends with their dentist and added not one extra word to their stock of half-a-dozen phrases in Shillong's local language, Khasi – phrases they threaded into their conversations with maid-servants and taxi-drivers.

Sophie's father taught English Literature in a government school for boys. Her mother taught history in a girls' school. There was something absurd about this parallel because Mr Das had a PhD and was once a college lecturer who'd considered a job at the university within easy reach. Instead, he'd moved down the scale while Mrs Das, who started by giving tuitions at home to supplement the family income, had moved up the scale. They were unhappy equals now and nowhere was this more evident than in their very different ways of marking test papers. Mr Das would plant large red circles around misspelt words, mixed tenses and split infinitives, often printing remarks in the margins in his neat upright hand: 'You have mixed up the sequence of events in the novel' or 'Answer the question! Do not digress.' He'd work his way through a pile of papers in an afternoon, then lean back smoking his cigarette, unperturbed by how rarely his students were able to meet his exacting standards.

Sophie's mother, on the other hand, would peruse each sentence carefully, her reading glasses slipping down her nose and her mouth a downturned curve.

'Nothing,' she might say occasionally, '... nothing this girl has understood,' speaking in a manner common to both Sophie's parents – a manner of addressing everyone present and yet no one. Long, pregnant moments of silence would follow as she pored over the rest of the answer. 'I have to fail her,' she would whisper then and the sorrow of this would make her sigh, tear off her glasses and step out into the garden for some fresh air.

Why had Sophie left that town where everything was so wonderfully fixed in its place? She thought back to that cold afternoon in November. She'd stood at the parapet that ran around the garden, smoking with her back to the house, the hand holding the cigarette well out of sight. Mukulika, her younger sister, was trying to kill a kitten. Her mouth was bright red with kwai, her eyes glittered and from one knee hung a dirty bandage with a dark spot of iodine on it. She was tying the kitten to the branch of a tree with a chewed-up pink ribbon looped around its neck and reciting an impromptu poem to it – 'The thought of suicide/ has never crossed my mind/ though I have always lived beside/ the orange tree.' Sophie had turned her back on her sister's scruffy evilness – Mukulika had for weeks been trying to fend off the boredom of being fifteen and unloved by inventing more and more advanced ways of tormenting the tiny ball of fluff. She had made smoky bonfires of her old school notebooks and swung the kitten over the topmost flames; she had left it madly scrambling in a dipper full of soapy water; she had climbed a mora placed atop a coffee table to leave it stranded on a high cupboard. There were months to go before school reopened and Muku's attention wandered away from the indestructible kitten. Whatever the object of her rage, however, Muku always wreaked the greatest damage on herself. Her body was like a tirelessly worked upon wall of graffiti – covered with little cuts of dried blood and chocolate-brown burn marks, multicoloured bruises and jellied wounds hidden under soiled layers of gauze – signatures of a mysterious provenance that nothing would erase. Now she let the snarling kitten unleash a frenzy of scratches on her hands as she tried to knot the ribbon around its throat. Sophie, meanwhile, smoked cigarette after cigarette from the packet stuffed in the pocket of her jeans and waited for that fated passer-by to notice her, recognize her and take her away to that contextless place called eternal happiness.

Then she heard the tapping of heels on the quiet pavement and saw Killer Queen approaching. As children, Sophie and her sister had named this local madwoman after the song for her demented stare, her habit of scolding strangers on the road, her fake crocodile skin purse, her clickety stilettos. Sophie watched as she came down the road dressed in musty black velvet and dark glasses, her bun enclosed in a cobwebby-looking hairnet – this permanent fixture of Shillong's streets. Watching the way she walked, with an assurance that belied the troubled nature of her mind, her head moving as alertly as a sparrow's, Sophie felt an overwhelming affection for her. Who was she, this unchanging relic from her childhood? Where did she go on these afternoon sojourns that Sophie and her sister had been secretly witnessing all their lives? Suddenly Killer Queen stopped short on the pavement and looked up at Sophie. Sophie looked down at her, unable to fathom the expression behind the goggles.

'What are you staring at?' screeched Killer Queen. 'Haven't you seen a good-looking woman before?'

Sophie and Killer Queen stared transfixed at each other and a terror took root in Sophie that would banish her to Bangalore. At that point, though, she merely shrugged, flicked ash from her cigarette and mumbled, 'I wasn't staring.'

But the image remained with her, seeping into dreams whose logic demanded only one thing – escape. Tracy Chapman singing, 'Don't you know you gotta run, run, run, run, run, run, ru-un, run?' Teeth-grinding, absolute, out of reach, never to be found again ... escape. The Killer Queen had summed it up – why was Sophie there at the parapet, when she'd spent a whole lifetime of afternoons there? What was she staring at when there was nothing to see?

So Sophie had, one year ago, substituted the view from that garden for the view from this balcony: a cow nosing about in the peelings left behind by cooks who had gathered the previous day outside the choultry to chop pumpkins, string beans, slice a small mountain of potatoes for the wedding lunch. Sophie tossed her cigarette stub over the wall onto a vacant lot and went back inside thinking, as she often did, that there was not a person in the world who would understand how she could have turned her whole life upside down because of a stray remark made by a passing madwoman. As soon as Sophie reached Bangalore, Killer Queen retreated into a fairy tale and casting about for a reason to be there, Sophie had attached herself to the first boy who understood the essentially shitty nature of her job and held her hand when they crossed roads.

Every morning, as Sophie was waking up, Swami, back home from his call centre shift, was getting into bed, cellphone in one hand and a slim, tattered novel in the other. Every morning he embarked afresh on the reading of *Swami and Friends,* a novel about a hapless schoolboy. Sophie had gifted him her copy soon after they'd met. Swami didn't really read but for Sophie's sake he tried every morning to penetrate this story about his namesake – it began with an account of an unhappy Monday at school. As soon as he got past the first few lines, however, a sudden black bomb of exhaustion would flatten him and, pinned under it, he would try to read faster and faster in order to get to the point (for in novels, as in everything, shouldn't there be a point?). But reading faster didn't help – the lines started blurring and soon the characters were speaking to him in the American voices he heard all day. He'd go under that glorious wave of sleep in which hours passed like a tight snap of the fingers and then he'd wake up and step over the fallen book as he rushed to the bathroom to shave and think about cars, car-loans, loans in general, what one could buy with them, how best to repay them, the importance of planning for the long-term, his longing for a promotion, Sophie, marriage, eternal happiness.

Even though fiction's apparent lack of a function annoyed Swami, the thought of *Swami and Friends* did sometimes weigh upon him as he sat in his fluorescent tube-lit cubicle and answered calls from people in business establishments across America, people who had problems figuring out how their credit card machines worked or who wanted to know how to set up an online transaction programme or understand what a Point of Sale system meant. Swami knew he had to get through the novel for Sophie to cooperate with him on the matter of the car.

Sophie was now heating up her iron and asking herself the question that was starting to become a routine, morning, accompaniment-to-ironing question, namely: what had changed? She had formulated an answer over the last few weeks, the answer being – everything. Swami had changed, she had changed, she and Swami as a unit had changed. Swami was once an echo of the child Swami of the novel – in constant flight from the intractable adult world of rules and responsibilities. The fictional Swami hated school and believed in spending his life playing cricket or sitting by the riverside eating lime pickle, but was frustrated at every turn by the obstacles adults flung at him. Sophie's Swami suffered no angst, drove his bike through the shocking traffic impervious to its mad howling, could get excited by an aeroplane in the sky or the year's first rain. He had that mixture of innocence and craftiness that would see him through without either hurting anyone or failing himself.

When Sophie first met him, he didn't have a job but in order to escape his Upanishads-quoting father he would spend the days away from the house – nursing a beer in a pub, getting his bike repeatedly washed, acting as a half-baked sound engineer when his friends – members of a deafening band called Little Idlis – played concerts. Sometimes, desperate for a little money, he would fall upon the strangest jobs. For a few weeks he was a subagent for the sale of battery-operated, Chinese-made, tennis racquet-style mosquito swatters, whose strings zapped the bloodsuckers with a satisfying buzz and crackle. Then, one of the children he sent out every morning to swarm the traffic junctions and peddle the racquets to motorists was run over and Swami no longer felt like continuing in that line of work. Another time he found employment in a company that exported fresh flowers to Europe, a job he abandoned one ghastly week in February when he had to take about a hundred phone calls from British and German retailers frantic to get in enough roses in time for Valentine's Day. They were going nuts because the African country that was their other major supplier had suddenly erupted into war.

Sophie had loved Swami's laid-back nature, even his laziness. He would often wait for her at their favourite pub in the evenings and she would tell him bitchy stories about her colleagues when she joined him after work. He'd say – fuck all this *working*, man. For what? They would get drunk on this and beer – the stupidity of all this working.

Then a speeding lorry trying to overtake him from the blind side knocked down Swami as he was riding his beloved bike. He managed to get away with just bruises; the bike, though, was mangled beyond repair. He almost cried with anger and decided he didn't want to ride bikes anymore. A car, he declared, was what he'd always wanted. But a car – not just any car but the best possible one – meant getting a car loan and one needed a steady income to get a loan.

For the first couple of weeks after joining the call centre, Swami told Sophie correspondingly bitchy stories about his colleagues but soon he appeared to be enjoying his work, enjoying thinking about the car he would buy, enjoying thinking about money in itself – the crisp purity of it. Sophie no longer quite knew what to talk to him about. They had shared this looking askance at Bangalore's frenzy and now he had joined it. And thinking, as she ironed a kurta, of the weddings in the choultry, Sophie realized that much as she appreciated them from a distance, she wasn't at all sure she wanted to climb those steps with the floodlights in her face and wait for Swami to join her.

~

The doorbell rang in a series of slowly fading peals.

'Madam, please remove your underwear,' said Mr Bhatt, the landlord.

'Huh?'

'Underwear, underwear,' said Mr Bhatt urgently. For a few moments, the impatient Bhatt and the incredulous Sophie stared at each other. It was only when he gestured in the direction of the balcony that she understood. He had peeked out of the window on the landing and was objecting to the panties she had hung out to dry. Meanwhile, two-year-old Mani, for whom Sophie felt a helpless and unrequited love, looked up at her with his long-lashed, intelligent eyes and then began moving decisively towards the kitchen.

'Chinnappa has become the Residents' Welfare Association Secretary. Yesterday he said to me: Bhatt if you want to keep single ladies in your house you please take responsibility. *We* cannot take responsibility.'

Sophie knew Chinnappa. He had called the police last week, halfway through a very civilized party. (Four people drinking their beer, passing around joints, guffawing not with the intention of breeding envy in the hearts of the Residents' Welfare Association office-bearers but simply because life looked at from the perspective of a chilled Kingfisher on a Saturday night *was* funny.) Sophie's friend Ringo Saar had drifted out to the balcony to take a phone call and, trying to balance his beer bottle on the ledge, accidentally dropped it. The bottle crashed outside Chinnappa's kitchen door which was wedged against the side of Sophie's apartment building. Half an hour later, two plainclothesmen were seen unlatching the gate downstairs. Finding nowhere to hide it, Anu, another friend, ran up to the roof and dropped a pouch with a week's supply of weed in it into the rainwater tank. Sophie pushed the boys – Swami and Ringo Saar – into the bathroom, so that it was just her and Anu who faced the law. The law, given the hints dropped by the two moustached men with identically quilted jackets, was asking to be bought, but Sophie pretended she didn't know what they were getting at. Then Ringo Saar spoilt it all by barging out of the bathroom and asking the men to leave. A protracted argument followed, with the men insisting that Ringo Saar come to the police station with them and Ringo Saar going out and knocking off one empty beer bottle after another to demonstrate how the original bottle had fallen off by accident and that no one intended to kill Chinnappa. And as for the noise, what noise?

One of the men grabbed Ringo and the other started cross-questioning Sophie about why she was letting people make all this 'galata' (that uniquely Bangalorean shorthand for trouble, whatever its origins and whatever its aims) in her house. Didn't she know this was a respectable neighbourhood full of educated people – judges and doctors and headmasters? Sophie said: ask my landlord. I never make trouble. Go across the street and ask him. Leave us alone. To which the man said – drinking and smoking and talking too much? What job do you do? Software aah? Too much money aah? That's why you can open your mouth.

Ringo bored his eyes into the policeman who was holding

down his arm and asked with utter calm, 'Who gave you the permission to touch me, you cunt?'

The abuse, incomprehensible though it probably was to the policeman, made him bark out angrily at Ringo as he pushed him into a corner. Sophie saw from the unblinking, hatred-filled look on Ringo's face (usually a cheerful, jokey drummer boy whom she'd never known to even get indignant) that he was readying himself to hit out. She appealed for restraint and quickly sent Anu to get Mr Bhatt who appeared at the door within seconds. He'd been peering from a crack through his door, waiting to see if the entire gang would be marched out. A long discussion in Kannada ensued and finally the men were throwing dirty looks all around and zipping up their jackets.

Since that evening, Mr Bhatt had scowled wordlessly at Sophie whenever he met her in the lane.

Sophie was one of his tenants in this garish pink apartment, which was just about big enough to accommodate a normal-sized family but which Bhatt had partitioned into four, cramped two-room flats, fitting each with a tiny bathroom and kitchen, thereby able to take advantage of people like Sophie who, despite her small budget, preferred to live by herself instead of sharing a larger flat with someone else. The other matchsticks in this matchbox-sized house were hard to pin down – they were usually college-going boys who stayed for a few months at a time and then disappeared only to be replaced with another, equally shadowy, set. Four or five boys would, optimistically, stuff themselves into each flat and if their doors were ajar when Sophie passed by, she'd notice the astonishing leanness of their lives. Except for piles of books bearing enigmatic titles such as *C++, Cobol, dBase, SQL, Basic*, the rooms were always bare: there was never any evidence of what these boys slept on, what they ate, where their clothes were, how their pasts were concealed. They would be sprawled at different angles on the floor, talking to each other, living, as if, on air.

The nicest thing about the building was that both the upper floor flats had largish balconies and it was this that had decided it for Sophie. Sitting on the balcony, she could look at the world and the sky as she smoked or rest her eyes on the few leaves the Bhatts had given her. This flowerpot-giving implied she'd been singled out from the Bhatts' other tenants because she was a girl and alone. They felt responsible for her in some way. Even though Bhatt made inspection visits to each of the flats and even though she sometimes heard him haranguing the boys too, the scolding she got always had a moral edge to it. He would not mind, for instance, if the boys hung out underwear to dry, whereas in her case it implied a shocking looseness of character.

Now Bhatt walked into her living room, noticed the ashtray next to her breakfast plate and announced, 'Again you are smoking inside the house.' Sophie shoved the overflowing ashtray under a shelf.

Mr Bhatt lifted a curtain between his thumb and forefinger and asked, 'New?' When Sophie confessed, he assumed without asking that she had paid more for the curtains than she ought to have and gave her a lecture on the idiocy of those who shopped without comparing prices, described the new furnishings shop in the neighbourhood that had cheaper rates than most places in Commercial Street, gave her the number of the bus that would take her to Cottonpet where she would get curtains at wholesale prices, and finished by remarking on the pointlessness of buying new curtains when she had old ones, curtains being, in his view, purely functional things.

He looked into the bedroom, noticed an old tea stain on the floor by the bed and embarked on a fresh lecture on how important it was that she keep a maid and not destroy his floor. Sophie resisted the idea of hiring a maid, while Mr Bhatt's concern that his flat be kept in proper shape overrode, in this case, his passion for universal thrift. Sophie thought it was a scandal that he paid his own maid so little and would have hired her only to somewhat redeem the maid's situation, except that her preference for keeping house herself superseded this concern.

Then she remembered Mani and rushed to the kitchen.

He was sitting on the floor, his face glowing white in the cold sunshine of the open fridge and his hand inside a bottle of jam. Around him lay the debris of plunder – milk trickling from a sachet, an upturned bowl of chicken curry, scattered carrots and bhindis, a slab of butter smeared on the floor, a plastic bottle of juice on its side. Mani opened his mouth and pushed a fist glistening with pineapple jam into it.

Sophie bent down and stroked his head. This was the third time he had raided her fridge – behaviour that in his own home would have earned him a slow twist of the ear and a swift slap on the face, which Mani would have answered with a two-hour, red-faced howling match. Sophie believed that if she let Mani go on emptying her fridge and cuddled him every time he did, he would reciprocate, in some Pavlovian way, the love she felt for him.

She had been trying to woo Mani, without success, for the past year. While he constantly directed urgent remarks at everyone else about some element of the environment – the neighbour's dog, a cow frozen in the middle of the lane, the sound of the flower-seller shouting 'hoovu' as he streaked by on his bicycle – Mani was majestically oblivious of Sophie. He regarded with utmost boredom her attempts to play cricket with him and walked past her into the house every time she opened the door to his grandparents.

Sophie's experience of infants was limited to the time, sixteen years ago, when her sister, Mukulika, was born. Her first sight of Mani, trailing after his grandparents, his saliva forming a long silvery skein between his thumb and the corner of his lips as he pulled his thumb out and opened his mouth to bawl, immediately filled her with a longing to win him over. She remembered her fascination with her baby sister and something from those years, some residue of tenderness and amusement, flared up in her.

Now she lifted a doggedly resistant Mani from the floor, gave him a piece of chocolate to stifle the howl of outrage that was forming in his mouth and surreptitiously kissed him. 'Darling sweetheart angel,' she whispered, while Mani rubbed his jammy hands into her freshly washed hair.

She could hear Bhatt shouting and carried Mani out. Her landlord had been on the roof and was standing by the door with the pouch of grass from the water tank. He held it, dripping, before Sophie's nose.

She denied any knowledge of it but Mr Bhatt told her that Chinnappa and the other members of the Welfare Association had, nevertheless, given him an ultimatum: unless Sophie stopped letting her noisy and bad-mannered friends visit, stopped smoking on the balcony in full public view or inside the house where she was likely to start a fire, stopped shamelessly hanging out her underwear to dry, stopped coming home at any time of the night she chose, she must be asked to leave or Bhatt himself was in trouble.

'I am helpless madam,' said Bhatt, dropping the pouch into Sophie's bin, good-humouredly clicking his tongue at the Mani-wreaked devastation, tightening his veshti and proceeding out from the kitchen door to the balcony to check if it yielded evidence of further misdemeanours.

Sophie followed him. Mani struggled out of her grasp and started stuffing chrysanthemum petals into his mouth.

'Chinnappa himself wanted to come and talk to you but I said, leave it. She has been my tenant for one full year. We can talk with each other. Why should she respect what you say? She will respect what *I* say.'

He squatted down and turned his attention to the first of the drooping plants.

Chinnappa was a humourless man except for his sessions at the laughing club that convened in a maidan twice a week, when its two dozen members held their sides and laughed helplessly at nothing in the belief that such objectless mirth improved their lives and lengthened their life spans. Men like Chinnappa and Bhatt, who turned livid at the sight of female underwear and did everything possible to draw attention to it, reminded Sophie of the nuns from her childhood who were always talking about sex in order to protect their students from it. Words like virginity, rape, ovulation, abortion and intercourse had rung through her high school moral science classes. Unlike Ringo Saar, though, who'd shown himself eager to fight back the arm of the law, however long, Sophie found it hard to openly challenge her neighbours. For this ambivalence it was the nuns, again, who were to blame. She had been so finger-wagged into submission by them and other figures of authority that she was never sure she was right and authority wrong. Perhaps, she mused, stroking Mani's cheek so he would learn that chewing petals too was among the activities that would be met with love, it was equally difficult for men like Bhatt and Chinnappa who had painstakingly built houses to rent out, but who nevertheless remained fundamentally suspicious of tenants – men trying to balance their greed with their morals.

Bhatt was insincerely professing helplessness, digging out cigarette stubs and bottle caps from the potted plants, saying it was all Chinnappa's fault. However much he wanted to, however much he complained about her underwear and smoking and stained floors, Bhatt could not himself deliver ultimatums to Sophie because she wielded a unique advantage over him. Her friend, Ringo Saar, was (besides the drummer of the band Little Idlis) employed in a financial services company that, among other things, functioned as a loan recovery agency for banks. Mr Bhatt had defaulted on several loans and on his credit card repayment and the company was on his case. Ringo had informed Mr Bhatt that the next stage of the recovery strategy involved publishing his photograph in the *Deccan Herald* along with the details of his crime. It was this ignominy Mr Bhatt had been trying to stave off by promising Ringo that he would not harass Sophie but let her stay and not raise the rent. It was the reason he had, that evening, talked the plainclothesmen into leaving, Sophie knew, slipping them the baksheesh they wanted once they'd gone out. He was only buying time, of course, and Ringo, who had got several defaulters to pay up and won the respect of the brothers who ran the company, had on the company's behalf promised him time. Bhatt would go far to protect his moral stature among the colony's residents, Ringo knew, so the *Deccan Herald* advertisement was an effective threat. Chinnappa, for instance, whose interests revolved around the Welfare Association and the laughing club, whose two daughters both had cushy software jobs and were married to men with cushy software jobs, didn't appear to know his neighbour was in the red.

Mr Bhatt was a monumental debtor. Apart from a building loan, he was repaying, or trying to, a car loan and a personal loan; the latter had gone into his daughter's – Mani's mother's – wedding (a woman who was now, along with her husband, doing a two-year stint in a hotel in Singapore – an attempt to salvage her father's situation by bringing back savings in a foreign currency). Mr Bhatt had taken loans to repay loans. In order to clear them, he had mortgaged both his houses. The building loan, taken to add an extra floor to his house, had long since been spent on stocks, all of which were doing badly.

For someone who had tied himself into such knots of

liability, Mr Bhatt was a marvellously unruffled creature. He cared about things like potted plants. He taught his grandson bhajans. He oppressed his wife. He went patiently through his last years as assistant manager in a company that made fake Ayurvedic health and beauty products, a company that for a time had done so brilliantly that everyone's salaries had been doubled. That was when, ten years ago, he'd started taking the loans and, as if he had discovered a source as inexhaustible as Aladdin's lamp, once he started he couldn't stop. All of this Sophie had learnt from Ringo who'd spent many hours trying to draw up a sensible repayment plan for Mr Bhatt. It seemed increasingly clear the man was reluctant to make good his debts, Ringo reported to Sophie, who'd begged him to put some sense into Swami's head. He seemed to be developing Bhatt's weakness for loans.

Mr Bhatt now frowned at his grandson, then without warning delivered a resounding slap on his cheek. Fear flashed through Mani's eyes before he let out a piercing wail and began retching out a chocolatey goo mixed with shreds of yellow.

'Don't hit him!' cried Sophie

'Please *remove* your underwear,' said Mr Bhatt coldly, lifting the screaming Mani with one arm, like a rag doll, and carrying him through the house and down the stairs.

Sophie swore under her breath, tore her panties off the line and returned to her toast and her *Bangalore Times*, sidestepping the mess in the kitchen. Was the usually calm Bhatt beginning to crack up? How much longer before he caved in, stopped caring about the photograph in the newspaper and turned Sophie out? The thought of losing Mani, of going over house after poorly built house for one that was inhabitable and suited her small budget, of dealing once more with dodgy brokers and nosy landlords, made her want to cry.

She shook out the newspaper angrily and scrutinized the partygoers featured in it, like she did every morning. The captions beneath them always referred to them by their first names – 'Daniel and Asha' or 'Juhi with friends' or 'DJ Rocky with VJ Sunny'. When she first came to Bangalore, Sophie believed that all these people were so famous, readers didn't need to be told their last names. But after a year, she knew better. The city's rich were too many and too anonymous and this way of appearing in the papers was for them a means of confirming their existence.

In Shillong, Sophie had known the rich to belong to two categories. There were the indigenous rich – genteel Khasi families (some with strong hints of British blood somewhere down the line) who lived in old bungalows with neat porches, took pride in their roses and despised all forms of showiness. Their wealth lay in the vast properties they owned, for the men and women in the family were usually in middle-class professions – doctors, university teachers, preachers and bureaucrats. Then there were the settler rich – mainly Marwaris from Rajasthan who'd first arrived in Shillong in the late nineteenth century, built up family businesses over generations and remained aloof from the locals by living in vast, dark, cavernous houses hidden away in narrow, open-drained alleyways. In Bangalore, however, the rich seemed to proliferate without history giving them that vital push into richdom – they were there every morning, one arm around another rich person and in the other hand a drink.

Sophie was a compulsive reader of these newspaper supplements and of glossy lifestyle magazines. She would read them furious at people who described their beach holidays, their self-designed bungalows, their favourite night clubs. She ground her teeth learning about wine appreciation evenings in swanky hotels, salsa competitions, champagne brunches and tips on where to get the best lounge furniture. Massive idiots, she would say out loud to those who considered going on cruise trips in the Mediterranean de rigueur, to those who were standing up in restaurants and telling the chef he had made a mess of the osso bucco, to those who swore by their Blanco shoes.

As a result of her reading over the past year, neither seemed real to her – the city in which people, all of whom were about 33, zipped home from work and hit the party scene, and the city Sophie saw when she walked in her neighbourhood. Here, the one or two tall new glassy stores that sold sports shoes or jeans or washing machines were still out-numbered by row upon row of small, one-room enterprises, all of them with grand names – the Paper Mart piled high with bundles of old newspapers; the Flour Mill where a certain number of floury people always sat waiting on folding chairs, calmly observing the street; the fragrant-smelling Coffee Works with its medieval-looking coffee grinder; the mishmash on offer in the Novelty Stores; the Iyengar bakeries; the Chicken-Mutton stalls; the Car and Motorcycle Wash; the Horticultural Co-operative Societies and their occasionally fresh vegetables; the hole in the wall Ladies Tailors; the Framing Works whose framing work tended to take over the pavement; the Juice Stalls with their line-up of faded mixer-grinders and their garlands of oranges and mosambis; the Motor Driving schools; the Free Reading Room with its broken window panes; the remarkably high number of Piles and Fistula clinics; the Hot Chips shops where one man would be out on the pavement slicing potatoes into an enormous cauldron of boiling oil and the other inside, mixing salt and chilli powder into them; the many gold and silver jewellery stores; the shed-like restaurants with their zany hyphenated names ('Have-More', 'Sip-n-Bite', 'Hasty-Tasty'); the Speak Good English coaching centres; the photo studios; the 'herbel' beauty parlours; the shops with sad rows of old TV sets needing repair or burial ...

Her doorbell ran again. It was the Bhatts' maid, with Mani, his face streaked with dirty tears, manfully climbing the steps after her. Sophie smiled at the maid and waited, while the latter drew in her breath to gather the little Hindi she knew. Finally all she said was, 'Pot, pot' and gestured towards the balcony.

'He wants the pots back?' asked Sophie in disbelief. Surely this was the first step in ousting her. The maid was relieved that Sophie had understood and strode off to the balcony.

Mani stood there deliberating whether to raid the fridge again or follow the maid. He looked up at Sophie, a cold, appraising look that seemed to ask – what are *you* doing here?

~

'There's a boy, Sophie. There's a boy.'

Her mother was crying on the phone and Sophie wasn't yet dressed for work. Mrs Das rarely cried and when she did, it meant the appearance of a crack in her world that stoicism or just regular complaining could not mend. When she cried, Sophie listened with all her heart rather than only half of it, as she usually did, the other half being reserved for her father.

But as soon as Sophie understood that it was about her sister, she felt relieved. Muku was always in trouble – it was only a question of how bad it was.

'She didn't come home last night. At 10 o'clock she calls and says she's staying with Priya. Then Priya comes on the phone and starts saying – Aunty this and Aunty that. She gives me a mountain of lies – that they were watching a movie and forgot to check the time. I tell Muku – if there's a boy I'm not letting you out of the house. And all she says is – it's too late to come home now. Priya's driver has left for the day and there are no taxis.'

'There's no boy ...'

'*Sophie, there's a boy.* I know from her voice. This is just the beginning. Wait and watch. I'll sit here alone wringing my hands while your father shuts himself up and answers my questions from behind a closed door. What should I do? Run out into the streets to look for her? Call the police?'

From the distance of a year, Sophie could view her mother's boy-paranoia with some objectivity. Mrs Das's respect for marriage was in inverse proportion to her hatred for boys. All girls, in her view, ought to care for nothing more than finding a good husband but somehow this idealized creature had nothing to do with the 'boys' that Sophie and Muku occasionally fell in with and whom they tried, without success, to keep hidden from their mother. Mrs Das knew about Swami too, in a theoretical sense. Sophie was certain that her mother had surmised, 'from her voice' or some equally arbitrary source, that there was a boy around. She knew that if she went back home, she'd have to face marathon bouts of questioning, the kind of persistent scrutiny under which it wouldn't be possible even for the city-hardened Sophie to hold out.

'Okay, so what if there is ...' said Sophie, trying to curb the impatience in her voice. She could not be impatient with her parents. She couldn't be at twenty-five what Muku seemed to be born with – a natural scorn for adults, an instant mocking of anyone who tried to instil in her that hilarious thing: a sense of right and wrong. At home, Sophie had taken her parents' side in the war against Muku but now, from this safe distance, she could feel sorry for her sister. Maybe a boyfriend will calm her down, she thought, going to the window to see if she could spot

Mani. But this was not something she could say to her mother who made the whole deal with boys seem so low, so *dirty*, that the minute Sophie tried to talk about the possible innocence of the whole thing, the big, disembodied hand of guilt would appear out of nowhere and smack her in the face. There was no way Sophie could betray her mother's boy principles.

Mani was down in the lane, bawling at some new injury, while Bhatt and Chinnappa conferred in low voices.

'I can buy her a cellphone as a last resort, but then why should she answer on a cellphone if she doesn't answer when I ask a simple question to her face? I told her this morning – Muku, look, at least tell your sister. You don't have to tell me. Just let Sophie know whom you're spending time with. Isn't that reasonable? But she just abandons her breakfast and runs out of the house without even closing the door after her.'

'I'd know if there was someone. She can't keep that kind of thing secret from me,' said Sophie with confidence, even though they all knew that the seemingly iron bond she had once forged with Muku was almost nothing now. In moments of weakness, Sophie felt like reminding her sister of the child she had once been – the curly-haired, chuckling toddler who called out to strangers on the road with the confidence of the beautiful, who held her bald doll on her hip in exactly the way that Sophie held Muku on her hip – the three of them welded to each other with a love now only a memory.

Mrs Das had stopped crying but that only made her shriller. 'What if it's someone much older than her? What if he makes her pregnant?'

'Maybe it's Priya's brother. Or one of her brother's friends. Those are the only boys she knows. But I still doubt ...'

'Sophie, you talk to her. I've done my best. She's sixteen years old, how long is this going to go on? And then there's the exam.'

'Mama. Office,' said Sophie sternly. If her mother started on the exam that would take another fifteen minutes – the torturous subject of Muku's high school leaving exam which was due in a couple of months.

There was complete silence on the other side.

'Hello,' said Sophie, hoping her mother had gone away.

'Sophie,' said Mrs Das in an entirely new voice. 'There's only one way out. Baba and I have decided. We're going to send

Muku to you. You're alone there and she's missing you here, even though she doesn't say it. You can take care of each other.'

It was Sophie's turn to be silent, suppress the immediate cry of 'No!' that rose in her. If her sister moved here, Sophie's secret would be out: the fact that she didn't work in a publishing house, like she'd told her family, but a BPO company. Business Process Outsourcing.

'Sophie, you're listening, no?' asked mother. She had lost her shrillness. This was her steely voice, the one that brooked no argument.

'What if she fails the exam?' said Sophie clutching at the likeliest straw. 'Won't she have to stay there and take it next year?'

'I know your house is a little small, but it's not as if you've both been raised in large houses,' said Mrs Das, deploying her usual trick of not answering a question she didn't want to by pretending she was being asked an altogether different question. Sophie had always assumed that her parents wanted at least one of their daughters to stay with them for as long as possible. That's what they always said – if Sophie goes, Muku must stay and if Muku goes, Sophie must stay. Why had that policy changed?

'You don't worry about us,' said Mrs Das with a readiness that made Sophie suspicious. 'Let's think about Muku.'

They wanted to wash their hands off Muku and they weren't even looking at it that way. They imagined they were saving her from herself. Her father out of an absent-minded world-weariness and her mother out of paranoia about the boy disease were going to send Muku to Bangalore and return to Sophie the supervisory role she hated.

'I can't have her here,' said Sophie but couldn't, of course, spell out the reasons. And she was afraid that arguing with her mother might reveal an ever deeper truth – the possibility that she no longer loved her sister, the possibility that she would be quite happy never to see her again. Besides, her mother was forestalling objections even before Sophie had voiced them.

'Sophie if you're thinking of money, don't worry. We'll support her. Money's not the issue. It's a question of where the best opportunities are. And Shillong has just gone down the drain. You know that. Why did you leave? You had to leave because Shillong has gone down the drain.'

'I'm late,' said Sophie wearily. Her mother hung up after reminding Sophie that charity began at home.

Sophie decided to feign menstrual cramps. She called Maya Singh, her boss, who was always the first to get to work and made all those who came late suffer. Maya bought the lies, but only provisionally, as Sophie knew from experience. She assumed that her staff lied routinely about all manner of things. It made even those who were speaking the truth think twice.

'Fine, fine, come when you're feeling better. Let's do lunch together, I need to discuss something important,' said Maya, then vanished, as she always did, before Sophie had a chance to respond.

Sophie lit a cigarette and stretched out on the divan, trying to calm herself down. She looked at the few books on the shelf beside her and reached for the selection of Vivekananda's writings that she had won in a school elocution competition for reciting, in the voice of someone being slowly choked to death, Alexander Pushkin's 'The Captive'. She had instantly turned into a Vivekananda fan and remained one for several years. She opened the book to a page on the subject of Karma Yoga.

'Karma, in its effect on character, is the most tremendous power that we have to deal with. The human being is, as it were, a centre, and is attracting all the powers of the universe towards oneself, and in this centre is fusing them all, and again sending them off in a big current. Such a centre is the real person – the almighty, the omniscient – and the whole universe is drawn towards this person.'

This was from a piece called 'Work without Motive'. At thirteen, Sophie told no one she read Vivekananda but she would for days on end try to follow his advice, mulling over his words as she walked back home from school, planting every step firmly on the ground, ignoring the school boys who whistled and hooted at her, focusing, focusing, noticing the precise way a raindrop slid from the top of the umbrella in front of her to its edge and then to the ground (for didn't the swami say that even the tiniest action counted, fed into the sum total of human character?). Then she'd get home and five-year-old Muku would have somehow reached up to her bookshelf and be drawing frenzied crayon swirls on the pages of Sophie's school notebooks, her mother would be grumpy with backache, her father would be in his chair in the sitting room, oblivious to the discontent around him because he was so steeped in his own. Vivekananda would vanish and Sophie would no longer be the person attracting all the powers of the universe towards herself but only a thirteen year old making tea for her parents, her head hurting with the futile mysteries of algebra.

Sophie remembered all of this but what the book in her hands evoked most strongly was not these separate details but the sense of that time, the feel of something left unfinished. She shoved Vivekananda back and pulled out the glossy brochures of American universities she'd accumulated in Shillong and brought along with her, remembering how she'd written for them and how she'd applied for a scholarship she never got. Those pictures – arcaded buildings, neat classrooms, groups of students sitting on sunlit lawns – were another lost world.

She began walking distractedly through the house with the lit cigarette between her fingers, back and forth through the kitchen, the small box of a living room, and her bedroom with its large ironing board which took up a lot of space but was important because Sophie loved ironing. She touched her things – the CD player, the jars in the kitchen, the pile of clothes on the ironing board, stopping once in a while at the window to look for Mani though there were only vendors down there now, shouting as they went by, and workmen calling to each other on the newly-dug up construction site next to the Bhatts' house. Nothing was ever still outside her window. Maids washed dishes or beat clothes viciously at outdoor taps; women darted after toddlers between the lines of washing hung on roof-terraces that stretched into the distance, above which the fronds of palm trees swayed, while cats stalked thin perimeter walls, keeping watch on the rustling undergrowth hiding vacant lots.

Sophie possessed all this – the view from the window, the tiny flat and every particle of air in it. She could cook what she liked, smoke to her heart's content, put every object exactly where she wanted it to be and know it would not move unless she moved it. For the first time in her life she was free. She stopped pacing around and stood under a fan, sweating and still.

Muku couldn't come here and destroy this.

If Wishes Were Horses

As Sophie's auto-rickshaw was coming out from under the railway bridge near the big hotel, with its row of multicoloured pennants on tall flagpoles that fluttered imperiously over her every day on her way to work, she saw him. There were hardly ever people on this stretch of road: just the looming white façade of the hotel half hidden by its boundary wall, the mysterious flags, the occasional thunder of a passing train and traffic: everyone locked into their modes of transport as if they'd been born in them. So it was doubly odd to see Ribor peering into the rickshaw, trying to make out if it was taken or not, tentatively flagging it down. The driver revved up the engine in response and sped past Ribor till Sophie cried, 'Stop, stop!'

He braked so suddenly, a cyclist coming up from behind nearly crashed into them. The rickshaw swerved, Sophie was thrown hard against the metal bars supporting the front seat, the driver cursed, and the stalled cars from behind them immediately began pounding their horns. The driver, still cursing, restarted the engine and pulled to one side. The cyclist shouted out as he pedalled away, making the gesture that every aggrieved motorist in Bangalore makes to every offender in his path – an extending of the arm with the palm spread out, a gesture that seemed only to be motioning towards the offender but actually did much more. It conveyed disgust, ridicule, anger. It said more than words could say, for in the universe of the streets whose only law was movement, it was not always possible to stop, cause a traffic-jam, push shirt-sleeves up, insult and be insulted in return.

Each of the drivers of the first few cars that went by shouted out their indecipherable complaints at Sophie and her cursing driver, but she didn't care. Her amazement at seeing Ribor in Bangalore, the man she could not picture anywhere but in his small, smoky music shop high above a Shillong street, overrode everything else, including the pain in her knee.

But as she jumped out and limped towards him she realized it wasn't Ribor at all – only someone who looked like him.

'Oh!' exclaimed Sophie, her mouth open, feeling she had been tricked, and then, as she continued to stare, suddenly too embarrassed to even try and hide her confusion. But the man only assumed that she wanted to tell him off for trying to stop the rickshaw and nearly causing an accident.

'Sorry, sorry,' he said backing off. 'I didn't know it was taken.'

Sophie waved away his explanation and climbed back into the rickshaw. Only when they took off again, the driver shaking his head in disbelief at her stupidity, did Sophie realize her hands were trembling. She ignored her throbbing knee because it was nothing compared to what might have happened if they had killed the cyclist or if the rickshaw had lost balance and toppled over. And to add to that were a whole array of even worse possibilities: What if it *had* been Ribor and he hadn't recognized her? What if Ribor was in town and hadn't called her, leaving their meeting to chance? What if she had, when she thought she saw Ribor standing there (a small man further diminished by the traffic, the pavements where no one walked, the towering walls of the hotel behind him), zipped out of the rickshaw to hug a complete stranger?

The last time Sophie was in Ribor's shop they'd talked about her going away and she'd found it hard to explain why she was leaving. All *he* knew were names and rumours – Bombay, where the bombs could go off any time and the commuter train rides were interminable; Delhi, in whose buses girls carried open safety pins to ward off lecherous, groping men; Bangalore, where too many people killed themselves and where everyone was on their way to getting rich. There was nothing nice about places that were not Shillong. He would never be found here – a piece of Shillong dwarfed by a Bangalore street. Yet why not? He could come and visit, perhaps he had cousins here. Everyone in Shillong had cousins who were somewhere else. They would take him to pubs and malls and rock concerts so that he could see for himself what they were like – the places that were not Shillong. And what would he say to it all? He'd say – it's okay. Things move fast. People mind their own business. They don't stand around gossiping at street-corners. He'd appreciate that – that people minded their own business. He would laugh if Sophie asked him too many questions, laugh the way people did in Shillong – not just when they were amused but also when they were surprised or embarrassed or didn't know what to say – laughter that could mean anything. Sophie remembered now how easily it came and how much it concealed.

Are you planning to move here, she would ask him.

No, no, I'm too old for that sort of thing. I'm going home.

But you'll come back?

An exquisite smile that was thoughtful around the edges.

I don't know. This is the first time I ever went anywhere.

Sophie had once been like Ribor – hidden in a small town, never seen the inside of a train or known what it meant to watch a plane land, never seen city lights, just watched television, imagined the world through MTV and Discovery Channel, listened to rock music, set store by lines in songs. But they weren't really alike. She had got up and walked out of the door one day. He hadn't turned his back on that town like she had, and he'd never been as lonely as she'd been when she first came here.

Maybe, if he was sharing this rickshaw with her now, he'd ask her how she was. You're okay here? he'd ask casually, and she, in order not to think about the conversation they'd had more than a year ago as they smoked together on the balcony of his shop, would tell him instead about Killer Queen. Did I tell you it was Killer Queen who got me to leave Shillong? It's funny how if you don't really believe in anything, it's possible to believe in the most absurd things. My father believes in Shakespeare, so he has some standard by which to judge other things, most of which fall short. But my sister and I – we're clueless. So when this madwoman – you know the one with dark glasses and the big purse who always looks like she's on some mission – asked me what I was doing standing there, I took it as a sign.

And Ribor would understand what she was talking about because he knew Killer Queen, everyone knew Killer Queen. This time he would not laugh; he took Killer Queen seriously just as Sophie did. She would tell him what happened after the Killer Queen moment. She started going to the little internet parlour near her house run by the charming college dropout, Vinetta, who sat around practising karaoke on her customers all day. Sophie was going to get out. She trawled through websites advertising jobs in big cities – Delhi, Bombay, Bangalore – looking for anything that required a combination of a BA, no work experience and a modicum of language skills. Which was all she had.

After weeks of searching, she applied for a job in a major publishing house based in Bangalore that was looking to hire twenty assistant editors. A Mr Sharma wrote back asking her to present herself for an interview. Her father was impressed when she named the publishing house though he continued to believe Sophie was cut out to go abroad on that scholarship he had himself never got, come back and teach in a university with high pay-scales and a free house. Sophie *had* applied for this dream scholarship once, laboriously typing out a two-page answer to the question of why she wished to study abroad and how she would apply her learning to a career back home. Mr Das noted with pride the earnestness of Sophie's tone and the felicity of her style and suggested changes only in a couple of sentences. He posted the application himself and then they all waited for the call. But it never came, that letter inviting Sophie for an interview in Delhi, the letter that would take her to the neat lawns and colonnaded university buildings advertised in the brochures.

Her father said, 'Look, these things happen. Competition

has increased these days. Try other scholarships.'

But Sophie knew that he, like the rest of her family, believed that she'd get it and that he was disappointed in her. She stood by the parapet and chain-smoked for three days, her teeth clenched as if holding down pain, and no one ever mentioned the word 'scholarship' again.

Now the whole thing seemed acutely funny to her – in a Shillong sort of way. She would tell it to Ribor like a joke on herself and then ask him for his news. He wouldn't have much. He might say, for instance, that he'd recently turned forty and spent his birthday with a friend, drinking rum in the shop till late at night, then driving home through the pitch-black streets. Sophie would try to find out whether he'd enjoyed this or thought it sucked. Perhaps neither. Perhaps he watched his own life go by with the same detachment that he watched the street outside his three-customers-a-day music shop.

He would ask her if she missed Shillong and instead of giving him the easy, ready answer, she'd tell him the truth, which is that what she really missed was Beauty. When people talked about hill towns, they imagined them as holiday destinations. They imagined them as places that offered a brief respite from reality and were for that reason adorable. They imagined them as a collection of views and things to do. But that was not what Sophie meant when she confided to herself and an imaginary Ribor about the thing she missed most. The white gushing of Elephant Falls or the green expanse of Umiam Lake were nothing compared to waking up early on a winter morning because you were in love with someone who hadn't noticed, and watching through the frost on the windows two boys in jackets and mufflers kicking a ball around in the football field and an occasional taxi rolling out through the morning mist. And then continuing to stand there and freeze as the light slowly changed and the yellow cast of morning deepened, touching now this angle and now that, till it was 8 o'clock and sunlight transformed the air of ancient sadness that hung over the scene – the lonely shouts of the boys, the milky mist, the cold, sleeping houses on the hill – into an ordinary morning.

Bangalore, on the other hand, possessed a great zest for

ugliness. Everyone just wanted to obscure the view, blot out the sky, erase the gaps. The city not just proliferated but kept reproducing itself. And so you never arrived anywhere in Bangalore. You never turned a corner and experienced an epiphany. You just got more of the same thing. Sophie had learnt to content herself with the minor things, therefore – the smell of flowers coming from pushcarts late in the evening, the view of a palm tree from an open window, the corners of certain pubs, the pleasure of seeing one's things neatly arranged in a room. That's why for so many people creating islands of their homes is their life's greatest pleasure, she thought. They need a place they can fashion in their own image because the city is not that place.

But Ribor wasn't there to share these thoughts with and the rickshaw felt enormous without him. Sophie usually took a bus to work, negotiating the morning crowds, the women packed into the front half of the bus, the men in the rear half, the khaki-uniform-clad conductor repeatedly squeezing into the sweaty throng of bodies to extract fares and then squeezing out, shouting 'munde hogi, munde hogi' as if any let-up in his insistence that the entire bus's population move up would cause the crowd to turn manic, knock him down, trample upon him.

Sophie allowed herself rickshaws on rare occasions but she wasn't enjoying it any more. She watched the driver speak into his cellphone and at the same time manoeuvre expertly between long sleek cars and thundering bikes and aggressive buses and other rickshaws that screeched so painfully Sophie had to momentarily cover her ears with her hands. The traffic sounded different from the way it did from a bus. Out here in the open, it became a powerful, inchoate din as overwhelming as the images that flashed past: the driver of a stalled bus yelling at a tempo-truck wallah, a fat woman balanced sideways on the pillion of a crazily speeding scooter, snatches of music emanating from a car painted with orange flames, a pair of girls dressed identically in black suits and pumps sailing elegantly through the traffic on two scooters and keeping an animated conversation going between them. There was an unmistakably insane tinge to the melee.

The pain in her knee was growing and she noticed then that a small dark patch had appeared on the outside of her jeans. She pulled the fabric up and examined the wound.

Real blood. Imaginary conversation. And then an idea came to her with perfect clarity, connected somehow with the vividness of the blood trickling down her knee. She would go to Shillong to see Ribor. She hadn't gone back once in the past year, unwilling to face her family and glad to see that despite her mother's occasional panicky phone-calls, all three of them were holding up without her. Perhaps Sophie had overestimated her role as a Das pivot. She would often march about her flat the way she had done that morning, touching the things that were hers and no one else's, congratulating herself on having got away.

But now the ache in her knee triggered other aches, all of them connected with this man who might even have forgotten she existed – the girl who often drifted into his shop to look over his CDs. She decided to go back for a week – not long enough for her family to reclaim her or foist Muku on her, but enough to find out what Ribor had really meant. He had said that she didn't really need to leave, that it might not work out, her going to an altogether new place. But what if he'd meant more than that? What if he'd simply meant – *stay*.

As if in logical consequence of this incredible thought, Sophie called Swami. He answered on the fifth ring.

'I'm sleeping, da,' he said.

'How far have you got?'

He yawned a long yawn, which seemed to soften him, make him tolerant of the world's demands on him.

'I read a few pages ...'

'Make a schedule. Read five pages everyday.'

'Do I really have to? Read this particular book?'

Sophie believed that if he did, some kind of irreversible mutation would take place in Swami – the same that had taken place in her when she read *Swami and Friends* at the age of nine and *Vivekananda: Awakener of Modern India* at thirteen and *Madame Bovary* at eighteen. He might become more like that Swami and less like the Swami that was hardening, leaving his sangfroid behind. It was all because of that call centre he'd joined, thought Sophie for the hundredth time. His income had upped the status of the entire family. It had given them something to talk about in the evenings, made them curious about the prices of real estate, the best mutual funds to invest in, the shops on MG Road they had never set foot in before.

'Don't read it if you don't want to read it,' said Sophie grumpily. 'It's no big deal.'

'What? I can't hear you.'

'My rickshaw nearly killed a cyclist. And I could have been killed too,' shouted Sophie.

Swami laughed. 'You can't die that easily.'

'I just can't stand being on these streets any more. I'm quite sure I don't want to go in your car when you get it.'

Sophie was obsessed with traffic accidents. She recognized well the sickening, explosive crunch of a bike spinning out of its rider's control and hitting the road, an SUV colliding with a scooter, a lorry crumpling a small car like a ball of paper. She'd seen people die on these streets, or knocked unconscious, or with their legs gone. They'd be folded up like bloody pieces of cardboard and hastily stuffed into the backs of rickshaws and cars to be taken to hospital. She didn't know if it was just her who attracted accidents or if other people witnessed as many as she did but were able, because of the brain-numbing excess of them, to remain indifferent. Nobody else seemed to think much about it, while Sophie had to work hard to suppress the idea, when she was out, that in the end everyone on the roads simply *wanted* to die. She was telling Swami now about a gruesome accident Ringo Saar had recently described to her.

'Ringo saw a man without a head, did he tell you? One minute the guy was driving his bike, trying to zip through a small gap in the traffic, the next minute his head was caught between two massive interstate video coaches and just came off ... Swami?'

He had fallen asleep. Sophie found it hard to believe, then immediately forgave him his great weariness because she knew what it felt like. As they drew up at a red light, she looked at the people standing near a traffic junction. Above them a woman on a hoarding held out a steaming bowl of pasta, grinning maniacally, while next to her a local film star's outsized face advertized gold jewellery. A knot of people watched a bus inching towards them; some broke away from the group and ran to board it before it reached the stop while others stayed where they were, looking indecisive. There was no telling if the bus would extricate itself from the maze of traffic and actually halt at the stop, or sail away leaving behind the rule-abiding but timid citizens who had not had the courage to board it when the opportunity presented itself. Sophie looked at them and she looked at the Ashoka trees lining the road and they looked exactly the same – bloodless and dusty.

She was going to drop everything and go home.

~

When Naomi Picks first appeared in office two weeks ago, Sophie had abandoned all work and just gaped. Naomi was fantastic; she was the living, breathing embodiment of all the films that Sophie had to watch day after day, so many films that she could no longer distinguish between them – they had all coalesced in her mind into a single American voice and an oceanic blur of images.

Sophie worked in a company called Star Titles, which had its headquarters in Los Angeles. It was the LA office that took on clients – the big American movie studios whose names had sent a thrill through Sophie on her first day at work. She sat upright at her computer in the brightly-lit, yellow and cream colour-schemed office and experienced, looking at the names of those studios, the same sense of anticipation she was used to feeling in a movie hall when, after the trailers and advertisements, the lion roared. Sophie loved her work for the first couple of months. What she and her colleagues were paid to do was transcribe the soundtracks of Hollywood films so that they could be marketed on DVDs. There were three kinds of captioning required – captions for the deaf included every single noise made on the screen (like someone coughing or the name of the instrument playing music in the background); captions for the hard of hearing were less rigorous – if a song was playing you didn't need to spell out its lyrics but just state – 'song playing in background'; and finally the third 'normal' level which required you to just subtitle dialogue.

Sophie mastered the system in days – figured out the software, experienced no trouble with American accents or American spelling or American references to American cars and supermarket chains and rock bands and cigarettes brands. She enjoyed the fixity of all the little rules of the captioning universe – how to place the lines in relation to the soundtrack, when to break a line, when to italicize, when to use an ellipsis, what an ellipsis with an extra dot signalled, when parentheses were called for. She liked the feel of being an important cog in the machine – fifty people strong – that hummed with energy through the day (and through the night when the technical guys worked on creating the master files). Maya had thumped her on the back and said, 'You're fast,' during that first month and then, in a lower voice, 'Just keep up and you'll soon be a client coordinator.'

There were two client coordinators for each of the three floors and they were all about Sophie's age – pert girls and boys with businesslike manners to whom clusters of hackers like Sophie reported. The coordinators got proofers to check and report back on what the hackers (or editors) had done, supervised a 'final simulation', gave the files to the technical guys to marry with the films. Then they were sent off to the eternally impatient people in the LA office who never really seemed impressed with how quickly Bangalore worked, how dutifully it transcribed the sound of every punch Arnold Schwarzenegger delivered, every Dirty Harry one-liner, every throaty Julia Roberts laugh, every violin accompanying every first kiss, every mysterious creak in every haunted house.

Sophie had thought that she would like to be a coordinator and throw her weight around a little and thereby also remain in Maya's good books, which wouldn't hurt because Maya was the director of operations and handled the day-to-day running of the company. Also, the coordinator positions were often vacant; coordinators routinely quit because there was no room for them to move up (if they tried they would bump into Maya). And they were too smart to be content with their positions for more than a year or two. All these girls and boys were set to apply to universities abroad; in their minds they were already in Boston or New York or Berkeley and their manner signalled an impatience with the slow ones, the ones who had to listen to James Bond six times before they understood what he was saying, the ones with atrocious grammar, the ones who had no ambitions other than trying to get Maya to talk to the big boss about salary hikes and better benefits.

Soon, though, Sophie came to think of her work as repellently mindless and she began to resent the coordinators and feel less and less inclined to be like them. She was also, without ever fully admitting this to herself, afraid of being promoted because that would mean that like the rest of these overconfident people she was preparing to eventually leave, fly away, embrace her destiny. Sophie had no such plans, however – she had nothing that could be described as an ambition. So, without trying very hard to, she fell into a gentle malaise and got on by doing just the bare minimum. She would tap in a few lines every morning, then go onto the Net to check the correct wording of some American slang and get absorbed instead in the blog of one of Maya's friends, who spent most of his time partying and who described his social life in riveting detail. She read his blog with the same mixture of fury and glee that overcame her when she read the magazines full of glossy people that lay in small piles everywhere in her living room. What especially fascinated Sophie about the blogger was how he never grew bored, how he never underwent an existential crisis about the meaning of it all. She would keep going back to his blog if only to check that he had still not cracked up from the endless rounds of theme parties and fashion shows and late nights out drinking that were his life.

Today Sophie felt at an even lower ebb than usual. She looked around for Naomi or Maya, then peeked over the cubicle wall at Shanthi Gowda who was working diligently, with large headphones clamped down on her head. Sophie often looked at Shanthi when she was bothered about something because Shanthi was a worker ant who was never going to give up. Her life was like a painting in which every inch of blank space is filled up with colour and detail – her conscientiousness, her unbreakable habits, her identical lunch boxes, her army of relatives, her temple-going, her favourite serials on television, her salwar-kurtas all cut in the same way and made from the same kind of fabric. There were no spaces left in the picture for doubt or idle daydreaming. On good days, Sophie liked Shanthi for her sober realism. On bad days she resented her lack of imagination.

Shanthi finally noticed her standing there and announced, 'I am getting married.'

'Good,' said Sophie, unsurprised and unwilling, despite knowing how churlish she sounded, to display any false excitement over this development. She could very easily see Shanthi climbing the steps to the choultry near her house, dressed in shiny silk.

'Please come for my wedding. I won't see you after that. Only one week more in this job.'

'You're quitting! Why?'

'No career advancement here. One can only become coordinator but after that what? I applied in an exam coaching centre and got the job. Salary is much better. You should try, Sophie. If you want to apply in my centre, I can give your reference. In a year's time you can earn double of what you're earning here. You don't have to go by bus any more, you can buy a scooter, you can take loan for a car, you can ...'

'That's great, that's great,' said Sophie hastily. 'But I'm okay here.'

Shanthi smiled at her, 'Please come for my wedding. Naomi's coming. She's very excited.'

Sophie nodded, then went back to her computer and looked at Halle Berry and Billy Bob Thornton frozen in the last frame of *Monster's Ball* – sitting out on the steps of the back porch, looking at the stars, eating ice-cream, Berry's character coming to terms with the revelation that Thornton's character is the man responsible for her husband's death. She put on her headphones and began to transcribe the last few lines of the film. Wrong, Sophie, wrong. Shanthi's moving on, she's not the sucker you thought she was. She's going to get ahead. But so what if she is? It's only about replacing one brain-dead job with another and who cares if the money's better?

Sophie did not notice, as she captioned the last few frames of the film, the shock and confusion on Berry's face or the gentleness on Thornton's. A film was no longer a human thing to her. It was a compilation of sound, colour, movement, faces, words. In her waking life she had become indifferent to this endless unspooling but at night when she tried to sleep, it pressed in on her. She couldn't have explained it to anyone, but there was something sinister about this vomit of images; in her half-dreams she experienced the horrible thinness, the unrelieved flatness of film, a two-dimensional world whose peculiar chemistry reduced everything to the same thing. Her insomnia gave way only when her dreams' camera eye could rest on a wide open landscape free of this ceaseless churning of image and noise and then she would sleep peacefully for a while. But as soon as morning broke and the focus shifted to people again – the landlord lecturing someone, the phone ringing its Swami ring – everything returned to the brittle and the insincere. Those were the moments when she felt that films had enveloped her daily life too – that the real world they gestured towards didn't really exist, that they were a fake world created on the basis of a fake world.

Sophie ran quickly through the entire film's captions before emailing the file to her coordinator. Then she tore off her headphones and wandered into the narrow corridor that linked the cubicles and led towards the kitchen. The balcony adjoining it was the only place where smoking was allowed.

She found Maya there, puffing hard on a Wills as she watched Naomi trying to pin a string of jasmine into her short hair. Naomi was the Vice-President of Human Resources in the LA office of the company; she had come down for a couple of weeks to conduct a leadership training workshop for the coordinators.

'I know I'm not gettin' it exactly right, but what d'you think?' said Naomi, turning to Maya and then Sophie.

There was something hypnotic about Naomi. She possessed qualities that made her seem like another life form altogether. What were these qualities? Enthusiasm, primarily. An enthusiasm of such stupendous proportions, an alacrity so alacritous, a willingness so willing, that when Naomi first crossed her path, Sophie felt the little energy she possessed being sucked out of her with the whooshing sound souls made when they were sucked out of bodies in horror movies.

'And then I'll wear a sari. White ... um, not exactly white but sorta creamish – silk with like a border here, a gold border. Shanthi's going to show me how to do it; we've gone through it once already. I mean Shanthi wore one herself, she's a real pro at it, she does it all in like twenny seconds and it looks so fantastic but I can never follow the steps, so I got her to do it slowly and I got that on my handycam. Which is cool, because I'm taking back two saris with me – the one I'm wearing to the wedding and another one I bought on MG Road last weekend. It's cobalt blue. The guy at the shop called it peacock blue ... gosh, that sounds so udderly exotic ...'

Another thing that singled out Naomi was how much she could talk. Her talk was like an orchestra, movement joining movement, the whole thing gushing towards some incredible climax till she'd be diverted by a small detail – a remark that her listener managed to insert into the torrent, or something in the udderly strange environment – and then the orchestra would change direction, take up a new theme.

Maya took a last deep drag on her cigarette, and said 'I'll see you guys later. Got to catch Ravi before he goes off for lunch.'

Naomi turned to Sophie. 'I'm thrilled about this wedding! Are you coming? Apparently, there's some kinda party the day before, you know where they paint everyone's hands with all those henna patterns. You have to sit for like hours without moving once you get the pattern on your hands, which is going to be the tough part for a jack-in-the box person like me, but I'm determined to do it for Shanthi's sake.' She lowered her voice. 'You know about her mother, don't you? She's really, really ill. Schizophrenia. Do you know how it happened?' Naomi paused here to ascertain if she could fill a significant gap in Sophie's knowledge.

'No idea,' said Sophie, lighting a cigarette, glad to keep Naomi going so that she could just watch her – the way she stroked the flowers dangling by her ear, the terrific mobility of her face, the expressiveness of her hands. Though in some part of her tired mind, Sophie did register that Shanthi, her colleague for a year, had never confided in *her* about her mother's illness.

'Well it all began when her brother went to Dubai to work. Apparently – the exchange rate being what it is – what he earned there translated into a pretty good packet even though he was only working as a bus-driver, you know – not the sort of thing he'd be doing if he were here. I mean I've met him, he's a really [elegant shrug] intelligent guy. He has a graduate degree in science but he only went there because the dad died. You know about that, don't you? Shanthi was just seventeen and her brother was twenny-one. She never complains about stuff, she's a brave girl but I know how hard it musta been for them. She told me that after their father died they were like eating only twice a day and they had to give up their gas connection and cook on a kerosene stove. Anyway, this guy, Sunil, goes off to Dubai and gets a well-paying job and then Shanthi starts working as well, right after college and suddenly the family is pretty well-off.'

How had this happened? wondered Sophie. How had two people, each set like jelly in the moulds of their separate worlds, effected this fantastic connection? More to the point, how had Shanthi – unassuming, down-to-earth, even rustic Shanthi – managed to silence the deadly Naomi Picks long enough to tell her all these stories within stories about her life? But there was no time to analyse; Naomi was rambling on.

'Their mother loves jewellery. She's been hoarding this little box full of stuff she got at her wedding. Even when they were like the lowest of low, she never let that box go. So the first time Sunil came back from Dubai he brought gold bangles for her. And then everytime he came back to visit he got her more gold stuff. She wouldn't let them keep it in a bank locker; she'd like sleep with it under her pillow, this little mountain of gold that kept growing and growing. Then one time he didn't get her any jewellery; he got her a shawl instead or something. And, boy, was she mad. Shanthi says she tried to attack him, like claw his face. They just couldn't understand what was going on. Around that time, she started wearing all this gold all the time. She would insist on going shopping or to their relatives' houses with all of it on and this was worth like a lot of money. And she started talking, having conversations with the jewellery about her life, about all the trouble she'd been through, about the family back in the village and how jealous everyone was about her possessions.'

Sophie suppressed a yawn, not of boredom but pure tiredness.

'She just got weirder and weirder. She'd say unconnected things, accuse Shanthi of trying to steal her gold and one night Shanthi found her on the bathroom floor, stark naked but with all her heavy pendants and earrings and bangles on. That was the last straw. Her brother flew back and they took her to a psychiatrist and he said she'll probably need medication for life. She's cracking under the pressure, he said. Just the pressure of having so much when once she had nothing.'

'How will she handle the wedding?' asked Sophie.

'Oh, she'll manage. I've met her – she seems to talk sense a lot of the time. Take me to the United States with you, she says. I don't want to be in India any more. All these people here say I'm crazy and it's not true. Of course, it's not true, Mrs Gowda, I tell her. The medicine really numbs her, but you can see it in her eyes.' Naomi lowered her voice. 'She's stark, raving mad.'

~

Sophie sometimes came to this bustling fast food restaurant with Maya. Its walls were painted red to match the red baseball caps and candy-striped shirts of the staff, all of them young boys who seemed to be injected with the robot drug. They all smiled and said 'Sure, ma'am' with their hands behind their backs in exactly the same tone when the food was ordered, unloaded plates off trays with perfectly identical flourishes and glided smoothly across the tiled floors like ever-multiplying figures in a computer game. Sophie could never tell them apart, but that didn't bother her. She focused on the food – the way lettuce drowned in mayonnaise squelched out of the chicken burgers when one bit into them, the uniformly golden colour of the French fries, the taste of spaghetti doused in ketchup, the searing fizz of a cold drink on a hot day. She'd been able to afford restaurant food only occasionally in her previous life; now, she could never eat it without reminding herself of her blessings.

She ordered a burger and a milkshake, Maya a salad.

'Only salad?' asked Sophie.

'I've got to lose weight, just look at me,' said Maya.

Sophie did and could see no difference. But Maya sucked in air through her teeth and said, 'I'm fat, fat, fat.'

When the food came, Maya began to eat her salad delicately, spearing one small morsel with her fork at a time, as if food were only something to fill in the pauses between talk, while Sophie demonstrated the opposite belief, wolfing down her burger and eating three French fries at a time.

Maya lived in a large apartment in a gated community that had its own golf course and spa and multiplex. In Maya's world, when you were hungry, you picked up the phone and told the janitor which topping you wanted on your takeaway pizza. You had your groceries home-delivered. You never went to any restaurant that didn't have valet parking. You never walked anywhere ever. You took your holidays in Rome and Maldives. You had plans to 'redo' your kitchen. Sophie was a tiny bit contemptuous of Maya, even though she knew that Maya was fond of her – she took her out to lunch sometimes, tended to overlook her sloppiness, tried to motivate her.

But now as soon as they'd ordered, she said: 'Sophie, I've been quiet about this for a long time but it won't do any longer. You're going from bad to worse. You haven't met a single target in the last six months. What's happened, Sophie? You used to be great when you joined!'

She looked at Sophie in the frank, intense way in which she always looked at people and waited for her to make her confession. That was Maya's way – she usually knew when her staff was fudging.

'But I was late this morning because my landlord conducted an unannounced raid on my house. He found – panties drying in public view, a pouch of weed in the rainwater tank, unnecessarily new curtains, a full ashtray and a stain on the floor.'

Maya laughed sarcastically. 'You're his entertainment, Sophie. His life would be just bhajans and vegetable shopping without you.'

'Then my mother called and cried. She's got something up her sleeve. She refused to put the phone down and I hadn't even got dressed.'

'She wants to marry you off and you're against arranged marriage on principle?'

Sophie nodded violently in the negative through her chewing.

'She's figured out about Swami and is coming here to put a stop to the evil?'

Sophie nodded again. Did Maya really know so much about her life? She couldn't remember telling her.

'She's guessed you've been lying about the job?'

Sophie swallowed and took a deep gulp of her milkshake.

'She wants to send my sister here so I don't have too much fun,' she said, recovering her breath. 'That's not good, according to my mum – too much fun is a sure sign of moral degeneration. Maybe because she never had any fun herself, she was so engrossed in trying to keep her head above water. She's spent too much time in the kitchen. It's the fumes, that's what it is.'

'Don't develop rubbishy theories, Sophie. Let your sister come. Look at you. Think of how you were afraid to take a rickshaw after ten in the night or touch a glass of whiskey. You've blossomed here.'

'You don't know my sister. She'll figure out the most dangerous things to do and do them. I'll have to babysit her every second. Otherwise she might kill herself or something, just out of spite.'

'I have the solution then. Take the exam with me. Get out of here. They can't follow you everywhere.'

'No, no, no!' said Sophie, shaking her head from side to side like an obstinate child.

Maya had for years been planning to apply to an American university, so that she could, like the coordinators, fly away. And not just that but emigrate. Marry, get a job there, live the life that fulfilled some television or magazine ideal so many of Sophie's colleagues were in the grip of. But Maya kept postponing her departure to paradise – see-sawing between the idea of going abroad and the idea of moving up in her job. Both were attractive options and she kept both alive without deciding on either. Lately, she'd been trying to convert Sophie to the dream of a foreign education but Sophie, having tried and failed once, was adamant.

'Why not, Sophie?' asked Maya in exasperation.

'We've had this discussion a million times. That's the wrong question. It's not why I don't want to go, it's why you want to go? Why anyone wants to go. Because everyone else goes?'

'No, because ... I mean just look at stuff here. Look at the traffic. And I'm always falling sick. My stomach keeps aching.'

'Maya, you're *not* always falling sick. When did you last take sick leave? Anyway, that's not a convincing reason for wanting to spend thousands of rupees on a foreign education you don't need. How do you know your stomach won't ache when you're living in your fancy condominium in Pennsylvania or wherever?'

'In the long run I can't stand India,' declared Maya.

Sophie tried to look stern but burst out laughing. 'That's like saying you can't stand yourself.'

But Maya wasn't listening, lost in her dream of abroad.

'What if you feel horribly out of place there?' asked Sophie.

'I can feel at home wherever there are supermarkets and people have manners. But the work is growing and I want to hang on for a while. I just spoke to Ravi – we're going to get this British company soon that LA has taken on.'

Maya described the new content they'd be working with – British comedies like *The Catherine Tate Show, Little Britain, A Bear's Tale* and *Dad's Army*. She spoke about the new challenges – mastering British accents, the crucial importance of maintaining consistency of place and people names in the files, given that instead of single films they would now be working on whole series. Sophie passed her hands over her eyes and wished a bomb would fall out of the sky and reduce the office to nothing.

Maya said, 'It'll be great for us – everyone can get the salary hike they've been nagging me about, but the pressure's going to go up, up, up. Which is good – there's potential for us to do much more. We're just sitting tight on our asses most of the time. I think we should prove to LA that they don't need to set up more operations, that right now we can handle everything they have.'

'You mean you think we're underworked?' cried Sophie.

She considered Maya's confident expression sceptically. How could she take this seriously, this retarded job of copying down lines people said in films, this hackwork LA sent them only because they did it cheaper than anyone anywhere else in the world? But of course Maya took it seriously. She earned a fat salary from it – it put the fuel in her car, the expensive cheeses in her fridge, the dreams in her head of belonging to some kind of international elite of cool.

'I think I just need a break. Can I go to Shillong for a week?' Sophie asked matter-of-factly, knowing that even though Maya took vacations herself, she was wary of her staff going off for more than a few days at a time. It weakened her hold on them.

'Are you having trouble with Swami?' asked Maya, pushing her salad aside and leaning over the table towards her.

'No, it's just this insomnia. I can't sleep till like five in the morning. And then I'm tired all day. It might help if I take a break.'

'Your coordinator came and complained to me and I just shut her up – I said you had a personal problem to deal with, that's why you were slow with the files. But I don't want her to go and blabber to Ravi. I promised her I'd talk to you.'

'Thanks,' Sophie mumbled. 'Thanks a lot, Maya.'

A tense silence followed. Maya was weighing the odds.

'Won't your folks drill this sister thing into you if you go home? Why don't you take a weekend off instead and go to Goa with Swami?'

'No, no, I need to go and talk them out of the sister thing. If I don't fix it, the next thing I know, Muku will be standing on my doorstep with whichever random boy she's currently seeing.'

'Okay,' said Maya reluctantly. 'Take next week off; I want you refreshed when you start on the British series. After you come back I'm going to see you meeting all your targets and I mean all.'

She looked at Sophie intently and Sophie, worried that the delight on her face might be too obvious, changed the subject.

'Are you sorry about Shanthi leaving?'

'No, of course not. I've already spoken to two new girls and they both seem good. I just need to decide between them. Hey, d'you think Naomi might have something going for Shanthi?'

Maya's voice was suddenly more animated – the transition had been made from work-talk to gossip and Sophie let off the hook. Whenever this happened, Sophie remembered Maya was a whole year younger than her, and that even though she controlled it well, she sometimes possibly had the same urge to not *behave*.

But what Maya was actually saying made no sense to Sophie. 'Naomi? Shanthi?' she asked, bewildered.

Maya, in keeping with her usual spirit of leaving all options open, thought of herself as bisexual, though as far as Sophie could tell all her heartaches concerned men. On the other hand, she was always noticing incipient gay affairs where Sophie saw none, so it was possible she was attuned to something that Sophie wasn't.

'What did Naomi do?' asked Sophie.

Maya clicked her tongue. 'She didn't *do* anything. But I've been watching how she pursues Shanthi – chatting with her at every available opportunity, praising her work, eating lunch with her and not with me and the coordinators which is weird and which everyone has noticed because Shanthi's not even part of the workshop. And now this whole wedding mania. She's extending her stay just so that she can attend the wedding. And that's all she talks about – the wedding, Shanthi, Shanthi's pushy fiancée, Shanthi's dotty mother ...'

Sophie tried to readjust her mental picture of Naomi to accommodate the possible fact that she was lesbian. It made her seem even more interesting.

'But why are you worried?'

'Sophie, you just don't understand how these things work. Right now it's all hunky dory but Naomi might reach a point where she wants to make a move that Shanthi resists – without actually realizing what she's doing – and then there's no knowing what'll happen next. There's going to be a big comedown. I can see it coming. Like this morning, she kept trying to convince Shanthi to come to the US for a honeymoon and Shanthi was uncomfortable but she didn't know how to deal with it.'

'Whatever else Naomi might be, she's not an idiot. She's a VP and she's down here on a work visit. She's not going to blow anything by being indiscreet. '

'Sophie, if she makes a pass at you, don't come complaining to me.'

'Makes a pass at *me*? But you just said it's Shanthi ...'

But Maya had already pushed her chair back and was striding out of the restaurant and out onto the street to smoke.

Sophie looked out of the window, completing her sentence in her head. Then, finding one of the robots hovering at her elbow, hinting wordlessly to her that she should give way to the next customer, she began to slurp milkshake through her straw at top speed.

The Fatness of These Pursy Times

Sophie tried to be earnest after lunch and started on a new film, but action movies left her cold, discerning each sound effect was a nightmare and a year's accumulated insomnia weighed down her eyelids. The usual, big picture, post-lunch questions began to trouble her – how, for instance, would a deaf person benefit from reading phrase after phrase that went 'glass breaking', 'heels clicking on pavement', 'gunfire', 'man's head being bashed against a wall'? If a film's deaf audience once could hear, wouldn't they be able to imagine the sound of a gun going off from the context? On the other hand, if these vast unseen audiences consisted of congenitally deaf people, then to what avail words that indicated sounds? Finding no answers to these fundamental questions, Sophie would start to probe deeper. What about the sound a man whose head was being bashed made, as opposed to the sound his head made? Further, what really was the sound of a man's head being bashed against a wall? Surely not this muffled thump of a sack of potatoes repeatedly falling from a great height? Perhaps none of these things made the sounds that the movies attributed to them. Maybe the day we actually hear a man's head being bashed we won't be able to recognize it because of all this bad education courtesy cinema. This is not just a boring job, it's an ethically suspect job, thought Sophie. I'm paid to mislead people.

This realization neutralized any guilt she might have felt about closing the movie files and deciding to spend the afternoon doing emails, looking for cheap flights home and playing online Scrabble. From the console on her right she could hear the faint but distinct sound of her colleague Johnny, who was always stoned, absorbed in a computer game. He hadn't thought of turning off the sound, so every now and then a long beep could be heard signalling another combatant felled by another poison arrow or some such imbecility. Johnny was only two months old in office and he wouldn't last very long but it nevertheless gave Sophie hope to see other people at war with their situation.

One new message. The email from her father was brief – a written equivalent of his spoken manner. When it came to worldly matters, Mr Das tended never to speak more than three sentences at a time and most often managed with one. He wrote that she should begin thinking of 'what course of study Mukulika might pursue in Bangalore' – he never shortened her name to Muku like Sophie and her mother did. He informed her that his project to translate *Hamlet* into Bengali was making slow but steady progress. And he ended with yet another suggestion regarding her insomnia – taking a brisk walk just before bedtime, not out in the streets where it might be unsafe but in her own living room.

Whenever Sophie's mother wanted to confirm that her daughter recognized Mr Das's great incorrigibility, she asked – 'You know Baba, na?' Mrs Das had been asking this rhetorical question for years and for years Sophie had ignored it, ignored her mocking of her husband's obsession with Hamlet-Shamlet, ignored her long drawn out laments about his negligence towards his family. But the truth was, thought Sophie as she stared resentfully at the screen, that she *did* know her father just as she knew her mother. Sophie read the email again and stamped her foot involuntarily, then groaned softly as her injured knee hit the drawer that held the keyboard. She wondered what might happen if she wrote back saying – *I don't care.* That would constitute the ultimate betrayal – to declare oneself free of responsibility.

Responsibility. The Das family spent much of their time apportioning responsibility amongst themselves and the rest of the world. Why had Mr Das not got the university job he deserved? A multilayered story of blame, implicating the university professors who did not advocate his cause as they should have, Mrs Das and her lack of complete faith in her husband's abilities and, to a lesser extent, the head of the English department in the college where Mr Das had once taught, who'd provoked him into resigning, thereby forcing him into school-teaching and reducing his chances of becoming a professor. Who was responsible for Mrs Das's relatives cutting off ties with her when she married Mr Das? On some days it was her natal family that was to blame; on other days, it was all Mr Das's fault. If he'd been nicer to them, they'd surely have accepted him and the marriage, but he'd merely scowled, refused to eat the tandoori chicken offered to him and contradicted everything that was said about the state of the nation by Mrs Das's father who supported a right-wing, fist-shaking party and had begun to suspect Mr Das of communism. Why was Muku not doing well at school and constantly answering back? Her teachers were responsible and her chronically ill-behaved classmates and her father's lack of interest in her (from her mother's point of view) and her mother's excess of interest in her (from her father's point of view). Why did Sophie not get that scholarship to go abroad? Sophie herself was responsible – she should have tried harder and the city of Shillong was responsible – it made one lazy and failed to instil a competitive spirit in the young (yes, cities could also be held to blame).

Sophie thought she had escaped responsibility when she left home, but here it was again in her father's three-sentence email. Unable, as always, to disappoint him, she wrote him a message of disproportionate length, describing the weather in Bangalore, what she had eaten for lunch and (since her parents believed she was an editor in a children's publishing house) the fictitious book she was currently editing – one about a child who spends a whole day being afraid of dying, having understood for the first time what death really means. Till then this six year old had believed, wrote Sophie to her father, that death was a simple confusion on the part of the dead person – like wearing your shirt inside out and not noticing till someone points it out to you. In this way, Sophie sidestepped her father's advice and requests like her mother sidestepped Sophie's questions and demands. A hide-and-seek family.

Then she clicked on 'Compose' and brought out a grubby one-year-old piece of paper. A whole compartment of her wallet had been devoted to storing this scrap whose weight and significance she'd been conscious of during her first few weeks in Bangalore. She had in those early days often considered emailing Ribor, then put the scrap away, embarrassed at the pretence of writing without really having anything to say.

One night in Shillong, a couple of months before the Killer Queen moment, the lights went out; her mother called for candles and her father yelled for everyone to stay where they were till he located the torch. They groped through the shelves and found that they'd run out of candles but no one felt like going out in the driving rain to buy more so they just sat like that, growing accustomed to the dark while Mrs Das finished her cooking by the light of the torch. Lying in bed, seeing the everyday shapes around her grow shadowy and mysterious, the rain pounding on the tin roof with so eloquent a sound it seemed to carry a meaning, Sophie suddenly found Ribor's face floating before her. She'd been going to his shop for years – looking for an old CCR or a new Moby, while Ribor chatted with her or, on other days, was strangely silent, standing out by the railing of the veranda that went around the building, smoking, while Sophie browsed inside. She'd never really thought about him but on that evening dark as blindness it was as if some hidden cache inside her – of things she'd unconsciously been noticing – suddenly came to life. She felt dry-mouthed panic at the thought of seeing him again.

She stayed away from his shop after that, but went back the day after Killer Queen brought her to her senses. She was exhausted with the endless arguments she'd been having with herself. One half of her felt this was a daydream, a fiction she'd created to salve her boredom, a ghost that would evaporate (and rightly so) as soon as she saw him, forcing her to *run*. The other half believed that she had no choice really but to return to the shop where Ribor sat among his music in his worn brown leather jacket and cowboy boots. She was helpless; her infatuation would – Madame Bovary style – spin things out of the control of her volition.

When she got there, Ribor was talking to a woman he seemed to know. Sophie almost turned back but she was there as a customer, she was there to ask Ribor to bring out his cartons of CDs, let him play a couple of tracks for her, buy something or perhaps not, especially if he said – this isn't such a good album, his last one was better. Or – take it home and listen to it, if you like it you can pay me later. Sophie found she didn't quite know what to do with her hands. She put them on the glass counter and looked down at the discs arranged face up below.

When he greeted Sophie, she saw how the emotion in his eyes tailed off from recognition and friendliness to something starker and more dispassionate. The woman ignored Sophie and paid Ribor.

'You tell me what it's like,' he said to her as he handed her some change. 'I haven't heard it yet.'

'Sure, sure,' said the woman, her mouth lurid with lipstick. 'How can Madonna ever go wrong?'

'Never,' said Ribor. Sophie knew he didn't believe that and yet he made the word sound like a promise of something. The woman dropped her coins, then asked, looking up from the floor, 'Tomorrow?'

Ribor nodded. 'I'll call you.'

Get lost Madonna, the eighties are over and you're past your prime, thought Sophie. As soon as the woman walked out, Sophie said to Ribor, 'She left her umbrella behind.'

Ribor, stacking the scattered discs, glanced casually at the purple parasol that had leaked a small puddle on the floor.

He shrugged. 'It's okay. It isn't raining now.'

They smiled at each other as if at a private joke.

'You're looking for something in particular?' he asked then, turning his back on her.

Sophie thought for a moment he had seen through her, and, furthermore, suspected that all the years she'd been coming to the shop it was for him and not the music. And the awful part was that Sophie herself was not sure. She appealed to Madame Bovary for help and with sudden intuition realized Ribor was thinking about the Madonna woman. He went outside and put his hands on the railing. Sophie thought – I have to get out of here. And even though she would afterwards put it down to Killer Queen, the truth was that she received her confirmation in Ribor's shop – the sudden need to change her life from beginning to end.

Ribor came back and picked a late nineties Dylan album for her when she didn't even care about Dylan.

'I'm leaving,' said Sophie, even though she had no clear plan yet. 'Town.'

'Why?' asked Ribor casually. 'I mean, have you got a job or something?'

'I need to find out what lies on the other side of the mountains as they always say in fairy tales.'

'It's hard. Many people think it'll work out but they come right back. They're embarrassed for a few weeks – you ask them what happened and they say – I couldn't find a good place to stay, or it's too hot, or everyone out there thinks we're Chinese and tries to rip us off. And then, after a while they forget about it and it's as if they never went. So why take all the trouble?'

Ribor had never stepped out of Shillong. Even though she had herself not travelled much further than Guwahati – a three hour drive away – she considered Ribor a lovely relic, except that she wasn't sure a relic of what. Perhaps of the faraway history of Shillong of which she knew only a little – the tiny tribal settlement, its people roaming the hills for millennia, carving little kingdoms for themselves, conducting a slow-moving trade with those in the plains of what was now Bangladesh, standing up to the mighty British with bows and arrows. Then the British had taken over and changed everything – put down native rebellions, acquired the limestone business. Seemingly out of nothing, Shillong emerged – the schools, the churches, the bungalows, the lake, the polo grounds, the golf course, the offices from where the colonials presided over

Assam, the winding road down to the plains. And with the town came the people – Calvinist Protestant Welshmen, German and Irish Catholics, Scottish Presbyterians, Bengalis bearing the message of Brahmo Samaj and Vivekananda, settlers from the lowlands of Assam, traders from Rajasthan who opened grocery shops. And much later, after the British had gone, after Shillong became the capital of a smaller state, the people continued to pour in – teachers, students, restaurant cooks, tailors, garbage collectors, construction-site workers, carpenters, bureaucrats, doctors. Sophie knew that Ribor had grown up during a time when it still made sense that the town accommodate people who spoke a dozen languages and didn't understand each other. She, on the other hand, was born when Shillong first started trying to throw off this crazy past and become the pure thing it had possibly never been – a place where one people of one blood lived. All through her life this had continued to be the town's defining characteristic – its search for purity and aloofness.

And now Ribor was saying that she should go by the experiences of his people when she wasn't one of his people, didn't look like one of his people and most certainly didn't have the luxury of going away, coming back and saying – doesn't work, it's too hot there.

'But I have to leave some day so ...' she said.

'But you've always lived here so ...' he said.

These incomplete sentences didn't need completing. Both of them knew what they were saying. Sophie was saying – of course *you* can't take off into India just like that – you with your secret language and your unique face. And Ribor was saying – even if you're a dkhar, even if my people have always wanted your people out, even if blood has been shed, you have the right to stay.

They stood outside and talked. Sophie didn't care, even though it was a risky thing to do because her father might walk by, shopping for groceries and spot her. (And who would be responsible for that? How many people could be implicated in this violation – Sophie smoking publicly and shamelessly with a middle-aged stranger, a random shopkeeper, in the heart of Laitumkhrah?) But Sophie wasn't thinking of that right then. She was watching Ribor as he asked her whether there wasn't something she could do in Shillong. There's nothing here, she said – the way she'd heard her parents say all her life, and he said – you can teach in a kindergarten, bake cakes and sell them from home, write newspaper articles, become an announcer in the local radio station. Right, said Sophie, smiling. Those are the kinds of things one does in this town.

And all the while she watched him – the delicate way his long fingers held the cigarette, the wrinkles around his eyes that suggested a history. He said nothing personal though she knew he had the Madonna woman to meet the following day. So despite how long she had waited to apply her Flaubertian education to life, Sophie decided not to be Madame Bovary. She took the strip of cigarette carton on which Ribor wrote down his phone number and email address, accepted the Dylan album as a parting gift and reached out reluctantly for the left-behind umbrella he offered her because it had started to rain again. She walked home without opening it, flinging it into the first swollen gutter she saw.

For so long she had let this frayed piece of paper lie untouched in her wallet, certain that Ribor and she had nothing more to do with each other, suppressing the memory of that last conversation. But neither had she thrown it away. Now she deleted the few halting, happy lines she'd written and logged out of her mail. She didn't need to announce it to him in advance. She was coming home.

~

The following afternoon, Sophie was in her favourite pub, waiting for Swami. All over the walls were posters advertizing events that had happened a long time ago. They were no longer announcements but yellowing commemorations: Pink Floyd's *The Wall* live in Berlin in 1990, The Who at the Marquee Club in London, Bowie's Changes One. Accompanying these were larger than life black and white portraits of Bob Marley smoking a joint and Frank Zappa on a commode. Above all this, painted directly onto the low ceiling, was an outline in black of the Beatles.

Sophie liked the feel of this place in the afternoon, the

scattered drinkers and talkers who always appeared a little derelict and yet engrossed in themselves, as if they led secret lives in this dim, castle tower-like pub while people went about their mundane business in the too-brightly lit world outside. The place started filling up only after six and then the music would slowly grow louder till, over the clamour of drunken voices and the shouts of waiters to each other down the spiral staircase, and the clinking of beer mugs, and the honks of passing traffic, its steely vibrations could be felt on a wall if one happened to touch it, and in one's chest if one pressed hands against ears.

But now the orange glow of the afternoon light from the tinted glass panes that ran along the staircase revealed what the night-time regulars would never see: how the sad little bow ties the waiters wore – like characters from a wayside inn in a Dickens novel – were fastened to their shirt-collars with fraying elastic bands, how the whites of their shirts had faded to grey, how the ceramic bowls they broke packets of popcorns into were exactly the same colour as their shirts – once white but now only aspiring to whiteness.

Sophie checked the time. Swami was late but she resisted the urge to call. A growing sense of guilt made her feel she ought to make a mental catalogue of Swami's virtues while she waited so that she wouldn't snap at him when he came. So he had changed. But intrinsically wasn't he still the Swami whose girlfriend Sophie had, with a self-conscious giggle, agreed to be once they'd gone for the standard number of movies together? He was kind. He was the sort who always ran to accident sites to help. He was untroubled. He possessed the composure of the innately clueless and though clueless herself – the eternal Alice falling down the eternal hole – Sophie appreciated how there was little that could make Swami anxious. Then, he was called Swami like the character in the book, even though he was unable to get past the first few pages. And he loved her. Here Sophie felt a pang of embarrassment. Swami's love for Sophie was a mystery best left unexplored. There was nothing to it – he just did. Sophie liked Swami less on some days and more on others and the cumulative effect of the days when she didn't like him at all lessened the potency of the days when she was grateful for him. But in Swami's case not one of their arguments, however corrosive, could change the consistency of his love for her. And in a strange way that's the problem, thought Sophie, abandoning her meditation on her boyfriend's noble qualities. That's the problem because given this rock hard love, nothing need ever change. He can go on being ridiculous and I can go on being irritated, she thought, grinding her teeth and pouring out more beer for herself.

She took several large gulps, breathed deeply and asked herself – what is it I'm irritated about? Her mind stayed vacant for a long time as she watched from the corner of her eye a couple having an argument. The girl apparently wanted to buy a particular type of cardigan ('I've already told you, I saw Jennifer Aniston wearing it on *Friends*, a little black cardigan!'). They seemed to have wasted all morning looking for it and had now repaired to this pub to vent their frustration on each other. 'I don't give a shit,' said the boy and the girl went very quiet so as not to cry.

Just then Ringo Saar walked in and came straight up to her as if he had expected to find her there.

'So what are you going to do about it?' he asked in a musical, mock Malayali accent.

The first time Sophie had seen Ringo Saar, he was coming out of Bhatt's house and getting into his car; he asked her the way to the nearest petrol pump, oblivious of Bhatt who came out after him and was trying to give him a flyer for the Bangalore guru Baba Sampige's 'One Truth, One World' spirituality workshop. Perhaps Bhatt believed that Ringo could be converted to gentleness via religion. After Sophie bumped into Ringo in the lane a few more times, she started inviting him to join her and Swami when they sat in her flat smoking joints on Sundays. Ringo, once he got to know the jobless Swami, invited him to help with the sound during the Little Idli concerts. To Sophie, Ringo had in those days seemed too placid to be either a drummer or a loan recovery agent but more recently he'd cut off his pony-tail and toughened in some way. Perhaps, it was the growing experience of the job that involved bullying people whichever way you looked at it; perhaps it was his parents' recent divorce. His mother ran a chocolate shop in Bangalore that thrived particularly on orders from software companies which, during festivals, ordered chocolates in their thousands with the names of each of their employees printed individually on every truffle or éclair. It was the in-thing apparently. Ringo's father was an alcoholic who ran a booming prawn farming business in Kerala and was shy of his son. Ringo could, if he wanted to, take it easy for a few years given his parents' successes but he refused to touch his father's money. Besides there was Rukshana, his girlfriend, who could be expensive. Sophie knew he was here waiting for her to join him.

'Your Bhatt is in trouble,' he said.

'Picture in the papers?' asked Sophie in alarm.

Ringo Saar nodded.

'What?' cried Sophie. Bhatt was always about to get his picture in the papers, always afraid that he would stand revealed before the smug Chinnappa and the rest of his loan-free neighbours, but Sophie had come to believe that this would never actually happen.

'You promised me you could do something.'

'We just discovered there's a second credit card company after him. And he's done nothing about our repayment. Not moved an inch. He's hollow, he just doles out one false promise after another. I can't hold out any longer, Sophie. My bosses are starting to breathe down my neck on this one. This is it. Come next Wednesday and the whole city will be in on it.'

'But he doesn't have the money, Ringo. You know that,' said Sophie, feeling personally betrayed.

'The bank has filed a case. If they get a High Court order they can seize his property as security till he pays back.'

'What property?'

'Two houses, Sophie,' said Ringo as if he were addressing an idiot. 'Plus he must have a small pile of gold hidden away somewhere. No self-respecting middle-class Indian his age can function without a hidden pile of gold.'

Sophie bit her nails. She felt absurdly sorry for Bhatt. And for herself – of course he'd throw her out now.

'What does putting his picture in the Deccan Herald achieve? He's just going to get more adamant.'

'Oh no, just wait and watch. He'll consider selling off his house and moving into a rented place.'

Sophie was starting to see how much Ringo enjoyed bringing defaulters to their knees, men much older than him, perhaps his father's age.

'There should be some way of writing off loans you know you'll never recover.'

'Oh, but with Bhatt we're nowhere close to exhausting all options. He has savings squirreled away – I can sense it. Let the picture appear and see what happens – some money will miraculously appear. Want to bet?' asked Ringo, cracking his knuckles.

'Suppose Swami were a defaulter, would you be as hard with him?' asked Sophie, but before he could answer Rukshana appeared – a woman Sophie had never quite managed to have a conversation with. Rukshana was always full of indignation at life. Always, some speeding biker had driven too close to her, some waiter in a restaurant had not grovelled enough, someone at the ATM booth had elbowed his way in past her, some friend had forgotten her birthday. So now Sophie merely nodded at Rukshana, as Ringo steered her out. They were going shopping. Sophie remembered the couple fighting over the cardigan and turned to look at them. They were still fighting.

Ringo stopped at the door and turned back. 'So what are you going to do about it?' he repeated in a mockery of his father's accent and Sophie looked at him with a woebegone expression and said, 'Don't do it.'

'But I have to do my job,' said Ringo wearily.

'Write him off,' pleaded Sophie. 'Go after someone else.'

'See, that's why I told you not to make promises to her,' said Rukshana with satisfaction.

'Sophie, I don't get it,' said Ringo. 'You don't even like the old bum. Look, I'll help you find a new place. I know a good broker.'

'And now you're making promises again,' said Rukshana triumphantly.

'Give him one last chance,' said Sophie and there was a new note in her voice, a note that meant – *I've known you from before you met this woman, I have a prior claim on your loyalty and you have to prove that loyalty now.* I will never speak to him again, she thought calmly.

Ringo saw the thought in her eyes and pulled savagely at his hair and said, 'Okay … okay. I'm going to give him another month. I'm coming over there tomorrow and I'll tell this to him in person – one month and no more.'

Rukshana screamed, 'How can you do this? You might as well just hand over your job to her.' Ringo tried to quieten her but she shook her arm free of him. 'You're putting your own future in that office on the line because of her? Take it back Ringo. Stop making promises to her.'

Sophie drank her beer and pretended she couldn't hear anything and Ringo said, 'This is nothing to do with you, I swear. I've known Bhatt for some time now and sooner or later we'll get his money. It's nothing you have to get worked up about.'

'It's her I'm worked up about,' screeched Rukshana and spat 'Bitch' at Sophie loud enough for the others in the pub to hear, turned on her heel and walked out.

Whoa, thought Sophie. But she was pleased. A month was a long time and the tide could turn.

Swami appeared, talking on his cellphone. He looked like he always did during daylight hours – unkempt. He was on a perpetual journey and dying to reach the point where he could stop travelling, have a bath, wear clean clothes, go to sleep and wake up refreshed. The bottom of his low-slung jeans brushed the floor as he walked, he spoke in a slur and his eyes always began to crinkle up when people spoke for more than a minute at a time. At night Swami sprang into life, however, as a smoothly-shaved, smartly-dressed executive who spoke crisply into his phone and never tried to fudge it when he couldn't be of help, instead patiently explaining to the caller the limits of his role. Swami's less confident colleagues had started to imitate him.

He gave her the thumbs-up sign. Every second minute his phone conversation sounded like it was going to end, and yet it didn't. Sophie looked at the fighting couple who were preparing to leave and whose argument had now shaded into one about which one of them should drive the car.

When Swami was finally done, he gazed at his phone as if it were a person. 'I need to humour this guy because he's the head trainer – if I keep at it, he'll promote me. There's just no way he can't, I've been working my ass off. No customer has ever complained about me, I haven't taken a single day off and I always know what the weather's like in every city of the United States.'

He kissed Sophie, took a sip of her beer and continued. 'He talks too much. He's a real operator – but man, does he know how to work the system, does he know how to work the system! The guy's rolling in money just from buying little bits of land all over the city – nothing bigger than what you can put a telephone booth on – sitting on them for a year or two and then selling them for as much as a 500 per cent profit. How does he do it? Because the areas in which he has these itsy-bitsy properties have developed so much in this short time that some guy desperately *needs* that bit of land to put his telephone booth on. Do you have any idea what's going on in this city, Sophie? You could get rich with your eyes closed.'

'So you're taking another loan then.'

'Land is gold, Sophie. I'm seeing this happen before my eyes – people in my neighbourhood, who just ten years ago ran pani-puri stalls and sold fruit from pushcarts are now driving Hyundai Accents and have three apartments each – none of which they live in. They cling to their poky old houses and put all the apartments on rent, clear off their bank loans in half the expected time, then invest the money in more apartments. This is getting fucking insane, man, I can't believe it.'

He was so excited he couldn't sit.

'So how come Bhatt is in such shit then if it's all so easy?'

'Bhatt?' asked Swami as if he'd never heard of him. He stopped a waiter and ordered another pitcher of beer.

Sophie suddenly felt a stab of extreme disorientation. Who, indeed, was Bhatt and why did it matter to her so much that he was in trouble? She and Swami met only a couple of times a week, yet they always ended up having these arguments about the future, about that horrid thing called the long-term. Swami was waiting to lie sprawled on a sofa in the living room of his *own* house, thinking – this is my house – and never tiring of that thought, never ceasing to marvel at the beauty of ownership.

Sophie wished herself back in the rickshaw with Ribor –

the imaginary exchange of small bits of autobiography, the recognition of shared experience in the form of Killer Queen.

'I'm going to Shillong for a week,' she said evenly, trying, as she'd done with Maya, to suppress the sudden, absurd sense of happiness.

'You got a whole week's leave?' asked Swami in disbelief. 'You have Mother Teresa for a boss. I couldn't even take two days off without jeopardizing this whole promotion thing. But I've really got to do everything to make sure it happens. Then I'm through with this all-night-on-the-phone shit – I have normal working hours, I have Saturdays *and* Sundays off, I don't have to deal with the transatlantic retards. Like the other night there was this taxi driver cruising the streets of Florida. My wireless credit card machine isn't working, he says – there's something wrong with the memory. It's supposed to hold up to a thousand transactions but it says full at a hundred. And I kept asking him – why do you want to store so many transactions, you should connect with your merchant account provider as soon as you can after each transaction unless there's something holding you up. But he just went on about his faulty memory and then it turns out that there were a thousand transactions stored in there – he'd just been reading the figure without his reading glasses! Brilliant. He's all apologetic and I ask – just to be nice – if he's cleaned his machine recently. And he says, 'Never, how does one do it?' He's had it for four years and never cleaned it!'

'Swami, you're losing perspective. How does it matter that some random taxi driver in America hasn't cleaned his credit card machine? You've got to find something else to think about once you leave office. Can't you read a book or something?'

'But I *want* their damned credit card terminals and their payment service systems to work. I want no one in America who calls me to feel like – heck, this guy's useless. The rotten thing is that if there's a real problem, we can't fix it. We can only tell them to wait while the technical guys do their bit. It's not real, what we're doing. That's why it's frustrating – because it's not real.'

'Like my job is real. Listening to those crappy dialogues and spewing them out.'

This silenced them for a few moments – the fictions of their respective jobs. Then a sloshing pitcher arrived and the hours began to melt. Slowly, the pub filled up, the lights dimmed, the cacophony grew so powerful that Sophie and Swami had to yell even though they were sitting right next to each other.

Sophie was telling Swami about Shanthi.

'She never complains about anything. She just goes on working like some low-level machine, takes fifteen minutes off to eat her damned lemon rice and then she's back at it. She makes me feel psychotic.'

Swami, now considerably drunker than Sophie, started giggling.

'Don't abuse the lemon rice, da. People might take offence. Suppose someone said 'fucking dal makhani'. How would you feel then?' he said through what was developing into a seizure of laughter.

'You can abuse dal makhani to hell. It's not like it's my fucking heritage. Anyway, this Shanthi is amazing. She's so completely accepting of everything the job demands. And now she's moving to another job, but it's not as if she's changed or is really dissatisfied. She'll make more money elsewhere so she moves. It's all mechanical.'

'Fucking dal makhani and fucking palak paneer also,' said Swami, embarking on another laughing spree, beer spraying out of mouth. 'But not kathi rolls. I like kathi rolls. So let's not fuck those please,' he shouted.

Some other drunk person caught the tail end of Swami's shout and yelled 'Yeah, man!' through the gloom.

'Shut up, Swami,' said Sophie. 'You're making an ass of yourself. You haven't heard a word of what I said.'

'I know these types, man. I used to laugh at them once but they're everywhere. My office is full of them. You can't let them bug you, da. The whole world is like that: people want to make their money and go home and watch TV and take holidays once a year in some bloody boring place like Kerala or something. That's the definition of life. And I'm starting to think – what's wrong with that? It's normal. *I'm* normal. I no longer want to say: no thank you, I'm an intellectual.'

Sophie desperately wished she could light a cigarette.

'There's nothing wrong with Shanthi. Stop bothering about her,' added Swami with unusual curtness.

'Okay, so there's nothing wrong with her. She's totally impressive. Yes, you're right. People like Shanthi are the world's backbone. If everyone was like me there'd be no fucking new economy running this city,' replied Sophie.

'Now you have problems with this city? Then what are you doing here, I say?'

Sophie gave up and Swami, despite his drunkenness, noticed her face fall. He put his arm around her.

'You don't love me at all,' he said.

Sophie tried to shrug him off. 'Don't keep saying that, Swami. I watch too many films. Words like love have lost meaning for me.'

'So prove that you love me then and I'll stop saying it.'

'I can't.'

'Kiss me at least then.'

Sophie kissed him on the cheek then moved away dextrously when he tried to reach for her mouth. The previous Sunday she hadn't (on the half-pretext that Bhatt was starting to get suspicious) let Swami stay over at her place, as he usually did on his off day. The fumbling lovemaking, the same talk before and after as if sex was just a commercial break, the jaded air of secrecy over his coming and going so that the Bhatt family wouldn't notice, the sense of casualness with which he held her – all of this had begun to depress Sophie.

'Let's go shopping,' yelled Swami suddenly. 'You need gifts for your folks if you're going home.'

~

The new mall was clogged with Saturday night shoppers and in the atrium, on a tiny ramp, a fashion show was in progress. Girls with jewellery glinting like mirrors, wearing richly embroidered saris of silk and georgette, walked up and down coyly and occasionally sat on a chaise lounge, considering each other wordlessly through eyelashes weighed down with mascara. Men photographed the models with their cellphones.

Things, things, things, thought Sophie with pleasure, as she and Swami soared up the escalator. What could she buy for her parents and Muku that in some way bore the impress of her one year in Bangalore? Shoes and sweaters, leather handbags, crystalware and cookie tins, ballpoint pens and shiny cars, scents, posies, wicker bins ... brandy, coffee, long umbrellas, novels, kurtas, strong white mints ... shampoos, trousers, cheeses, flowers, sandals, knives and ...

Swami swaggered into a menswear shop and Sophie stopped her silent singing. A shirt in this store cost a third of Sophie's monthly salary. They both knew this but faked confidence – pulling out soft woollen pullovers with Fair Isle designs, checking the price tags on jeans, marvelling at how the shirts, rainbow-like, ranged from light pastel colours to violets and indigos. Sophie walked through rows of jackets and T-shirts as if in pursuit of something she could not find till the salesgirls with their rehearsed smiles started coming up and asking, 'Can I help you ma'am?'

'Let's go,' she whispered to Swami, who was immersed in his cellphone near the socks and underwear.

In the next shop, Sophie sprayed perfume after perfume on her wrist and on the inside of her elbow, had eager salesgirls draw thick lines of lipstick on the back of her hand, which she studied intently, trying to guess if her sister would prefer pink to chocolate brown, or like neither and instead be content with 'Plum Crush'. She sniffed at body sprays and checked the prices of hair gels, examined creams for under-eye repair and overnight rejuvenation. Then she carefully put the jars back on their shelves and looked for Swami who was waiting for her outside, having bumped into someone from the call centre.

'Check this out dude,' said the boy to Swami, holding out a CD of techno music. Swami took it with an even expression.

'It's totally orgasmic,' said the boy excitedly. 'Fucking intense.'

Swami passed it on to Sophie, saying, 'Get this for your sister.'

Sophie passed it back saying, 'No, she only listens to Lordi.'

In the food department, Sophie, with Swami trailing behind her, asking if she'd bought anything yet, ran her eyes past grape-jelly streaked peanut butter and potato chips in thirteen flavours and American candy bars and cheese from Denmark and kiwi fruit from New Zealand and smoked herring from Canada and nectarines from San Francisco at three hundred rupees a kilo, with skins that looked like they were painted, crimson and gold. She longed to touch one, but walked on, her feet beginning to ache.

They stopped outside a bookstore.

'I have to leave soon,' said Swami. 'Can't be late. That guy … Pritish … saw me, so can't even say it was the traffic.' Swami's office was around the corner. He sometimes came here to eat hotdogs. Occasionally he'd buy a CD or watch a film in the multiplex on the top floor with a large cone of caramel-flavoured popcorn wedged between his knees.

'I need to check out everything first, before I decide what to buy,' said Sophie.

'Everything?' asked Swami in concern, as he followed Sophie into the bookstore. 'There are a hundred shops in this mall.'

Sophie said nothing. They looked at the hardbacks on display in the front of the small store, and then walked through the low shelves stocked with management books and computer books, cookbooks and children's books, returning to the one shelf that had novels. Sophie saw a copy of *Swami and Friends* on the lowest rack. She balanced on her toes and looked at the spine, not daring to pull it out and compare this edition with the tattered one she'd read as a child. She had an obscure fear that it might turn out to be different in some way.

'Let's go,' she said.

'Buy a book for your dad,' said Swami. 'He's a professor, right.'

'He's not a professor,' said Sophie with her back to him as she walked out of the bookshop and forged ahead through clamouring toddlers and women in sequined clothes and men with bulging shopping bags. 'He's a school teacher and he doesn't read anything written after the Second World War.'

Swami caught up with her as she was entering a music store. 'What does your dad need then? Anyway, the point is that I have to leave by nine.'

They didn't buy any music or films. They didn't buy any handmade soap or fresh-fruit shower gel in the shop selling those things, nor wine, nor assorted candy, nor watercolours and drawing pads, nor saris, nor silver jewellery nor warm jackets, nor … nothing, in short.

Sophie's feet hurt badly in her hard-soled slippers. She put her hand in the pocket of her jeans and felt for her credit card. They were on the highest floor, and looking down they could see that the ramp used for the fashion show had been replaced by an improbably long car with a huge red ribbon tied onto it with a bow.

'Mercedes Benz,' said Swami. He couldn't see a car and not name it. But it wasn't enough to curb his exasperation.

'What's your problem?' he asked Sophie. 'Surely there's *something* you can get. Otherwise forget it. Let's go. I have to report to work in ten minutes.'

'There are just too many people here,' said Sophie listlessly, unable to explain the sudden paralysis that had come over her. She was starting to feel that the general ocean of things in the mall would come rushing down and engulf any specific thing she bought. But neither could she leave till she had proved this absurd fear unfounded, till she had taken *Swami and Friends* out of the building and found it unchanged despite how diminished it looked, or till she had bitten into a nectarine and discovered that even if a hundred thousand nectarines rained down on her they would not dilute the sweetness of the one she was eating. She looked down and saw how, from that height, people appeared to be driven by a mechanical impulse: swarming into the atrium, thronging the escalators, spilling out of stores. No one was still. Sophie felt dizzy. Swami caught her by the elbow as she leaned out, but she shrugged off his hand, laughing.

'You can go shopping by yourself some other day,' said Swami.

'I don't have time, I'm leaving Monday,' she said.

'*Then please buy something,*' said Swami, yanking Sophie's hand off the railing and attempting to lead her away. A few teenage boys looked at them with interest.

'What the fuck is wrong with you,' asked Sophie in a low voice. 'Don't pull at me like that.'

They walked away from the staring boys to a corner near an ATM. The effects of their binge in the pub had worn off completely.

'Sophie Das,' said Swami gazing intently at her. 'Are you confused?'

Sophie returned his gaze and then looked away, trying to

fight the sense of extreme irritation she felt – at him and at herself.

A sudden scream rang through the air, echoing eerily in the vault and dying out slowly. There followed a minute of absolute silence in which Sophie breathed out, feeling everything would be okay if only they could leave at once and not have to find out what had caused the scream. But then the din resumed with greater intensity and the woman screamed again and there were people shouting now. Swami ran to the railing as did everyone else on each of the four levels of the mall. Sophie remained where she was, feeling trapped in the beginning of some exitless nightmare. They were imprisoned in this tower with its gleaming cancer of things, things which had now started to conspire against them. She looked around her and could see no openings that let in air, no breathing holes.

'I'm going down,' yelled Swami as he disappeared.

'What happened?'

'Some kid fell down ...' he shouted and then vanished in the throng. Sophie pushed people aside and saw a child sprawled face down on the Mercedes Benz, whom she recognized at once because of his blue and red Superman suit. It was a child she had earlier seen surveying the crowd, high on his father's shoulders, and she'd stopped short for a moment because he looked so much like Mani. It hadn't been Mani at all – it was just that abstracted look of a two year old that had attracted her, the look that seemed to be taking in everything and processing it into an altogether different intelligence from the regular adult one.

She tried to make her way after Swami but was blocked by people pounding down the escalators, eager to find out what had happened, fuelled by that enthusiasm for tragedy she could never understand. She noticed it whenever there was the horrible sound of vehicles colliding in the street and people in shops or offices would drop what they were doing and run out with that inexplicably eager expression on their faces.

She had lost Swami. By the time she got to the ground floor only the after-effects of the accident remained – a crush of people who all seemed to be talking at the same time. The red bow of the Mercedes Benz was a little askew and there was some blood splattered on its white top but apart from that it was unchanged, its hard inanimateness unaffected by the soft, living thing that had crashed into it. Yet people, some leading children by the hand, continued to enter the mall with a look of innocent expectancy on their faces as if nothing bad could ever happen in their world.

Sophie, her mouth dry, asked the woman at the information desk who sat there looking helpless, 'Do you know what happened to that child?'

The woman said, 'He's been taken to the hospital, ma'am. We don't have any other information at the moment.'

A man standing nearby, holding a giant burger made of tan-coloured felt (with squares of yellow, green, brown and red felt poking out to represent the cheese, lettuce, meat and tomato, respectively), said, 'He's dead.'

The burger could have been anything – an oversized keychain, a CD wallet, a work of art. Sophie stared at him. 'He died on the spot. I saw it happening. I saw him falling, I saw him hitting the car, head first. His eyes were wide open when they lifted him up. He was bleeding from the head. They didn't want a scene here so they whisked him away.'

Sophie asked, 'What's going to happen now?' even though she wasn't really sure what the question meant. But the guy had no idea. He seemed dazed. Others in the crowd were asking if they should help the parents of the child file a police complaint against the mall. A man with a mop was washing away a trail of bloodstains. Nobody seemed to think that the car should be removed – the murder weapon.

Sophie heard stray remarks which to her seemed to have no connection to what had just happened. 'Bloody stupid parents. Now they'll blame the mall authorities when the problem is that they can't mind their own kids because they're so busy shopping their brains out. This will generate so much bad publicity. And it's one of the best malls ...'

'He couldn't have been more than two years old ...'

'I saw it happening – he was sitting on the banister and his dad held him with one hand and had tonnes of shopping in the other. And at some point he lost his hold ...'

'It'll be in the papers tomorrow. Come on. We'll get your swimsuit another day.'

'What's the problem? Is your bank balance low? You want me to lend you some money?'

'A kid just fell down three floors ...'

'What?'

Sophie looked through the massive doors and saw the traffic streaming past. Swami had disappeared. Maybe he'd gone to the hospital. She went back up and into a vast food court, got herself a coffee, found an empty table, poured a sachet of sugar into her cup, stirred it, blew on it, took a sip and shut her eyes. Her claustrophobia had given way to an intense sadness. She tried to focus on the matter of the gifts before the shops closed but all she could think of now was the dead child, the murdered, secret brother of Mani's and the unmoved and unmoveable car onto which he had fallen. And when, after another cup of coffee and more sadness, she was finally able to think about the gifts, she realized that nothing in this mall had any connection with her life. How was it that once a bottle of Coke, a pair of sandals, nail polish of a certain colour, a new notebook with crisp white sheets, were things so filled with secret emotion they could alleviate all sorts of suffering – the feeling of being slowly killed off by boredom, the belief that one lacked a personality, the conviction that one would die unloved, the fear that no one understood? Things once had essences they gave off slowly, filling long, empty days, making time bearable. Now that they had proliferated – all these things she had spent her childhood longing for – it was as if they had returned to their hard, closed shells and were nothing more than their functions. Now when she had the sharp rectangle of the credit card pressing against her thighs, now when pleasures were graded for her and lay stretched out in every direction like some version of paradise, all she got was suffocation, death, people screaming. She was Madame Bovary all over again – pressed into her lover's arms after being wrung through tragedy and yet thinking – doesn't this in truth sicken me?

Guru

The next morning, Sophie ironed clothes and thought, uncharacteristically, about God. Since the time she had fallen under Vivekananda's influence, she'd come to understand the Vedanta principle that God was to be found in the consistent practice of high-mindedness and selflessness and that he was not modelled on Santa Claus. Striving towards this version of God required a lot of work. And it didn't help that Vivekananda frequently compared religion to chemistry – just as to succeed in the lab there is some amount of accidental dropping of acid on oneself involved, so also religion is a process of trial and error and you can get your fingers burnt. So when Sophie completely messed up the maths paper in her school leaving exam, she found herself praying to the other God, the one found in school chapels, the Father glimpsed through the dead eyes of Christ, invoked with humility and desperation and nothing of the cool scientific approach Vivekananda advocated. She *did* pass and for a while after regarded the divine with shy admiration. Then she discovered cigarettes and love and forgot about both Vivekananda and God. Her father was an atheist and her mother's God was transcendental – he was everywhere and nowhere. Mrs Das never went into temples and only occasionally reminded her children about the invisible divinity she believed in.

This Sunday morning, however, Sophie was going to take part in a satsang in honour of Baba Sampige. Returning alone from the mall the previous night, empty-handed and full of a feverish gloom, she had run into Mrs Bhatt in the lane, trying to prevent Mani from embracing a street dog the colour of gutter water. Mrs Bhatt went briefly into the house and returned with a flyer for a satsang the following day in honour of Baba Sampige's birthday. Though Mrs and Mr Bhatt were both fanatic followers of the guru, they appeared in other respects to live on different spiritual planes. Mrs Bhatt was ninety kilos of stoicism. She spoke little and when she did it was only to make minor demands on the world – such as now when she offered the pamphlet to Sophie and said, very simply, 'Please come.' Mr Bhatt was often lecturing Sophie on Baba Sampige and thrusting notices on her to do with the guru, which she threw away as soon as she came upstairs. But the gentleness with which Mrs Bhatt invited Sophie, the patience with which she tried to wean Mani away from the dirty dog, and Sophie's awareness that Mani had been saved from death by karmic centimetres (given how much the little dead boy in the mall had looked like him) made her say, 'Yes, I'll come' even though she had not thought of God in particular or the spiritual realm in general since that maths exam. She had long outgrown Vivekananda and his rousing exhortations to a nation of weaklings and cowards ('If there is one word that you find coming like a bomb from the Upanishads, bursting like a bombshell upon masses of ignorance it is the word *fearlessness*.').

But despite her overall indifference there was still lodged within her an insistent shard of nostalgia for this single-minded man. She still thought of it sometimes – the idea, instilled by Vivekananda and reinforced by parents, teachers, nuns and Jesus Christ, that one was put on earth a weak-willed, selfish, pleasure-loving imbecile and one's work was to redeem oneself ('This world is the great gymnasium where we come to make ourselves strong'). So even though Sophie barely noticed the photographs of Baba Sampige whose moustached, wide-eyed, innocent face advocating lovepeacetruth stared down from every second lamppost, shop-front, banner and hoarding in the city, she occasionally felt she had unfinished business with the idea of God or with that of self-improvement, which she believed to be the same thing. Climbing up the stairs the previous evening, she studied the pamphlet and looked for the first time into the reputedly saintly eyes of the guru. It was his thirtieth birthday and the satsang would be one of dozens organized around the city, the country and the world in his honour – a wild contagion of a birthday bash. The Baba appealed to Bangalore's citizens not to cause traffic jams by heading en masse to his ashram but instead celebrate his birthday by holding local prayer-meetings.

Perhaps, she thought, as her pile of ironed clothes steadily grew and she tried to shut out the image of the crushed child, if she showed up briefly at the satsang that would also improve her standing with the Bhatts so that when it came to the crunch (as it would one day, despite the time she had wrested from Ringo), and the whole colony had learnt with initial surprise and eventual glee about Mr Bhatt's shameless borrowing, her landlord would not hold her singularly responsible for his troubles.

She wondered (purely hypothetically because not smoking would be death) what would happen if she chose to follow all of Bhatt's dictums. What would he say to her if he came to her apartment on one of his spying missions and found he had nothing to say to her? But that could not be. In his eyes she was doomed because of who she was and not what she did. Who was she then and how had she come to be on this godless plateau? She remembered how as a child there would sometimes well up in her the fierce urge to be good. Some rare moment of pure love for her parents (rather than merely concern or pity) would trigger this resolve in her. And it was always easy to know what adults wanted. They wanted silence, clean hands, no tears, no questions and report cards without red marks. Sophie would live in that fantasy for a day or a week – the sterilized white world in which she was never scolded and she was never upset. That it always crumbled didn't mean she stopped trying; her Vivekananda-following had been one of those tries too, a last-ditch attempt at penetrating the goodness everyone else seemed to have a grip on but which she – who fell in love too readily with strangers, failed in maths and didn't understand chemistry, squabbled constantly with her sister and yearned for an excitement that had no name – could not achieve. The question had remained with her – the question of who and what was good, of human goodness, of which bits of the people she knew (herself included) could be considered unequivocally good. Her thoughts returned in slow, gentle spirals, via this lofty route, back to Ribor as if he were the only pure thing left in the world.

Sophie wondered if the satsang would provide a sign, a confirmation of her feeling that Ribor was where she had left him, waiting for something he couldn't put his finger on. Since there was no Killer Queen on hand to offer the vital hint, perhaps Baba Sampige would do the job. Sometimes she'd see them – Killer Queen's brothers and sisters – but because she was too shy to reveal herself to them, they never saw her. They usually had a bull with them, decorated with so many embroidered clothes, so many bright pompoms and splashes of paint, so many bells and garlands and strings of seashells that the animals looked like walking shops. These itinerants went barefoot from door to door chanting invocations, blowing on their nadeswarams, and begging for alms, while the cattle waited wearing expressions of human gravitas. Sophie would watch these wanderers surreptitiously from her window, admiring their bohemian aplomb.

She started to smooth out a pair of cotton trousers. Ironing was her peculiar obsession – a way of withdrawing from a faulty world into a perfectionist's universe. Here was symmetry, as when the right sleeve of a shirt could be folded back in exactly the same way as the left, because they were of exactly the same proportion. Here was elegance – in creating a knife-edge out of a rumpled trouser cuff. Sophie often thought, when she ironed, about one of the few films she'd seen that hadn't dissolved into just pixels of colour – a painful, violent, sneering film by Werner Fassbinder. Its aim appeared to be to establish that everything its characters felt or said or did was a ridiculous sham. The protagonist trying to impersonate a famous dead poet, the policeman investigating a murder, a woman fan of the poet who professed to love him – all of these people turned out to be either deceived or deceiving. Against ninety minutes of coruscating cynicism stood out a moment of exceptional tenderness. The poet – ageing, desperate, cruel – visits the house of his mistress and, as he is talking to her, irons a pair of her panties. The sincerity with which he does this, the calm of perfection that envelops him as he works on this tiny triangle of silk had made Sophie smile in the dark and redeemed the film for her.

She put away the clothes and went out.

The house-in-progress next to the Bhatts' seemed to be shaping into one of those gigantic, laughably showy creations with Roman style fluted columns supporting its terraces. A construction worker at the site sat her toddler on a pile of sand and tied a thick rope around one of his ankles. The other end of the rope she wound around a large block of granite. The child was engrossed in breaking his rattle, unaware as yet of this clamp on his freedom. The woman looked up at Sophie, her eyes crinkling in amusement at her own ingeniousness and Sophie smiled back. She wished she could help, take the child back home and look after him while his mother balanced trays of pasty concrete on her head as she climbed up the scaffolding. Don't be foolish, Sophie said to her herself as she walked on, but the woman's smile stayed with her.

There was a terrific hum in the air from all the construction activity around. When Sophie first moved to Bangalore, it was just the nerve-wracking whine of the stonecutters' drills, shaping tiles to lay on the floor of the newly-built house next door. But Sophie soon realized that there was nothing temporary about this noise. This was the very voice of the city – this whirring, manic hum of urgent construction. It followed her everywhere she went – the growl of mixers churning cement and sand and gravel, the shouts of constructions workers relayed from floor to floor through the shells of the buildings they were creating, the buzz of sparks flying from the torches of men welding gates and window grilles. And all the while, the little and large squares of land filling up like in an animated film with beauty salons, game parlours, jewellery shops, bakeries, clothes stores, cafes, apartment buildings and then, often in just the space of a year, morphing into something else – bungalows torn down to make way for office blocks, gift shops becoming travel agencies, internet parlours converted to coffee shops, everything succumbing to this fantastic flux.

One of Sophie's friends, Anu, had recently acquired a boyfriend and to celebrate this, Sophie had the previous week invited her, the new boyfriend, Ringo Saar and Swami for lunch that afternoon, so she started by shopping, then lugged her heavy bags to the choultry. Outside was a long, proud row of cars, each of a size that would have doubtless met Swami's standards of car heaven. Sophie stopped for a moment, a little intimidated by the fervent singing that emanated from the building; it struck her that it might be vaguely sacrosanct to enter with the beer she had in the bag. It was too late to do anything about it, however. She kicked off her sneakers, clasped her bags to herself to prevent the bottles from clinking and went in.

People were packed into the hall, some of them sitting cross-legged on rough jute mats, their hands joined together and their faces reverential as they swayed with their singing. Sophie tried to slip, unobtrusively, into a corner, then noticed Mrs Bhatt signalling to her from the rear and went to sit beside her. Mani, his face knotted with restlessness, was jumping violently in his grandfather's lap. He registered Sophie's presence with a loud, inarticulate exclamation and a rare, angelic smile.

Then the singing stopped abruptly. A man got up, bowed low before a giant picture of Baba Sampige's heavily garlanded face and began to elaborate on a banana metaphor in an adroit mixture of Kannada and English. From what Sophie could understand, he was saying, after Baba Sampige, that the ritualistic elements of all religions are like the skin of the banana, while they are in their essence, shorn of their rituals and symbols, like its flesh. Because of our emphasis on the difference between religions we are left holding the skin, forgetting that the flesh is the point – the flesh that stands for lovepeacetruth regardless of the religion. Sophie considered the metaphor. If the skins of these metaphorical bananas are what we end up focusing on because they signal the differences between religions, shouldn't all these skins at least *look* different so that you can tell a Christian banana from a Hindu one, notwithstanding the fact that when you peel either you get the common lovepeacetruth within? Perhaps he could have explained his point better by talking about green, red and yellow bananas, thought Sophie, because then at least you can tell them apart from their skins. On the other hand, green, red and yellow bananas have entirely different kinds of fruit and you can't convince someone who wants a red banana and nothing but a red banana to take a green one instead – the green ones are meant to be eaten cooked and the red ones raw. As for yellow ones they come in so many different shapes, sizes and tastes that to attempt any metaphor of universality based on them would be sheer folly.

She stopped listening to the Banana Man and tried to get Mani, now weeping from the frustration of all this enforced stillness and tearing at his grandfather's moustache, to come to her. He advanced cautiously, then stumbled on the edge of a mat and fell heavily into her lap, turning up his wet, injured face to her to see what diversions she could offer. An aarti commenced and this temporarily quietened him down. A pundit, the ample brown folds of his bare stomach glistening, waved a brass tray with a flame in it before Baba Sampige's picture. He rang a small bell with one hand and muttered his lines; the flame danced in the breeze created by the rotation of the tray. The smoke of incense and camphor made a haze around the picture; more flowers and tinsel were now being draped around it.

Mani knew the bhajan that the devotees had launched into; he clapped his tiny hands in glee, out of sync with everyone else. Sophie had the watchfulness of a new mother, careful not to curtail Mani in any way, now that he seemed to have, in a moment of absent-mindedness, recognized her. Some of the other worshippers turned to look at them with curiosity – an imperiously clapping child and a girl with torn-at-the-knees jeans.

As the bhajan merged into another and then another, Mani fell asleep and Sophie tried to formulate her thoughts on the question of faith. She closed her eyes and saw the school chapel into which she had sometimes followed her more prayerful classmates, where the emphasis was on silence and where Christ would always disturb her because of the infinity into which his suffering stretched. Why was the Banana Man so anti-symbol? Didn't they need the Baba's picture now to fawn upon, this flowery centre which everyone faced as they sang their bhajans and clapped their hands? One of Hamlet's lines came to her, a line that her father often repeated. It was the King, *Hamlet's* uncle, praying for the forgiveness of his sins and yet aware that he was not sufficiently repentant. 'My words fly up, my thoughts remain below, words without thoughts never to heaven go.'

So she mentally cleared her throat and whispered into the void: please let a week be enough. She had postponed the pleasure of imagining her return, but now, with her eyes closed, Mani nestling comfortably in her arms and the singing growing as foggy as the incense smoke through which she heard it, Sophie was back in Shillong. She had already reached the airport, flown, landed, been driven up the hill road in a beat-up Sumo taxi, unlatched the gate of the house in which she had lived for twenty-four years. It would be like a film played backwards – every step in the reverse sequence would erase the equivalent of that step in the forward sequence, so that by the time Sophie was sitting down with her parents to eat a lunch of rice, dal and fried fish, she would have become a Sophie who'd never left town. The same streets, the same rooms, the same winter, the same longing.

The sound of a bottle crashing rang through the hall with horrible clarity. Sophie leapt up and it was only when she saw the swelling puddle of beer on the floor behind her and the proud look on Mani's face as he stood there surveying his handiwork that she realized she had fallen asleep. The bhajan-singing died out. A man came over and pulled the bag with the remaining bottles away from Mani and Mani away from the broken glass and yellow puddle. He turned out, devastatingly, to be Chinnappa, the laughing-club member, the man who had set the police on Sophie and her friends. Beer bottles seemed to pursue this strict vegetarian teetotaller wherever he went. The remaining bottles clanked loudly as Chinnappa examined her bag. A crowd formed and Sophie cowered. Chinnappa said, 'Oh ho, ho, ho, ho! Madam, what is this? Why you are insulting our guruji?'

Couldn't he be my guru too, thought Sophie, her face burning, but there seemed to be no way of proving it. Besides, the Banana Man's speech hadn't worked for her. Baba Sampige was no Vivekananda – he didn't seem to have a plan of action. All he offered were generalities to do with lovepeacetruth and breathing techniques supposed to calm down people like Chinnappa, except that Chinnappa was so angry now that even if Baba Sampige had appeared in person it wouldn't have helped.

Mr Bhatt was screaming at Mani whose look of smugness was beginning to crumble.

Others in the hall were pressing down on them, eager to scrutinize the evil puddle. The priest, whose bare, fat torso now seemed frightening to Sophie, pushed his way through the crowd. He summoned a tattooed old lady sitting on the steps outside to mop up the beer and sweep away the shards. No one seemed sure what Sophie's punishment should be. They started a debate in Kannada.

Sophie gathered her other bags together.

'Sorry,' she said. 'I was listening to the bhajan and didn't realize ... had to do some shopping urgently ... should have gone home first ... I am trying to learn about Baba Sampige's message ... I thought the child was asleep ... this is for some friends ...' Every explanation trailed off and she sounded horrible even to herself.

She straightened up and said, 'I think I should leave now. I am disturbing all of you. Sir, can I have my bag back please?' she asked Chinnappa.

'No, no, I will handle it.'

The priest surprised everyone by proclaiming in English, 'Wherever people are coming together and praying, that place is like a temple, madam. What you are thinking? People are doing holy things here. Satsang, satsang,' he said loudly as if she were deaf. Perhaps he'd mistaken Sophie for a dim-witted foreigner, which she admittedly was in some ways. The priest's remarks seemed to diffuse the sense of purpose in the rest of the group.

The Banana Man, who had been running his eyes over her body in a leisurely fashion, now addressed her breasts. 'It must be by mistake no, that you came here? These are all decent family people, ma. This is not a party zone.' He laughed in a macabre way, his eyes still boring into her, and Sophie started to inch away from his look. She caught Mrs Bhatt's eye, but Mrs Bhatt turned away, embarrassed, and pulled Mani towards her before the still-shouting Bhatt could slap him. Sophie crept slowly along the wall towards the door. The centre of authority in the hall had been Baba Sampige but since he was now reduced to just a picture, it seemed unclear to the others who should decide on the next course of action.

Chinnappa noticed Sophie sidling away and said, 'Madam, please come here.' Before she realized it herself, she was running down the length of the hall. Instructions were shouted out about stopping her but she was already pounding barefoot down the stairs and sprinting down the burning street. A left turn at the new apartment block, then right, then right again and now she was almost home. She slowed down a little, panting. They knew where she lived; they would find her. Yet the feel of those men standing in judgement over her, her beer and her body had made her panic. (And suddenly there'd been just men; the women had retreated to the back.) She felt hot and angry at the thought of all that wasted beer and the loss of her sneakers, then heard a painful shriek coming from the construction site she'd passed earlier.

The baby was on the mound of sand, straining at his leash now and crying with the effort. Sweat and tears glazed his small round face. All activity on the site had ceased and none of the labourers were around, but from inside one of the blue plastic tents in which they lived came a sound Sophie recognized at once – the sound of a man beating a woman. Sophie could see the tent shifting shape as they lurched inside it – the man's drunken and slurred shouting interspersed with his wife's shrill pleas. Sophie was torn between rescuing the woman and urgently calling Swami to come and save her from the incensed pack of Sampige-worshippers who might at any minute turn the corner of the lane and descend upon her.

She took a step forward; gravel pricked her feet. 'What are you doing?' she shouted in Hindi. The baby paused in its crying to look up at her. A small iron pot came flying out of the tent, narrowly missing the child. The labourer appeared, dragging his wife with him. He tottered as he explained incoherently to Sophie what the problem was, all the while hitting his wife, aiming blows at her stomach and chest and face. The woman kept talking to him as she tried to dodge his hands. Blood from her nose was trickling into her mouth.

'Stop it,' screamed Sophie, trying to separate them. There was something frightening about the way the woman clung to the man, more intent, it seemed, on persuading him to stop hitting her rather than breaking away from him. There was nothing left of her earlier insouciance. Her hair was a mess and her face was twisted with crying.

'Madam you simply cannot run away like this,' called out Chinnappa from the head of the lane. Sophie suppressed the desire to flee and waited for him. Bhatt came huffing and puffing behind him, signalling, with wild gesticulations, some message Sophie could not really decipher except to broadly understand that she had better behave and submit to whatever Chinnappa wanted.

'He's beating her. Phone the police,' she said.

Curiosity made both Chinnappa and Bhatt glance at the construction site but as soon as they saw who was beating whom they lost interest.

Chinnappa said, 'Madam, you must come back. You have spoilt the whole satsang and we must have a meeting and decide what to do. We must do a puja to purify the choultry – how can we continue to do our prayer-meetings there, how can we have marriage ceremonies there? And who will pay for all this? And what report will we send to the guruji – we must send reports on all the satsangs we do and this was a special one. It is his thirtieth birthday ...'

'Get him to stop hitting her.'

Bhatt, who was always more conciliatory in Chinnappa's presence than he was on his own, said, 'Leave it, ma. They won't do anything. Police and all can't do anything. These people behave like this only. They simply get drunk and beat each other. Better you don't get involved.'

Sophie hopped from one bare foot to the other on the hot asphalt. She looked around and noticed another of her neighbours, a young guy in shorts and a Yale University T-shirt washing his car and pretending he hadn't noticed anything. She went up to him and cried, 'He's killing her. Can you stop them?'

The man grimaced. 'These people behave like this only. They simply get drunk and beat each other. Better you don't get involved.'

He splashed a mug of water onto the car. Sophie felt a few drops hitting her face.

'Yale University bastard,' she whispered to herself. The

labourer and his wife were still locked in a bloody embrace, oblivious to their audience and Chinnappa and Bhatt were going on about the unique insult meted out to Baba Sampige and the importance of concealing it from him lest he disown their chapter of his vast spiritual realm.

Sophie went up to the drunken man again and warned him that she was calling the police if he didn't stop. At the mention of the word 'police' another labourer emerged from the shadows of the half-built house, smoking a beedi; Sophie realized, with surprise, that he'd been sitting there all along, unmoved by the violence. He grinned at Sophie and shrugged, seeming to share the general view about the pointlessness of paying heed to this scene of routine domesticity. Nevertheless, conscious of her distress, he went up to the wife-beater and called out genially, 'Muthu, ai Muthu.' Muthu continued unabated, so the man gave him a hard shove with one hand, holding his beedi in the other. Muthu was forced to slow down and his wife finally pulled herself out of his grasp. She bent over the sand pile and untied her baby, paying no attention to Sophie as she angrily wiped her tears. Her husband continued to yell at her from a distance. The smoker took one last puff of his beedi, flung it away with a casual gesture, returned to where he'd been sitting and began breaking stones with a hammer.

Chinnappa was now talking about calling for a Residents' Welfare Association meeting and serving a legal notice on Sophie. Bhatt is useless, declared Chinnappa. He cannot manage his tenants, and now, not content with making trouble in the neighbourhood, his tenants are defiling the neighbourhood's sacred spaces. Sophie's attention was focused on the wife-beater; she tried to determine whether his anger was spent or if he would attack his wife again.

No one noticed two hefty men get off a bike, strap their helmets to the handlebars, run their hands through their hair, push their Ray-Bans up their noses. It was only when they came up to Mr Bhatt, each taking hold of one of his arms, and started talking to him in a low and friendly murmur as they led him to his house, that both Mr Bhatt and Sophie realized something weird was going on. They stared at each other in mutual comprehension and Sophie thought – they're Ringo's goons!

She gaped in horror while Chinnappa continued lecturing her, oblivious to the torture Mr Bhatt was undergoing in broad daylight. Sophie rushed past Chinnappa, ran up to her flat, heated up her iron and began smoothening out creases in the only way she knew.

~

Sophie heard the men on the bike ride away in a thunder-burst and she waited for her doorbell to ring and Bhatt to come and give her the longest lecture of his life, followed by Chinnappa, followed by the priest, the Banana Man and every other upholder of public morality. Strangely, Mr Bhatt did not come, and Sophie, who always ground her teeth at the noise, found the silence disturbing. She ironed till there was nothing left to iron, then wondered how to improvise a meal for her friends now that her groceries had been stolen.

Swami called to announce that he wouldn't be coming for lunch because he had yet to fulfil his weekend quota of sleep. 'I'm reading Swami and Friends,' he added with pretended casualness.

This show of initiative on Swami's part touched Sophie and her many worries faded briefly.

'I like this Rajam fellow, the Police Superintendent's son. Ten years old but he won't take nonsense from anyone. Totally sorted guy.'

'But he's one smug rich kid throughout, whereas Swami and his other friends – they have to fight for a few pennies or the permission to go out and play. It's a daily war,' said Sophie.

'I want to follow this Rajam guy. See where he gets with his air-gun and his khaki shorts.'

'You're not concerned about Swami?'

He apparently wasn't. Swami had met Swami and failed to recognize him. Sophie thought of Mani and the amusements he strained so hard to wrest out of his circumscribed situation. Would Mani grow up to be like her boyfriend too, after all these anti-establishment efforts? On the other hand, it was astonishing to hear Swami talking about something as sentimental as a novel. Just to prolong that astonishment, Sophie continued arguing with him about Rajam, while Swami, through his yawning, tried to defend his idea that the brat was the novel's true hero.

'Can I stay over tonight?' asked Swami suddenly in his little boy voice and for a moment Sophie had nothing to say – no rebuff, no excuse, no put-down.

Then she said the obvious thing. 'It's the worst day possible. I went for a satsang with some shopping and a bottle of beer broke right there in the hall and as if that was not enough Bhatt has been beaten up because I begged Ringo not to put his picture in the papers and he agreed but then he must have felt he needs to do something else to prove ...' She stopped simply because of the too-convoluted nature of her circumstances.

'But I've read two chapters ...' she heard Swami saying as she, out of sheer helplessness, gently pressed the red button on her phone.

She began half-heartedly hacking at a dried-up onion, then wiped her face with a kitchen towel as her phone rang again.

It should have been Swami but it was her sister.

'You're crying?'

'Onions,' Sophie said. 'I'm cooking.'

'You're crying.'

Sophie and her sister tended to disagree about the basic facts. Despite this, Sophie knew from her tone that Muku was her good self today. She could be mocking, cruel, intransigent some days and reasonable, eager to talk, even funny on others. Each of these halves was sustained by the other – the difficult half needing the redemption of the good one (because even by her own standards Muku sometimes went too far) and the good half needing to take recourse to the difficult one when she felt, as she usually did, that everything sucked. Muku was, in a way, a mirror image of their parents' relationship, Sophie felt – that combination of pigheadedness and tractability – but their parents didn't appear to have noticed.

Muku had called to talk about her new boyfriend, Pavan – a topic Sophie didn't particularly want to discuss. Her parents had gone for a funeral and Muku was taking advantage of the empty house to share secrets with her sister.

'He has a CD player from Singapore,' she announced.

'How long have you known him?'

'His parents are cool and I mean cool. They just let him do

what he wants. Everyone leads their own lives in that family.'

'Mama won't let it go on.'

'His father's a big shot. He was promoted to chief secretary last week. They have two Alsatians and a real chic house near Ward Lake. You should see it. French windows, a piano, carpets in all the rooms. All the children have their own computers and Pavan also has a mini gym.'

'Is he doing okay at school?' asked Sophie on a hunch.

'Did Mama tell you something? It wasn't a big deal. He just got into trouble because of some other boys. They called in his parents for a talk but nothing happened.'

'Was it drugs?'

When Muku shouted a vehement 'No!' Sophie knew she had guessed right.

But it was important for Muku to always have the upper hand, so she calmed down at once and said smugly, 'I tried smack with him. It's all right.'

Sophie was quiet, refusing to fall for the bait.

'Don't tell parents, please,' said Muku then by way of a joke. She knew Sophie had long given up believing that complaining to their parents would deliver her from her sister.

'So you passed a syringe around and now you're going to get AIDS and die, all because of your need to impress this idiot,' said Sophie, flat-voiced.

'What about all the grass you smoke? From parents' point of view all drugs are the same. Also from God's.'

Just hearing Muku's voice shattered the romantic image of home that Sophie had started to build up. She would have to spend a week fending off Muku, even though neither of them would ever win this battle of pinpricks, this sourness in the blood, this fight that was so old and repetitive it might as well have been themselves the two were fighting.

'Of course we didn't use a syringe,' Muku said then, discomfited a little by the silence. 'We just snorted a bit and that's all, but it was 10 o'clock when I remembered to check the time. Luckily, Priya lives next door so we went to her place and got her to call home. Mama complained and complained and she's still grumbling.'

'So what did you expect?'

'I'm not moving to Bangalore.'

'It's not my idea.'

'Tell parents then. They're just waiting for you to get here so that you can brainwash me.'

'I have to go and cook. There are people coming for lunch.'

'You know what I figured? I figured you don't really work in that publishing house you always talk about.'

You little witch, thought Sophie, in dismay. But she knew that it was mutual. The sisters had through the years developed an unerring instinct for each other's lies.

'So you have to get parents to drop this Bangalore idea. Otherwise, they'll be heartbroken about your fake job when they hear about it. And as for what you really do, I'm not even *trying* to speculate ...' said Muku breezily. The line went dead.

Sophie returned, furious, to her onion. Who was responsible, she asked herself, raising the eternal Das question, for the fact that she'd been lying about her job? It wasn't her at all, it was Mr Sharma – the man who'd sent her an email saying openings were available in the publishing house of which he was the personnel manager, the famous imprint whose books Sophie had read as a child. Her application was shortlisted and she was asked to present herself for an interview in Bangalore. The interview was a five-minute affair during which three men in ties, including Mr Sharma, had each asked Sophie one question – was she married, was she comfortable reporting for work at 8.30 in the morning and was she familiar with word processing software.

When she went back to the reception to wait for the verdict along with what seemed like at least fifty other people, she got talking to a girl with her cropped hair dyed burgundy and multiple rings in her ears. Chewing ferociously on her gum, the girl watched Sophie as she described the interview and wondered about its outcome. Then she said in a profoundly American accent, 'I feel bad about saying this, but you got it all wrong, you know. These *are* the same guys who publish children's books and all that stuff. They're old and respectable. But right now they're into outsourcing.'

The girl explained. Opus was growing into one of the world's biggest providers of back office services to international publishers. It was cheaper to edit copy, have pages typeset and jackets designed here rather than in the West. So Opus just took over all this work, hired hundreds of people to work cheaply and made a lot of money in the process.

'But how does that matter?' asked Sophie. 'We're still working with children's books.'

The girl nodded her head and clicked her tongue. Sophie was beginning to find her annoying.

'Sorry again. You won't getta work on literary manuscripts, no way. You won't even get near 'em. They don't outsource that kinda stuff.'

'So what does one do starting from eight-thirty in the morning then?'

'Grunt work. You got an economics background, right?'

'It was one of my subjects in college. How did you know?'

'They edit tonnes of business journals from across the English-speaking world, so they need people to work on those. Most people in this room have done some economics, some even have PhDs. A bunch will be hired as language editors, the rest as copy editors. It's hackwork pure and simple. You just gotta go through manuscripts and make sure they're in keeping with some kinda handbook – presentation, referencing, spelling, grammar, usage of technical terms, etcetera, etcetera.'

'How do you know? Did they tell you this at the interview?'

'I have a friend who works here. They won't tell you anything at the innerview; they're not interested in you. They need manpower, somebody who can slog it out for nine, ten hours a day. And they pay shit. But I'm going to take it if they hire me coz I need the money. I'll chuck it up in a few months, soon as I get something better.'

Sophie stood up and looked at the dozens of people around her, as if threatened by each one of them, and then, without a word to the burgundy girl, walked out. When Florence, the friend she was staying with (also from Shillong, and a nurse, as befitted her name), heard about Sophie's plight, she'd slapped her forehead in an exaggerated gesture of shock.

'Are you mad?' Florence asked. 'Do you know how many people come out here from the Northeast? Just for jobs like these? There's no way you're going back!'

So Sophie called her parents and told them she was joining

the publishing house. She spent the next few days searching the Net and scanning newspapers for job openings or just sitting around in Florence's apartment whose Shillong-style cosiness (lace curtains at the window, a gleaming aluminium tea kettle, a woven cane basket with fruit on the table) only heightened her homesickness. Sophie remembered the unremitting harshness of the light outside the window, the claustrophobia of buildings that blocked out the sky, the sewer smells, the clamour raised by maids clanging the pots they washed in the well of the apartment, the dust thrown up by the traffic wobbling on the rutted road nearby. Everything seemed to impress only by its contrast with the town she had left behind.

In the two weeks that she waited for something to turn up, Sophie met scores of Shillong nostalgics who passed through Florence's always open home – girls and boys who had their parents send them bundles of kwai leaves and jars of tungrymbai – fermented soyabean chutney – with every Bangalore-bound Shillong youth; people who could not wait to go back home and who, once they went back, could not wait to return to Bangalore and its liberties. Online, as an extension of this flesh and blood community, Sophie discovered deeply sentimental boys who had once gone to school in Shillong; bloggers who upheld the view that growing up in Shillong made you special, forever battling those who believed it didn't; blurry photographs taken on visits to the underground caves or the living roots bridge; tacky hill station memoirs that inevitably involved Assam-type bungalows, doting grandmothers, frisky dogs and picnics at Ward Lake.

Sophie was eventually interviewed by Star Titles, offered a job at a reasonable salary and told to join at once. Soon she moved into her own place, started out on her brand new life and begun inventing for her family the lies about her life as an editor of children's books that she would sustain for a whole year.

~

Anu and Ringo arrived bearing the bottles of beer Sophie had urgently messaged them to get. With them was a tall boy with a ponytail – Shiva, Anu's latest boyfriend. Sophie had, rudely, not extended her lunch invitation to Ringo's girlfriend, Rukshana, but Ringo seemed oblivious of this slight.

'You creep, you creep, you creep,' chanted Sophie to Ringo as soon as she opened the door.

Ringo shrugged and asked for a bottle-opener, then said, 'No, you can't complain now. I did exactly what you asked for and pushed off the newspaper threat. But you're not going to tell me how to do my job. That I won't take.'

'What are you talking about? He's an overweight man whose heart is probably going to give way any minute; his wife understands nothing about money, they have an infant to take care of, and you send these brutes to beat him up. This isn't doing your job. This is enjoying being criminal.'

Sophie had seen the confident way the men marched Bhatt into the house. Perhaps this very minute Bhatt was lying in a shattered heap. But that could not be; Mrs Bhatt would have come over and asked for help if anything that bad had happened. But what if Mrs Bhatt had fainted from shock?

'What if Mani is alone right now with a pulped Mr Bhatt and an unconscious Mrs Bhatt?' demanded Sophie.

Ringo said, 'Don't be stupid. They're well-trained men. They didn't bash him up or anything idiotic like that. It's all psychological – debtors are already frightened people and these chaps just play on that fear. They may push people around a little, they may raise their voices now and then, but to you and me their behaviour won't really seem intimidating. It'll only seem scary to the person who's guilty.'

'Someone please talk to me,' called Anu from the divan where she had flung herself. She had a somewhat grubby look – the result of sleeping on a mattress on the floor of the apartment she shared with a bunch of ex-college mates, eating cheap takeaways or whatever she could find in the fridge and wearing clothes out of cupboards stuffed with things the girls collectively owned. Anu was human proof of the fact that it is possible to get by without doing *anything*. Her argument was that she tried. She went for job interviews at newspaper offices and welfare organizations but lost her nerve halfway through and bluffed her way out. She dressed up to assist friends at corporate dos and product launches but would break into hysterical, client-insulting laughter at the wrong moment. Anu was congenitally unsuited to work. A boyfriend was integral to this existence and she squeezed all her successive boyfriends dry, her great regret being that she had not yet managed to bag one with any money to speak of.

Sophie told her about the only bright thing in her life – the break she was taking the following week.

Anu sat up in excitement, 'Hey, can Shiva and I borrow your place when you're gone?' She winked at her and started to tell her in a low voice, as Ringo and Shiva drifted out to the balcony for a smoke, how it was out of the question spending time together in the shared apartment – there were so many girls lodged there now it was hard to know who was who. And since Shiva lived with his parents there was nowhere she could spend a few private days with him.

'We could try out your place and if it works I can convince him to get us a flat,' said Anu.

Sophie started to feel safe with Anu around. Nothing dislodged the fundamentals of her world – cold beer, a secure source of food, a little credit, parents who were intolerant in specific ways but generally indulgent, boyfriends who could be relied on. Sophie watched her as she crammed chips into her mouth and asked about her plans for Shillong. Sophie loved Anu's casualness, the way she took whatever came to her; something of that attitude had rubbed off on Sophie too. The one-year ago version of Sophie who had walked out of a job seemed laughably alien to her now. She could have taken it and chucked it up as soon as she got something better. She ought to have learnt right away how to drift in this city of drifters.

Sophie didn't bother answering Anu's question about borrowing the flat, though. The very thought of facing Bhatt was terrifying.

Instead, she shared with Anu the horror of the previous evening. It turned out that Anu knew, in a casual kind of way, the dead child's parents. She described the couple to Sophie as Shiva returned and tried to pull the bowl of chips away from her.

'These guys wouldn't come back home from work till like ten in the night. The kid would be with the maid. He'd watched so much TV he was brain-dead. He didn't know he's supposed to say something when you ask him a question so he'd just give you a blank look and return to Cartoon Network. That's probably why he fell off that escalator. He imagined he was Superman or something.'

'Anu, stop eating,' said Shiva.

Anu continued: 'They got wiped *out* when the dotcom bust happened. They'd left their cosy marketing jobs, got some venture capitalist to put in a humungous amount of money in a start-up that helped young entrepreneurs turn their ideas into online businesses. They loved talking about those days. It was like you could pluck an idea out of the air and as long as it sounded daring enough and you weren't older than forty and had a good track record, you could get someone to bankroll it. It was pure oxygen, everyone was getting high on it. These guys were a totally sensible couple, but they got sucked into it. Okay, it did go fabulously for a couple of years. They hired three or four people, everyone was earning fat salaries, they bought themselves an apartment and paid off the loan for it in fifteen months flat. They still talk about it with like awe or something. And then, of course, simply because so much money had been put into this shit and there wasn't any sign of a fraction of it coming back, people started getting restless and the bubble burst. Their VCs ran out of money and wanted their investment back, the advertisers started pulling out, salaries and employee-stock options went down, and in a matter of weeks the whole company collapsed. Eventually they had to dig into their savings and sell their flat to pay off their dues. They needed to wait out the storm a bit, living in a small rented space and trying not to snap at each other. Then things picked up and they both went back into marketing, had a baby, started moving up again, bought a new place. They'd throw big parties and let the kid run around screaming till midnight. That's the only time he made noise – when the house was full of drunken people.'

Sophie listened with a horrified fascination. Shiva finally succeeded in tearing the bowl away from Anu. 'You've been eating since morning. Sophie put that away.'

'No, don't be a pain,' said Anu, reclaiming the chips. 'Okay, I'll eat slowly. I'll eat one chip at a time. Oh guess what, Mia's leaving the country.' Anu relied on broad strokes and never took unnecessarily long with any story. Mia was one of her housemates. She was called Mama Mia for the way she mothered the other layabouts in the house – cooking for them, making rosters for bathroom cleaning and dish-washing, looking for cheap furniture, taking anyone who fell ill to the doctor. Sophie thought the girls exploited her outrageously. Then she'd got a job assisting a leading fashion designer.

'One month into the job, she's got a whole new wardrobe, three months and she has a car, five months and she has a boyfriend who *also* has a car, seven months and she's moving to England.' Anu struck each item off her fingers.

'She probably never has time to do regular things any more,' said Ringo, coming in and opening more beer bottles.

Sophie kept her eyes averted. She could not forgive him.

'But who wants to do regular things? If I could, I would never even cut my own toenails, or change my own bedsheets, or make my own coffee,' said Anu.

'Anu,' yelled Shiva as she continued stuffing herself.

'Shiva,' she screeched.

'Pay attention to what you're eating, then you'll eat less, like that religious dude says,' said Ringo. 'That Baba whatever. Apparently he has spiritual solutions to problems like overweight people.'

'Baba Sampige?' Sophie spluttered.

'Yeah, apparently fatties check into his ashram and meditate on a grape for hours every day before they eat it.'

'He doesn't have a single worthy point to make,' declared Sophie, 'Vivekananda said it all.'

'I'm not fat,' said Anu pouting. 'Not in the absolute sense. As in, I'm a fat thin person. Not a fat fat person.'

'You look thinner than before, actually,' said Sophie

'Thanks darling,' said Anu. She blew Sophie a kiss and took another chip, glancing at Shiva from the corner of her eye.

'You into this Baba Sampige guy?' Shiva asked Ringo with a laugh.

'No, don't give a shit but he's everywhere, man.'

Shiva said, 'My cousin's actually infiltrated the inner circle. She's donated so much money to the ashram, the guy has noticed her. She's chucked up her software job for him. Runs his website or something. Wants me to go and see him, can you believe that? Me with that dude? It'll be fucking embarrassing.'

'Maybe she's in love with him,' said Ringo.

'Hadn't thought of that. My uncle and aunt have been trying to rig up a marriage to rid her of the Baba mania but she's not budging. She's the dude with the money so she calls the shots.'

'Why does she want you to see him?' asked Anu.

'The master holds the key to my future,' intoned Shiva. 'Except that I used to know him as a kid and he's no master, and there's not a chance in hell I'll see him except to remind him of what he once used to be.'

It turned out that Shiva and Baba Sampige were boyhood friends and neighbours before the latter became a guru and changed his name from the insistently singular Raghavan to the double barrel Baba Sampige. They'd started life as social beings in the same cramped primary school and had collaboratively committed minor acts of betrayal such as peeing in a corner of the classroom, creeping up on the aunty who came to read stories to the class every Friday and trying to poke lit matches into her cloud-like hairdo, and noisily regurgitating their lunch-time idlis in order to feed them to their more pliable peers.

When they were both seven, they'd seen a truck driver beaten to near-death on the highway near their homes – a man who had just run over the grocer from whom Raghavan and Shiva's parents bought their vegetables. Witnessing this double act of brutality – the death of the smiling vegetable man and the frenzy with which his friends from neighbouring shops fell upon the reckless truck driver – Shiva, in a Buddha-like moment, lost his sense of humour. He ceased to play their evening games of cricket with the same gusto while Raghavan became even more blasé than before. He cheated relentlessly at carom, made girls cry, laughed at teachers. By the time he was twelve, he developed a side business at school – offering the smokers, the gamblers, the porn addicts and all others among his school mates who were dependent on ready cash, small loans at ten per cent interest. This became a weekly rate of interest after the first month and a *daily* rate of interest by the third month. He'd then do all he could to avoid repayment, rushing past his debtors who would have taken to waiting outside his classroom and waylaying him with threats and appeals for mercy when he emerged. By the time Raghavan was willing to accept the repayment of his loans, they'd grown so monumental and so clearly out of the reach of the twelve and thirteen year olds who had taken them that he had no option but to enlist the services of some of his beefier classmates. The mini-defaulters were compelled to steal from their parents in order to bring their misery to an end. Shiva, his faith in mankind irrevocably destroyed after the grocer incident, used to once admire the ruthlessness with which Raghavan ran his evil empire.

Then abruptly – at the age of eighteen – Raghavan announced that he was renouncing life as he had known it and joined the Baba Kakda ashram. Shiva believed it was a ploy to avoid going to engineering college, but Raghavan insisted it was all due to the goodness of Baba Kakda. Baba Kakda did not speak but that did not deter devotees from flocking to him in their hundreds, receiving the sacred ash and going into a collective trance. Raghavan, who had never expressed spiritual leanings before, happened to visit Baba Kakda with an uncle. Upon returning he reported to Shiva that as soon as he saw the ash-smeared hordes of men and women in the courtyard of the ashram with their bodies leaping frenziedly and their eyes rolling, while their souls achieved Bhava Samadhi, that ecstatic state of almost oneness with the Super-Consciousness, he decided this was where the party was and decided to become the Baba's disciple for good. When the old Baba died, Raghavan – only twenty-four – stepped into his shoes and in just a couple of years achieved perverse levels of global fame under his new name – Baba Sampige.

'Wow,' exclaimed Anu. 'You could have been in his position today if you'd just been smarter.'

Shiva threw a beer cap at her and said, 'Don't talk like my infantile cousin.'

'So this Vivekananda guy then, what was he all about?' asked Ringo turning to Sophie with undisguised sarcasm in his voice.

'He was speaking to the cowards,' said Sophie. 'He was saying to them – stop sending your servants to fight for you, move your ass off the soft cushions where it's been planted for centuries, take up your sword and fight.'

Ringo burst out laughing. Anu and Shiva maintained a

respectful silence.

'He would have despised you Ringo,' said Sophie trying hard to be spiteful but Ringo was still laughing.

Sophie realized, to the sound of Ringo's derisive chuckling, that there was something terribly archaic about her and that to no one would her ruminations make any sense. She thought of the disaster of the morning and suddenly she didn't want to refer to Vivekananda any more, not even in passing. It's over, she thought with a sudden finality. It didn't exist – that army he had tried to raise of well-built, football-playing, proudly ascetic men with muscles of iron and nerves of steel. 'My faith is in the younger generation ... They will work out the whole problem, like lions. They will spread from centre to centre, until we have covered the whole of India.' Wrong, thought Sophie. We aren't there. We have flown away from the wheels of the world machine. And only half-listening to Shiva as he continued to describe Baba Sampige's great fakery, she imagined with something approaching grief, a similar moment of insight in the future when she might have to give up Madame Bovary too and forego all ideas of romance. For they were all tied up together in her, weren't they – the lady with the marvellous blue-black eyes, the man with the large orange turban and the small boy who was afraid of his father. *Ribor,* she thought weakly, and as always the name was her talisman and enough to make the room retreat a little.

Ringo stood up. 'Okay, I have moved my ass from the cushion where it's been planted for the last one hour, and I am taking up my sword and going across to wave it at Bhatt.'

Anu cheered. 'I'm coming with you. I'm going to ask him if Shiva and I can stay here next week when Sophie is away.'

Sophie found this hard to believe. 'Have you lost your minds? Here I am hiding, afraid that he's going to arrive any minute and evict me ...'

Ringo said, 'Sophie, why don't you understand that the tables have turned? He's seen now that I'm no longer going to come here every week and drink coffee with him and make elaborate Excel sheets that he can happily ignore. Now at last he's going to understand the seriousness of this.'

'So let's try this idea on him then. That we take care of

Sophie's house while she's not here,' said Anu.

Shiva noticed the shock on Sophie's face and said, 'But only if it doesn't make things worse for you.'

But Ringo was already striding out and Anu followed and then Shiva, shrugging. Sophie stubbed out her cigarette and ran down after them, feeling betrayed.

Mr Bhatt was peering through a crack in the door at her friends. He was bare-chested, with only a veshti, and turned away as soon as he saw Sophie.

'Probably gone to call the cops,' said Anu. 'He can't deal with the sight of your ponytail, Shiva. And as for you, Ringo ...'

Mr Bhatt returned wearing his trademark white vest and opened the door a little wider this time. He glared at Sophie but she could see Ringo was right. The glare concealed fear and she understood with a pang that he had still not recovered from the shock of having his arms twisted. He hadn't been able to gather his wits and lapse back into his authoritarian state in order to come and give Sophie a lecture. There was a slight tremble in his voice as he said, 'Nothing I have to say to you. You saw those goondas who had come? You saw them? They know everything. Everything they know. They know the exact size of my plot. They know all my bank details.' He seemed almost impressed by the extent of their knowledge.

Ringo said, 'Can I come in and talk to you for five minutes? I need to explain why these men were sent and why my bosses are putting so much pressure on me.'

Bhatt kept his hand firmly on the door and did not so much as even look at Ringo. To Sophie he said, 'If I see this man's face one more time, that is it. You are out. You understand?'

Sophie opened her mouth to speak but found she had no defence to offer.

Ringo said, 'Mr Bhatt, you have reached a dead end. That is why those men were sent to talk to you. This is the last private appeal we are making. After this, we take the public route. Your photo and all the details of your dues appear in the newspaper. And if that too does not have the desired effect then we go to court.'

He was speaking in the loud, declamatory voice of one who represents the law.

Bhatt, with a look of pure hatred on his face, forced himself to look at his nemesis.

'You don't know anything,' he said

'I used to be able to help you, remember? We used to have long chats and all you would say is – Ringo Saar, you are holding out your hand to a drowning man. But you didn't do as I said and now it's all out of my hands. I could have prevented what happened today but no one cares now when I say – give him a little more time. That's all I wanted to tell you.'

'You don't know what I can do. I will write to Baba Sampige,' said Mr Bhatt.

'You can write to the President, it won't change anything.'

'Baba Sampige!' exclaimed Anu. 'His cousin works for Baba Sampige,' she said pointing to a Shiva who looked like he wanted to evaporate. 'She is his right-hand woman.'

Bhatt didn't appear to have heard. He averted his face from everyone as he said to Sophie, 'You go. You go and smoke and drink and dance. If the police come to your house, don't come running to me. I have done enough for you ...' He trailed off as Mani zipped out of the house, across the lane and straight through the gate of Sophie's apartment. Soon he was working his way up the stairs one at a time. It was clear that he had figured out that the door to her house would be open and the fridge waiting to be raided. Sophie ran after him and he giggled as he tried to outrun her; then, screaming in glee, he accepted defeat and let her carry him back. For the second time in a day, the child had acknowledged Sophie. Perhaps the bribe of the jam had finally starting doing its work.

Mrs Bhatt came hurriedly to the door, wiping her hands. She seemed to have heard the mention of the Baba's name. She mostly cooked; she had spent so much time waiting for the dosas to brown, the mustard seeds to splutter, the rice come to a boil, the idlis to rise and had become so used to the predictable patterns of these things that she responded to all occurrences in the extra-culinary world with the same expression of weary neutrality she wore while she cooked. Her face betrayed not the slightest interest, but Sophie could tell from the way she hushed Mani that she wanted to know more.

Mr Bhatt reluctantly explained to her the connection between his enemies and His Holiness. Mrs Bhatt's eyebrows rose.

'Can you take me to him?' she asked Shiva, her look still impassive. 'My hernia problem…'

'No, no,' said Mr Bhatt, stepping before her and blocking her off from view. 'For that you need operation, ma. What can Baba Sampige do?'

'He has cured thousands of sick people,' said Anu. Nothing in her tone suggested that she had first heard of Baba Sampige just an hour ago and knew nothing about what he did for sick people. 'People go to him with all kinds of problems. Illness, debt, bad stars,' she continued authoritatively. 'And Shiva's cousin can get you a special private darshan with him. We just have to tell her you are close friends of Shiva and she will do it.'

'I want his darshan,' came Mrs Bhatt's muffled voice from behind her husband.

'Anytime, anytime. As long as Baba Sampige is in town – you know that he travels a lot,' said Anu.

Mrs Bhatt pushed her way past her husband. 'Next week he is in Bangalore. I know. He is addressing a big rally.'

'Wonderful. Give us one or two days and we will organize a darshan for you.'

The two women were talking as if the others did not exist. Baba Sampige had fired up something in Mrs Bhatt and she commandeered Bhatt now with a volley of uncharacteristically forceful Kannada.

'It's a once in a lifetime chance,' pitched in Anu helpfully.

Shiva surreptitiously twisted her elbow; she shoved it into his ribs in response. Ringo and Sophie stood uneasily to one side.

'At least half-an-hour, that much we can guarantee,' said Anu as Mr Bhatt appeared to be running out of good reasons to turn down a chance to meet God in private.

To compensate for losing the argument, he glared ferociously at Anu. 'You see this Sophie Das may be your friend, but she has given me too much trouble. Appa! She is driving me mad. Day and night she is smoking inside, not swabbing the floors, coming late in the night, cooking non-veg food…'

'Kaage,' announced Mani, pointing to a crow that had swooped down onto a large twig in the middle of the lane.

Sophie made encouraging noises at him, so he said 'Iruve' next, identifying for her a column of ants that disappeared into a crack in the gate post. He allowed Sophie to cuddle him as he then delivered a short commentary in Kannada on the neighbour's dog who was always kept chained and who barked in savage misery through the day.

There was a final overriding burst of enthusiasm from Mrs Bhatt, which is when Anu – displaying a perfect sense of timing – delivered her ultimatum.

'The thing is that Sophie is going to Shillong next week, so I think Shiva and I should stay here and swab the floors. And we'll accompany you to the ashram. Shiva will arrange a taxi. Without us the darshan will not be possible.' She addressed this exclusively to Bhatt – riding on the fact that he had confided in her about Sophie's failures. 'We are engaged,' she added at the first glimmer of doubt in his eyes and Sophie saw that neither he nor Mrs Bhatt believed this for a moment but were trapped now in the attraction of meeting Baba Sampige.

Bhatt even managed to grumble with something of his former irony: 'There are lots of vaastu problems with the house. If people come and go like this, what will happen to the energy in the house? It will become worse. I am not saying I have anything against you ... you are good people, you have good jobs, I'm sure. Anyway please remember this is a good locality. Gate is locked at 10 p.m. and please do not be making any noise. And don't steal the clothes line. I put a new one there just last month.'

Sophie and her friends went away with their heads bowed and waited till they had reached her house to break out into whoops of joy and angry recriminations.

Anu started right away on Sophie's lunch, a large pot of rice boiled together with whatever odds and ends she had found in her kitchen – sambar powder, dehydrated peas, onions, old cashew nuts, dates, an egg, fish pickle, port wine, lime juice, dried methi leaves and red chillies.

'This is ghastly, Sophie,' Anu said through a mouthful, grinning.

Sophie grinned back. Despite Bhatt's anger, she felt better now that the confrontation with him was over.

Shiva said, '10 o'clock? Is he nuts?'

'You can jump over the gate, it's easy,' said Sophie.

'Just ignore Bhatt. Sophie has been a good tenant and paid her rent on time, so as long as you don't burn down the house all else is permitted,' said Ringo.

'You haven't lived here Ringo. You don't even know what is and is not permitted,' said Sophie.

'Sophie, you've been complaining for months ... for months about how this man can't let you alone over a simple thing like having a smoke in your own living room. You can't decide to champion him now just when I get tough with him. Make up your mind, whose side are you on?'

Before Sophie could stop herself her anger with him boiled over and she said what she hadn't meant to say. 'It's because of Rukshana isn't it? You sent those goondas here to prove to her you weren't cowed down by me. You must be delighted now that I'm on the point of being thrown out of the house.'

Ringo's eyes grew still and cold. She saw the same anger she'd noticed when the policemen gripped his arm.

'Don't bring Rukshana into this, I'm telling you Sophie,' he said. 'And anyway, who the fuck are you to tell me what I can and cannot do?'

Anu yelled, 'Go easy Ringo' and Sophie was amazed to discover that she had lost him. She wanted to say something to bring him back into their argument but he was already past caring.

A moment of awkward silence followed which was broken by Chinnappa calling to Sophie from the open door and announcing, as her surprised friends looked on, her punishment – a thousand- rupee fine and a written apology to the committee that ran the local chapter of Baba Sampige's One Truth One World Foundation. Sophie could tell from the triumph on his face that he had come to her via Bhatt and knew that she had been roundly scolded. Behind him was the tattooed cleaning lady. She advanced towards Sophie, dangling by their laces, like a pair of dead rats, the sneakers Sophie had abandoned in the choultry.

Don't Stop the Noise

When they got to the open-air amphitheatre later that evening, Sophie tried to pay attention to the heavy metal boy bands that came on one after the other, all of them given only twenty minutes to perform yet each spending absurd lengths of time on sound checks ('more monitors on the bass, please ... sorry, more bass on the monitors'), before launching into songs that all sounded alike to her, especially because most of the singers were fantastic howlers but couldn't carry a tune. After an hour of this she gave up. The sky was streaked with a sunset glow and it was nicer to lie back on the broad stone steps and lose oneself in the purple spotlights bouncing off the metal sheen of a guitar or the occasional wizardry of a drum solo. She was a year into weed but it still surprised her – how life slowed down, how the things that were near came vividly near but those that were far seemed to belong to another lifetime.

Then Little Idlis came on and Anu took the joint from her, visibly tense. This was a rock music competition and L.I. was a strong contender. After the argument with Ringo,

Sophie didn't want to come for the show, but Anu insisted that she couldn't sit at home alone and mope and Ringo was prevailed upon to apologize. He said a perfunctory sorry but Sophie knew it meant nothing and that the truth was what she had read in his eyes.

The lead singer, whom Sophie had minutes ago seen cradling his cellphone lovingly, clearly talking to an actual or potential girlfriend, was now transformed into an angry beast, striding up and down the stage and seeming, through his raw shrieking, to berate his mostly male audience. At intervals he flipped his long crinkly hair over his head and swung it violently with the beat, with the crowd (including Swami who sat some distance away from Sophie) following suit. Ringo was obscured by his drum-set which he thrashed so wildly Sophie winced every time she looked at him. He seemed almost embarrassed to be playing in a band called Little Idlis, whose lead singer was less a little idli and more a moron.

'Make some fuckin *noise*,' said the singer, after the set-your-teeth-on-edge distortion of the guitars had died down and the applause was loud but not rapturous.

Noise, thought Sophie. She knew that these head-banging boys in their black T-shirts with one or the other avatar of the devil printed on them were fundamentally nice boys unlike those at concerts in Shillong for whom the violence was often physical and who would, once they had smashed bottles and slashed auditorium seats, badly want a face to punch. Whereas these boys were all replicas of Swami and Ringo and Shiva – boys who loved their masala dosas and respected their parents and held hands with their girlfriends in cinema halls. Yet weren't they frustrated deep down, wondered Sophie, if they could swing their heads with the uncontrollable frenzy of epileptics and so freak out on the noise?

Sophie sneaked a look at Swami and then looked away. He was watching the show with the credulous expression of a child and she wanted to say – no, don't believe so readily. He wore the look that had first drawn her to him – the *Swami and Friends* look. Without Swami she'd be lost in this raucous city, still standing at some kerb and waiting for the traffic to slow down so she could cross the road. It was only with him that she had learnt how to do it – take on the city's insanity and remain essentially unaffected. Why was it all wearing off now, that early sense of adventure?

She started thinking about the first time she'd met him. It was at the wedding of one of her colleagues, a joyless affair in a cavernous hall without panes on the windows, at the far end of which the newly-married couple sat on gilded red thrones, while people hung about in small groups waiting for dinner to be served. Toddlers in miniature suits ran about screeching, their natural hysteria heightened by the perfume-and-biriyani-scented hysteria of the atmosphere. Sophie stood in a corner, her only silk kurta over a pair of jeans. She wished she hadn't come – none of her other colleagues had turned up and Malini, the bride, seemed unable to make ordinary conversation in a wedding sari. Sophie had had to make do with Malini's mother – a woman not without a sense of irony, who seemed to find poetic justice in the fact that the couple would get to eat only much after the guests had eaten. She turned out to be a schoolteacher and was much taken by the fact that Sophie's parents were teachers. She asked Sophie a great many questions about Shillong – as if the height of the town's tallest peak or the depth to which its temperature could sink in winter had been the enduring mysteries of her life. But after a while she had to go and attend to the other guests whom she referred to as 'those fellows'. She called out to a boy in a white shirt, gel glistening in his wavy hair, and introduced him to Sophie as her nephew, Swami.

'You talk to her, she's from Shillong,' she told Swami as she ran off. Swami shook hands with her, then looked her in the eye and asked, 'You getting bored here?'

Sophie was disarmed. Back home any such encounter would be awash in self-consciousness but here was Swami and he appeared to be completely at ease talking to a woman he'd never met before.

The next band was now absorbed in their fussy sound check; Anu offered Sophie a half-eaten chicken roll and Swami shuffled off to get more cigarettes.

'I hate this kind of music,' said Anu and they grimaced at each other in shared pain.

'Have you heard the lyrics of some of this shit? They practice on our rooftop so I'm forced to listen. It's all so stupidly violent – kill someone, hate women, drive the devil into your soul. It's like they would be embarrassed if anything they sang had even a touch of decency to it.'

'But you want the band to win?'

'Of course! There's a ten thousand prize. Ringo's promised us a party if they win.'

'You're a pig.'

'I know.'

They laughed, then stopped, looked at each other and laughed even harder.

'They call this music,' said Anu and hiccupped. Then she sobered up and said, 'I'm glad we have this week together in your place. I can talk things over with Shiva. I love our gang but finally I just want to get out of here.'

Sophie groaned inwardly. She'd just been admiring Anu, but realized now as Anu started to elaborate, that she was corrupted like all the others by the glamorous dream of escape.

Swami returned, talking on his cellphone, flung a packet of cigarettes at Sophie and flopped down on the steps again. He was pissed off with her about the ban on staying over. She let him be. His sulks were always short-lived; one or another of his enthusiasms – cars, loans, Sophie herself – would very quickly take over. Swami had to work hard to stay grumpy just as Sophie had to work hard to stay pleased. Meanwhile, a three-member band invoked Joe Satriani and went on – speechlessly – to display their guitar skills. The crowd cheered.

Anu had it all worked out: she wanted Shiva to find a job in Australia, emigrate there on a work visa so that she could follow, marry him and live happily ever after. But Shiva has no interest in Australia, Anu wailed. He was full of complaints about Bangalore but would not budge from the city. Anu was working on him and was confident he would relent. Someone had once mentioned in passing to Anu that it wasn't hard for Indians to get jobs in Australia, relative to the US or the UK, and ever since then she dreamt of cities by the sea – Brisbane, Sydney, Melbourne, Adelaide. Her present life became shadowy. She no longer minded sharing an apartment with her friends, eating disgusting food and never having enough money because she knew that eventually she'd make it to that antiseptic place untouched by India's messiness. What she did there was immaterial, what Shiva did there was immaterial. Sophie held back, though she wanted to scoff, like she scoffed at Maya's plans to fly away. She found it increasingly hard to challenge the fake clarity of her friends' dreams. They were envisioned in black and white, these dreams – the shabby present, the pristine future.

Anu couched her dream in the language of the hard-boiled realist, however.

'Doing a two-bit back office job and hanging out with the guys is all right for now, but soon his parents will throw him out and he'll have to think of a career. He'll have to cut his hair and wear clean clothes and wake up early every morning.'

Sophie thought of Ribor in his faraway shop, which she knew brought in just enough to keep him going. She thought of her parents and their teaching jobs which they would hold on to till they retired. Suddenly there was something embarrassing about the modest nature of these lives. How had that happened? wondered Sophie. How come Anu was confident of taming Shiva, but Shiva didn't appear to pose any challenge to her, didn't say – 'This is who I am, take it or leave it.'

'Swami's getting his act together,' said Anu. 'Why don't you guys consider Australia as well? I'll tell you what. As soon as we move there and get a grip on what's going on, you can join us. Can you picture it? All of us in the same city, Swami and Shiva working in the same office. And we just hanging out maybe, if what they're bringing in is good enough. Just having kids or something. Can you believe how much fun it'll be?'

Sophie pretended to give this thought; Swami roused himself as the guitar wizards left the stage and came over to Sophie for a cigarette. He seemed to have just realized that Sophie would leave for Shillong the following day.

'When you come back, I'm going to take a few days off. Right now I'm going crazy over this loan. The head trainer has given me two options – a loan at fantastically cheap rates, except that the dalal he took me to seems a bit shady, *or* a loan at the regular bank rates. I've got to decide quickly because the HT has found this fantastic little parcel, thirteen hundred square feet, just right for a nice three-bedroom house with a basement garage, and right in the middle of a colony where all the plots are being snapped up. Soon this will be gone too. The HT knows the owner and he's willing to sell it at just under current market rates because he's in Singapore and needs the money quickly for some restaurant business he's expanding. HT said he'd buy it himself if he didn't have his cash tied up in so many properties. He thinks I'll be an idiot not to take it. Even if the Singapore wallah was selling it at the market rate, I could sit on it for a few years and then make a killing on it, but the fact that he's in a hurry, is willing to take whatever he gets and trusts the HT, makes this a marvellous deal ...'

But Sophie was no longer listening because the Shillong Blues Band – invited to perform as a finale to the competition – had now taken to the stage. Their front man was Uncle Rock, a short, pale, skinny guy with a thick, ragged mop of hair who had the canny look of an operator but who, Sophie knew, was a gentleman and a lover of the music of passing things and bittersweet love. He was a middle-aged one-man band though he occasionally grouped around him, as he had today, a bunch of identically angel-faced musicians who drifted in and out of bands as Ribor had once done till he gave up the idea of being some kind of a *personality* and settled down in his shop. Uncle Rock on the other hand was little besides personality. Sophie remembered Ribor telling her that Uncle Rock had once famously said to someone who'd suggested he form a real band – 'Does Bob Dylan have a band? Does Van Morrison?'

So the Shillong Blues Band was fictitious but they looked good – the trilbies, the boots, the drainpipes, the little black satin waistcoats with pointy fronts were all part of some self-devised style that was unmistakeably Shillong's. The band could have dropped out of the sky, they looked so wonderfully out of place. The metal heads were temporarily silenced.

Uncle Rock played a quick riff on his guitar, then shouted 'Good evening Bangalore' and was greeted with shouts of approval. Sophie felt herself implicated in their applause. They started with 'Going Down Blues' from Uncle Rock's latest album. The whole band joined in the chorus enthusiastically – like in a school concert where the true function of the many superfluous side characters is only revealed when they deliver the various jolly numbers that punctuate the action.

The Shillong Blues Band performed their songs with an old-fashioned restraint – all at the same tempo, all followed by polite 'thank yous' and bashful waves of the hand. There were long guitar solos. A jazz note here, a reggae tune there. A smattering of the blues. Cheesy lyrics that forced words like 'sunrise' into rhyme with words like 'French fries'. Earnest songs about corrupt politicians. Playful songs about philandering men. Plaintive songs about true love.

The sense of expectancy in the amphitheatre slowly started to fizzle out. The crowd seemed to be waiting for the band to do something to justify their status as special invitees and lure them out of their metal-hardened shells. But, exactly like the metal heads, the band was hiding behind the music rather than speaking through it, Sophie realized. Uncle Rock, who could prance about the stage and holler wildly to draw out his audience, now seemed to have gone on auto-pilot and more or less refused to meet their eyes.

Someone shouted 'Slayer!' in the scattered applause following yet another sweet number. Somebody else laughed and yelled 'Korn!'

'They're very laid back,' observed Swami.

How could this have happened? How could Uncle Rock, who'd sounded charming to her all her life, have now turned into this clownish figure whose half-baked songs and flimsy tunes spoke of a small town diffidence in the face of the big world?

'They're going to be killed,' said Anu.

'Give them a chance,' said Sophie.

'They're too polite,' said Swami.

'They're from Shillong,' said Anu.

'Give them a chance,' pleaded Sophie.

Uncle Rock grinned into the mike. 'As you know we're all big fans of Dylan here. This is young Dylan coming into New York town where the people are going down to the ground and the buildings going up to the sky. And he's blowing his lungs out for a dollar a day, trying to make it in New York.'

So he wasn't completely unaware of his indifferent audience then, and of the city he was in. He drew took out a harmonica from his waistcoat pocket and blew his lungs out for nothing. Sophie knew about the Dylan obsession. Bah Lou, an older and more well-known Shillong musician, had started it all by organizing birthday concerts in honour of the singer every May, and these parties had eventually developed into a full-blown cult with its competing Dylan impersonators, serious Dylan aficionados, charlatans, sects and groupies. In concert after concert stretching back over a few decades, the first half of the Dylan catalogue had been exhaustively explored, digested and then regurgitated to be explored again. Uncle Rock was one of the better known Dylan worshippers but by no means the only one.

But at the moment Dylan was letting Uncle Rock down. The sudden excess of autobiography, the plain-speaking voice, the simple, raw rhythm of the harmonica was the last straw. The Shillong Blues lost its audience. The applause had been replaced by a roar of impatience, a sea of yelled comments – from names of heavy metal bands, to ironical 'I love yous' that generated howls of laughter, to 'Goodnights!' to the unequivocal 'Shut up, you boring fuckers'. Gangs of boys started to walk away as the Shillong Blues Band sang on, unaware or unconcerned.

'You said they're big in Shillong,' said Swami, raising an eyebrow at her. Anu sighed and took off to look for Shiva.

The band remained untouched by their failure and as the amphitheatre emptied in pockets, they seemed to grow more relaxed and started strolling away from their frozen positions, smiling and nodding at each other.

A little later, abandoned completely by her friends, left with a handful of stragglers and the few thin stars that showed through the polluted darkness, Sophie heard Uncle Rock announce his best song. He always saved it till the end and Sophie was relieved to find it unchanged – this one song, sung in the deep nasal voice of experience, always managed to capture a real sorrow. This is when it all came together, when Uncle Rock turned around and faced himself and described what he found.

For exactly five minutes, Sophie was taken out of her body and suspended in the clear fluid of memory. She shook her head rapidly to clear the ridiculous tears that pricked her eyes at the insidious ache of the song's melody, at the battering she had taken that day and the evening's shameful failure, at the thought of Ribor, at how she had for years walked down the same streets of the same town, always imagining that those dreaming walks were some kind of prelude to her entry into the real world. And now the song that had once seemed like a promise of future riches had turned upside down and become a remembrance of past pleasures.

~

'If you kick off with 'Going Down Blues' it's going to be downhill from there all the fucking way,' said Ringo Saar, who was driving the car. Little Idlis had not won the competition so there was a touch of aggression in his voice.

'But the audience was shitty,' exclaimed Anu from the backseat. 'Imagine asking a blues band to sing Iron Maiden. It's like asking Eric Clapton to wear eyeliner and smash up a guitar.'

'They're metal heads, man,' said Ringo Saar. 'They're the best. I mean, ask me, I've played in Delhi, Chennai, the Northeast ... these guys are the most kick-ass metal heads in the world.'

'Forty-five different kinds of metal,' announced Shiva. 'Okay, forty-five is an exaggeration, but man, who's heard of things like doom metal and grind metal and hair metal and stoner metal ... these guys are neck-deep into this shit. Bringing down a blues band was a dumb idea. It was an insult to hype them up just to have people ask them to shut up. They should have invited some good local band to keep the crowd happy, someone like ...'

Swami cut him short. 'The whole idea is to get people down from other parts of the country, man. Everybody's heard the local guys a million times.'

'They had Parikrama down last time. Everybody loved them, and they're not metal,' said Ringo Saar.

'There are tonnes of bands in the Northeast. They could've got someone with more life in them. They have some pretty mean metal heads in Imphal, in Shillong ...' said Swami.

'What's this metal fetish about anyway?' asked Shiva. 'Swami, you say, you're one of those hardcore types.'

'It just feels good, that's all,' said Swami, his voice suddenly awkward. 'It's the only way to protest.'

'Against?' asked Shiva.

'I don't know, man. Against the idea that one shouldn't protest.'

'Who says you shouldn't?'

'Everybody mostly keeps quiet when they see stuff happening. Or ... or they don't say what they really think. If you listen to metal you can say what you really think.'

'That's a load of shit,' said Shiva.

Swami went quiet. He always avoided confrontations.

Shiva said, 'As a culture we're in love with noise, that's what it is. The stuff that makes the greatest racket wins. Take my neighbours. They're one of those ultra-religious types and the latest thing they've got is an electronic temple noise-maker. You plug it in and the bells, gongs, drums, cymbals all go off at once, like they're being played by a fucking ghost on speed. They keep it going for an hour every morning and an hour every night. It's killing, but when I try to talk them out of it, they don't get what I'm saying. That's the killing part. They don't understand why noise should be offensive, especially noise in the service of religion. I mean, wouldn't the most sensible thing be to ban loudspeakers in temples and mosques ...'

Sophie did not defend the Shillong Blues Band. She had started out by considering their failure her failure, but was now, hearing the talk in the car, pivoted to a place her friends would never know, a place where university students sang in the backs of buses, prodigies went to Europe to study piano in famous conservatories, churches resounded up to heaven, there were impersonators galore of everyone Elvis downwards, every boring government 'function' was preceded by a chorus doing wonderful harmonies, taxis blasted metal, restaurants still played Queen hits, the local radio channel never stopped saying bye-bye to Miss American pie, and carollers took over the streets every Christmas. So she let everyone's memory of Uncle Rock be drowned out by this talk of metal and noise and drifted out of the conversation. Through the window she could see a plane, discernible only because of its twinkling lights, beginning its ascent. Tomorrow this time, she would be home.

She yawned and checked the time as they got out of the car and took the elevator to Anu's fifth-floor apartment. It was already 10 o'clock. As soon as they trooped in, Shiva switched on the television, continuing to analyse the intimate connection between Indians and noise. The once cosy apartment was in a mess. It looked like it hadn't been cleaned since Mia had got absorbed in her fashion designer job – she was the only one of the girls who knew how to cook a meal, deal with servants, pay electricity bills, source the cheapest groceries. Sophie noted, disapprovingly, the dining table's food-stained tablecloth, the CDs without their covers strewn all over the sofa, the shoes piled higgledy-piggledy by the door, the dust balls created by the breeze from the fan. She strolled into the kitchen for a glass of water and screamed. An enormous cockroach was nibbling at something near the gas cylinder.

'A cockroach aah? I thought you were being murdered or something,' said Swami who had rushed in to rescue her.

'The place is full of them. We've tried all kinds of poisons, but nothing seems to work,' said Anu coming in after him.

Sophie poured out the glass of water without drinking it. She followed Anu into a bedroom.

'It's all because of Rukshana,' said Anu in a whisper. 'She'll eat half a biscuit and just drop the other half on the counter. Or she'll leave leftovers on her plate instead of putting them in the bin. She's a world-class pig.'

Sophie hung around while Anu moved dizzily between the two bedrooms, both in a state of complete disarray and appearing, between them, to be home to an army of girls. They all seemed to be out on Sunday evening expeditions; there was no one around except Rukshana (Ringo Saar's snooty girlfriend), who sat on the floor in a T-shirt and shorts, painting her toenails, while in the other room Mia lay on a mattress writhing with menstrual cramps.

'It'll get better in a bit,' said Anu soothingly, as she peeled off her jeans.

'It's not getting better,' cried Mama Mia. 'Increase the speed of the fan.'

'It's on max,' said Anu.

'Fuck this cramp,' said Mama Mia.

'When did you take the painkiller?' asked Sophie.

'Half-an-hour back,' said Mama Mia.

'Sophie, you think this skirt is okay?'

Sophie inclined her head as she considered it.

'I know it's a bit too tight but what the hell. Is my butt sticking out?'

'Not very,' said Sophie.

'Mama Mia, are you crying?' asked Anu.

'It's not getting better,' said Mama Mia, wiping her nose with the back of her hand. Sophie knelt by her and stroked her forehead. There was something depressing about this hyper-organized go-getter reduced to a helpless heap on the floor.

'Maybe you should eat something,' said Sophie.

'There's nothing in the fridge except milk and I don't drink milk,' said Mama Mia.

'Shit,' said Anu, trying to find the reflection of her lower half in the small mirror on the wall. 'Rukshana just ate the last egg.'

'I'll tell Swami to get something,' said Sophie.

Sophie went out to the living room, where all the boys where hypnotized by a cricket game, and gave instructions to Swami. Rukshana called out to her when she returned. For a moment Sophie was horrified – Rukshana's face looked like it had been mauled to a bloody mess. But it was only a mud-coloured, slimy-looking face pack. Along with doing her nails, she was also eating what appeared to be breakfast (cornflakes and milk, a fried egg, coffee) and watching a movie on a computer on the floor. Clothes and shoes lay strewn everywhere, but in one corner, as a kind of clue to the homes these girls had left behind, stood a beautifully polished, antique dressing table without a mirror, the only piece of furniture in the room. Rukshana chucked the DVD cover at Sophie.

'It's dumb. Tom Hanks is getting on my nerves.'

Sophie saw no reason to speak to Rukshana after their exchange in the pub, but Rukshana behaved as if she hadn't declared Sophie a bitch or gnawed at Ringo for paying attention to her.

'You work in that company that does these subtitles right. They're so crappy. They make a complete hash of what a person's saying,' said Rukshana. Though she was baiting Sophie, there was also, Sophie realized to her surprise, a desire to make up.

'These are all done in sweatshops in Hong Kong or

somewhere,' said Sophie. 'The films we caption for never get released in India. They're for Europe and the US. And they're absolutely accurate. We get hauled up even if there's a comma in the wrong place.'

'Really?' asked Rukshana, smiling sceptically as she slurped milk and cornflakes from a soupspoon.

'Why are you eating breakfast?' asked Sophie.

'Because my day is just beginning, darling,' she said, touching her face pack gingerly. 'I do the midnight to eight in the morning shift.'

She turned to the screen.

'Look, look,' she yelled, reaching out to the keyboard to freeze the frame. 'Now this is the climax of the movie, right. This is when the man says to the woman – I loved you all along, I just didn't manage to tell you. And the woman says – I loved you too, I just wasn't sure ... And before she can complete her sentence he kisses her. And then wham, bang and happily ever after. We've seen this a million times right, we know how it goes. But it makes us cry. Why?' She spoke to Sophie in a teacherly voice but Sophie couldn't tell what she was getting at.

'I don't understand how mush works. I've tried to discuss it with Ringo, but he can't distinguish between mush and everyday life. When we watch movies together, I cry because even though it's sentimental shit, it still manages to affect me. The harder I try not to cry, the more I cry. But Ringo is different. He cries because he believes that's what life's really like and he's completely unembarrassed ...'

'Ringo cries?' asked Sophie with interest. She found it hard to believe.

'He weeps copious tears. Then he comes out and he'll be his usual cynical self, plotting which goons to send out to punch which insolvent rickshaw-wallah. But these films ... isn't it your job to analyse them? You watch hundreds of them.'

Rukshana seemed different from her usual outraged self. Perhaps this upside down morning was her time, the time when she saw that things had a life of their own and didn't exist just to antagonize her.

'The only way to survive in my job is not to think about movies at all. They're just one frame after another. Ninety minutes of talk and sound effects. The stories disappear. The emotions are nothing. I can only remember two or three movies from the last one year,' said Sophie. She didn't want to go deeper into her distrust of Hollywood or describe how her problems with films had started when the ploys became apparent to her: the same kind of music to express the same kind of emotion, the same choreography between a man and woman who will soon kiss, the same switch of perspective from an intense, focused moment in a room to a wide open landscape, the same primitive ethic – what goes around comes around and there are no free lunches and love conquers all and the good guy doesn't always win but the bad guy usually loses.

Rukshana clicked her tongue disapprovingly. 'That's the easy way out. You need to think about this. Maybe we've all seen so many movies it's hardwired into our brains – the idea that there this a moment when it all comes together. Maybe there is no such moment. You get me? Maybe that's the illusion we're chasing and we cry when we see it on screen.'

Her eyes stood out, glittering against the oily, brown mask, as she waited for Sophie to respond. She looked faintly scary.

'Sophie, just come here for a sec, *please,*' said Anu from the doorway.

Sophie followed her, glancing at her cellphone. Ten-thirty. She was hungry.

'I'm not getting better,' said Mama Mia, sitting up abruptly, her voice breaking with helplessness and pleading.

'Sophie, could you please iron this top. I wanted to wear another one, but I just can't find it in all this mess, and I have to finish my make-up, it's getting bloody late,' said Anu.

Swami came into the room with a bag of chips.

'She can't eat that Swami, she's having cramps!'

'Everything's closed in the neighbourhood. I had to borrow Ringo's car and drive a long way out before I found even this.'

Mama Mia had collapsed in a heap with her back to the world. Sophie wondered if it was possible to die from cramps. She pressed the top quickly and left it where it was, then stepped over the prostrate Mama Mia and looked down at her. She was conscious but her eyes were closed. Her skin was a strange colour.

Sophie went in search of Anu. She and Shiva were having an argument in a corner of the living room, above the cricket commentator's urbane murmur.

'Then why did you *ask*?' said Anu.

'Relax, man. I didn't mean it's looking bad or anything. I just asked to make sure you're comfortable in it,' said Shiva backing off.

'Of course, I'm comfortable in it. Why would I wear it otherwise?' hissed Anu.

'What's up?' asked Sophie.

'He asked me if I was entirely sure I wanted to wear this skirt to the party,' said Anu.

'Exactly. Now is that a crime?' asked Shiva.

'It means that you think I look stupid in it.'

'You're saying that. Not me.'

'Guys, Mama Mia looks quite ill. What do we do?' said Sophie.

'Ringo, please pick up some food for Mia after you've dropped Rukshana at work,' ordered Anu. 'She needs more painkillers and she can't have them on an empty stomach.'

'Will she be okay all alone?' asked Sophie.

'Oh, come on! Anil will kill us if we miss this party. I'm going to change into something else,' said Anu.

'Why on earth?' asked Sophie in despair. 'You're fine in that.'

Rukshana came into the room with her mudpack washed off and her face glowing. 'Hi Ringooo! I'm so sorry you guys didn't win.' Ringo looked morose as she skipped across the room to hug him.

And Sophie, standing there blinking, was suddenly overtaken by a powerful sense of disorientation. *Who were these people and what place was this and why was she here?* For a moment she had no clue.

~

Anil, the birthday boy, was wearing slacks in a camouflage print and Gucci shades; his hair was dyed blond and sculpted into a frenzy of vertical shapes. Sophie couldn't understand how he saw anything through the shades or why he wore them. She had met him once before, at another party, and all she remembered was a long conversation on the differences between their cellphones, the difference between Anil's present cellphone and his earlier one, the difference between the cellphone he had and the one he was going to get, the difference between his cellphone and his girlfriend's cellphone ... Sophie had drunk too much beer to really care, but afterwards she remembered that he was some kind of richie rich. It was hard, now, not to be impressed by the vast apartment rooftop with its also spiky-haired DJ in one corner (a smooth blur of activity behind the thundering techno heartbeat of his machine), its sparkling bar in another corner, its strobe-light lit dance floor in a third and its loaded food tables in a fourth, complete with pasta counter and salad counter and barbecue. Sophie couldn't remember who of her gang knew him well; it was possible that they weren't quite sure themselves. Nevertheless, Anil seemed to recognize her at once and pulled her into a hug when she stretched out her hand to wish him happy birthday.

'Come and dance,' he said into her ear. He shouted out perfunctory questions about her work over the din of the music, then started telling her about himself – the BMW his parents had given him for his birthday, the fact that the DJ was on hire from the town's poshest nightclub.

His cologne was overwhelming. Sophie turned away from him as soon as there was a break in the music, but he was already talking to another girl in a haltered red top, dancing in a slow, solipsistic way. She had the inscrutable look of the very beautiful.

Shiva was by the bar, ordering a drink.

'You have to check out this pile of bricks,' he said to Sophie in a loud whisper as soon as he saw her. 'Every resident owns six, yes, six parking lots, and enjoys spending a few minutes every evening wondering which of the four swimming pools to use.'

Sophie thought she was in just another luxury apartment; her party-going of the last one year had taken her to a few and she had quickly learnt how to mask her amazement with a slightly tired air of polite appreciation – they all did this, she and her scruffy friends, as if they weren't impressed to the point of disgust at the scale at which their hosts lived, and as if they weren't starving for the lavish food and thirsting for the exotically-coloured cocktails. But Sophie wasn't aware, till Shiva explained to her as they waited for their Long Island Ice Teas, that she was in Bangalore's most exclusive piece of heaven. It just didn't get better than this. The figures he spewed – to do with per square feet rates and rentals – didn't mean much to her but when he started describing how there were only thirty families in the humongous building, each living in apartments the size of football fields, with a 360-degree panoramic view from every house, and how, in order to acquire a piece of this cake, you had to not just be super-rich, but prove you were – culturally, ethically, spiritually – a clone of the existing residents, Sophie started to experience that familiar lurch of nausea mixed with awe that wealth in all its forms evoked in her.

She took off immediately for the loo.

Instead of the elevator they had come up in, she went down the winding ivory-coloured marble staircase. Each gleaming step was large enough to go to sleep on. She got to Anil's floor, and walked down a corridor with gilt-framed mirrors on the walls and mahogany tables holding fresh, tall-stalked gerberas, and notepads with golden pens laid across them at a stylish angle for those who wanted to leave a note, and a settee if you wanted to rest in the interval between ringing the doorbell and being admitted into heaven, and a huge filigreed wooden holder on the wall for the post. The relative smallness of the black and silver plaque that carried the family's name and the apartment number was offset by the fact – which she would not have noticed unless Shiva had told her – that all the four doors in the corridor led into the same apartment. She rang the bell on one and heard nothing echoing within but the door was opened instantly by a maid who, in her well-fitting salwar-kurta, her bouffant, her discreet make-up, her manicured toes peeping out from high-heeled sandals, looked about ten times better groomed than Sophie who was still wearing the offensive torn-at-the-knees jeans she had gone to the choultry in and the once ironed but now crumpled shirt. The maid gave Sophie a dazzling smile, stood aside to let her in and told her in proud English: 'Hello my name is Priya for the bathroom go straight down and take the second door on the left.'

Sophie did not have time to wonder how she knew. She would have liked to wander through the apartment on her way to the loo but the maid, who said, 'No, there's no need,' when Sophie started to take off her shoes, was clearly going to keep an eye on her. Despite the maid, however, Sophie stopped short. The living room, which was so large that it got positively blurry at its far reaches, was like a posh version of the minotaur's labyrinth. Everywhere were tables crammed with gleaming silver jugs and urns, bronze figurines, bells and busts, polished paan holders, enamelled ashtrays, gemstone encrusted jewellery boxes, brass trays, and crystal vases. Some tables held ornate lampshades matching the walls, or piles of coffee table books, while others displayed foot-high miniature universes of painted porcelain – an Indian village complete with lazing cows and a flautist Krishna or English gardens with women in flowing white dresses dreaming in their bowers. Wall mirrors multiplied this gleaming assembly of useless things into a treacherous ocean in which it was hard to tell the real from its reflection. Any way you moved you were liable to knock something down. Somewhere in the centre of this madness was a collection of bright orange sofas numerous enough to seat all the fifty-odd people at the party upstairs but which held just the minotaur – the woman trapped in the heart of the labyrinth on whose neck and ears Sophie could, even from that distance, see egg-sized pearls softly glowing. The surprising thing was not the size of the pearls but the way the woman sat, staring into space with her hands clasped in front of her. She looked dressed up to go out but for all Sophie knew these could be her nightclothes and nothing could simply be what she did every evening.

'Hello,' Sophie murmured though the woman had not looked up. It didn't matter; Sophie would have had to shout to reach her.

She wove her way gingerly though the tables with the maid following and then, as they went down a corridor lined with more objets d'art, she glimpsed in passing the bedrooms with their wall-covering paintings and giant chests of drawers and parquet floors and plasma TVs. Finally they were at the door of the bathroom and the maid let her go. Sophie shut the door and entered a dressing room the size of her living room. She opened dark teakwood cupboards and found nothing on the hangers, as if in an unoccupied luxury hotel room. She sank back into a brand new deck chair, picked up a magazine, studied herself in an artfully spot-lit wall mirror and briefly contemplated her life. Then, guessing that the maid would be hovering nearby, that the success of the maid's evening possibly hinged on her properly escorting Anil's guests to and from the bathroom, she went in, took off her slippers and sank her feet into the thickest rug she had ever encountered. Everything, starting from the CD player and down to the toilet seat, the patterned tiles, the voluptuous carving of the mirror frames and the fluffy towels, was pink. The bathtub, which looked like it had never been used was in a third room all by itself. Sophie lingered for as long as was possible without compelling the maid to knock politely on the door, trying out the perfumes in their pink bottles and going through the tacky CD collection of Bollywood hits and Grammy awards compilations.

The maid was nowhere to be seen when Sophie emerged but as soon as she started down the corridor, Priya slipped out of one of the many doors and gave Sophie another blinding smile. The lady of the house was still bravely doing absolutely nothing but sitting and staring. This time Sophie saw her turn her head towards her – she was too far to decode the expression on her face, but she heard what the lady said with a sudden loudness: 'There's just no point trying to catch it.' Sophie stopped short; it took her a few moments to realize that the remark was not directed at her but was part of a mysterious conversation the lady was conducting with herself, a conversation she'd possibly kept running over uncountable similarly blank evenings.

Sophie felt like Alice leaving wonderland as she thanked Priya and Priya shook hands with her. She went back to the roof-top in a thoughtful mood; there was something she had been reminded of and it was only when she was back in the comforting techno boom and mixed food smells of the party that she realized what. It was her walks in the by-lanes around her home. Whenever she dug deep enough into those parts she started to see a pattern. The least well-to-do people lived lives that pressed up against narrow lanes where children tried to murder each other with catapults and stray dogs licked the dripping taps of communal water tanks. The open-doored houses here consisted of two or three bare, tiny rooms and walking by you would glimpse a woman standing by a gas flame, a wall calendar with a picture of the Alps, a bicycle leaning against a wall. As one moved further out, the lanes widened. As soon as the houses got fractionally bigger, their owners would fill up their living rooms, still visible from the street, with gargantuan wooden sofas, and they'd stuff glass-fronted showcases with great bunches of plastic flowers and bronze-coloured papier-mâché Ganeshas and lurid booklets – displayed face up – brought back from religious pilgrimages. That's what Anil's apartment reminded Sophie of – those showcases full of colourful trash that people in her neighbourhood lovingly created to signal that they had moved up, that visitors no longer needed to sit on mats on the floor (in rooms that people slept in by night) or have nothing to look at but a dusty technicolour vision of Switzerland. And Anil himself – despite his expensive shades or perhaps because of his eagerness about those shades – was exactly like those people who had moved up from not starving to the fringes of respectability. When Shiva handed Sophie her drink and asked her what she thought, she laughed out loud and asked him if he had any grass. They repaired to a corner to smoke.

As she described to Shiva the impressive pinkness of the bathroom and the strangeness of Anil's mother, Sophie could see Swami in the distance, drinking his whiskey and talking to Anil. His look alternated between animated and despairing – she knew without being able to hear him that the first signalled car-talk and the second loan-talk. It was a relief to observe him from afar – from this distance she could wish him happiness and forgive him his lapses.

'I hear you're from the Northeast. What a tragic place,' said Shiva, no longer interested in the apartment.

He was turning out to be a compulsive pessimist, this Shiva. Sophie said nothing, never quite sure how to live out this role as someone from the tragic Northeast – that amorphous, eternally misty region whose people apparently spent their lives either fighting each other or resisting the bullying arm of the Indian state.

Shiva said, 'I had a friend who was working there, teaching in an engineering college, enjoying it. He was going back after a holiday in Bangalore and the 'boys', as they call them there, blew up his train as it entered Assam. They never found a scrap of his body. He just vanished – poof!'

Perhaps Shiva was like her – always confronted by the bad things – except that she sometimes also saw good things. She could have sworn, for instance, that it had been Ribor the other morning, trying to flag down her rickshaw.

Shiva said, 'Who cares, really, about the idea of India. Do you? I mean if people want to raise their own flags and form their own little countries why is that such a problem?'

Maybe it was the weed, but the word 'India' lodged itself in Sophie's brain. Somewhere in the depths of her childhood she had formed the idea that India was an exact feeling, a fixed series of things in contrast to everything else in her environment which was simply what it was and had no relation to India. And even now, the residue of this belief clung to her. The words of the Rabindranath Tagore poem – 'Into that heaven of freedom, my father, let my country awake' – sung during the school assembly on Independence Day were India. The yellowed pages of her history book when she was eight, filled with stories about King Harshavardhan and scenes from the Mahabharata, were India. The little flags with their dripping orange and green watercolours, which she and her sister used to laboriously paint when they were little, were self-evidently India. Vivekananda ('Shall India die? Then from the world all spirituality will be extinct, all moral perfection will be extinct, all sweet-souled sympathy for religion will be extinct ...') had for her once been India in its noblest form. At school, the girls who oiled their hair and worried about exams reeked of India, as against those who wore their skirts short and who, already at thirteen or twelve, understood the mysterious workings of sex. Amar Chitra Katha comics, the 9 o'clock news on TV, diyas on Diwali, the gaudy colours of the idol during Durga Puja, the Republic Day parade, the mithai shop from where they always bought their sweets, where the flies floated without drowning in the basin of rosogullas and the laddoos were so sweet they gave Sophie a head-rush – all of these were uniquely and indisputably India. *Swami and Friends* was India. The vague past her parents came from was India. Often the subject of their quarrels was India, though they didn't know it. Sophie's mother would say –

'Nothing these girls are learning in this town, nothing. Where is their culture? What are their values?' And her father would stamp his foot impatiently and say, 'Don't mix things up. You can appreciate Hamlet sitting in a village.' For Hamlet-Shamlet was his touchstone, his pole star, his single point criteria.

As far as Sophie could tell, this was the only legacy of having lived in Shillong – the sense that India was far away even though it managed, now and then, to manifest itself. When Sophie moved to Bangalore, she'd expected to be overwhelmed by the excess of India, and for the first few months she had approached everything with caution – the alien-looking mangoes, the little heaps of blood-red, deep fried gobhi manchurian in roadside stalls, the gloomy recesses of the temple, the astrologer's consulting room (a man whose signboard announced 'Since from 50 years stay in Bangalore. Know your future. Visit your problem in education, job, trade, love, marriage, court problem, family matters, politics'). But over the past year, she had by implication herself become India and now the opposite seemed strange – the idea that she could have lived the first twenty-four years of her life believing in her foreignness.

It would have been impossible to explain any of this to Shiva who had, meanwhile, moved on, driven by no apparent logic, to the subject of stray dogs. 'There's no sense of balance in anything we do in this city. Take this whole campaign to kill all the stray dogs. I mean, for years if not decades, nobody thought the stray dogs were a problem and now, suddenly, they're rounding them up and shooting them in the head. There's a sweet dumb mutt who's adopted our office and he hangs out there wagging his tail without a break, living on the scraps the watchman throws him. Now that dog's got a life, right? He's not getting in anyone's way, he's just happy to see the lot of us in the morning and know he's not alone in the world. Frankly he's a lot more decent than most fuckers in my office. But they took him away yesterday.' He shook his head and rubbed his eyes.

Sophie found it hard to tell how much time had passed and whether the joint she was smoking was the one Shiva had first rolled. Her friends were where she had last seen them; Anu was deep in conversation with a couple Sophie didn't know; she was eating from a plate piled high with food from which strings of spaghetti hung and legs of chicken protruded. From time to time she tried to feed a forkful to the woman and then the man. Sophie's hunger had turned into a sharp acidic feeling in the pit of her stomach. She left Shiva sitting cross-legged on a carpet, expostulating on the city's latest dog-decimation statistics and shuffled off towards the buffet.

Anil welcomed her as if he had just met her, told her he knew just the thing she should eat, gave a few instructions to a chef. Sophie giggled without good reason and felt like eating the chef's hat – it looked like it was carved out of a huge block of vanilla ice-cream. Anil tried to ascertain whether she was having fun and she tried to figure out if his mother sat alone like that every evening, talking to herself. ('My mum?' asked Anil, lost behind his shades. 'She's fine. She knows how to have fun by herself.') He handed her a plate of steaming clams freshly tossed in butter and garlic. Sophie stood alone in the centre of the terrace and ate them with her fingers; they tasted so singularly of happiness, she was reminded of Emma Bovary who, when she attends her first ball, realizes that she has never seen pomegranates before nor tasted pineapples. Sophie went back, got herself another plateful and, bypassing Swami, headed towards Anu.

Shiva was already there, embarking on a new rant. Drink seemed to have unloosed something manic in him. 'Do you know what these nouveau rich guys in the city's posh areas do? They gift us their shit and this is how it happens. When they're building their fancy houses, they encroach on municipal land so that they can extend their already huge plots. Their garages, for instance, cover the storm drains. Then, to save costs, instead of taking a proper connection to a sewer pipe, they let all their sewage leak into the storm drains. And this shit starts to travel all across the city. In our neighbourhood, we have muck from as far as three kilometres away. My parents have filed a public interest litigation, but the judge says, this muck has come from somewhere else. I can't solve your problem unless someone addresses the problems with the whole city. Millions of people and all of them thinking only of themselves. Why? Why do we have to wallow in other people's shit?'

'Please ... I'm eating,' said Anu, scooping up the last morsel into her mouth, then skipping away to get more. 'Change the subject. Shiva meet Anand and Anandi. Anand and Anandi meet Shiva,' she said over her shoulder. The couple offered wan smiles. They seemed not to be enjoying the party, while Shiva was clearly a party animal.

'Try a funny story,' said Sophie. She felt herself becoming a feather, a snowflake, a sparrow. Soon nothing would touch her.

'Okay, consider this,' said Shiva. 'They've built a new mall near my house. This hideous UFO has appeared, like overnight – decorated like a Christmas tree, lots of parking space, giant posters of chicks in the windows, great discounts. All the suckers in the neighbourhood go there on opening day, and this is *not* a rich neighbourhood, these are accountants and postal clerks and insurance salesmen. But how can they not go when this marvellous object just appears on the side of the road one day? Everything you can think of, right there on the shelves. It's not about what you need, man. It's a trip. So my mum goes too, the poor sucker, and she comes back trembling. She says – Shiva, I was caught in a stampede, I nearly died. It turns out that there was some exchange offer – like you give them an old frying pan or something and you get a new one. And people had gone berserk. There were rickshaw drivers waving their pressure cookers in the air and then it was closing time and like hundreds of people still hadn't got their thrills. So then there's a stampede. People get hurt. My mother manages to get away with just a bruise on her arm, just a tiny little bruise. And, then of course, everyone comes out and starts stoning these giant glass walls, and the police turn up and we know the rest of the story. And what I'm thinking is, if my mother had been killed, I'd have died of shame. How could I have gone around explaining to people – you know, my mum died in a shopping mall stampede. It was opening day and she'd heard you could get two packs of toilet cleaner for the price of one.'

No one laughed. Anand, in fact, seemed to be wiping tears. Anu returned with another mountainous mess of food and took her place in the centre of the group.

'Shiva, I said change the bloody subject.'

She apologized to Anand but Anand was sobbing openly now, drawing in every breath as if it had grown thorns. His partner was struggling to hold back her own tears.

'He was going nuts after the cremation this morning, so Anil suggested that they drop in for a while. That way we can all keep an eye on them,' whispered Anu in Sophie's ear, and then, imagining, as people sometimes do, that replaying a tragedy, bringing in all the witnesses, would lessen its horror, she turned to Anandi and said, 'Sophie was there ... Sophie saw what happened.'

So they were the little dead Superman's parents! Sophie ceased floating and fell to earth. She didn't want to look into their eyes; she was afraid of what she would see. The disorientation she had felt at Anu's place gripped her again. Why was she the chosen recorder of other people's suffering? It was as if things that should happen behind closed doors and drawn curtains were being performed in full public view, with Sophie inevitably there, trying to keep her eyes averted yet forced to look – the labourer woman wiping the blood from her battered face, the man mopping a dead child's blood from the floor, the metallic smell of blood in the hot closed room where they had left Mama Mia crying with pain. And once Sophie had been forced into this spectator role she felt weighed down with responsibility.

But she was too stoned to trust herself to say anything, and she knew, from the crazy pain that twisted Anand's face, the tightly reined-in grief on Anandi's, that silence was the only recourse. Shiva had been silenced too. Anu tried to cheer everyone up by feeding them seekh kebabs dripping with paneer gravy but no one was hungry. What are they doing here, thought Sophie frantically, and tried to think of more appropriate things for the parents of a newly-dead child to do. But what *could* they do? Anu had a bright idea.

'Sophie tried out a Baba Sampige session this morning, just to see what he's all about. You think it might help to visit him, talk it through with someone who's detached and stuff?'

Shiva started running agitated hands through his long hair. He wanted to tell his Baba Sampige story but Anu was not going to let him. She silenced him with a forced forkful of fried rice. Anu was treating tragedy the way she would treat hunger – a vacancy, an emptiness that urgently needed filling. 'Anand and Anandi, *please* don't listen to what other people say,' she said. 'Just go to the ashram and talk to him.'

Garden City

Two o'clock and the party was starting to wind down. Shiva, finding that the potential audience for his interminable stories recoiled at his approach, had lapsed into a moody silence. Anand and Anandi were put into a taxi and sent home. Swami was drunk. The previous night, a man from San Francisco had been frantically trying to place an online order for a book and when he'd understood that Swami was Indian, he'd asked for an American agent.

'I told him – you search, you won't find an American agent. If you find an American agent call me back and I'll quit my job this minute.'

Swami went quiet after this, his chin sunk into his chest.

'What did he say?' asked Anu impatiently.

'He said he'd been waiting for weeks for this book to hit the stores. He can't stand being put off now by some fuck-up in the systems. I told him – sir, it's 3 o'clock in the morning here and I'm trying to do my best. He went on about the payment to the online bookstore that refused to get authorized. And I kept giving him my retarded, robot line – please check with your bank, sir.

Our systems do not authorize or perform any evaluation on any transaction. And he kept saying – I've checked with the bank. They haven't got the transaction request, there's something wrong with your system, get me an American agent. How can an American solve the problem is one question he couldn't answer. How can someone, just because he has a different accent and a different skin colour ...'

'What was the book?' asked Sophie, since Swami was drunk and had to be helped along in his story till he got to some kind of conclusion and they could all go home. She felt she could collapse right there, but on the other hand she knew that as soon as she did all those images would come crowding upon her, all the poisonous tentacles of her insomnia.

'Some gardening stuff ... How to Grow Grass at Home.'

'How to grow grass ...' Sophie repeated slowly. They looked at each other, and Swami, understanding for the first time, erupted into laughter. Soon they were helpless, Swami spluttering, 'Was I really awake at 3 a.m. trying to help a junkie? Was I really trying to get him to understand from halfway across the world ...'

Nobody else found any reason to share in this mirth, but Sophie and Swami, Sophie and some shadow of the old Swami, some obverse of the Swami who usually just worried about the limitations of his job, were ecstatic with their shared recognition of irony. Then Swami, as if suddenly realizing that being there on the floor laughing so hard might further weaken his hold on reality, started trying to lift himself up. Sophie didn't help him, so he rose by degrees, first squatting, then kneeling, then hoisting himself up by holding onto the edge of a table.

'Hey, I hope you enjoyed the pardy,' called out Anil, coming up to them.

'How can an American agent prevent the whole shithouse from going up in flames?' Swami asked him.

'I hope you enjoyed the pardy,' repeated Anil, reaching out a hand to steady him.

Swami raised his drooping head to look at Anil. 'There's no food left. What kind of host are you, I say?'

Since his eyes were veiled, Sophie looked at Anil's mouth

to see how it reacted to Swami's insult. The mouth looked genuinely shocked. He turned to the catering staff.

'Sorry sir, the live counters are closed but there's some salad and rice ...' said one of the chefs, whose shirt – as if signalling the lateness of the hour – was poking out of his waistband.

Anil waved him away and said, 'No one goes hungry at my pardies. Just give me a minute, I'll see off some friends, and then we'll go and get you some dinner. I know a place that is open late.'

Swami vomited explosively in response and they all leapt back.

I'm finished with this, thought Sophie, though she'd been smiling a minute ago. I'm through with this.

Anu rubbed Swami's back gingerly, while he explained to her between further bouts of vomiting why the man who had wanted an American agent had been so fundamentally wrong, how he'd undermined the whole system by imagining that any of this had anything to do with race.

Fifteen minutes later they were in Anil's new BMW.

'If you got to puke, you got to puke,' said Anil.

Anu's phone rang. She listened for a moment, then said – 'Mama Mia. Stomach's still hurting. Ringo never got back with the food. Doesn't know what to do.'

They'd all forgotten about her.

'We'll bring you something,' said Anu into the phone. 'Just hang on for a bit.'

Sophie looked out at the city. The lights of the occasional all-night pharmacy flashed by, there were people asleep in bus stand shelters, and cars whizzed past with a speed denied to them by day, some leaving sounds of loud music and laughter after them like a vapour. The city smelt different at this hour – a putrid smell, the smell of food gone sour, the bad water in the city's lakes, the mangy bodies of stray dogs and the garbage decaying by the minute at street-corners. Swami insisted on holding Sophie's hand. Norah Jones sang about love on the stereo and for a while everything was smoothed over by the movement of the car, the music, the comfortable silence.

The restaurant Anil knew was shut.

'Damn it. They even have a hookah bar,' said Anil, as he started up the car again. He seemed almost nice, despite the shades. Intent on finding food for his hungry friend.

'Taj,' said Anu. 'Best chicken rolls in town.' They drove to Shivaji Nagar, slowed down before a restaurant called Taj.

'Not this one, not this one!' cried Anu in horror. 'This is multi-cuisine.'

They passed another Taj, which wasn't the right one either. It had a string of party lights over the entrance and they caught a glimpse of faded plastic chairs and tables laid out in a balding garden.

'This city has fucking multi-cuisine coming out of its ears,' slurred Swami.

Anil flew down an empty street, took a sharp left turn with a dramatic screech of brakes and came up against a posse of six policemen.

'What the hell ...' he whispered as he slowed down.

A police jeep stood to one side and the occupants of another car were being questioned.

An officer came up and tapped on Anil's window.

'Get out. Everyone get out,' he said.

A drunken driving check? wondered Sophie.

The officer was joined by two other cops and they barked out their questions. Where were they coming from, where were they going, how did they know each other, what were their names, why were they out this late, had they noticed a WagonR speeding. The last question made everyone prick up their ears. Someone was on the run.

The officer sniffed Anil's breath and said, 'Drinking aah? Give me two thousand rupees.'

Anil tried to divert his attention by asking him what was going on.

The officer spoke into his walkie-talkie in Kannada while one of the policemen announced – 'Murder'.

'Murder!' echoed Sophie.

The cop started to behave as if he'd told them too much and ordered them back into the car. 'Go home, go home. Not a good time to be on the streets.'

His superior told Anil over the voices crackling on his walkie-talkie, 'Give me two thousand rupees, otherwise he will take you to the police station.'

Anil began bargaining with him while Shiva slipped away to eavesdrop on the two boys the other policemen were questioning.

'I'm hungry,' said Swami. Anu found an old piece of chewing gum in her handbag and gave it to him. It was unbearable to her that someone should go hungry in her presence.

'Don't move to Australia,' said Sophie suddenly. 'Who will you call if you're in trouble?'

'Australia?' asked Swami.

'I know, I know. But there are compensations,' said Anu. 'Sophie, will you talk to Shiva?'

'Why me?'

'He'll pay attention if someone else says it. I've been bugging him about this for weeks; it's just noise to him when I talk. All I want him to do is apply for a passport. That's the first step. Apply for a passport.'

'Who'll be left then?' asked Sophie with a stoned gentleness, more to herself than Anu. 'Even the stray dogs are going.'

'I sometimes feel I don't understand people.' This was the closest Anu had come to making a philosophical statement. Sophie looked at her intently and wished someone had a smoke. 'Happiness is so easy to define. You can be so clear about what you want. Isn't that amazing?'

Swami, who had no taste for philosophical discussions, shrugged and said, 'These cops are screwing Anil, man. Two thousand bucks? That's a rip-off.'

'And yet people are so weird because they don't do it. They could identify what would give them happiness and that's half the battle won, but they're just not able to take that simple step,' continued Anu.

'But what happens afterwards, after you've got everything you wanted?' asked Sophie.

Shiva came over and said, 'I got the full story.'

A few hours ago, a boy had apparently stabbed his call centre employee girlfriend to death and dumped her by Ulsoor Lake. A couple who happened to be taking a late night walk had seen the body and called the police. The dead girl's phone was in the pocket of her jeans; the police called the last number she'd called and understood from the friend who answered that the girl's boyfriend dropped her to work every evening. She gave them his name and number. The boy did not answer his phone but they found a landline number for him in the dead girl's phonebook and his mother answered. Her son was at home, asleep, she said. By the time the police got there he'd vanished.

'They have cops posted all over. They'll get him. He's been only driving for the last half an hour. Poor sucker,' said Shiva.

A cold silence descended on the group.

Sophie felt like her head would burst, but another part of the same head knew that it could sustain this feeling for hours without anything happening.

Anil had managed to beat his fine down to a thousand rupees.

'Go home,' said the officer, putting the money in his pocket.

'Let's *go*. Mama Mia might have passed out by now,' said Sophie.

Anil sped down Mahatma Gandhi Road. There were two policemen on the Brigade Road corner, looking indifferent. They didn't flag the car down. But twenty minutes later, on Bannerghata Road, they could see them from a long way off – the police jeeps with their rotating beacons. Anil cursed as he slowed down and Sophie started to feel that the night was moving in reverse and soon it would be the morning of the day that had gone by, not the day to come. When she closed her eyes, all that came to her were the crazy fragments of films – people screaming, monsters and zombies, exploding cars, the ripe laughter of children, some woman always talking somewhere, summing up life in some impossibly eloquent way. As Anil drew up, she tried to formulate in her mind the words that would convince the cops to let them pass. She thought of Mama Mia's blue face and of the killer driving alone, sobbing in fear, and she realized that Swami was right – the shithouse was going up in flames.

But she needn't have worried about the policemen because they were all piling into their jeeps and leaving. Anu's phone rang. 'We're almost there, darling,' she cooed.

'Mia's crying,' she said to the others then in a strangely trembling voice and dropped the phone in Shiva's lap as if it were on fire. 'She's saying something about cops coming to the house and asking about Ringo. I don't know what she's going on about.'

Shiva put the phone to his ear, his eyes growing impossibly large. 'Holy shit, it's Ringo. Swami, it's Ringo. Swami ...'

'Ringo what?' asked Swami impatiently, snatching the phone from him. He listened to Mama Mia for a few moments, then shouted, 'No, no, no!'

~

Ringo Saar had killed Rukshana. For the first hour after they got to the apartment, this was so shockingly absurd that they just sat down together, unable to look at each other, everyone trying desperately to grasp this. Again and again, someone broke in to say in a cracked voice – *He murdered her? It can't be.* After a while, other questions were asked and the tears started spilling and the shock only grew. He had a knife in the car? He stabbed her till she died? He dumped her by a lake? What was the question to which Ringo had decided the only answer was murder?

Swami, his drunken slurring suddenly gone, whispered, 'I'm not believing anything till I've met him.'

Mama Mia's phone rang but she ignored it.

'Why would he run if he didn't do it? He can't get away, he can't,' she sobbed, then repeated what the cops had told her. She seemed unable to stop saying them – those horrible words. Anu started shouting at her to shut up.

Mama Mia said, 'But they were here half an hour ago. They said – we found her phone and she'd spoken to you at 11.30 p.m. I said, I wasn't feeling well and she wanted to know if I was better.' She launched into the whole story again; then her face contorted and she bent over with cramps.

Swami said, his face pale, 'I just don't get it. Whenever I dropped by in the evenings, Ringo Saar would be here making her breakfast while she yapped on the phone. Or he'd just be sitting around waiting for her, so he could drop her to work. He was constantly buying things for her. He took her parents out when they were visiting. Why would he do this?'

'Pray that he gets away. That's the only hope left – that he drives right out of town and never comes back,' said Shiva.

'I told her not to play with him,' said Mama Mia. 'I told her he's going to snap one day. And she'd laugh and say – Ringo is sentimental. He cries at movies.'

Anu was laid out flat on the floor, her hands over her eyes. 'It can't be true, it's just not fucking true. Somebody else did it. A psychopath ... one of her colleagues who was jealous ... it could be anyone.'

Mama Mia said, '11.30 she calls me and two hours later the police call me. She never makes it to work. They called her office and checked. She had no plans to meet anyone else ...' She moaned and asked Sophie to get her another pill from the bedroom.

Sophie asked, 'Have you been eating pills on an empty stomach all night? I'll boil some rice for you.'

She went into the kitchen; grains scattered everywhere as she tried to measure out some rice with her wildly trembling hands. She held on to the counter to steady herself, no longer aware of the giant cockroach which, for its part, seemed to sense her harmlessness and didn't scuttle away. Her mind could only form images; no thoughts – Rukshana's screams that no one heard; Ringo begging Rukshana to wake up for once, wake up and consider how he felt; Rukshana begging Ringo to take her to a hospital; the look in Ringo's eyes when he'd told her off earlier that day; the look in Rukshana's eyes when she had told Ringo to stop indulging Sophie the previous afternoon. She acted now as if Ringo's life depended on her carefully boiling some rice, as if she just needed to focus hard enough for him to get away. Drive, drive, drive, she whispered. *Drive.* She could hear Shiva saying that Ringo wasn't answering his phone. Then Mama Mia's phone (whose ring tone was a girl's voice trilling 'tring tring') went off and Sophie heard Swami taking the call. Already there was a glimmer of normality in the sounds coming from the living room, while Sophie felt unable to face her friends, unable to breathe properly, unable to pick up any one of the many threads of her life.

Then slowly, despite her not wanting to, things started of themselves to fall into a sequence and she thought of the pressure she had put on Ringo and the pressure Rukshana had undoubtedly put on Ringo to undo his promise to Sophie. He cracked up, she thought. Guilt turned her legs to stone, while her hands shook harder. She tried to think of other, larger reasons for what had happened. Rukshana did cheat on him and yet so compelled him that he could not leave her; his work had brutalized him; he had grown-up watching his parents fight. There were so many reasons for Ringo to let go, yet the only reason Sophie could think of for why he let go *that* night was what had happened between them over lunch. Any other night but tonight would have overwhelmed her with pity and horror but now she also felt shame. He was mocking her, even as his hands were covered in blood and his face was wet.

Swami came into the kitchen, gripped her arm and said, 'They got him.'

And then there was no reason not to cry.

Swami looked grim but he wasn't breaking up. Even the most horrible things have a logic that must be followed to the very end – that's what his expression suggested, whereas the more clearly Sophie saw what had happened, the more helpless she felt. I don't understand anything, she said and meant – I don't know what would have been the right thing to do. Swami thought she meant – how do we deal with the randomness of this and he tried to comfort her, to show her that the rock solid things would always stay that way and that the world cracked only if you let it. She grew angry at Swami then and shouted through her crying. Why hadn't anyone seen this coming? Why had no one cared when she said Ringo was changing?

Swami tried to calm her down but Sophie only felt things go darker and darker till the flashes of disorientation she had earlier experienced started to seem like premonitions – she was in the wrong place. She could suppress her horror for a moment to admire Swami's restraint but even that meant nothing because hadn't Ringo been the same in the early days, in control and laid-back and quiet and laughing till he started showing glimpses of pure hate? She could do nothing but stand there limply and moan as Swami hugged her and said, 'Anil, Shiva and I are going with his mother to the police station. You guys stay here and stay calm.'

'What will I say to him when I see him?' asked Sophie, wild-eyed.

'Nothing, you don't need to meet him right now. But *we* still need to help him. Rukshana's gone, there's nothing …' He broke off and studied the floor.

'I shouldn't have ever come here, I shouldn't have got to know him.'

Swami looked at her uncomprehendingly and said, 'Just sit with the girls. I'll be back soon. Mia's not in good shape, Anu won't get up from the floor.' He tried to squash the cockroach with his foot but the cockroach was faster.

'How can anyone help him? He's beyond all of us. This is what he wanted. He wanted to make someone suffer hard so that he could suffer himself. He didn't even drive fast enough. Couldn't he have gotten away at least, driven that goddamn car a little faster?' Sophie continued to burble in misery, but Swami had turned away and was punching a number on his cellphone.

She followed him out.

Mama Mia was talking to herself. 'What have you done with Rukshana, Ringo?'

Anil had finally taken off his shades and Sophie saw that despite the advantage of money he was like the rest of them – a frightened twenty-five year old who didn't know what to do when life turned shitty.

~

Sophie and Swami, smoking joints in her flat at 5.30 in the morning. They'd left Mama Mia fed, drugged with painkillers and finally sleeping, Anu talking to Rukshana's parents on the phone, and Anil and Shiva watching over them. They'd jumped over a locked and spiked red gate to which Sophie did not have the key because her landlord didn't consider it necessary – if Sophie returned home late that was her problem.

The silence was acute. This was not the silence of dusk when things are slowly withdrawing into themselves – small boys going back home with cricket bats under their arms, dark kites winging across the sky, the last of the soppu-sellers; not the silence of 9 p.m. when a motorbike suddenly spluttering into life in the lane could cause Sophie to start; not the silence of midnight through whose impenetrability she could hear the faraway barking of dogs, bark relayed to bark, the whole adding up to a ragged, improbable chorus. This was a silence that lacked the remotest hint of noise to give it definition. Sophie knew it well; it was like sitting in the dark for ages and then suddenly realizing you've gone blind.

The weed had spread to the far corners of her brain, making things so sharp they hurt. She could have gone on just staring at all the razor-edged, brightly-coloured objects in the room, and tried to erase the last few hours through such a meditation. She'd only spoken to Rukshana a few times and never really paid much attention to her, but death was slowly rendering her unforgettable. Maybe there is no one moment when it all comes together – those had been Rukshana's last words to her, which seemed like some kind of joke now because a few hours later it had all come together. Everything about her was now overlaid with the fact of her death – it would never be possible to separate the two and ask who Rukshana had really been. Who was she? Sophie wondered and could only remember reports from Anu and Mama Mia about this haughty, beautiful ex-classmate, whose instinct for glamour they enjoyed but whose perennial complaining and slob-like tendencies they didn't. She plays around with Ringo, Anu would sometimes say, and Sophie would ask for details but they were always sketchy. Rukshana kept her purported extra-Ringo affairs well-hidden.

Swami was talking about Ringo Saar. Sophie, her eyes like the lens of a powerful and impersonal camera, focused on him. He appeared so vivid to her, half-lying there among the cushions in a corner of the room, addressing not her but a pinkish gecko that was making cautious progress across the ceiling.

Ringo's mother had been given fifteen minutes with her son, and Swami had wheedled his way in along with her, explaining that she suffered from extreme hypertension and might have a stroke unless he was on hand to calm her down. In a small dusty room, across a bare table, with a picture of Gandhi hanging slightly askew on the wall above his head, Ringo, flanked by an armed policeman, tried to explain why he had done what he had done.

'She went too far. I know it's horrible, but it was horrible before. It's not worse now.'

Ringo's mother had broken down repeatedly and not understood anything, and Swami found it hard to say much given the policeman, the dusty Gandhi, the handcuffed Ringo and the inescapable nature of what he had done.

'She was going to leave me. She didn't understand what was real and what a game. As long as she was having fun, she didn't care. Can you live like that? No, you can't live like that. You need to take some things seriously. I showed her the knife just to make her see that you need to take some things seriously but she just laughed at me. I thought, if I hear her laugh one more time, I'll have to kill myself. You know the feeling? Swami, don't stare at me like that, man.'

'Did he say anything about me, about how I was harassing him?' asked Sophie.

Swami said, 'All he said was – tell Sophie she can keep Bhatt now. She'll be happy.'

Sophie felt she had shrunk to the size of an ant, while Swami expanded as he talked loudly about Ringo. Lots of people knew him but no one knew him well. He neither loved nor hated his job. He wasn't worried about the men (they were always men) whose lives he made difficult, unlike Swami who grew anxious when customers two continents away banged their phones down in disgust. He could drink a lot of beer. He didn't talk much. He practised on his drums a lot. He loved Rukshana – that was for sure. And Rukshana was always threatening to leave him, though she never did. He'd discussed this a few times with Swami, his fear that she would actually leave. For a laidback guy he was surprisingly obsessed with her. And they could all see it, couldn't they – that she was using him. She wanted to have Ringo Saar around, but she also wanted to hang out with other men if she felt like it and she often did. There were times when she'd disappear and not answer her phone. Ringo would go a little crazy then and say – this is it, this is the last time – but no one really thought about what he meant. Now it was clear, said Swami. He meant that he'd kill her. But then, each time, Rukshana would return and tell Ringo Saar – you're free too. Why do you have to sit here and call me, like, seventeen times a day? If you don't stop doing this, I'm going to leave you. And he'd say – okay, fine. You have it your way.

But all Sophie could think of was the part she had played. She told Swami about what had happened the previous day and all the earlier fights she and Ringo had had about Bhatt. Swami smiled sadly at her and took her hand and spent a long time trying to convince her of the inevitability of what Ringo had done.

'She's dead simply because a moment came when he wanted her dead, that's all Sophie,' he said finally, his voice rasping. 'You know what I think. I think he murdered her when he realized he *has* to leave her and he can't do it. That's kind of scary, isn't it – he had the guts to stab her but not to let her go.'

For the first time in what felt like months, Sophie found herself going along with Swami. She felt hollowed out and Swami's voice – even though cracking from tiredness and sorrow – was confident and she let it fill her in order to have something to hold on to. She felt desperately thirsty but the kitchen seemed miles away and opening the fridge and getting a bottle of water seemed to require the dexterity of a tightrope walker.

'It was just like Ringo Saar said,' said Swami. 'She thought it was a game. As long as she kept threatening to leave, he would hang on and never take her for granted. He'd beg her to stay and then she would and he'd be grateful and the game would go on. But of course, she never meant to leave him. He was incredibly nice to her. He heard her out and cooked for her and dropped her to work every evening. He took her out shopping and to restaurants and paid for everything.'

Sophie said, 'She didn't think in absolutes and he thought in absolutes. In some basic sense they just didn't get each other. Ringo loved Rukshana yet hated her for not seeing it. Rukshana enjoyed ambiguity. Maybe she did try to make this thing with Ringo work but just gave in to other temptations.'

She felt the pain that arises when death changes from a single, shocking fact to a mist that blurs all of life. The whole city, all their various lives in it together, all that she and her friends imagined they wanted – Australia, love, cars, heavy metal, tolerant landlords – none of it seemed worthwhile any more. Ringo was mocking at everything from his prison cell. Away, away, away, he was saying. He was echoing what Anil's mother had understood – there's just no point trying to catch it.

Swami pressed Sophie's face in his hands.

'Was there something you wanted to tell me earlier, at the concert?'

'Water,' said Sophie.

Swami got a bottle from the fridge and they sat side by side, their bodies pressed tight against each other for comfort, drinking greedily.

'You've been angry with me,' said Swami, embracing her so hard, her chest hurt. They lay down and suddenly it seemed as if they could not get close enough, even when leg was entwined with leg and groins touched and their mouths were on the sides of each other's necks and their hearts beat in each other's ears. Sophie closed her eyes; the weed was starting small fires the colour of blood and orange peel all over her mind's dense black.

'I will never sleep again,' said Sophie, but holding onto Swami like this as they freefell through their separate stoned darknesses, even that thought was manageable.

'I called my dad and told him what had happened and he said – it's because you people don't sleep and eat at regular hours. The old man's got it all figured out.'

'Has your dad ever not woken up at 5 o'clock, ever not drunk coffee at 7.30 a.m.?'

'It's not just the routine. It's the whole tradition and progress funda. His great grandfather probably had the same idea of life. It's kinda okay. You don't have to worry about whether what you're doing makes sense because so many people have done it before you.'

Sophie had met Swami's father once. He'd greeted her in a stately fashion, with his hands pressed together and a fixed stare. He did an hour of yoga every morning, went for a long walk, had a bath and then immersed himself in his puja. At 8 o'clock he would launch on the 'progress' part of the day. He ran a school on the premises of a temple, owned by the temple math. This he had been doing for twenty-five years. Sophie found him both fascinating and scary.

'Tradition and progress,' repeated Sophie. 'I have this weird feeling all the time that I'm moving backwards. I have to tell myself every morning – today is what I yesterday thought of as tomorrow.'

'So you want to go back to Shillong?'

Sophie was quiet for a moment. 'I have to get away from all this for a while,' she said. 'What are they going to do with him?'

'I don't know. His dad is talking to some big-shot lawyer. He had that knife in his car so it's premeditated murder. If they'd had an argument and he'd just grabbed a kitchen knife and stabbed her …'

'It's this city. When you're out on the streets, you feel you could kill someone every day.'

They had relaxed a little and loosened their hold on each other, so they hugged fiercely again but it wasn't possible any more to feel each other through cloth so they unbuttoned each other's shirts and pulled off their jeans and lay down again, feeling each other's warm skins as if for the first time, their ache closer to becoming one ache.

Swami said, bringing his face very close to Sophie's, 'We must get married.'

Sophie went limp for a while, then sat up abruptly and stared at her boyfriend. She was so shattered that if he'd suggested anything else she'd have gone along with it, but those clear words put her life together again. She looked at Swami in shame and started putting her shirt on.

'Please Sophie please,' said Swami, trying to pull her back. 'I know we've always said we should wait till things are settled but I don't want to wait any more. After tonight, I don't want to wait.'

Sophie shook her head in amazement. 'No, no, no. You've got it all wrong.' And now that she'd opened this wound, she decided to do what Ringo had done and wipe it all out in one clean sweep.

'I can't see you again.'

She hated herself; she wanted them back on the floor, together without words. But that was a lie: nothing was possible without words. The truth was that Swami wanted her all for himself, he wanted her to fit his little world.

He was looking at her as if he'd been shot.

'You've been kind to me. This is not your fault but there are many mornings when I don't even want to talk to you.'

Swami sat up angrily. 'You don't know what you want. When we were in that mall the other day …'

'Don't talk about the mall. We haven't had a proper conversation for months. You've become obsessed with something else, so it's better you follow that, whatever it is, wherever it takes you.'

'I'm just making sure I lead a comfortable life, my parents

lead a comfortable life, you ... I'm doing it all for you. I don't want to be like Ringo. See where he's ended. I have a plan ...'

Sophie took a deep breath and touched his arm. 'No, Swami. I can't do it. No more plans.'

'You want to go back to Shillong, is that what you want?' he asked again.

'I don't want to lie to you any more.'

'Sophie,' said Swami in a small voice. 'I don't care. I'll wait and wait and wait for you.'

Sophie just lit another joint. She couldn't tell if it was a few minutes or many hours later that she heard the sound of his Nikes hitting the ground as he jumped over the gate.

~

Sophie submitted to her visions. Someone had whipped away the everyday part of her mind and revealed the glittering life underneath. Here everything was a whirl of colour and activity, a fairground of impressions that spun teasingly past her – toy-like faces, their eyes horrifyingly alive; an assembly line of identically dancing figures, glinting silver and ruby and turquoise; chattering people who melted into rivers of chocolate; floating pencil sketches of cityscapes in which certain things – a lit window here, a cigarette-tip there – glowed with a painful orange intensity. Everything led to something else, triggered yet another merry-go-round of images that hurried past her on their way to somewhere important. Everywhere she looked was this nauseating carnival conspiring to kill her. She felt she should open her eyes but the idea was remote, like the thought of something one intends to do in a few years' time. She wanted to scream but they would hear – these masks with eyes, these talking ghosts. So she let them fight each other while she stood at the brink of the precipice – the very precipice into which Rukshana and Ringo had fallen.

Aeons later the whirlpools began to slow down and Sophie opened her eyes and thought – where did I get them from, these tacky cartoon images? It's the films, that's what it is. That is all my mind can yield.

I've learnt nothing, she thought then. When, two years ago,

she had failed to get the scholarship that would take her to the magical universities of the West, Sophie had spent a few days looking out at the street (the eternal street, the Killer Queen street). The question Sophie had asked herself repeatedly, the assessment she had tried to make was – What did she really know? Given that life had not prepared her to fly away and become the scholar her father dreamt of (some superior version of himself), was there anything else she was equipped for?

Sophie had clenched her teeth and tried to think. Bits and pieces of her education had flashed through her mind, surprising her with their futility. The names of parts of a flower, how to determine the time difference between various cities from their longitude, the dates of wars and the composition of a cell, lines of poetry and novels about English lives, how ox-bow lakes are formed, the behaviour of ocean currents, the meaning of parallelogram, what happens when sulphuric acid is heated, the names of the emperor's sons and their sons, the reason why it rains in the afternoon. What did she really know? She could quote long speeches from Hamlet-Shamlet because her father had fallen in love with the play at some point in her childhood and never outgrown it. She could cook, though not elegantly or with any sense of tradition. Everything she cooked became a nameless concoction that was sometimes edible and sometimes not. She was a decent shot at volleyball. The news on television was as meaningless to her as it might have been to Madame Bovary. Going over the paltry results of her self-examination, Sophie realized she, in fact, knew nothing and was, therefore, condemned to always view the world through the same fog that was at that very moment clouding her vision. Then, of course, she had called upon the trinity (Emma, Vivekananda, Swami) to see if they could in some way redeem this sad conclusion.

And now a memory within a memory came back to her. As she'd stood there cross-questioning herself, she'd suddenly remembered the time she was eighteen and it was the start of the winter holidays. Feeling like she would have a nervous breakdown if she heard a minute more of the snarled metal that exploded from her sister's stereo from morning to night, she'd walked all the way to the city library without really planning to, and found it closed. As she'd flopped down on the steps, unwilling to go back home, a man had climbed up past her – one slow step at a time. Sophie noticed that he limped. He returned when he found the door locked.

'It's closed on Mondays. I always forget,' he'd said and Sophie jumped. Strangers never addressed her; she never addressed strangers.

'You're waiting for someone?'

Sophie nodded dumbly.

'Mind if I sit here?'

Dumb nod again.

He'd shown her his book on planes and another of photographs of everyday things – a mug of beer, a parked car – rendered poetic. She had no books to show him in return; she hadn't visited the library since she was a child.

He didn't ask for her name but told her a little about the aeroplane book – an illustrated history of the aircraft used in the Second World War.

'Here's a Spitfire,' he'd said, opening a random page, his voice full of pride, as if he was in some way responsible for its existence. 'Here's a Dakota.'

When Sophie returned the following day he was there again. He limped up to her as she was craning her head to look at the top row of a shelf of novels in the Stack Room.

'Shall I pull down something for you?' he asked and she was too embarrassed to refuse, randomly saying, 'Madame Bovary'. That was how she came to read the novel and that was how, when he stretched up and the leg of his trousers rose a little, Sophie saw the glint of metal where his ankle should have been.

'How long will you take to read it?' he asked her as they were getting their books issued.

'Maybe a week,' she said.

Exactly a week later they were both there.

They'd met a total of five times. They'd slowly climb up to the Reading Room on the upper floor. He'd point out to her articles in *Time* and *National Geographic* about genetic engineering and the history of the Vikings and underwater explorations. She'd describe to him, in a low voice, while people rustled the pages of encyclopaedias and newspapers around them, the doings of Madame Bovary. He'd ask for motives when she told him what a certain character had said or done. But she hadn't known about motives. Motives had always been mysterious to her.

Then he vanished.

Sophie returned to the library every week for the remainder of the winter, walking through the Stack Room, then sitting in the Reading Room, looking up every time someone came in.

She remembered that first awareness of loss – how numbing, how world-altering. She'd cry at night till she felt feverish, all the while suppressing even the smallest sniff in case her sister heard. It all looked so different now. He probably wasn't that old – maybe about as old as she was now. He'd just happened to notice someone presumably keen about books and got talking. He hadn't been in the least bit interested in her and disappeared when he sensed Sophie was growing attached to him. Maybe she'd shown an eagerness about something that contrasted too sharply with her former shyness. Or maybe she was completely wrong and it was her younger self she ought to trust. Maybe he had loved her more than she could imagine and hoped they would spend the rest of their lives meeting in the stone-cold Stack Room or upstairs where the afternoon light slanted in gracefully through the windows, but had then been run down by a bus.

It was answers like these Sophie was after – the truth about people's emotions, the logic of people's motives. And that's how her long night ended – with her ironing all over again a pile of already ironed clothes, and realizing she'd been on the same quest when she was eighteen, when she was twelve, when she was eight and started to understand that adults never notice anything. Despite Swami, despite Ringo Saar mocking at her from his prison cell, she was going to give herself one last chance.

We Want the World

As soon as the sun was up and the lane had awoken into everyday life, Sophie went across and rang the Bhatts' doorbell. Mrs Bhatt opened the door. Mr Bhatt and Mani were out; the former had joined the laughing club at Chinnappa's insistence. He would now be out two mornings a week and perhaps develop into a more affable man, although Mani was likely to return in a foul temper, scratching and tearing at his grandfather, physically trying to break out of the lifestyle that had been imposed on him. He seemed to have been born with an inherent awareness of his grandfather's tediousness. Though he did reluctantly give in to select activities like bhajan-singing (mainly because he was allowed to clash the manjira all out of tune), most of his energy was spent resisting his grandparents. Left to his own devices, Mani would probably build up a full-fledged alternative lifestyle out of chewing garden plants, kissing stray dogs, wandering in and out of cricket games and raiding fridges.

Mrs Bhatt invited Sophie in as soon as she noticed the look on her face. Sophie sat on their battered sofa and told Mrs Bhatt everything. There was comfort in describing her night to someone whose world moved along a different orbit, someone who would never party till dawn, never have a friend turn murderer, never long to rewrite her life-story. There were moments of awkwardness, of course. Only yesterday Sophie had desecrated the choultry and been shouted at. And since Ringo had been the devil pursuing them, it would not have been out of place for Mrs Bhatt to express relief at this turn of events. Instead, she went into the kitchen and came back with a plate of hot idlis arranged around a dab of coconut chutney and handed it wordlessly to Sophie.

Then she said, 'You must meet Baba Sampige some day.'

She started describing the Baba's genius. The first time she saw him he was addressing a huge gathering in a dusty field. He was a small white butterfly in the far distance that had come to rest for a while at the edge of this ocean of people, yet his voice boomed like God's through the loudspeakers. Mrs Bhatt had lost her younger sister; it had been two months but she still cried every day into her cooking. Then she heard Baba Sampige narrate the story of Vishnu and the sage Narada, and all the years became as light as moments. The story went thus: once sage Narada asked Vishnu to teach him about the unreality of the world and Vishnu said – first go and fill this pitcher for me from that well. As Narada was drawing water, he noticed a beautiful girl by the well and fell in love with her. He followed her to her house where her parents welcomed him and after some time, with their permission, he married the girl. They were happy together and over the years they had three children. One rainy day Narada and his family had to travel to a nearby village and to do so they needed to cross a swollen river. When they were mid-stream their boat capsized; Narada tried very hard to save his wife and children but couldn't. He managed only to drag himself to the safety of the other bank. As he lay there, he heard a voice calling him – Narada, Narada, where is my pitcher of water? I've been waiting for it for nearly two hours!

'You understand,' asked Mrs Bhatt, giving Sophie a ghost of a smile.

Sophie nodded. The years did not become light as moments, she would never be a Baba Sampige fan, Mrs Bhatt didn't know that her God had once joked and cheated his way through life, and Ringo had still killed Rukshana. Yet something lifted fractionally in her. The floors had just been washed; outside the birds were singing and the idlis were perfect.

'He will be happy,' said Mrs Bhatt sighing and Sophie knew she meant Mr Bhatt. His enemy was now out of the way and Sophie could, unproblematically, remain his tenant. She and Mrs Bhatt nodded at each other in mutual irony, as Sophie reluctantly made to go.

An hour later in Anu's place, Vishnu's lesson to Narada about the unreality of the world was clashing in Sophie's head with one of her father's old lines – murder, though it have no tongue, will speak; murder, though it have no tongue, will speak. The apartment was full of people, and some of the boys, sitting stiffly in their seats, may or may not have been Rukshana's boyfriends-in-passing. Sophie caught a glimpse of Rukshana's parents in one of the bedrooms, stiff like the boys, their faces crumpled and dark from grief and exhaustion. They've forgiven Ringo, Anu whispered to her. They were highly religious and considered it God's will. Sophie had seen it in their faces too – not anger but resignation. Everyone seemed drained of volition, constantly drifting to and returning from the room where Rukshana lay swathed in a blinding white sheet on a durrie on the floor. There were prayers led by a maulvi and Sophie sat by the entrance to the room and watched, choking on the smell of incense and death. Swami was in the crowd on the far side, trying to catch her eye, and she kept her face averted. Why doesn't he see this is an example of the rot, Sophie thought with a sudden anger. The local TV channel that morning had been full of what it described as a 'call centre murder'.

And how stupid Sophie had been to imagine she could avoid stepping into the path of other people's sorrow – it was everywhere now, that sorrow. Anand and Anandi were there, their faces wooden. Mama Mia had been crying (the dripping tap kind of tears, the sniffling kind, the anguished sobbing kind, the sudden water in the eyes kind) all morning. Anu looked inconsolable and Shiva had fever. I cannot leave them, thought Sophie. Yet she so badly wanted to get onto that flight and go home, she was afraid it showed on her face.

The moment came to take Rukshana away and all the grief

in the apartment ballooned into something hot and powerful and ready to burst. It was her parents everyone was watching but they managed to restrain themselves and let Rukshana go as if her going was in the tragic but natural order of things. Sophie was amazed at their dignity. As Swami emerged from the room holding on to one end of the shroud-wrapped body, he slowed down and whispered to her, 'Go. You need to go.'

Sophie watched the men file out, then went to sit with Shiva, Anand and Anandi. Shiva was, with red eyes and weakened voice, running down Baba Sampige ('Who's this dude who's suddenly learnt how not to trip over a robe and turned messiah? Who's this freak, you know, at whose feet people fall in outlandish places such as Chile and Iceland and Cambodia? Who's this guy with a limited vocabulary – lovepeacetruth – who's raking in millions?'). Anu half-heartedly tried to get him to shut up, but Anand and Anandi seemed, despite Shiva, to be leaning towards the idea of visiting the Baba's ashram. Anu had mentioned him the previous night; and this morning their son's playschool teacher had insisted they go and see him. Anandi said that what he actually said to them didn't matter – just being in a place where suffering was understood, where there were people each harbouring some small or great tragedy of their own, might mean something. Is that why they are here this morning? wondered Sophie.

Shiva tried to talk them out of it; he promised them only disappointment. Anand interrupted Shiva and started describing Superman in a whisper. He didn't talk about his dying, he just talked about him – the chocolate cornflakes he loved, his favourite shows on Cartoon Network, his reactions to being inside a plane for the first time when they'd gone to London for a holiday, the initial look of disbelief on his face when his parents got back home every night, his cynicism with regard to all the spooky stories his father made up to satisfy his hunger for spookiness. Anand went on talking about his son as if he intended to put everything into words – every remark, every habit, every attribute.

Sophie caught Shiva's eye; he had finally fallen silent. There are more things on heaven and earth, Shiva, she thought. She looked surreptitiously at her watch. It was almost too late to catch the flight now.

Anu noticed and said, 'Go.'

'I could stay.'

'We're all here together and, anyway, you're back after a week. Go!'

So Sophie gave Anu the keys to her house, pulled out the rucksack she had kept out of view and ran out of the house.

Sophie was on her way to the airport in a rickshaw, wearing sunglasses and frayed jeans, the cool breeze blowing into the by-lanes of her heart, clearing its passages, making space for departure, making space for arrival. The winter light had a mellowness that cut through the pollution and the needlessly honking cars. All the trees seemed to have lost their flowers but suddenly there would appear a leafless tabebuia with its effusion of lavender blossoms, the burst of colour bringing streets to life. Over all the hoardings lay a fine dust from two rainless months, and on the corners of pavements little piles of golden leaves mysteriously left behind by sweepers danced in the breeze. This was Sophie's favourite season – this gentle sunlit, blue sky time whose memory she carried over from Shillong. She looked out at everyone and everything with a terrific sense of pity – the people asleep, their heads lolling, inside overnight coaches powdered with the soot of other towns; the grocers unloading sacks full of fresh vegetables from the backs of tempo-trucks; the boys, with flannel dusters and lifestyle magazines, funny plastic masks with bulbous noses and Gandhi-style glasses, dodging the rickshaws and cars to get to the people inside them. She felt sorry for them only because they existed so transiently on such a transiently beautiful morning.

She urged the driver to go faster and just then they shuddered to a halt at a red light; the driver tried to manoeuvre his rickshaw into the tiny bit of space between a bus and a shiny red car. The car-driver leaned on his horn, an unambiguous sound that meant – What the fuck do you think you're doing? Then the light turned green and the rickshaw started up with a growl. Her driver was going to overtake the red car. They caught up with it soon and he honked brazenly – a sound that meant, move over, you jerk. But there was no way that the big car was going to move over. The car-driver looked out contemptuously – a glance that meant – you're nothing, I see nothing when I see you. But in that split second his attention had been diverted and the rickshaw swerved to the right and zipped ahead. Now the red car was angry. Now its driver could certainly see something when he saw the black and yellow rickshaw ahead of him, swaying like a happy bee. He blasted his horn – a sound that meant – pull up, I need to fix you. And the rickshaw-driver's pulling up and braking abruptly meant – we'll see who fixes whom.

But as soon as they were out of their vehicles, as soon as the two fat men from the car pounced on the small-built, bony rickshaw-driver, the rules of the game changed. This was no longer about the brazen upstaging that can seem impersonal when it happens from behind the wheel. This was about two big guys repeatedly hitting one small one and the small one so disadvantaged, so weak, so afraid, that he wasn't even going to protest.

'Behenchod, shaan dikha raha tha?' said Daddy as he hit.

'Saala, kya kar raha tha tu? Tu kar kya raha tha?' said his son as he kicked.

Sophie jumped out.

'How dare you beat a defenceless man?' she screamed.

No one noticed her at first – a small, boy-like girl trying to shout louder than the men and the unconcerned traffic whizzing past.

She went up to big daddy and said: 'How dare you beat a defenceless man?'

He stopped momentarily to stare at her.

'He's misbehaving on roads,' he said and punched him again.

A wife and a daughter had emerged from the car and stood watching from a safe distance. A neat quadrangle of a family – father, mother, son, daughter. They'll beat up anyone who challenges the unwritten law that fat men in fat red cars have the right of way and can never be overtaken by small men in battered rickshaws.

'How dare you beat a defenceless man?' asked Sophie. She was paralysed by that one sentence; she just couldn't think of anything else to say.

'We'll report him to the police,' said the son.

Mama and daughter kept their eyes averted. A small crowd

consisting of the only kind of pedestrians often to be found in the city – construction labourers, daily wage earners, stick-thin men, women and children who walked in groups from one site to another with their possessions balanced in bundles over their heads and the handles of their steel lunch boxes slung over their wrists – had now gathered around.

'I'll report *you* to the police,' said Sophie glaring at him, and then, suddenly conscious that she was glaring, glared even harder. 'For beating a defenceless man.'

'These people are just not worth it,' said Daddy getting back into the car and shutting the door with a decisive bang.

His son was dusting his hands, filmi-style. Pappu, thought, Sophie. That just had to be his name.

Miraculously, two policemen appeared. Their bike was painted like cheetah skin, yellow and brown. They parked it calmly, as if they had an appointment with just this group of people at exactly this time. Daddy got out of his car and shut the door with a second decisive bang.

'What's up?' asked the first of the policemen in Kannada. He wore gold-rimmed goggles and his hair was slicked down, every strand in place despite the fact he'd been riding the bike. The second one held a truncheon he slapped energetically into the palm of his left hand. He called out to the onlookers to scoot.

A tiny shiver of panic ran through Sophie when she noticed the leisurely demeanour of the pair. This was going to take time. She ought to take another rickshaw. She said nothing. Let Daddy and his kin explain. She edged towards the road and scanned the oncoming traffic.

Daddy was bristling with self-righteousness. 'Good thing you saw us and stopped, sir. This man was threatening us ...' he started in Hindi, and then, to impress Sophie perhaps, switched to English. 'He was abusing us and threatening us. Pehle toh, he's trying to overtake from the blind side, and when we stop to ask – why are you doing this, he starts shouting at us in his own language, calling us names. You only tell us what should one do? My son is driving in peace and all of a sudden people come out of from nowhere and start harassing us and waste our time and make a scene ...'

The lying bastard, thought Sophie, lifting her rucksack onto her back and digging into her pockets for the fare.

The first policeman cut Daddy short and began barking at the rickshaw-driver who still seemed unconcerned about defending himself. He muttered softly beneath his breath while the second policeman continued to smack his truncheon into his palm and then flourish it in the air so that the daily-wage labourers with their air of ancient stoicism slowly started moving away. Sophie sneaked a look at the women who continued to stand there, watching and waiting, though the older woman's expression seemed ready to crumble into something nasty – whether that would be manic rage or just regular exasperation was hard to tell.

All the rickshaws that streamed past were taken.

The son had taken up the reins of the lies that Daddy had invented.

'He should pay us a fine. He would have scratched our car if we hadn't braked in time.'

'Whyfore he should pay fine?' asked policeman number one. He spoke his first English sentence with a panache that Sophie found impressive.

He caught sight of her and called her over. 'Swalpa illi banni, madam.'

'I don't speak Kannada,' said Sophie on cue.

The cop shook his head in mock despair. 'Staying in Karnataka and not speaking Kannada? You should learn, no.' He was jovial – the whole episode seemed to strike him as buffoonery, enriched by the fact that two of the three parties didn't speak Kannada. It contributed to their idiocy.

'Madam, you are sitting in this rickshaw-aah? You can tell me the truth. I will naat listen to all these people. You are ...' here he broke off to confer with the truncheon-wielder about the right word to use, '... anh, you are the *witness*. Helli madam.'

Sophie felt herself stopping to think for a moment. She was the witness. She had sole access to the truth. The truth seemed to shrivel in the face of this responsibility. But she had to speak.

'These people are the cause of all the trouble. First, they started beating up this man. They just got out of their car and started hitting him, both of them, without asking any questions. And now they're lying,' she said. She felt utterly secure standing in the policeman's shadow, even though she distinctly saw Pappu mouth the word 'bitch'. 'They're telling lies,' she added, in case the policeman was not perfect with his tenses and missed her point.

'So they are beating him and he is innocent. Nothing he has done?' asked the cop.

'He was driving roughly and trying to overtake. But everyone does that. All these people with big cars, they are the ones who behave as if they own the road and it's like if anyone smaller goes past them they feel insulted.'

'You must all come to the pulis station. I cannot understand anything.'

'Sir, I have a flight to catch,' wailed Sophie. 'I'm running late, I have to go.'

'Why are you poking your nose in other people's business if you have a flight to catch? Just go!' said Pappu.

The cop seemed to notice him for the first time and fixed his goggled eyes on him.

'Why are you talking to that chit of a girl, sir? You ask my son, he was driving the car ...' said Daddy.

'License,' said cop in reply.

Pappu dashed up to the car and began rifling through the glove compartment.

'Kahan hai meri license?' he asked the silent women but they seemed to have turned to stone in the sun.

'License,' repeated the second cop, leaning on his bike and enjoying Pappu's discomfort. He seemed to know in advance that this was the behaviour of people who had no license to produce.

Sophie went up to him and asked, 'Can I go, sir?' but he just shrugged and gestured in the direction of the first cop.

After his son searched fruitlessly for a few minutes, Daddy tried to redeem the situation.

'He's very young. He must have forgotten it at home. Tomorrow he can come to the station and show it to you. We have to go now, bahut late ho raha hai.'

The cop got onto his bike and his partner got on after him. 'Pulis station,' he thundered but before he could ride away, Daddy was beside him pulling out his wallet.

'Sir, I know it is very difficult for you to take care of all these things. Hamne bhi duniya dekhi hai. What to do? There is so much traffic these days, these kinds of things happen once in a while.' He slipped a five hundred-rupee note into the cop's hand. The latter quickly stuffed it into his shirt pocket and declared, 'This time it is okay but next time you please make sure. No license, beating up people on the road … ai,' he called out to the rickshaw-driver, and delivered a similar-sounding warning to him. The driver appeared to agree with everything he was told, probably relieved to be saved a visit to the police station.

The cops rode away, completely ignoring Sophie. She put her bag back into the rickshaw and they took off.

'Fools,' she yelled as they whizzed away. Pappu was berating Daddy, perhaps for letting on that he was the driver and bringing up the unfortunate issue of the license.

'Sorry,' said Sophie to the driver.

He didn't reply. Perhaps he was as disappointed as Sophie was to learn that the truth was dispensable, the poor shrivelled-up truth that had done its duty but not been deemed good enough. The truth needs something to defend it – something that can counteract the five hundred-rupee note and the brutality of Daddy and his ilk, thought Sophie, clutching the handrail as the rickshaw flew over potholes. What would that be? she wondered, but couldn't think of an answer.

She checked the time, groaned, called the airport and was told her flight had just left.

~

Sophie paid off the rickshaw and then stood stock-still in the middle of the pavement with her rucksack at her feet. She didn't know which way to turn. Everyone was a stranger; she couldn't remember how she had come to be on this road where the cars kept braking and then starting up jerkily as if remote-controlled by someone playing a video game badly. For a few moments, all she knew was her name and that she badly wanted a cigarette. Then she called her father and tremulously explained that the plane had left without her. Come tomorrow, her father said, without any trace of panic in his voice, while Sophie felt hers only rising, knowing he was more than three thousand kilometres away. Tomorrow felt like another continent and where was she to sleep? Her only house key was with Anu and she could not face the gang again, she could not talk about Ringo Saar or dodge Swami. Okay, okay, she told her father, then flagged down another rickshaw and went to office, where Naomi was at large on the balcony in a pista-coloured salwar-kameez, engrossed in a conversation with Maya about why men in India urinated in public.

'You can stay with me tonight,' said Maya, completely unsurprised to learn that Sophie had had to postpone her departure and that her place was taken. 'You know, I drove past this guy the other day who was talking on his cellphone, peeing and giving me the eye – all in one go,' she continued.

'That is so *funny,*' said Naomi. She always pronounced things funny instead of actually laughing at them.

Gross, gross, nothing but gross, thought Sophie. She asked Maya for a cigarette and drifted away. She switched on her computer; the murder was front page news on the website of the local TV station. Seeing Ringo's unrepentant face, staring frankly into the camera, the painful heartbeat of fear and guilt started up in Sophie again. But she felt less vulnerable here in office where no one knew him. For once, office was safe – the ridiculously diligent expressions on everyone's faces as they worked at their films made her bloody weekend seem far away. Even if it only had to do with bits of Hollywood trash, there was at least a play at seriousness here that she could for a little while take refuge in. She picked up her headphones, then put them down again. She thought of Emma Bovary who, after she discovers she is in love with the young and ardent Leon, responds by drawing the blinds tight around her world – going to church regularly and taking a sudden interest in the housework – so that behind this outward veil of dutifulness she can revel in thoughts of him. In Sophie's world the equivalent of that chastisement would be captioning all four parts of *Die Hard* without a murmur.

She stood up and peeked at Shanthi Gowda who noticed her at once and started to struggle out of her headphones in order to say something. Sophie waved the unlit cigarette at her and slunk away to the balcony to look for a light.

Naomi was discussing the saris she had bought Shanthi as wedding gifts.

'Wrong, completely wrong,' announced Maya.

'What d'you mean?' said Naomi, a look of disproportionate shock on her face.

'Far too gorgeous ... stuff she won't ever in her whole life have occasion to wear. You think she's the kind of person who wears brocade on silk on a weekly basis? I would give people clothes that suit their station, you know.'

'What *is* her station?' asked Naomi with an unusual edge in her voice.

Shanthi appeared. 'Sophie, can you help me just for a minute. I cannot understand one line that Catherine Tate is saying.'

Maya gave Naomi a look that suggested – there's your answer. Then she turned to take the lighter back from Sophie and raised her eyebrows. Sophie remembered the lesbian theory and tried to gauge if Naomi's expression revealed any hint of passion for Shanthi. She was worked up over the sari topic – it was clearly important to her that she get the wedding gift right. Shanthi was meanwhile giving Sophie her hard, expectant look even though Sophie didn't have the faintest clue who Catherine Tate was.

Maya said, 'Do you find it funny at all?'

'What?' asked Shanthi guardedly.

'You'll never understand what Catherine Tate is saying if you're going to be so uptight, Shanthi.'

'That is not part of my job description. To enjoy dirty serials from Western society.'

Maya groaned. 'Oh come on, what about the crap you watch on TV when you go home?'

'Hey Shanthi,' said Naomi, going up to her and seizing her arm. 'You were only meant to work half-day. You're on leave now. Come on, time to go.'

'Where are you off to?' asked Maya in her bossy voice.

'The old town. Shanthi knows those parts; she's going to show me the flower market and we're going to get some dried fruit and other stuff for the wedding like ... er, kumkum and henna and bangles. Actually, I'm really looking forward to that 'coz you know MG Road and all of that is fine but what I've really been wanting to see is an Indian market. And of course, Shanthi will be the best guide because before all this happened – with, you know, her mother falling ill and her father passing away and her brother going to Dubai – they would go to Chickpet every Sunday and eat mutton biriyani at Mohan's Tiffin Room, and then they would ...'

Maya exhaled a sarcastic plume of smoke into her face.

Naomi was momentarily silenced by this piece of rudeness and turned to Sophie.

'I've never been there,' Sophie mumbled.

'You've never been there?' said Naomi in surprise. 'And neither have you Maya?'

'Are you joking? I would never go and tramp about in cow-shit and have men feel me up just for the sake of saving twenty bucks on curtain fabric.'

She tried to keep her voice jokey, but Sophie noticed a sudden, mysterious glimmer of pain in her eyes.

'But Sophie will go with you; she needs to get almonds. Look how pale she is. Look how tired she looks,' said Maya.

Sophie opened her mouth, then soundlessly swallowed her protest when she understood that Maya was sending her on some kind of spying mission. She was supposed to go after Naomi and Shanthi and report on whether the two were holding hands, what they were gossiping about, what they thought of Maya. There was something new and raw in Maya's voice. And even though she was desperately tired, Sophie would have to go for Maya's sake because Maya always took her part. She rubbed her eyes and said, 'Sure' trying to think back to the last time she had slept. Rukshana had made it there, to the country of eternal sleep. She was finally free of people's voices, phones ringing, ceaseless thought, there under the cool earth, sleeping at last where it was dark and not in the unnatural daylight with an eye mask over her face. Fuck, I'm going to crack up if I think about her, thought Sophie, and then continued imagining the fresh smell of the earth down there, the small rustlings of creatures who, temporarily shocked at the upheaval, would now rearrange themselves around Rukshana, the way the white shroud would already be stained with mud, while her freshly painted nails remain, in some callous way, permanently glossy. If Sophie could somehow penetrate through the horror there was peace on the other side. A pastoral kind of peace to be found in dying and breathing earth at last, leaving behind the ugliness and fatigue of streets and car exhaust and high-rises and the endless pressure of other people's wants. But Maya was sending her back into that world and she couldn't say no.

'Run along now, Shanthi,' said Maya. 'Sophie's not working on those files. She can't really help you. Ask Priya.'

'Hey Maya, what's your problem?' asked Naomi, acknowledging for the first time that there was one. 'Why are you always so edgy when it comes to Shanthi?' Her face was flushed. Maya's right, thought Sophie. There was definitely a special vibe between these two women but what was it and what name should one give it?

Shanthi said in an unnatural, high-pitched voice, 'Let it be, Naomi. She's not worth it. She spends all her time in MG Road, Brigade Road and you talk to her about anything else, she'll say – crap. Crap, crap, crap – that is her favourite word. As if walking down Brigade Road drinking cold coffee in a styrofoam cup is not crap.'

'Shanthi, everything you're *saying* is crap. Look, I don't want to start an argument. Just go back to your desk; we'll talk about this later,' said Maya.

'You can't order her around, Maya. She has the right to say what she thinks,' said Naomi in a steely voice.

Maya threw her hands in the air. 'Naomi, I'm the one who has to deal with them. Shanthi's forgetting her place. You heard the tone she just used with me. I can't have other staff getting used to that kind of tone. I really appreciate how friendly you are with everyone but you're only here for another week. If I were you I wouldn't mess around with the already established relations between people, you know. I would focus on my work and leave people alone.'

Naomi, her face now a blaze of red, said, 'Maya, this is going too far.' And then, as if by common consent, both she and Shanthi walked out.

Maya and Sophie looked at each other in mutual confirmation.

'Go forth into the boondocks and bring me some juice, my lovely,' said Maya putting her arm around Sophie. They finished their cigarettes, inhaling along with them the fumes of the 3 o'clock traffic down below – the smoky, burnt-out smell of the city. Maya talked about how everyone, because they couldn't get the accents, was screwing the British comedies to hell.

After she had booked a new ticket for the following morning, Sophie, Shanthi and Naomi took a rickshaw to the old town. Sophie, in her mind distanced from the city and already, in a different version of events, on that plane home, looked at the streets with new eyes – the people eating their cheap meals in the fast-food Darshinis, the IT executives with their glossy identity cards slung around their necks, chattering animatedly as they waited to cross the road, the woman who sat at the edge of a pavement in a surprisingly clean sari but feet that looked like great fungal life-forms, the stench of sewage that contrasted with the towering apartments on whose distant balconies Sophie could see clothes flapping in the wind, a tiny shop selling gutka and cigarettes and tabloids, the vast store window in which stood a row of mannequins wearing silk saris in a dozen different shades of yellow, the billboard that advertized Sunday brunches with an hour-long massage thrown in. Sophie felt she could go on being driven through the streets all day and never arrive anywhere – only find more shops, more apartments, more streets, more houses. No hill or sea or river or valley to put a natural stop to this mad proliferation.

There were just too many people – it was a kind of calamity, the sheer number of them. Every year more arrived with the kind of idiotic hope in their hearts Sophie had first felt when she saw her brightly lit office cubicle. Boys from smaller towns in the state coming to study in engineering and medical colleges; girls from the Northeast coming to work as waitresses or run tiny beauty parlours; men and women from one or another big city moving here because Bangalore seemed to urgently need designer boutiques and five-star hotels and architectural firms and advertising companies; couples from the North relocating for software jobs; whole clans moving from the neighbouring states to work on construction sites and live in their flimsy plastic tent homes; wave after wave of people arriving and at once establishing their own passage through the city. And the city, as if it were a living thing with a generous heart, taking them all in uncomplainingly.

Soon after the three got off and made their way into the

dense alleys packed with shops, they began to be followed by a whistling teenager on a bicycle whom they were able to shake off now and then only to find him shooting out from another corner and cutting into their path again. To Sophie his aim seemed to be to demonstrate how well he knew this confusing network of streets, but Naomi, on whom his interest was focused, and whose body he kept brushing with his hand every time he zipped by, started to grow pink and flustered, while Shanthi's look grew more and more thunderous.

'Why is he making these terrible sounds?' whispered Naomi as the boy, sucking, whistling and mewing tore into them, and they parted hastily to give way.

These alleys were new to Sophie. In some, lorries stood parked in long rows, piled high with bulging sacks containing dried fruits and coffee and spices, in between which rats scurried and around which stood clusters of men shouting instructions to coolies. Other alleys opened out to shop after shop selling hardware and computers and electronic goods, while strung across them and obliterating the sky were hundreds of painted banners advertising these things. Overlaid on the banners and crisscrossing madly between either sides of the lanes was such an astonishing jumble of electrical cables that it seemed as if someone had taken a black pen and drawn frenzied loops across the whole scene. Sophie stopped to gape, but Naomi was rushing on to evade the obscene cyclist, who this time, as he whizzed past, yelled, 'Darling!'

Without meaning to, Sophie burst out laughing. Soon she was hysterical and had to lean on a wall while Shanthi and Naomi looked on in concern. She looked back at their bemused faces and the world seemed to tilt behind them. 'I'm falling,' she thought and even that was funny. Stop, she told herself then. Stop, stop, stop. She could not crumble here and have to explain all the bloodiness to these two nice, ordinary, gentle girls. *Why am I laughing*? She straightened up and said, 'So much work for one word. He'd probably kill for a whole conversation.'

Naomi said, 'No, he's seriously frightening me. I think we should go to the police. I mean what if he follows me home, what if he …'

'I will cure him of this English disease,' said Shanthi. When they came upon him next he was face-to-face with them and as they parted to avoid colliding with him, Shanthi shot out an arm and held fast to the handle-bars. He was forced to brake suddenly and tumbled off the bicycle though this did not prevent him from delivering his punch line to Naomi, which was 'Hey sexy, do you want to have sex with me?'

Sophie cracked up again, her face turned away from them so that they shouldn't feel she was mocking them – mocking Shanthi's embarrassment that something like this should happen on her turf or Naomi's fear that a little boy on a bicycle would rape her. She laughed as if laughter were air and she hadn't breathed for days, while Shanthi, still holding on to the bicycle, delivered a long and angry lecture in Kannada. Little by little the boy's shoulders sagged, his face dropped and he lowered his eyes. He mumbled something with the word 'sorry' in it, climbed onto his bicycle, and rode away, pedalling slowly.

'He will not trouble you again,' said Shanthi, her teeth clenched. 'He thought even I was an English type.'

Having thus established that this was her territory and that the 'English types' needed her guidance and protection, Shanthi undertook to show them the flower market, which was spread out in the well of a cavernous building. They leaned over a railing and surveyed the scene below them. The place was suffused with blazes of contrasting colour – everywhere one looked were blossoms stringed and coiled into huge mounds or baskets heaped with petals or buckets packed with flowers still on their stems. Shanthi proudly pointed out pink and purple asters, delicate orange kanakambara, saffron marigolds, yellow chrysanthemums, pearl-like jasmine pods, rich purple rudrakshi chendu, gladioli and gerberas on tall stems, roses shading from peach to burgundy.

Naomi let out cries of 'Fantastic!' from behind her handycam while Shanthi drew their attention to the figures painted on the large pillar standing like a shrine in the centre of the market – the goddess Chamundeshwari on her tiger (the local version of Durga), the local god-like actor Raj Kumar, Tipu Sultan, Shiva and Parvati, and Ram and Sita surrounded by their devotees. When they emerged into the bright afternoon and walked past the open-air vegetable market, Sophie realized it was from such a centre that they all emanated – those figures who conducted a precarious commerce in the city and seemed to totter at its edges, pushed out by the supermarkets and shopping malls – the flower-seller, the vendor of greens, the chap with the pushcart full of lemons, the scrap-dealer who carried his shop on his bicycle – they were all released like birds into the city from here.

As they continued walking in the teeming, narrow lanes, Sophie forgot her life for a while. Naomi was her cheerful, over-enthusiastic self again; she had done some reading and explained to Sophie that this was Bangalore before the British came at the end of the eighteenth century and built the cantonment on the eastside of town – this network of gullies, this once-walled city with a small fort to its south. She drew up suddenly and asked them to look down the length of a road and observe how underneath the hundreds of new shop signs and massive jumble of electricity cables one could make out the shells of old buildings, two-storied shop-houses, and sections of old city gates. But Shanthi didn't look out for crumbling walls or old-style balconies – for her the market was organized according to what could be bought where and the two girls followed her as she expertly wove her way around sugarcane merchants, iron merchants, nut merchants, coffee merchants, cloth merchants, high class perfumers, ghee stores, sugar candy works. They stopped to buy glass bangles and henna. They passed through lanes full of the clatter of looms made by hidden weavers and dark shop interiors in which spools of golden zari gleamed and vats held skeins of cotton soaking in dyes. They turned corners and came upon doorways to tiny temple courtyards with tranquil old women sitting on stoops wearing magnifying-glass spectacles, and younger women inside watering tulsi plants.

They stopped at the ancient Sri Prasanna Coffee Club – its tiny window shutters painted red and its floor a chessboard. Sophie blew on her coffee and imagined that the owner had been preserved in this time capsule too. He'd been sitting there at the cash counter since the twenties, frowning at his patrons, with a sign above his head that said 'Do Not Wash Your Hands in Your Plate'.

Naomi sighed and said, 'I've got to come back here.' Sophie thought she meant the coffee club, but she actually meant India.

She realized then that this was probably the last time she'd see either of these women.

'So ... are you looking forward to this new job?' Sophie asked Shanthi awkwardly.

'Yes, yes,' said Shanthi impatiently. 'Money is better, no.'

She and Naomi began discussing Shanthi's mother. Sophie remembered the story about how a sudden glut of gold had driven the lady bonkers, but she had never heard Shanthi talk about her mother before. Shanthi described with admirable calm the many fictions that collided inside her mother's head – the enemies that, despite the medicines, had not been completely vanquished and could at any time show themselves at the window, the dead husband who was out on an eternal shopping trip but would be back as soon as he had eaten a dosa at his favourite café, the particular vegetables she couldn't stand because they made faces at her and a new tendency to walk out into the street with her sandals strapped to her head, talking animatedly to herself.

Sophie remembered resenting how Shanthi had shared her life-story with Naomi but not her. She listened avidly now as Shanthi revealed more – describing how, early in the treatment, her mother had woken up one dawn and walked two kilometres in just her blouse and petticoat, her always neatly bundled hair flying loose. She had gone looking for my father in that café he always went to, Shanthi said, and when I found her she looked more afraid of me than of the people who had gathered around and were questioning her.

Naomi went unusually quiet.

But sometimes *I* am afraid of her, Shanthi continued with a laugh, and described how her mother had once jumped upon her with a big coil of plastic rope and tried to tie her to a chair, accusing her of spying on her when she was bathing. Shanthi and her brother had hired a nurse to look after Mrs Gowda. Mrs Gowda meekly submitted to the nurse on the days she imagined her to be the dead actress Soundarya. On other days things didn't go as well.

'And then, of course, there is the gold,' said Shanthi sighing. 'In the end, everything comes back to the gold.'

'Do you think if Sunil had never gone to Dubai and never

started bringing back gold none of this would have happened?' asked Naomi.

'But look at how our lives improved after he got the Dubai job. You think we could have afforded this expensive treatment for her without his salary?'

'Yes, but without all the gold bangles he brought back she wouldn't have needed the treatment in the first place.'

Shanthi ignored this conundrum. 'Do you know what my mother did before she married my father? She used to live here in one of these gullies with her grandmother; her parents had died early. At dawn my great-grandmother would cook fifty balls of ragi mudde and two big pots of sambar and the two of them would go and stand outside the market where the lorry drivers and rickshaw-wallahs hang out and sell them breakfast. And if anyone got too friendly my mother would say, 'Remember you're eating ragi mudde. When you start eating masala dosa for breakfast then talk to me.' They would go back home with their empty pots and she'd change into her uniform and run off to school. When she married my father she became a tailor. Women tailors don't sit in the tailoring shops, certainly not shops for men's clothes, so every morning she would take clothes home from the master tailor, stitch them and bring them back the next day. The people who wore those shirts and pants never knew who stitched them. When my brother and I were born she stopped and after we started going to school she got a job as a peon in a bank. When my father died, we had to manage on her salary and she used to find everything funny – how she had to start making ragi mudde like her grandmother (because it's poor man's food, you know, Sophie), and how because of the jewellery that she always wore (which my father had given her and she never let go), the neighbours never got to know how poor we really were. Then Sunil got this job in Dubai and we told her she shouldn't work any more. That was the wrong decision. We made that one mistake. She had always worked and now her mind was empty. And suddenly she had all this gold but it had no purpose, you know. That was the horrible thing. For her money always had a purpose, but now it was just something sitting in her cupboard, growing and growing.'

It's the jewellery fetish, that's what it is, thought Sophie.

Perhaps Shiva would have something to say about this – the connection between the lust for gold and mental illness among urban Indians.

'My brother and I, we don't want to earn so much money that we forget money has a purpose. But also, we don't want to stand outside the market and sell food every morning, you know,' Shanthi was saying. 'See, people like Maya will never understand because they want everything to be fixed in one place. You are one type of person or another type of person and you should not try to act as if you belong where you don't belong.'

And Sophie wondered if she meant her as well, for wasn't she the cold-coffee-in-a-styrofoam-cup-drinking type whom Shanthi had dismissed a few hours ago? She wasn't sure she wanted to know exactly what Shanthi thought of her and when their eyes met, Sophie's were the first to turn away.

Wasn't it obvious to Naomi, though, she wondered, as Naomi asked her again – 'Now what exactly is Maya's problem? We got on *wonderfully* the first week, but she's become so strange.' Sophie said it was the stress to do with the British serials – apart from the problem with the accents, some found the whole thing too disgusting (one girl had even refused to work on an episode of *Little Britain* where a teenage boy feels up his friend's grandmother).

'They need training!' exclaimed Naomi. 'There's nothing here that can't be solved with a two-hour lecture on British humour.'

Shanthi said, 'No, no, it is not about work. She thinks because of my background I shouldn't be so friendly with you.' Shanthi started to explain but Naomi seemed to not quite understand the way these ancient class hatreds worked. She believed Star Titles was some kind of a benevolence in the shape of an office, that it could just appear overnight and wipe out all the old differences. She thought Star Title's high staff incentives meant that the most earnest workers, such as Shanthi, would move up and the indifferent ones, like Sophie, fall by the wayside.

Sophie remembered her own mission and said, 'I think Maya has a point though. When she says that favouring some members of the staff could lead to problems …' She trailed off at the look of severity on Naomi's face.

'What does Maya fear? Shanthi and I are friends – how

does that affect my relations with anyone else? And anyway, I'm leaving soon.'

'She just feels that ...' Sophie wasn't quite sure what to say – she just feels that the two of you are in love? She grew flustered and Naomi noticed at once and started cross-questioning her. Sophie hadn't seemed particularly keen to come out with them; was it Maya's orders? Had she sent her to check on them? Did she think they were up to something fishy? Did she think Naomi had instigated Shanthi Gowda to leave the company? Did she fear that Naomi was going to spirit Shanthi to the US and get her a better job than Maya could dream of?

'It's nothing,' said Sophie foolishly and then blushed. It was too late because Naomi saw everything – the heat rising to Sophie's cheeks, her fingers nervously fingering the strap of her bag, her sudden looking away. There was a long moment of silence and when Sophie finally, with a show of defiance, returned Naomi's look, she knew Naomi had guessed and in that same instant she also realized Maya's theory was pure rubbish.

It was only now (as Naomi ordered more coffee, and Shanthi, not understanding the sudden awkwardness that had crept in, tried to resume the conversation) that Sophie understood. Maya was jealous, that was all. Perhaps she was starting to feel diminished by Naomi's American verve, her enthusiasm, her ability to in three short weeks inspire the client coordinators and make them talk with a slight American lilt in their voices and walk with a bounce in their gaits. Naomi inspired confidence. Maya just got people to obey her.

Naomi, her eyes still fixed on Sophie said, 'Shanthi, I've been trying to get you to change your mind about leaving the company but now I think it's the best possible thing for you. Move up. Be ambitious. You appreciate money in a way that none of us can because you've seen it destroy your mother but you haven't given up. Do you know what you're going to do? You're going to try and perfect that dream that swallowed your mother and you're going to make it.'

Sophie stood up, unnerved by that stare, and as she was leaving the café she heard Naomi say in a loud clear voice, 'And as for Maya, she's going to regret what she started.'

~

Sophie stood on the balcony of Maya's eleventh floor apartment, surveying the beige and white high-rises of Diamond Bay, the small heads bobbing on the sunset-coloured swimming pool, the red-tiled roof of the spa and fitness centre, the velvety green of the empty golf course, the cars drawing up outside the community centre, whose pleasures, Sophie knew from her previous visits here, included three restaurants, a coffee shop, an ice-cream parlour, a supermarket and a three-screen multiplex. Whenever she stood there surveying Maya's world, Sophie tried to pick out a jarring note, but there was none – the fountains radiated water, elderly ladies in silk saris were dropped off at the spa in soundless golf carts, lush palm trees were planted symmetrically along the walkways. The only discordance was Diamond Bay itself – for surrounding its high walls topped with concertina wire, and visible from this height, were the half-finished apartment blocks, traffic-filled flyovers and dusty hoardings of the perpetually in-transit city. Sophie was hypnotized by the gleaming freakishness of Diamond Bay.

'Want to see pictures?' asked Maya, flinging a pile of photo-albums onto the couch. On the way, Sophie had tried to tell Maya about the trip to the market and get her to understand that Naomi had sniffed out something, but Maya absolutely refused to hear. She behaved as if the scene in office had never happened. Sophie didn't know what to make of it.

Maya pulled her into the living room, planted herself next to her and opened one of the albums.

'We'll start at the beginning. With Mummy-Daddy and Maya-Rohit. And the charming life they lived. Here they are, smiling real – not fake for-the-camera-say-cheese – smiles. They are delighted because little Maya has just spoken her first complete sentence. Or because Rohit has just learnt to tie his shoelaces. Or because Daddy loves Mummy and Mummy loves Daddy.'

Sophie knew a little about Maya's family. Her father was a brigadier in the army. He would wake up his children at six every morning and run fifty laps with them around the lawn of every house they'd lived in. They lived in seven different cities till they moved to Bangalore where Maya stayed on for college and then for work. All their houses came with large lawns as well as orderlies who polished her father's shoes and went grocery shopping for her mother. But the orderlies didn't mow the lawns or do the dishes or drive the family around. Those were the functions of the maali, the maid and the driver, respectively. Maya always spoke about her family in a tone of amused indifference. The army cut her father off from the world, she said. It made him believe that running fifty laps around the lawn every morning prepared you for life. She said less about her mother but in these pictures Sophie saw the pretty army wife who stays at home and keeps an elaborate domestic machinery running.

Maya was flipping the pages of the albums so quickly, Sophie barely had time to see – those pictures of birthday parties and picnics and school plays and marriage anniversaries that had no parallel in her own life (her short and undocumented childhood), but which were nevertheless starting to provoke an anguished nostalgia in her.

'My parents never took photographs, so I don't even know what I looked like as a kid. My mother noticed this gap in our history one day when my sister was about five years old, so she got the husband of one of her colleagues to come over and take pictures of the whole family. We all went out and stood in the garden. My dad looks grumpy, my sister is crying from her arms being held tight so she doesn't run off and I look just plain ugly, you know the way one looks at thirteen – stricken. My mother is the only one who looks charming – like a lily in the mud.'

'No photographs? That's not normal, Sophie.'

'I once asked my mother how I looked as a toddler. And she just couldn't tell me. It's not like she'd forgotten – she just didn't know how to put the image into words.'

'I'm going to take pictures of you right now,' said Maya and disappeared into the bedroom.

Sophie took up the album she'd left lying open. Mummy-Daddy, Maya-Rohit. A neat, four-cornered family like the one she'd encountered in the red car that morning. In one picture, a five- or six-year-old Maya in a flouncy white birthday dress was held aloft by her father, who smiled expansively into the camera. Maya on the other hand considered him solemnly, the expression on her profile detached, almost cold. She could be thinking – I'm too old for this nonsense or, more to the point – how did I get stuck with this chap?

'What were you thinking when this picture was taken?' she asked when Maya returned.

'I don't have a clue. I'm probably just dying to eat the cake.'

'You mean you don't actually remember? I thought one always remembers what one is thinking at the moment of being photographed. That way a photograph is a record of both an image and a thought.'

'Well, you thought wrong. Like right now, for instance,' said Maya holding up her digital camera. 'And now … and now. See, I already have three pictures of you and you barely had time to think.'

'Wrong. I was thinking about the man who took the first pictures of us. He committed suicide later. Hung himself from a tree.'

'Dear Sophie, what a morbid life you've led.'

'Really? I thought it's in the very nature of family histories to be full of uncomfortable stuff no one wants to talk about.'

'Stop right there.'

Sophie froze self-consciously, then said, 'You're making me dizzy jumping around like that. Maya, we need to talk about Naomi. It's not like you thought …'

'This is the last one … Okay, now we're done.'

'Lemme see.'

'Wait, not yet. You have to do something to deserve it first.'

'Like what?'

'Umm, don't know. We'll have to think of something. Here, take a picture of me first,' said Maya throwing the camera at her. Sophie grabbed it and took a few shots of Maya making outrageous faces.

'Is there any booze in the house?' Sophie asked then.

'There's some in the cupboard. Are you hungry?'

'Later,' yelled Sophie, already in the kitchen pouring out whiskey.

She handed Maya a glass. They could hear the faraway clamour of small children riding tricycles on the concourse and the warning shouts of their teenage nannies. The room was filling with evening shadows, but neither of them got up to switch on the lights.

'I like this,' said Maya softly. 'That you came here and we can just chill out like this.'

'Absolutely,' said Sophie, examining her bare toes, suddenly embarrassed. 'So this thing about Naomi ...'

'Oh hang Naomi,' said Maya. She took a large gulp of her drink. 'Let's talk about you and Swami?'

'What about us ... we're fine.'

'Why do you clamp up whenever I ask you about him?' asked Maya.

Sophie looked at her in surprise.

'It's strange how you never really talk about him, the way normal girls yap in a normal way about their boyfriends.'

'Maybe I'm shy.'

'Or maybe it's not going so well?' said Maya.

Sophie tried to work through the logic of this. It was wrong to pretend everything was hunky-dory with Swami, yet she didn't see why this should be anyone's business but hers. It struck her again that she was devastatingly tired. The last thirty-six hours, which had started with her praying to an absent God, seemed to stretch, when she tried to recollect them, over weeks. She couldn't understand why she and Maya were having this perfectly pointless conversation.

'Maya, don't you sometimes feel we're all damned?' Sophie asked. 'I'm starting to believe I took a wrong turn somewhere. I thought moving here would make it all different but here I meet people equally lost.'

'You look wasted,' declared Maya. Then she looked at her more closely and asked, 'Have you been crying?'

Sophie hadn't meant to but she blurted out: 'A guy I know murdered his girlfriend last night and he's in jail right now.'

Maya's eyes widened. 'Not the thing that was in the news?'

Sophie nodded wordlessly.

'Wow,' whispered Maya.

'There's nothing obvious about it, believe me. Even though he'd been getting weirder and weirder and I couldn't really talk to him any more. We quarrelled just yesterday afternoon. But it still doesn't square up the way people assume when they see something like that in the news. You can put it out of your mind because you think – of course, that person must have been inclined that way all along. Only now I understand that it's not like that at all. He's not a murderer.'

'Why didn't you call me? Where have you been all weekend?'

'It's over now. I'm on my way home. But everything's changed. All the things that seemed so important before. So when you ask me about Swami, I think: how does it really matter? We're all trying to reach some kind of understanding with ourselves. That's what's important – being okay with ourselves. Liking the story of our lives. *Finding* the story of our lives to begin with.'

They sat quietly for a while and the room seemed to darken by the minute.

'And what happens if you can't? If the wrong turn is too far back and by now you've lost the plot?' asked Maya.

'I don't know ...' said Sophie. 'Make peace, I guess. Ringo couldn't make peace. He wanted to follow his anger all the way down. But they don't see it. Swami doesn't see it. He thinks it was just some kind of a blip. A very big and painful blip, but a blip all the same. He thinks he can just go back to talking about his bloody plans. He's just ...' Sophie nodded helplessly.

Mays said: 'Some people need to keep up with the pretence. That's the only way to go on. Take these photographs.'

'These photographs?' Something in Maya's voice made Sophie get up, switch on the lights and sit on the couch facing her.

'It's all lies, you know. All those fucking happy pictures year after year.'

Maya was smiling but in her eyes was the shine of something like pain.

Leave, Sophie told herself. Just *go*. Whatever it was she didn't want to know. She didn't want more sadness, she didn't want more terror. But she stayed exactly where she was.

'What I hate most is that I've never ever confronted them. It's not just that they led their screwed-up lives in their screwed-up way because that's everyone's prerogative, right? But I just don't have a language in which to speak straight with them. The kind of language you have when you're just learning to talk, when a word means exactly what it means – nothing more, nothing less. That simple language has been defaced by layers and layers of hypocrisy.'

'I'll get you another drink.'

Maya continued talking in the same low voice as Sophie went into the kitchen, as if it wasn't really her she was addressing. Sophie imagined her sitting there alone in the evenings, talking to herself.

Maya's story emerged slowly – pulled like thread through the needle of three large whiskies and a bout of crying and several cigarettes. Her story did not concern the neat four-cornered family any more and no one was joined to anyone else in a cosy pair. Neither Mummy-Daddy nor Maya-Rohit featured in this narrative. This was, instead, about Maya's mother – an eyes-outlined-in-thick-kohl, seventies-style fringe, chiffon-sari-wearing person – who'd fallen in love with an army captain when Maya was seven years old and who'd been methodically punished over the next ten years for this transgression, become a clinical depressive, tried suicide twice and detested her husband with a rage that bound her to him in what Maya felt was the most hateful marriage in the world. Then there was Maya's father who drank heavily every Saturday night – started on his litany of self-pity with his second glass of rum, began roundly abusing his wife as he poured himself the fourth and by the sixth graduated to that unique form of torture he had devised for her – waking up the children at midnight, calling out for them from the living room where he and wife sat facing each other like two people engaged in civilized conversation, making them watch while he whipped her with the buckle end of his leather belt. He always hit where the bruises wouldn't show – on her upper arms, on her stomach, on her back, on her groin. Then he'd put the whimpering children to bed, while his wife remained where she was, never saying a single word, not even when he called her a lying bitch, a stupid cow, a saali haraamzaadi and jerked her hair back so she was forced to look him in the eye when he addressed her.

Brigadier Singh was a disciplined man. On all other evenings, he drank moderately and joked with his wife at the dinner table. He planned birthday parties for his children, pored over schoolbooks with them and, of course, jogged with them round the lawn. The Singh family entertained every month; went on holidays twice a year. By the time Maya was ten she had stopped crying during these weekend torture sessions – she knew exactly what would happen and she speechlessly watched her father's brutality in living rooms across the country, trying every week to pull him away from her mother and never succeeding. Her younger brother – who'd urinate in his bed in fright – would cry in the whining way of a puppy that never gets used to being kicked.

As for the captain, whose name Maya didn't mention or didn't know, he had long since been dealt with. Much after her mother had for the second time sawed open one of her wrists with the knife that was (decorated with a satin ribbon) used to cut birthday cakes with, long after Maya had left home, her mother told her what happened – her lover had been thrown off his scooter by a civilian jeep coming at full speed from the opposite direction, a week after Brigadier Singh discovered his wife smiling for no obvious reason at the mention of the captain's name. 'I don't think he wanted to kill him,' she said to Maya. 'He wouldn't have the guts. Just frighten him.' And he was too much of a coward to do it himself, Maya said. He got Premnath, their orderly at the time, to do it. The captain broke his arm, and when it healed, the jeep appeared again. He stopped riding the scooter, but the jeep would still zip into his path, Premnath grinning evilly from behind the windshield, till the captain sought a transfer out of Pune. He never crossed paths with Mrs Singh after he was found out, but her punishment followed her everywhere the family went – Jabalpur, Nasik, Darjeeling, Hyderabad, Bombay.

'I've never shared this with anyone else,' said Maya, a note of pleading in her voice.

'Does it still happen?'

'After she cut herself the second time, she changed. She stopped pretending. She stopped talking to the other wives. She stopped cooking dinners for all these people my father would invite home. She stopped caring about how the house looked. My father didn't know how to handle it.'

'So then he stopped?'

'He woke us up as usual one night. I screamed and said – I don't want to go. Let me sleep. And he just took hold of my wrist and dragged me out. I was seventeen years old. He forced me to sit and he said – Maya listen. Look at your mother. You think she has any self-respect? She has no self-respect. She has no nothing. Remember that – without me she has nothing.

'I tore myself away, ran back into my room and locked the door. Until then, I'd never lock the door. I'd wait for the beatings to start, wait to be called, always pretend I didn't want to go and then go. I felt that as long as I was watching nothing fatal could happen to her. If I wasn't watching he might kill her. But that night I locked the door. He kept shouting, but I wouldn't open. He realized it wasn't going to work anymore – my brother had turned into a gibbering coward, I was no longer going to play audience and my mother had openly started telling people that her husband beat her. She didn't care if the whole damn Indian Army was in on it.'

When Sophie stepped out onto the balcony there was a low, luscious, creamy moon in the sky, the colour of the jasmine in the flower market, and Diamond Bay now looked more like its name, evenly-spaced, globed lights outlining its frontiers. The whiskey was making her sway. She tried to think of something more to say. Did Maya's mother actually have a full-blown affair with the captain or merely smile at the mention of his name? Was she still depressed? Facile questions that Sophie needed answered for the story to feel complete.

She went back inside and sat down next to Maya; Maya put an arm around her. They stayed like that, ear pressing against ear, till Sophie started feeling a little suffocated in that embrace.

'Let me get some water.'

But Maya held fast to her. 'That was my wrong turn ...'

'Have you ever spoken to them about it?'

'I can't talk to *him*. The only language we share is the language of everyday things. I tell him how I'm doing in the job. He gives me some army gossip. It's a solid façade and nothing will crack it. I have to be *polite* to him, Sophie. Otherwise he'll start making me feel guilty. It's too complicated to explain.'

'You have to try. Say the first sentence. Speak it in the voice of someone else.'

'No, I'm going to fly away from all of this,' said Maya. 'I'd be okay just never having to talk to him again. He's sickeningly healthy – he's going to sit there till he's hundred watching the rest of us die. So the only way to get rid of him is to disappear into somewhere and it's got to be America because that's where people disappear into, don't they? You meet them all the time – hello, I'm doing my PhD at Harvard, hello, I'm a surgeon in New Jersey, hello, I'm a filmmaker from New York and there's that look on their faces as if that's enough of an explanation, as if this place they've come from is so mysterious and grand, there's just no way they could say more. *That's* where I want to be.' She gripped Sophie by the shoulders. 'Will you come?'

Sophie smiled and shut her eyes.

Maya said, 'Okay, I'm sorry. I just made up all that crap about Naomi and Shanthi.'

'I know.'

'I didn't want you getting as friendly with Naomi as Shanthi. I don't care about the two of them, but I'd feel terrible if you liked Naomi more than me. And I can see you're very taken with her.'

Sophie shook her head in astonishment. 'I ... I think she's great but ... I don't like her any more or less than you. Is this some kind of a competition?

'Yes it is,' said Maya without irony. 'All of it is. Look at how quickly Shanthi's moving despite being a total rustic. Anyway ... let's talk about you.'

'What about me?'

'I know you're not happy with Swami but you don't want to analyse why. By the sound of it, you don't fit in with that gang. For God's sake Sophie – this boy actually killed his girlfriend? No, don't say anything. You just can't be hanging out with people like that.'

Sophie could not say that she had just turned her back on Swami. That would vindicate Maya in some way.

'I want you to leave that dump and move in here. There's so much space. We could prepare for the exam together. We could be a force, Sophie. Have you thought about it?'

Sophie looked at Maya's eager face and, for a moment, she did consider that different life but the thought quickly dissolved into another kind of horror – the contradiction between the plastic perfection of Maya's outer world and the secret at its core.

So instead she said, 'We'll see about that. But right now you better watch out for Naomi. She's angry.'

'She doesn't matter. Sophie. I'm counting on you. You know, I've never told anyone about my family. Not one living soul and if I ever run into people from any of those army families we knew, I pretend I'm someone else. No, I'm not Maya Singh, I say, and run away. Only you know now about Maya Singh.'

She brought her face very close to Sophie's and touched her cheek gently. 'And I'm counting on you.'

Flight

The plane banked to the left and there at an angle, rising to meet her though actually moving away, was Bangalore, its mile after mile of flat-roofed, colourless houses packed together in a way that suggested only unpleasant things – haphazard construction, claustrophobia, over-population. Somewhere far away a tiny Ringo was crying, Rukshana was being eaten by earthworms, Swami was sleepily trying to phone Sophie, Mrs Bhatt was grinding coconut chutney, Maya was waking up empty, Anand and Anandi were missing their son, and Shiva was lamenting the city's water problems ('Did you know that this city needs one and a half times more water than we actually have? Do you know how low the water table's dipped because of all the bore-wells people drill into their backyards?'). Already there was something inconsequential about their lives. I won't go back to India, Sophie thought, and even though she was just testing the words, they seemed to turn off some switch in her brain and she promptly fell into an hour of silken sleep untroubled by dreams or anguish.

When she opened her eyes, Bangalore had been replaced by clean white sunlit snow that unfurled in every direction, extending till the horizon which glowed with an unearthly red. She sneaked a look out of the corner of her eye at the man sitting one seat away from her. He read his newspaper with the calmness of someone who is used to looking out of a window and seeing heaven. She grew drowsy again watching the clouds move with a slowness that contradicted the actual speed of the plane. Just then, a harried-looking air-hostess marched up to Sophie's row of seats and told the little man with the wild hair and aviator sunglasses who was following her: 'Here's a vacant seat. Is this okay?'

'Any seat's okay for me ma'am. I'm not the grumbling type. As long as no one's puking in my lap, I ain't complaining.'

The girl smiled with forced graciousness.

The man eased himself into the seat next to Sophie's.

'There are babies giving people hell up there in front,' he told Sophie, gesturing with his thumb. 'Puking, screaming, falling into people's food trays. D'you know why God made babies?'

It was Uncle Rock!

'To remind us how we start out. We all start out being disgusting and someone has to pay by wiping the crap off our asses. It's very embarrassing when you think about it. Hi, I'm Uncle Rock ... and you?'

Sophie extended a shy hand to meet his outstretched one.

'Aren't you from Shillong?' he asked.

'How did you know?'

'I've seen you before, somewhere on the streets when I'm walking. I walk everywhere. If you live in Shillong, sooner or later you'll bump into Uncle Rock with his bags of mushrooms and his honey jars,' he said and laughed heartily as if in acknowledgement of the unfunniness of this. Sophie decided not to let on that she had been at his concert. The man on the seat by the aisle shook out his newspaper in a way that seemed to suggest he didn't approve of loud, hearty laughter on flights.

'What was it like, being in Bangalore?' asked Sophie.

'Not bad, not bad. I did a great open-air concert ... Good

crowd, nice people too – the guys who'd invited me. But I told myself – this is the first and last time Uncle Rock is coming to Bangalore. Of course, I didn't tell them that, you can't say crappy things to your hosts especially when they put you in a hotel room with a bathtub, give you a bottle of whiskey, call you 'sir'. Imagine that. No one calls Uncle Rock 'sir'. I met a nice chick too,' he said, winking through his shades. 'Now she was a very charming woman. Married and all that, the cousin of this guy who was organizing everything – Joseph – but man, was she coming on to me, was she coming on. I just shook hands with her and said – thank you for coming to my show, ma'am. The dame keeps asking – when will you come back Mr Rock, when will you come back? That freaked me out – no one calls Uncle Rock, Mr Rock.'

'So why don't you want to come back?'

'Something about the feel of the place – it's not right. I didn't get the right vibe. No one really has the time to have a conversation. And whether you're from Shillong or Assam or Nagaland ... the whole damn Northeast – it's all the same to them. They can't handle us – our strange names, our strange languages, our strange accents. And if someone happens to actually sit down with you, buy you a drink, wants to listen to your stories, his damn phone will ring. After this happened a few times, I said to myself – Uncle Rock's not coming this way again. How long are you going to be in Shillong?'

'Just a few days.'

'You've got to stay on till next week, miss. I'll tell you why. Because Bob Dylan, yes, that's right – the man himself – *is going to perform in Shillong.* Bob Dylan, the original, the real thing. We've been trying to get him to come for decades and his people keep ignoring us – why should they care about some little Indian town with a bunch of fans? They're just controlling the business, they don't have any feelings. But this time I wasn't going to take no for an answer. So I gave it to them. I said, see, it's simple – we know him, he doesn't know us. We love his voice, he has never heard ours. We know all the people and places in those songs but ask him where Shillong is and he'll probably say – China. There's something weird about this. I mean we worship this guy, we've been keeping his music alive ever since our leader – Bah Lou – sang "Blowin' in the Wind" back in the seventies and lit a fire that will not die out. Doesn't Dylan owe us something? And guess what? He wrote back himself! Yeah. He had signed that email in his own name. Why? Because he understands that it's all about the music. Nothing else matters. So now it's all settled.'

He pulled out a bundle of newspapers from the inside pocket of his jacket. All of them were Shillong papers from the past week and all reported the imminent visit – some in outsized headlines ('Bob Dylan coming on Maiden Visit to India; To Perform Only in Shillong') and some in more sober fonts but on the front page. Sophie scanned and then returned the papers. She was excited on Shillong's behalf, but she wasn't really a Dylan fan. She thought of him as excruciatingly old: he had become symbolic of History or Time or some such thing.

'Most of the tickets are sold out but give me a ring and I'll arrange one for you. We have a few special passes. Shillong will never be the same again,' he declared as he wrote down his phone number on her boarding pass.

'And what about you? Bangalore's treating you well?'

'It's nice to live on one's own.'

'That's right. I've lived on my own since I was thirteen. Now I have a wife, of course, but she doesn't mess with my life. I have the shed at the back where I grow the mushrooms ... have a little apiary. Give some honey to my neighbours, what my neighbours don't want I sell off in the Laitumkhrah market. That's okay for me. Doing a few concerts, playing my guitar. I'm not in this game to make money. This Joseph guy kept asking me – when will you come back to Bangalore sir? He called me twice after the show. I didn't tell him I'm not coming back. I've been to Delhi a few times and Delhi's the same. Nice people, well-meaning people, but everyone's chasing something. Me, I'm not chasing anything. You don't look happy? You're not feeling well, scared to be so high up in the sky?'

'No, just tired. Haven't gone home for a year.'

'That's right. No place like Shillong, actually. It's fine to travel and see the world and all of that, but in the end I just want to go back to my own little place and shut the door. Time is an ocean but it ends at the shore, like Dylan said. We all need to find our own shores, moh.'

He nodded sagely, then flipped down his tray table and reached out for his lunch.

Calcutta airport. Sophie lost Uncle Rock somewhere in the melee. She sat at the edge of her seat, waiting for her flight to Guwahati to be announced. The Northeast was already starting to come into view – that country within a country whose hallmark was multifariousness. Voices on the PA system announced flights to towns like Aizawl and Agartala. Faces from the Northeast stood out – a woman with slanting eyes wearing a checked shawl, a nun with flesh-coloured stockings, a boy with naturally spiky hair. Occasionally someone with a paper cup of Coke in one hand and a cellphone in the other, or someone wearing stylish loafers and pulling a brand-new strolley, would move into her line of vision and draw attention through his glossy presence to the generally decrepit air of the airport.

Bangalore airport, on the other hand, in a way that was symbolic of Bangalore city, crackled with affluence. It was hard to tell where people came from given their branded jeans and homogenous accents and conversations that sounded like excerpts from a play on the brain-dead middle-class. (Is Mr Murthy going to be on this flight? No, he's taking a later flight. I asked Mr Choudhury to send the car. That's good. What did you do for the New Year? I threw a little party, actually. Good? Good. Plenty of drinks ...) In Calcutta airport it was possible straightaway to tell where people belonged. This is what Sophie had always understood as home – a place where everyone is a different ethnicity from you and where your ethnicity defines who you are.

Two hours later she was on the winding road from Guwahati to Shillong in a rented, beat-up Sumo with a driver who sat at a rakish angle to the steering wheel, pressing on a broken horn that sounded like a faint whistle. Trucks lumbering down from the opposite direction raised dust so thick it was difficult to see anything. But as they climbed higher, the sand piled on both sides of the road thinned, the air cleared, the light grew soft and everything spoke to Sophie of home – the red soil; the kongs with conical baskets of fruit or washing slung on their backs, slowly walking up hill-paths; the upright teak trees. As they crossed over the border to Meghalaya at Byrnihat, the road got steeper and the vegetation more lush. There were patches of rice and occasional bushes of tea and the sudden glint of a spring. People led whole lives at the sides of the mountain road – picking lice off each other's heads, killing chickens, washing clothes, selling small pyramids of the world's sweetest pineapples and oranges, running tea-shops. There were check-posts where they were stopped to ensure they weren't smuggling in Bangladeshi immigrants; huge crashed lorries, their cargo still strapped to their backs, lying like dead elephants on their side; hoardings advertising holiday resorts; other Sumos, their sides streaked with the yellow vomit of their car-sick occupants; long army convoys going in the opposite direction; faded signs at hairpin bends saying 'Accident Prone Area'; and wooden crosses at the side of the gorge to commemorate people who had fallen into it and died. The Sumo kept turning blind curves unnecessarily fast and at each turn they came upon the same scene – the outline of a mountain cutting diagonally across the horizon and in the foreground a field coloured an unreally vivid green. And when, finally, they were at the bejewelled lake that had once marked the outer limit of Sophie's world, she recalled what Emma Bovary thought when 'it seemed to her that certain places on earth must bring forth happiness, as a plant peculiar to the soil, that cannot thrive elsewhere'.

Where the lake had once been her gateway to the undiscovered larger world, it was now the point at which the world began to shrink. She knew how Uncle Rock felt. Everyone who lived in high-up, magical places must feel the same way. You come down into the world and you mingle, but all the while there's something calling you back.

A High-up, Magical Place

If Sophie had read the Shillong newspapers Uncle Rock carried rolled up in his pocket, she would have seen that shoring up the news about Dylan was story after story about the upcoming elections to the state legislative assembly. Most of these reports concerned scandals, intrigues, insults and manipulations to do with money. Many candidates in the state were openly bribing voters in their constituencies. Ambulances, sheets of tarpaulin and umbrellas were among the gifts distributed by politicians suddenly gone benevolent; more imaginative ones sponsored picnics for busloads of all too willing day-trippers, while cunning ones laid foundation stones for football stadiums that might or might not be constructed once the elections were over. Some candidates, going from door to door to appeal for support, had to part with hard cash. A higher price was demanded from 'sitting' candidates, that is those already in power and seeking re-election. A town elder who did not want to be named was quoted as saying, 'People will take the money given to them by a candidate on the grounds that he will become a thief when he is elected.' In the villages, meanwhile, candidates were compelled to hold daily feasts of rice, pork and beef to which hordes of people, young and old, flocked, 'to make hay while the sun shines.'

The election fever led citizens to unearth a remarkable number of ghost institutions, supposedly built from funds managed by Members of the Legislative Assembly. The MLAs in question gave statements to the papers refuting these charges (their favourite word was 'baseless'), accusing the accusers of trying to cover up their own sins by such allegations, inviting them to scrutinize their accounts and in some cases filing defamation suits. The premises of a sports and cultural club, an 'office-cum-residence' supposedly built for the headman of a village, a market-stall on which an amount of Rs 2,00,000 had purportedly been spent, improvement works on grounds meant for traditional dances and extension works on a crèche – all these had been identified by vigilant citizens as fictional projects.

Responding to allegations that his party was shamelessly buying up voters, a higher-up party representative announced from Delhi that elections are festive occasions, not funerals, and that some money is therefore needed to keep people's spirits up. In response to this, a young member of a new party called Fourth Time Around educated the higher-up on the indulgences that even funerals in the state of Meghalaya can be. MLAs were expected to host lavish parties every time an elder died in their constituency. 'Pray tell me,' he was quoted in the papers as saying, 'where does the money for the two pigs and the ten chickens come from each and every time?'

Meanwhile, an outlawed local political organization had called for a bandh on the occasion of this higher-up's imminent campaign visit to Shillong, on the grounds that the higher-up's party was trying to get rich at Meghalaya's expense by mining all the uranium out of the state. As a sort of corroboration, the following day police had arrested six persons at the Indo-Nepal border, smuggling four kilograms of low-grade uranium from Meghalaya into Nepal. The uranium was estimated to cost ten million rupees in the international market.

If Sophie had read all this and then returned to the headlines about Bob Dylan, she would have noticed that despite the big photographs of the curly-haired singer, this news item now seemed the tiniest, dwarfed by the excitement and horror that the elections, like some ritual cathartic exercise, had brought forth.

~

Sophie had always loved going into other people's homes. As a child she would be sent down the road to their landlady's house on a vague daily mission called 'keeping Kong Elsa company'. Kong Elsa – a well-to-do, elderly widow – lived alone and it was on these afternoon trips to the large bungalow, perched above a curve in the road, that Sophie developed to perfection her theory that her real parents (as against the ones she was stuck with) came from a similar world of crackling coal fires, the smell of freshly-mowed lawns, large glass-enclosed portraits of dead men and women blurring to white at the edges, little wooden doolies with wire netting for storing the butter-dish and the hard-crusted loaves, polished brass vases for roses, full-length mirrors that swayed on their joints and old chests of drawers filled with clean white handkerchiefs and warm tartan shawls. Sophie had not wanted any of these things in a specific way; she wanted the life that went with them.

Her first awareness of Shillong took the form of the realization that the differences between people could be traced to the differences in their houses and, growing up, she thought of houses with the care one usually reserves for people. She remembered how their maid, Kong Bina, had put all her savings into building herself and her daughter a two-room doll's house out of golden, unpainted planks of pinewood that had over successive monsoons dulled to brown, with a little patch of mustard leaves out in front. She remembered going with her parents into a cottage in Pohkseh (its tangled garden, its smooth red ferric oxide polished floor) built in the early seventies by one of the thousands of settlers from the lowlands of Sylhet. She remembered eating cucumber sandwiches in the beautiful refectory of St Mark's college where the wooden floorboards creaked with age and the windows were like paintings – full of light and leaves – while her father and his friend, the stuttering Irish monk, Brother Meddoe, co-lover of *Hamlet*, discussed the play. At sixteen, she had gone to the village of Nongkrem for the annual dance led by the Princess and was told that the Syiem's thatched house that stood on the far side of the compound was built entirely without nails. Another time, she had spent a whole morning in Garikhana searching for the house of a friend, and was surprised to discover, when she found it, that the house was not a separate entity at all but a haphazard collection of rooms buried somewhere in a catacomb-like building in which lived the multi-limbed Marwari business family to which her friend belonged. She felt she had entered another city and continued to feel that way as her friend passionately discussed the need to build a temple on the site of the demolished Babri mosque.

As she grew older her fascination grew. She discovered that Shillong had moved over to the sturdy Assam-types bungalows after the Great Earthquake of 1897 that flattened the town; she paid attention to the stained glass in the windows of the Cathedral; she sought out the houses in which Tagore and Vivekananda had spent time in Shillong and gaped at the summer residences of the Maharaja of Tripura and the Maharaja of Mayurbhanj. She was afraid of a time when there would be no built structure left to like and no house with a history. Several years before she left town, they had already started replacing the bungalows (sloping, corrugated tin roofs, small-paned bay windows, whitewashed walls held up, Tudor-style, by dark beams, rusty gutters to channel the heaving Shillong rains, tiny skylights) with ugly, flat-roofed, multi-storied, reinforced-concrete-cement structures. Already the hills were hidden away under slums.

At twenty-five, Sophie was ancient. She was unprepared, therefore, for the sense of surprise that overcame her as she got off the Sumo, climbed up the steps and gazed at her old home. She had always taken for granted that she would never live in one of those grotty houses that were swallowing the town, but now it seemed amazing to her that her parents had managed to remain tenants in a house that, seen against Shillong's growing squalor, was a faded piece of luxury – a cottage with a tiny lawn, moss on its rusting roof and lemon and orange trees out in front. They had lived for years anticipating that their landlady (not the kind Kong Elsa, who had died, but her hard-nosed sister, Kong Salty) would evict them so that she could tear down the cottage and build something larger and more rent-worthy on the land. For some reason (perhaps because she was so busy managing all her other lucrative properties), she had let them stay and even allowed them to add two rooms at the rear at their own expense. These extended to the compound wall, so the childhood thrill Sophie had derived from running *around* the house, circumambulating it as a way of expressing love for it, had at some point been lost.

As she was standing for a few meditative moments in the green patch that passed for a lawn, her mother noticed her from the window and rushed out, asking, her joy creased with a frown, 'Sophie what are you doing there? Are you okay?'

For a moment Sophie imagined her mother had read it all from her face – the grief and the hurt of the last few days, the lies, the insomnia, the confusion. But then she realized Mrs Das had seen nothing and they smiled at each other in relief and hugged. Her father was standing by the door and watching them.

As soon as she had answered her parents' primary questions about her well-being, Sophie toured the house, struck by the dumb beauty of things that had with the tenacity of the living put down their roots where they stood. She'd never noticed their loveliness before – the large cupboard without doors that had been the family's common wardrobe when she was younger, the old sitting room carpet with its patterns of black and red on beige, the woven cane baskets in the kitchen for onions and potatoes, the timeless bookshelves with her father's faded editions of the English masters. Outside, at the far end of a football field, was the hill, topped with a pylon, which she would gaze at whenever she was longing for something as a child. She stopped by the window, thinking about all the utterly tawdry things that had once made up her idea of fulfilment – a TV set because all her classmates had one, though her father hated the idea, a pair of strappy white sandals that could come to represent all the world's sophistication, or, the most abiding fantasy, her real parents.

She went and sat across from them now, her real parents in their familiar clothes, wearing expressions she knew well, framed in postures she clearly recognized – her father's clasped fingers resting on a crossed leg, her mother's ever-busy hands hemming a kitchen towel. She greedily ate a second lunch of rice, dal and fried fish, while Mr and Mrs Das watched over her and talked to her. The principal of the government school where Mr Das taught had been replaced and he didn't think much of the new chap. He was aggressive where the previous one had been retiring and while that one had adopted a permanent attitude of mild neutrality, this one seemed to want to play on the insecurities of his ever-quarrelling staff. What concerned Mr Das most were the arrears. Sophie knew about the arrears. They were five years overdue, the order to release them lost in some bureaucratic wrangle linked with the transition of the school from a grant-in-aid to a fully government-supported one. Mrs Das's school life was less anxiety-ridden. The husband of one of her colleagues had been discovered to be unfaithful; another colleague had fainted at her own wedding; a third had just had twins.

Then Mrs Das cleared her throat and said, 'It's been difficult for us.'

'She knows, she knows,' said Mr Das. 'Sophie, you know all about this.'

'Sophie knows, but still, the last few months have been very difficult. Muku is hardly at home.'

'But Sophie was never like this.'

They always said this – that Sophie had been different, not like Muku at all.

'Take a simple thing like eating – she doesn't eat at home. She goes out and eats on the streets. She eats what her friends give her,' said her mother.

Mr Das clicked his tongue. 'She's rebellious. It's all part of the same problem.'

'I asked your father to forbid her from seeing that boy but he doesn't say a word about it. He hardly talks to her.'

'You're talking to her all the time. Has it made a difference?'

'It's worse after she met this boy. No one can ask him any questions because his family is rich. He got into some trouble in school and they just let him off with a warning.'

'Who is this person?' asked Mr Das, as if he'd just heard of him.

'He takes drugs,' said Mrs Das, lowering her voice, and Sophie suppressed the urge to laugh.

'What does he want with her?' asked Mr Das gripping the sides of his chair in agitation. Normally, he just grunted in response to his wife's complaints about Muku or quoted Polonius by way of an oblique reference to his younger daughter's waywardness: 'This above all – to thine own self be true, and it must follow, as the night the day, thou canst not then be false to any man.'

Sophie saw from her Bangalore perspective how comfortable her parents' lives were. Reacquainting herself with the things that bothered them – Muku's boyfriend, her father's unpaid arrears, her mother's aching back – only heightened this realization. As Mr and Mrs Das, in their faded cardigans and knitted socks, went on with their futile discussion on Muku, Sophie put away her plate and crept closer to the glowing electric heater, watching the early evening light filter in through the windows. She remembered this sense of security from a time before her sister was born, when they would all sit quietly like this on winter afternoons and she would feel, without really being conscious of it, the slow contraction of the light, the fall in temperature as a breeze stirred the shadows of branches on the floor, and the curious fading away of the car-horns and shouts of boys playing football as the afternoon wore on. Before she could stop herself, Sophie was fast asleep.

Her parents stopped talking as soon as they noticed and when Sophie stirred they started talking again in soft voices about Muku.

Sophie yawned. When had it started – the slow shattering of that peace? Mr Das had been ill-tempered and jobless when Mukulika was born and her mother, resentful and overworked. And as soon as Muku was old enough to know what not caring meant, she stopped caring. Muku personified disregard. As a child, her first public crime had been stealing from other girls' lunch-boxes. She started smoking in school, carrying the forbidden photo-romance glossies in her school bag, writing threatening notes to girls who challenged her dominance, sniggering behind the nuns' backs. At home, she poured mud onto the heads of people passing on the street below their house, put salt into Sophie's tea, pulled the chair away from behind her just when she was going to sit, told her demented lies as a matter of course, refused to talk to her for days on end, screamed at her mother, stole from her purse, repeatedly failed every subject, and calmed down only when her father let out a single explosive word – *enough*. Things would be quiet for a couple of weeks before they started up again. Eventually her rebelliousness hardened into a rage that could not be stemmed. A few days before she left, Sophie noticed that Muku had been hoarding Ibuprofen tablets. She didn't know what taking twenty or thirty of those tablets at a time might do to a person but she knew that Muku intended to find out. The sight of those metallic strips tucked deep under the mattress had sparked in her an anger so electrifying, that for a moment it had seemed perfectly rational to Sophie to make Muku eat every last one of those pills. The two had scratched at each other till their mother came rushing to separate them. Mrs Das had flushed the tablets down the toilet and told Muku – thank your stars your father is not at home. Muku had responded by breaking a cup.

Sophie stood up, stretched and found herself drawn again to the window. She didn't see her childhood fantasies reflected back to her when she looked out now, but only what was actually there – cold, boxy pink and green concrete houses built by people who didn't care about Beauty, people who might of an afternoon appreciate the white gushing of Elephant Falls or the green expanse of the Umiam Lake but who for the most part didn't think about what they saw outside their windows.

She went to the kitchen to fill a kettle with water for tea. The incident with the tablets had shaken her up and on the phone from Bangalore she'd begged her parents to take her sister to a psychiatrist. No, no, she's improving, they'd said. She misses you. Sophie had stopped thinking very much about her sister till the phone calls started coming again. A new problem had arisen – Muku was seeing boys. She had discovered the universe that suddenly opens out between a sixteen-year-old girl and those boys on the street, on buses, in the houses of her friends, who notice her, smile at her, begin to watch her so intently that she is compelled to watch herself. Her parents were flabbergasted at the idea that Muku should be seen sitting in the Madras Café alone with a boy, that she should speak with strangers on the phone, that she should move about in Police Bazaar with gangs of sly-eyed boys and coquettish girls.

Sophie took the tea in and waited for her parents to say what they were dying to say – can you please take Muku away so we can wash our hands off this problem? Her mother asked her instead about the prices of groceries in Bangalore, the personal lives of her colleagues, what she cooked for dinner every night. She wanted to know if Sophie had made any new friends (a loaded question), if her landlord was friendlier than before, if she was managing on her salary. She suggested Sophie see a doctor for her insomnia, grow her hair, eat more to make up for the weight loss she was quite sure she had noticed. Her father drank his tea and disappeared into his study and, as if on cue, Mrs Das switched on the TV.

'Have you seen his room?' asked Mrs Das under the sound of the 6 o'clock soap.

Sophie nodded; she'd glanced into it during her sentimental tour of the house, seen the books in their place on the shelves by the door.

'Didn't you see – he's moved all sorts of things in there.'

'What sorts of thing?'

'His bed, a hotplate, all his clothes.'

Sophie hadn't noticed anything.

'He makes his own tea. He's bought his own kettle and spoons and cups and everything. He washes his own clothes. He sleeps in there. He doesn't eat with us any more. He comes and gets the food and eats by himself. He sat here today only because you were here. He hardly speaks to me, and to Muku, almost never.'

Sophie found her mouth going dry, less at this utterly strange behaviour on her father's part and more at the unemotional voice in which her mother was describing it.

'He's turned his back on us. He sits there all evening when he comes back from school, trying to read Bengali poetry. He hardly knows Bengali, you know that. He moved to Delhi when he was a teenager, whatever little he remembered from Calcutta was all forgotten. All his life it's only been English, English, English. Was there ever a Bengali book in this house?'

It was true that Sophie's father had always stayed away from

Shillong's Bengali community, from the Durga Puja celebrations and the Bangla Sahitya Sammelans. The smattering of Bengali his daughter learnt was not from him but from her classmates at school. Mr Das did not seem to have any use for the fact that he was Bengali. When he emailed Sophie six months ago and first told her he was translating *Hamlet* into Bengali, initially with the help of an old student of his, she hadn't known what to make of it. But distance had softened her view of her parents. In Shillong this might have seemed odd to her, this reclaiming of a language Mr Das had resolutely ignored all his life, but in Bangalore it only seemed like a minor and harmless eccentricity on the part of an ageing man.

Her mother had grown absorbed in the television, now that she had delivered this disturbing bit of news to her daughter. Sophie went and stood by the window for the third time. She looked at the garden with its faded winter colours. She and Muku had spent every vacation hanging out there, squabbling and squabbling and once in a while, because they had no one else, grudgingly making up. They never went away to visit an extended family, like the rest of their settler or dkhar classmates. Their father's parents were dead and he considered his other relatives a waste of time. Their mother's relatives had cut her off for marrying their father. This is our only context, thought Sophie. This town. We have no business now to try and claim some other, invented context for ourselves.

~

Muku didn't return all evening and Sophie, unable to bear the shrill TV voices, went for a walk. She noticed that new shops, which offered 'PC solutions' or stuffed toys, had been built above and next to the old shops. She could see in the smart takeaways, in the boutiques selling lacy clothes and frangible jewellery, in the tight little malls into which she aimlessly drifted, where phone booths and travel agents and information technology training institutes were packed into the unlikeliest nooks and corners – that this Shillong was uglier and more prosperous than the one she had left behind. It was mainly women who ran these shops but this was not new. They'd slowly been taking over – spunky young local women (edging out men from the plains who had once run most of the city's businesses), dressed in the international uniform of jeans and Converse shoes, fishing out chickens with one casual finger from the freezers in delicatessens, filling up the fuel tanks in the petrol pumps, styling hair, standing with a proprietorial air in the doorways of Chinese restaurants and sitting, with expressions of extreme boredom, behind the counters of tiny bookshops.

Sophie looked up at Ribor's shop as she passed it. He wasn't outside, leaning on the railing, but the lights were switched on. It was enough for now to know he was there. She imagined going back home and calling him. He'd answer the phone and as they talked, his eyes would pass over the discs under the glass and those on wooden racks held in place by springy wires and she imagined that these familiar things would suddenly look different to him seen through the prism of her voice.

She came to the ancient Fine Bread Shop with its bright blue shutters, thick-crusted bread with cotton-light insides, sweet biscuits with a single, chewy drop of jam in the centre and muffins baked in waxy paper. Sophie bought the loaf her mother had asked her to. Nearing home, she stopped at her favourite paan-wallah, Jagjivan Ram, who, as always, gently shook the water off a leaf before spreading masala on it. To Sophie that familiar gesture was comforting.

An over-sized paan stuffed into her mouth, she started making her way home and noticed, under the dim streetlights, a girl walking towards her in smart winter boots and a leather overcoat, accompanied by a boy holding her hand, whose clothes similarly gave off the distinct whiff of money. Sophie had thought, driving into Shillong, that her living on her own, her job with its seductive ring of America to it, her credit card and stylish cellphone, possibly made her a little cooler than the people she'd left behind. But she was wrong. Sophie could see in this couple's gait that they personified the Shillong contempt for other people's supposed coolness and they were going to go clicking past her in their expensive shoes without offering a fraction of a glance.

The girl, however, not just looked at Sophie but immediately stopped and announced in the voice of a woman, 'Pavan, this is my sister.'

If Muku had been reborn as Britney Spears, Sophie would not have been more surprised. Where were the frayed jackets of a year ago, the tangled, unwashed hair, the scarred, peeling elbows and knees, the perpetually running nose, the pout that signalled Muku's permanent state of rebellion?

'Sophie?' asked Pavan, extending a hand to be shaken, as if they were executives at a meeting. Sophie's speechlessness was compounded by the fact that her tongue was trapped in layers of leaf and various sweet spices and slices of supari.

'We're just coming back from the lake,' said Muku, so amicably that Sophie wondered if she had forgotten the bitterness on the phone last week, if she lived her life without making connections between the things she said and did from day to day.

'How long are you in Shillong?' asked Pavan.

Sophie shrugged, chewing furiously.

'She's going back next week,' said Muku.

'Come over to my place some time,' said Pavan. 'Come on Saturday for tea.'

'They're going to have a swimming pool soon,' said Muku

Sophie tried to think of an appropriate, elder sister type thing to say. She thought of her parents and their belief in Pavan's rottenness.

'Bangalore's a cool place. I have a cousin there,' said Pavan.

'But Pavan doesn't want to move there, he'd rather go to Delhi,' said Muku.

'That's because I want to study fashion design,' he explained.

'You *think* you want to study fashion design. You might change your mind when you get there.'

Sophie found it hard to believe that these were delinquent sixteen year olds talking. She would suggest to her parents that they meet Pavan and see for themselves what a marvellously good influence he seemed to be on their daughter, though her rehabilitation was clearly costing a lot of money. How had Muku managed to keep that coat secret from her parents? Muku and Pavan were watching her. She had chomped on enough of her paan to say, 'I'll see you later. Just remembered I have to make a call.'

She thought she must call Swami and say a decent goodbye, then realized it was Ribor she really wanted to call.

Pavan put his arm around Muku's waist with a movement

that suggested a seasoned familiarity, an almost sibling closeness.

'Nice to have met you Sophie,' he said, holding up his other hand in a gesture of farewell. His eyes reflected a moment's worth of curiosity.

Then the teenage lovers kissed right there on the street, while Sophie gaped. As Pavan turned away, Muku said to her sister, 'I'll walk with you. Need to tell you something.'

They turned back towards Laitumkhrah, Sophie feeling an uncommon awkwardness.

'Did you tell parents that I don't want to move to Bangalore?' Muku asked without preamble.

'No, but in any case what you want doesn't matter. I think they've made up their minds.'

'But they'll listen if you tell them!' said Muku, her voice thinning to a wail. This, all at once, and despite the glossy lips, the lovely coat, the flush of happiness, was the Muku of old. Sophie took a perverse satisfaction in knowing that she and her sister would probably not last the rest of this walk.

'So what's the deal with Pavan?'

Muku's walk changed, became a little slower and more self-conscious.

'He's going to be here for another two years and then go to Delhi. I've already told parents that I want to go there later.'

'Are you nuts? You'll wilt in the heat and have your bum pinched by men in buses. You don't know anything about Delhi.'

Sophie felt unable to directly address the subject of Pavan. She didn't know how to deal with this weak spot in an otherwise iron-souled girl.

'I'm going to Delhi, that's all I know,' said Muku.

A taxi went by, loudly playing 'Tequila Sunrise'. Could it be that everything was the same, thought Sophie, with a sudden confusion. That depressingly-lit restaurants were still playing old hits from the pop group Europe, that the announcer on the local radio station was still saying, over the slowly rising nostalgia of the song, 'And of course it's Mary Hopkin again with "Those Were the Days" ...'

But Muku wasn't nostalgic. 'You don't want me in Bangalore. So that's perfect,' she said. She pulled out a lipstick and wrote an inverted 'P' with it on her wrist.

'Do you know why parents want to get rid of me right away?'

Sophie shrugged, struck by the absence of pain in Muku's voice. Her sister knew that her parents didn't want her here; she knew Sophie didn't want her there. Yet she spoke as if all this animosity was completely natural.

'They're finished. They're going to ...' She brought her palms together and slowly took them apart.

Sophie stopped walking but still didn't fully understand.

'They'll tell you soon. She's going to live in Benaras, he's going to rent a house in Shantiniketan.'

Sophie gripped her sister's arm. '*What*?'

Muku had the advantage of having learnt this gradually: over the last year her parents who, she felt, had never been particularly nice to each other, had come to realize that they'd rather be alone. To her it only seemed like the lifting of a veil. Besides, she'd been witness for so long to their troubles that she believed, sub-consciously, that this was the way of all parents – all middle-aged couples were scornful of each other, all mothers complained about all fathers, all fathers believed all mothers to be fundamentally stupid. It satisfied a deep-seated sense of rage in Muku to see that her parents were now going to separate and be lonelier than they already were. The only problem was she needed them to be in Shillong as long as Pavan was here. After all these years of fighting everyone, Muku had latched onto one person with the desperation of a drowning woman.

Whereas Sophie, who had since childhood dreaded the fights between her parents and considered them aberrations when they were over, felt weak with shock.

'What did you do?' she stuttered.

'*I* didn't do anything. It's not because of me.'

'They were fine when I left. What happened?'

'Nothing. She just prays all the time. And he goes to his room and shuts the door. I think they're just bored.'

Sophie breathed a little easier. 'Maybe if they spent a little time away from each other ...'

'No, they're serious. They're so serious they're not even fighting about it.'

'They can't do it. They'll die the minute they step out of Shillong. And what about us?'

'You're already fixed. Once I go to Delhi I'll be fixed too.'

Sophie felt like slapping her mindless sister right there in the middle of the pavement.

'Don't even mention Delhi. You'll never get to Delhi. We have to put sense into their heads. Why can't the four of us sit down and have a conversation about anything anymore? It's always they talking to me about you, Mama complaining about Baba, you complaining about them. We're always waiting to be alone with someone so we can start the bitching.'

'You try having your civilized conversation. But I know what I know. Why is he always talking about that friend of his who's moved to Shantiniketan? Why has she been sending money to that dharamshala in Benaras? They've been planning it.'

'The dharamshala is just charity. And Baba's been talking about going on a visit to Shantiniketan, not moving there for god's sake!'

'But why do *you* want to cling on? You managed to get out. Even parents don't want to cling on anymore. I can't even understand why you came back.'

'Muku don't talk like that. I can't stand it when you treat everything as dispensable.'

'Sophie, this is the first time they're *doing* something. So far all they've done is talk. Mama is always threatening to go to that dharamshala but she never had the guts and Baba hates travelling anyway. So what are we left with? Two people tired of each other but shit scared to do something about it.'

'You have no idea what you're saying, you little idiot ...'

'Don't give me a lecture!' shouted Muku. 'I'm asking you a question – what's the point of holding on to the past? Just answer me.'

The answer materialized in the form of Killer Queen. She was walking towards them with her red handbag and hairnet and sunglasses. She looked exactly the same – unapproachable in her madness. Sophie's heart began to thump, absurdly, because she knew Killer Queen would never recognize them – they didn't mean anything to her. Yet she felt as if she were in the presence of an oracle and had just a few seconds to ask that vital question. Except that she didn't know what the question was or she didn't know how to state it in a way that would encompass all the questions. She and Muku parted on the narrow pavement as Killer Queen drew near. She was mouthing something, exuded a musty perfume and held up a veined hand in a kind of gesture of defence. Her nails were painted maroon. Sophie realized Killer Queen was talking to her:

'Child, can I borrow a hundred rupees? It's for my dog, you see.'

The two sisters looked at each other. It was impossible to ignore her; she might invoke a curse or attack them or take off her sunglasses and turn out to be a walking corpse.

She turned to Muku and asked, 'Do you want to buy some old stamps from the Queen's time?' She opened her handbag and stretched it out towards Muku who gave a little scream when she looked inside. Sophie saw it too – something slimy and crawling.

Killer Queen gripped Sophie's arm. 'I'm organizing a garden fete next week. You must come.'

Muku was already speeding away. 'Sophie run,' she called out without turning back.

Sophie tried to look through the dark glasses as she handed her a hundred-rupee note. 'When will it end?' she asked, and then again to make sure Killer Queen had heard: 'When will it all end?'

And from somewhere in the jumble of non sequiturs that was her mind, Killer Queen drew out a miraculously logical answer. 'It will end on the last page.'

Sophie pulled her arm out of the old lady's grasp and walked away, ignoring her requests for a sheet of blue inland letter paper to write to her daughter in Bombay.

Lovesick

Mr Das paced about his old-books-smelling room talking about Hamlet. He explained to Sophie, who had heard these very views stated in these very words countless times, how there was no play whose hero is sicker with life and yet no play that as passionately embraces life's fundamental mysteries. No play so taken with death and no play that does so little to redeem death's tragedy. No play that so mocks at love and no play that so grieves over the loss of a loved one. In other words, Hamlet had died but the questions lived on. These conundrums were timeless.

Sophie had never read *Hamlet* because her father had read it too much. There was nothing in his universe that could not be explained or illustrated with a quote from the play. This was an unbroken refrain running through her childhood – words words words murder most foul there is nothing either good or bad but thinking makes it so frailty thy name is woman give every man thy ear but few thy voice what's Hecuba to him or him to Hecuba something is rotten in the state of Denmark brevity is the soul of wit to die to sleep to sleep perchance to dream.

Sophie questioned herself about her father. Why had he once given up his Bengaliness? But perhaps he hadn't really disowned it, just kept it on hold till he needed it. All these years there were other things defining him – his Bihari mother; his coming of age in Delhi; his Hindi-speaking wife; his years in Shillong; his solitary nature; his distrust of friendship based on a common ethnicity or language; his belief, derived from the volumes of Shakespeare and Dickens that sat yellowing on his shelves, that the essential truths had already been expressed; his absolute faith in the beauty of the English language.

He was now quoting the lines she, in keeping with some old ritual, was obliged to repeat along with him without being in the least bit touched by them, as if they were the chorus of an overplayed pop song or a prayer that's gone dead from overuse. 'Thus conscience does make cowards of us all;/ And thus the native hue of resolution/ Is sicklied over with the pale cast of thought,/ And enterprises of great pitch and moment,/ With this regard, their current turn awry/ And lose the name of action.'

Sophie found, once she had dutifully recited this refrain, that she could not challenge him. Even if Hamlet meant nothing to her, once the prince had been invoked it was no longer possible to talk about everyday things in an everyday way. Hamlet rendered life oblique and it seemed crude to ask the plain question – are you and Mama going to separate? She could not ask it and her father could not answer it. Hamlet, once a bridge of affection between them (father and daughter grocery-shopping in the by-lanes of Laitumkhrah, the one reciting some poetic fragment and the other hearing it as a pleasant background buzz against which daydreams could leisurely unfold), had now become a wall. Here in her father's island of a room, she started to feel that her question was stupid because the answer to it so obvious. He had already cut himself adrift, his isolation was a slowly forming rock-shelf made up of tin spoons and empty cartons of washing powder and scattered sheets with Hamlet's lines rewritten in Bengali.

For the truth was that Mr Das had been unhappy for a very long time. Like Hamlet, his despair was the most important thing about him. It had become his very nature so his family had stopped noticing. Sophie did remember a time when her father played Helen Shapiro and Connie Francis records on an old turntable; a time when he came back from work and joked with his wife; a time when he was expecting to become a university lecturer and all of them would live in a free accommodation on a leafy campus on the outskirts of the town. Then he had fallen out with his department head, resigned from his college job, never got that university post, been forced to take up school teaching. And acquired the burden of permanent sadness. Her father would always stay this way – he would come back from school scowling, complain about the retardation of his students as he drank his tea, read Shakespeare, go out to get the groceries, take some interest in Sophie's plans but very little in Muku's and apparently none in his wife's. Just like Muku took it for granted that all parents were fundamentally bored with each other, Sophie had come to believe that the lives of all parents were basically static.

She was wrong. Things had been changing in the Das household. The disembodied god of Mrs Das's imagination had now acquired a human form and she had in the past year turned into a dedicated Krishna worshipper, while Mr Das, who'd been heard to speak Bengali only on rare occasions and never ventured near a Bengali newspaper, had now embarked on the ambitious task of translating *Hamlet*.

When Hamlet was exhausted and the silence between Sophie and her father grew awkward, he declared, 'I'm going to Shantiniketan.'

'To meet a publisher for your translation?' asked Sophie.

'No, I'm planning to rent a house there.'

'So will Mama go with you?' asked Sophie begging him silently to say 'yes'.

'She doesn't want to come.'

'It's too hot there!' exclaimed Sophie. 'And mosquitoes …'

Her father hated travel, hated the obligation to adjust that new places forced on him. And here he was talking about relocating to an entirely new town only because … only because, what?

'It's an experiment.'

'What kind of experiment?'

This was hard, this asking of simple questions and this answering on the part of a man who never answered. Mr Das had always considered the logic of his actions self-evident. He avoided explaining himself to the world and so had remained essentially inscrutable.

'There was a vacancy in the university,' he said in a low voice and then went silent.

So that's what it was – his old dream of becoming a university lecturer. Sophie wondered whether the reason her father had never reached the heights of academia was his great belief in *Hamlet*'s truth. Could it be that this obsession obscured his movement forward, that the native hue of resolution was indeed clouded over with the pale cast of thought?

'So if you get it, then ...'

Mr Das, by the standards of his usual reserve, suddenly turned garrulous.

'No, no, I don't have the qualifications. Debashish, someone I used to know in Delhi, applied and got the job. And now he tells me – there are plenty of openings in colleges, you can start by getting a few years of experience in a college, and slowly work your way up to the university. Now there is no guarantee, but he is there so I feel more confident. What's the harm in trying? I have ten years left before I reach retirement age and if out of those I could spend even one in a university.'

Each man to himself then, thought Sophie bitterly. She tried to think of the good side of this. Maybe he would make it, maybe he would be happier than he had ever been – that elusive happiness which through his love of Hamlet he had always mocked at.

'You can come and visit me there,' said Mr Das, smiling a rare smile. 'Closer to Bangalore than Shillong.'

How could it be that he didn't recognize her desolation? To her father she had become a visitor– someone who'd taken her real life with her to the town she'd moved to. He wasn't betraying her by going away because she had already left him behind.

Her father started to recite some other Shakespearean dregs but Sophie wasn't going to listen anymore. Soon she would forget all the speeches and poems she knew. Despite her sadness, the thought was liberating. There was something fusty about the prince who constantly went round in circles, thinking his fevered thoughts, century after century. His mantras were of no use to Sophie. She left her father there, lighting a cigarette, his eyes alight with *Hamlet*'s truth, while hers were wet. She went out of the house and down to the street and headed in the direction of Ribor's shop.

At first, she kept starting over, smiling foolishly, trailing off, going silent. It didn't matter because Sophie felt not the slightest doubt that eventually everything would be possible. Ribor's shop was outside the two cities she knew, unlike any room she had been in, high above the streets of the whole planet. It was beyond time too. Time was no longer the leaky bucket, the ocean without a shore, the hole in the sky. In Ribor's company it became marvellously whole and restored. It was a magic carpet, this shop to which no customers came, which in its smallness and neatness, its smell of tea and wood and cigarettes seemed to Sophie a place she could comfortably spend her whole life in.

Ribor didn't seem surprised to see her. How could he be? She had thought of him so often in the past year, while to him she was just the occasional customer, the girl he had casually shared a smoke with a year ago. Sophie stopped pretending she was there to browse and tried to find a way to talk.

She told Ribor she'd met Uncle Rock on the plane.

Ribor said: 'He has all that style, all that charm, but what does he do with it? He just walks about town talking to people he doesn't know, boasting about his honey bees.'

'Dylan is coming.'

'Apparently. To check out the competition,' said Ribor grinning. Sophie just kept looking at him, wondering about the lines around his eyes and about the Madonna woman whose umbrella she had thrown into the gutter.

'I used to do all the Dylan stuff with him and the others. Then I realized Dylan's a traveller. He needs to move on all the time. That's when I stopped doing the same old thing because I thought – heck, this is ridiculous, this has nothing to do with Dylan.'

Sophie thought of the conversation on the plane and Uncle Rock's decision not to come to Bangalore again. He was certainly no traveller.

'It's getting pathetic, all these Dylan clones trying to outdo each other as if his music is all about getting high on some kind of song contest. But if he does come it'll be like Judgement Day – all the little mortals meeting their creator.'

'I hope Uncle Rock's not disappointed,' said Sophie.

'Fifteen years ago this friend of mine – Aman – and I, we'd write letters to Pink Floyd. He sent them his poetry. We believed it would make a difference somehow, they'd write back or send us some kind of a sign. We were so goddamn serious about it. But Uncle Rock is going to be forty and he's still waiting.'

'Is that why you stopped playing? Because you need one or another illusion to be a rock star?'

Ribor laughed with a self-deprecation so genuine that Sophie felt her heart contract with love.

She wanted to ask him more questions but dreaded the answers. Was he married? He wore no ring. He'd told her once that he used to paint. He'd dismissed his guitar playing; painting was the real thing. But the family liquor store business needed to be taken care of so there was no question of going to art school. This was about the only thing she knew about his past – just this one tiny fact on which to base a whole person.

He pulled a bottle from under the counter as Sophie continued to linger. His grandmother made wine. She had a little setup in a loft where she coaxed wine from cherries and pineapples and sold it for seventy rupees a bottle at Christmas fetes. Ribor poured Sophie some in a teacup from the leftover stock. She took it and instinctively put her hands around it to warm them, before realizing the teacup was cold. It was a dreary January evening, the kind of day when you finally notice that the sun hasn't appeared for a long time and the grey depression in the air seems invincible. The first sip of the sweet wine burned a straight line into her, a bright, vertical streak of joy, stark against the winter's cold fuzziness.

She watched him methodically prepare to shut down the shop – empty an ashtray, count out the notes from his drawer, put on his jacket.

'Do you know of any jobs I could do in Bangalore?' he asked.

'No you can't!' cried Sophie. She would not believe this. Ribor, who was the reason she had made her way back, whose shop was the last vestige of the slow-paced old town Sophie had grown up in, who was so self-contained he had never needed to come down from the hills, this Ribor was now, like everyone else, speaking of leaving.

'I've been doing this for the love of it but it's getting kind of tiring. And I just about break even. A change of scene might be nice.'

'But ...'

'If you can do it I can do it. How hard can it be?'

The whole of the past week weighed upon Sophie – Mr Bhatt, Swami, Ringo, Rukshana, Maya. Wasn't Ribor meant to liberate her from all that?

But Ribor had troubles of his own.

'Some days I don't even feel like opening this hole. I just drive around till there's nowhere to go and I have to get drunk. Sophie, will you do this for me when you go back, look out for something I could do?'

'But,' said Sophie again, biting her lip. 'Things are messed up for me right now so I need to get Bangalore out of my head. Let's talk about something else.' Anu and Shiva would have been to see Ringo and he'd have asked – where's Sophie? The pendulum of guilt and pity started swinging in her head again. She had an overwhelming urge to tell Ribor everything – lay out all the disconnected parts of her world. There's got to be *one* person to whom you confess everything, who is allowed to see your life whole. Or was the ironing board to remain Sophie's lifelong confidante?

Ribor took her arm and led her out as if it was something he did every day. They lit cigarettes on the balcony and talked, as they stood there in the twilight, not about life's big choices but about what had changed and what hadn't in the street below – the new grocery shop with overflowing shelves which you could actually walk through and pick out what you liked, the wily cats that prowled between the fish stalls, the pyramids of fruit that the kongs piled up in baskets before them, changing colour with the seasons. They talked as if they knew each other intimately and for them life moved very, very slowly.

~

Sophie woke up to the muffled sounds her mother made in the kitchen in the icy early morning. Sleep ebbed and flowed in her, her insomnia cured as soon as she'd returned to her childhood bed with its worn-out mattress under which she used to hide all kinds of precious scraps and which she, even now, expected to turn over and find a half-filled notebook, incandescent with nostalgia. As her mother put on the tea kettle and then began to pray in a distant mumble, Sophie lapsed into half-dreams set in these very rooms whose frosted windows eclipsed the world. Things strewn around her, which the previous evening had only signified the house's general disorder, now, in the early morning light, looked like they were all sculpted out of a common shadowy substance.

For a while, her mother's chosen form of escape didn't seem ludicrous because it was at just the right distance from her, not close enough to wake her up and not so far that she'd lose sight of it altogether. She started to believe, in her fuzzy state, that the idea of her parents going away had been a complete misunderstanding – they were only moving to different rooms in the house – her mother to the kitchen, her father to his study. The dream segued into that of another winter when Emma Bovary is sick to the point of throwing up with boredom, when the dew has formed a lace upon the cabbages and the only sound that occasionally breaks the long silence of the windy day is the hollow rattling of the hair-dresser's signboard. Emma does not know it, but Sophie does, that *this* is peace. And while Emma recognizes the stirring of the signboard in the wind as the only paltry sign of life, Sophie would have been happy to command even that one unfixed thing to stillness.

Several hours later, walking with Ribor, this sense of peace remained and she forgot the tears of the previous day. When she'd got to his shop, he suggested they go and meet a friend of his and had bolted up the place so quickly it was clear he was glad to escape from it.

As she and Ribor stood waiting to cross the road, they heard Uncle Rock call from afar 'Just like I said. You walk in the streets of Shillong, you see Uncle Rock.'

Ribor crossed the road in a flash, leaving Sophie to shake hands with Uncle Rock. He wore a huge cowboy hat and had fat coils of a faded tartan shawl wrapped around his neck, almost obscuring his small white face.

'Miss, you must come for the concert. You will never forgive yourself if you don't – it's going to be the biggest night in town.'

He had clearly forgotten her name. 'You never called about the tickets but I have some right here so you can have them. They're only five-hundred rupees – a special rate just for you. I'll be opening for the big man. The little man and the big man.'

He winked at her.

'And I don't know what he'll play but as for me I only play the old stuff. For me it all ended in 1976. I'm going to tell him too when I see him. Mr Bob, I'm sorry to say this but I think for you it all ended in 1976.'

Sophie fished out money for two tickets to a concert by a singer whose career had apparently ended before she was born. Uncle Rock narrowed his eyes at Ribor, who had his back turned to them. 'Do you know that man?' he asked, and for a moment Sophie looked objectively at Ribor – just a man across the street, buying cigarettes.

She wondered if Uncle Rock had noticed them together. 'No,' she said.

'He's a strange one. Used to play for me and then just quit one day. I don't know why. Uncle Rock's philosophy is – if you have a problem with someone, come out and say it. Let's discuss, moh. You may not want to be my friend, but I don't want to be your enemy.'

The man who ran the hotdog joint was called Mama Jo and his café was just three large squares of corrugated tin, a fourth one balanced above to make a roof. A shutter of thin wooden planks with hinges had been partly pulled back, accordion-like, to allow people to enter this little cabin. There was a narrow bench up against one wall for customers; the other walls were fitted with bright yellow shelves that held bottles of ketchup and cooking oil, hotdog buns, a fresh head of lettuce, a row of faded tapes, disposable plastic cups, towels. Mama Jo himself took up the rest of the space, sitting on a low stool, slicing an onion, his skin glowing pink in the heat of the single burner gas stove on which he fried his hotdogs and made coffee.

'Haven't seen you for a long time,' he promptly said to Sophie though she had never met him before. Nor did this joint exist when she lived in Shillong.

'Happy New Year, brother,' he said to Ribor, throwing his

knife up into the air where it somersaulted before he expertly caught its handle and reached for the next onion.

Sophie told him she worked in Bangalore. 'You're a hardworking woman,' he said. People were always saying that. If you left town it was assumed you were going some place where all you did was work.

He wiped his hands, fished frozen sausages out of the basin of water in which they'd been thawing and slipped them into hot oil. Then he sat back, tapping his knife on the edge of the basin in tune with the music. Who was he? He wore an ironed white shirt and clean blue jeans and looked like one of those people whose roots are tangled up in old time Scottish and Welsh missionaries, or entrepreneurial Englishmen who stayed on after 1947.

Ribor was studying a xeroxed flyer for the Dylan concert pasted, lopsidedly, on the wall with the words 'Coming Soon' scrawled below a photo of Dylan.

'They're fighting like cats over him,' said Mama Jo grinning, and then explained. Political parties usually got well-known singers to campaign for them during elections. Since the Bob Dylan concert coincided with the elections, the burning question was – who would Dylan sing for? Mama Jo read out a few paragraphs from the day's paper lying rolled up next to him, according to which Dylan would do well to consider this question with some seriousness. He had a chance to give songs like 'It's All Over Now Baby Blue', 'Knocking on Heaven's Door' or 'The Times are A-Changing' a whole new lease of life were he to sing them in the context of the muck-raking, blatant bribing of the electorate and lack of ideological clarity that were the Meghalaya elections. Given his moral stature, the man needed to do some research before he put his weight behind any particular party. He could, for instance, alter the tenor of state politics if he decided to support the small but significant group of independents – for they were the only ones who regularly updated their websites, used words such as capacity-building and concentrated on issues like rainwater harvesting, instead of, like most of the others, stuffing their already befuddled electorate with rice beer and jah-doh in order to prevent them from thinking.

'They've lost their minds,' said Ribor. 'What are they imagining? Dylan dancing in the back of a truck, shouting with the rest – Ka vote jong phi phin ai ia no? Nga ai ia BDI!'

Mama Jo wagged his knife.

'It's all about money. If any one party can cough up enough dough then. The concert organizers will put up the posters of that party at the concert venue. And Dylan won't even need to know!'

Mama Jo's sentences often stopped at idiosyncratic junctures which heightened their impact. He spoke with the authority a cowboy might have or a fisherman – someone who completely understands how things work in one particular sub-universe.

'That'll be fun – to see Dylan supporting the Rooster party without realizing it,' Sophie said.

'*If* there is a show,' said Ribor. 'I mean how can we take Uncle Rock's word for it? He goes around saying he got an email from Dylan, which is like saying you heard the voice of God. How can one verify a claim like that?' he asked Mama Jo.

'But he is coming. I just bought tickets for the show,' said Sophie. 'For you too.' The look on Ribor's face made her go hot with embarrassment. How could she have been so stupid? Did anything in their conversation during the past two days imply that he'd want to go to a concert with her?

But it wasn't Sophie's forwardness that was causing Ribor to look horrified.

'Tickets? The man's gone mad. Take it from me – Dylan's not coming.'

'How?' asked Mama Jo. 'Do you know?'

Ribor said nothing, waiting for Mama Jo to continue. Mama Jo seemed to be his version of Killer Queen – Sophie noticed a glimmer of respect on Ribor's face every time he spoke.

But Mama Jo was quiet now as he sliced buns, slapped the sizzling sausages onto them and then carefully piled on onions rings, bits of lettuce, slices of tomato and mustard. He handed out the hotdogs, beaming like a proud mother, then put on water for coffee.

Ribor said, 'Why would he come? He's never performed in a big Indian city, why would he choose Shillong? It's not worth the bother.'

'But would Uncle Rock just make it up? I don't understand,'

said Sophie.

Mama Jo said, 'Ribor is a born sceptic, moh? But we should be proud. Because we have the best audience in the country, they know all the words. You missed the New Year concert ... open air ... more than a thousand people. No drunkenness. No one hitting anyone with broken booze bottles. No booing. What do you say to that?'

Sophie knew about the concert. They were still playing the footage on the local television channel.

'Ended at two in the morning. People danced out in the streets all night. You know what this proves?'

Sophie didn't.

'It proves that we can have fun and behave ourselves. At the same time.'

'Amazing.'

'People don't want trouble. They're tired of trouble. Dylan will come and everything will be peaceful, there'll be so much dope and good vibes going around, this town will be like fucking Woodstock. Things have changed. Around here.'

Sitting with her shoulder comfortably nestling against Ribor's, Sophie did not find it hard to believe things had changed from the time her father, out during a curfew imposed after a riot between the local Khasis and the settler Bengalis, had been slapped in the street (and in turn slapped the slapper). From the time when groups of boys who were part of a protest march going past their house had shattered their window panes with the small sharp stones they sent whizzing through the air. From the time Sophie had been asked to give up her seat on a bus because it wasn't her seat after all, or her bus, or her town.

'What's Bangalore like?' asked Mama Jo.

'It's hard to see.'

'MacDonalds everywhere?'

'Or its cousins.'

'Don't send any here.'

'They'll come anyway,' said Ribor, his voice low and calm again. He had eaten his hotdog in three large bites. 'Where do you think all these politicians are getting their money from? Fat cat companies. And what do you think the companies will want once the elections are over?'

'These are the highlands, brother,' said Mama Jo. 'Things work differently. In the highlands.'

'But the money's coming in and money flattens everything.'

'I support the anti-railway guys. We can't have trains here, too much will come in too soon.'

'You don't need trains to destroy things. You just need greed and stupidity.'

Mama Jo handed out plastic cups of coffee. Sophie chewed slowly, wanting to make her hotdog last, wanting to make the whole evening last. She'd heard conversations like these too many times before and she didn't care. She just wanted to think of Sophie and Ribor, Ribor and Sophie. It was like a poem in which two completely unrelated things have been umbilically joined to each other.

Mama Jo said, 'Your brother was here yesterday, talking about his latest business plan. Sounds good, sounds good. He's set up a company called Big Orange.'

'Great,' said Ribor. 'As long as it doesn't involve me.'

'He's going to set up an all-American store.'

'I wouldn't have believed it if he'd told me, but since you're saying it ...'

'He's going to import stuff from all over. Bangalore, Chennai, Thailand, Malaysia. Sell it at a 300 per cent profit,' continued Mama Jo.

'What kind of stuff?' asked Sophie.

'Clothes, knick-knacks, shoes, accessories. The point is that they'll be American brands, so people will go crazy, they'll pay through their noses. And you know what the point is?' asked Mama Jo as he changed the music to the Grateful Dead.

Sophie didn't.

'According to Max, the point is the American stuff isn't made in America. People don't give a damn where it's made. All you must figure out is how to source. Seconds from DKNY and Tommy Hilfiger factories. That's it. What he says is – you can sell this stuff out of any hole. But if you set up a really nice place, a kind of place this town has never seen before, with good lighting and stylish display and space to walk around then that's half the battle won. People pay for how things look. Not what they are.'

'You should advise him to drop these half-baked plans. He'll listen to you.'

Mama Jo smiled a wise smile. 'People talk. I listen. I'm not running anyone's life. I'm okay. Doing the hotdogs.'

'The little dough that Max has is all stolen,' said Ribor.

'Stolen?' asked Sophie.

'He used to steal from rich businessmen or get his goons to extort protection money from them. Even went to jail once for shooting a man. Got out after eight years because one of my uncles became a minister and saw to it that he was freed. Now he's trying to clean up his act and go into business but his money – what's left of it – is still dirty.' Ribor sighed. 'Why do you think I want to move out of this town?'

Sophie was silent, thinking – *I didn't come back to hear you say that.*

'What's your New Year Resolution?' Mama Jo asked Ribor, even though it was the end of January.

Ribor shrugged.

'Come on, brother. Say something.'

'If you really want me to say something then I'll just quote Robert De Niro in Taxi Driver.' Ribor said, then raised a finger and announced – 'Some day a real rain will come and wash all this scum off the streets.'

~

The following morning, Sophie listened again to her mother slowly moving about in the kitchen, and found it possible to believe again, in the mushy greyness of a winter morning, that peace was within reach. If she listened hard she could hear Mrs Das saying her prayers. What did she pray for, a woman who had largely ignored the great imponderables – God, love, death – and put her faith instead in the day-to-day? Hadn't that been the sustaining force once – the idea that even if Sophie had failed to make it to a foreign university, even if Mr Das would never become a professor, even if Muku was unrepentant, there was nevertheless the breakfast to make every morning, the school to go to, the buttons to stitch, the shopping lists to make, the TV serials to watch? Sophie had always felt that tragedy would never penetrate Mrs Das: she had built an invincible wall around herself and nothing gladdened or worried her too much. But now as she boiled the water for tea, she also read the *Bhagavad Gita* aloud to herself, she also sang a bhajan or two.

Sophie suddenly wanted to stop her mother from praying. She went into the kitchen and asked for tea, then she sat warming herself by the heater, still half-asleep.

Mrs Das said, as if resuming some ongoing conversation – 'All this has been going on for some time. You don't know, naturally. You haven't been here. But even before you left … even before you were born …'

Sophie sat with her nose in her tea, flinching at every word her mother said, for much as she believed in the power of the past, it was actually only her own past she was sentimental about. The realization that her mother had one too and that, for the first time, nothing was going to stop her from talking about it, embarrassed Sophie.

Mrs Das had married without her parents' approval. They had violently opposed the idea of her marrying an out-of-work lecturer, a Bengali and a possible communist (a mistaken assumption because Mr Das was actually allergic to politics).

Mrs Das's parents ran two hugely successful restaurants in Delhi; Mrs Das's brother wanted to emigrate to Europe and start a branch there; her parents wanted her to marry the son of a hotelier whom they'd known since she was a little girl; her mother had once told Mrs Das that she wasn't good-looking and ought to consider herself lucky that this chap had been waiting since he was nineteen to marry her; her father hated communists (and all outspoken people were potential communists); her brother believed that Pakistan should be bombed off the face of the earth; they all prayed together in the puja room every morning; they all believed that the only thing more important than money was honour. Mrs Das insulted honour and mocked at money by marrying an unemployed man who visited them only once and neglected to eat the whole tandoori chicken that had been ceremoniously placed before him – the perfectly crisp on the outside and succulent on the inside chicken on which the fortunes of two generations of the family rested. This was virtually the only thing Sophie had known about her parents' past all through her childhood and up to the present: that her father had spurned chicken in her mother's house and that her maternal grandparents therefore cut them off.

As a child she found this story completely plausible; growing up she knew, of course, that there must be more, but she didn't want to know. She didn't want to know where her parents came from: a deliberate lack of curiosity that she now had to pay for. She couldn't budge when her mother described in a completely even voice, how difficult it had been for them in those early years in Delhi. The rejection of the tandoori chicken acquired a sinister symbolism – there was never enough money to cook the food that Mrs Das had been used to eating all her life, let alone go out to a tandoori restaurant.

Then, once Baba got a job in Shillong and they moved here, things got better. Mrs Das described how her kitchen started to smell exactly like her mother's and how this made her feel that she didn't really miss the family that seemed to have no use for her. All the same, she'd written them a letter from Shillong, telling them about Sophie's birth and giving them her address. She opened a small window, just in case. But they clearly didn't care. She learnt many years later that they'd all moved to Amsterdam, all on the strength of a cousin who'd lived there for long years and was convinced Amsterdam badly needed another tandoori restaurant. Whenever Mrs Das had fights with Mr Das, she'd pull out, to comfort herself, the invitation card for his wedding that her brother had sent her – the only piece of communication she had received from them in twenty-five years. Afterwards she would hide the card away – Mr Das never learnt about its existence – and go back to the only life she knew.

Then, six months ago, something changed. Someone called her and said – your mother passed away. It was an anonymous phone call – the foreign-sounding woman hung up before Mrs Das had a chance to say anything. She thought about this for many days and concluded that she had been forgiven. As she lay dying in a strange city, Mrs Das's mother decided to secretly let her daughter know she was missed.

'For years I barely thought about my parents,' she said, sniffing, to Sophie. 'But I feel guilty now.'

Sophie imagined the old lady dying beside the canals and the tulips, oppressed not so much by them as by their distance from her. Maybe she had been sad in the way Sophie imagined elderly Indians trapped in foreign locales to sometimes be. But Sophie had never known her grandmother and it was easy for her to treat her death as a general symptom. Sophie's mother, on the other hand, was taking this personally. As long as her mother resented what she had done, Mrs Das was more or less indifferent; but as soon as the elder woman reached out to her, the daughter felt she'd done her mother a great wrong. Everything was made worse, Mrs Das said, by the fact that her mother was dead. She had spent twenty-five years without speaking to her family – the shock of this struck home only then. After months of praying, she'd decided the only meaningful thing would be to renounce the material world. Her mother was dead, her husband had locked himself into a room to obsess about some mad man in a play, Sophie had found her own way and could take Muku under her wing. In Bangalore Sophie had imagined these conversations with her mother would centre exclusively on the subject of boyfriends, but Mrs Das seemed to have already embarked on the path of renunciation.

'That's why I've decided to go,' she said. The light touched everything now; it was making the city rumble and melting the frost. Little rivulets ran like tears down the cheeks of the windows. Mrs Das wanted to move to Benaras – a city Sophie had never been to but which she strongly associated with death. People went to Benaras to die. Mrs Das had decided to acknowledge death. Some months ago she had embraced God. And now she was talking about her mother, a person she might, more or less, have invented, so strange did the idea of a grandmother appear to Sophie. Sophie looked up from her cold tea and considered her mother's profile as she bent over, kneading dough for the parathas. Sophie realized as if for the first time that her mother was beautiful. And if beauty is a kind of fate then Mrs Das had definitely not fulfilled hers. She'd been standing here morning after morning, making parathas, the closest thing to Madame Bovary Sophie would ever know. And Sophie, instead of saying something in recognition of this insight, said the desperate and selfish thing.

'No,' she said. 'I don't think you should go.'

Vinetta sat in the centre of 'Vinetta's Hotmail Parlour' and tried to outdo Alanis whose voice boomed through the small room which had bubble-gum pink walls overlaid with multicoloured polka dots. Trailing green plastic vines, bunches of fake sunflowers and unnaturally scarlet roses competed with clusters of heart-shaped balloons and crepe paper streamers that hung from the ceiling – decorations for an inauguration party that Vinetta seemed to have been anticipating for years. In addition to offering Internet services on five computers squashed into tiny wooden booths, Vinetta also had on sale the madly eclectic contents of a tall glass-fronted cabinet. Crammed into this were small jars of sweets, handmade baskets, Christmas decorations, cigarettes, condoms, little hardbound books of inspiring quotations with multiple red hearts on their covers, screwdrivers, bottles of orange honey, stereo speakers, cold cream, chewing gum and countless other odds and ends, none of which Sophie had ever seen anyone buy. Vinetta didn't seem to care. Making money out of this enterprise seemed to be an afterthought. The primary purpose of 'Vinetta's Hotmail Parlour' was to reflect Vinetta's personality, which, judging from the place, was maniacally cheerful.

Sophie's inbox, when she accessed it on a computer black from overuse, contained so many emails from Maya that she feared a calamity of some sort and shut her eyes. It was still new in her – Maya's lacerated voice and her hands on Sophie's face trying to extract a promise of something Sophie had not dared closely consider.

'I adore shopping in Bangalore,' sang out Vinetta, unseen, over the music. She was saving for her next trip and catalogued for Sophie's benefit the best places to buy handbags, the friends she had made among thrift shop owners, and the incredible bargains to be had on ladies shoes.

Sophie opened her eyes to the first of the emails, which came with the photographs Maya had taken of her, and Sophie, who very rarely saw photos of herself, was flabbergasted. She didn't look in the least bit familiar. She looked like a girl who might have her own thoughts and wishes, separate from, even in opposition to, Sophie's.

Vinetta described a new excitement – the interiors of a

nightclub in town, it's first proper one, which she was going to help design. The theme would be seventies pop and the colours would be red and black combined with lots of smoky mirrors and bead curtains, and the waitresses would all have fringes and wear bellbottoms.

Sophie interjected with 'oohs' and 'wows' from her cubicle. She was glad to have her talking – she needed Vinetta's bubblegum happiness and uncomplicated heart-shaped love to offset this – this deluge of mails from Maya who had suddenly turned scary to her. The next mail was full of gossip about Shanthi's wedding. Maya hadn't attended but heard from those who had that the opulent wedding reception started well but degenerated when Shanthi's schizophrenic mother shouted at Shanthi's newly-acquired father-in-law, accusing him of staring at her 'with big, big eyes'. And Naomi had cried along with the others when Shanthi left for her husband's house. After which she'd flown back to LA with henna patterns on her hands and was reportedly working out some way to come back to India. 'If she comes back to Star Titles and gets into her damned sari fetish again, I'm going to have to fucking run,' wrote Maya, and Sophie smiled, then stopped smiling, because the next mail was a kind of love letter. Maya swore that the whole Naomi thing was a joke and that Sophie was the one. She outlined in detail the kind of life they could share (where they could holiday, where they would go shopping in the weekends, how they would redo her kitchen) if only Sophie gave up her 'bloody boyfriend fixation'.

Sophie stared, riveted, at the screen. So this is what Maya had meant when she said – you have to do something to deserve seeing the photos. Outside, traffic rumbled past making the room vibrate. She felt trapped in that little booth but dared not emerge from it at once for fear of what her face might betray. She breathed deeply a few times, and then noticed, right at the bottom of her inbox, a mail from Swami. She could not deal with Maya whispering into one of her ears and Swami into the other; she deleted his message without reading it, turned her chair around and leaned against the cubicle wall. Maya would never find her. She would disappear into a place like this, the kind of place that was Shillong's hope. Once the town had been full of them – dusty second-hand bookshops with catatonic owners, alcoves in which dignified men stood selling hardboiled sweets out of massive jars, pakori shops that blasted heat into the street from their eternal frying. Nowadays most shops were housed in unpainted concrete boxes fitted into larger concrete blocks, and enterprises like Vinetta's parlour and Mama Jo's café and Ribor's 'Strings' and the bread shop of her childhood had become magical by contrast. One of Sophie's adolescent dreams was to start a tea shop in some tucked away, sun-filled room and spend her days dozing there or reading magazines, while the day's two visitors came and left. It seemed the most romantic thing then, before her father convinced her that nothing stood between her and a good scholarship and before her mother reminded her that dkhars were not encouraged to run establishments in this town.

Sophie emerged without reading the last mail.

'I hope it's a boy because then I can call him Dylan,' said Vinetta. She patted her pregnant stomach proudly.

The boy she was talking to – whose hair was so severely gelled that the spikes looked like they could hurt – believed that it was a CNN report that had changed everything. 'It was on the CNN, that we love Dylan. I mean, people must be asking him – have you heard of this little town in India where they worship you, and he'd have to say – nope, I know nothing about it.'

'For him, it's like going to any old place but for us it's such a big thing, moh. Just deciding what snacks to give him with the tea is making people nervous. My grandmother is worried if he'll like kwai or not.'

The boy clicked his tongue. 'We don't have to please him. It's because of people like us he's so big in the first place.'

Vinetta brought out a T-shirt with the words 'Bah Bob is Coming Home' printed above a cartoon sketch of the singer, his already large mop of hair exaggerated, and what looked like a beedi in his mouth. 'Only eighty bucks. They're selling like hot putharo.'

The boy suddenly looked worried. 'I hope we don't screw up things. I hope the sound is fantastic and the stage doesn't look like a rickety Durga Puja pandal.'

Sophie was trying to determine what exactly she owed Maya, for the thought that she did owe Maya something had started to bother her now. So despite not wanting to, she went back in and clicked open the last of her mails. In this, Maya informed Sophie that they'd both been fired from Star Titles. The CEO, Ravi Patil, had been discreet enough not to tell Maya why he was asking her to move on, but Maya knew it was something to do with the 'American bitch'. 'What exactly did you tell her about me?' Maya asked, and Sophie shifted in her chair in discomfort, though the truth was she hadn't told Naomi Picks a thing.

Ravi had added insult to injury by firing Sophie (whom he knew was Maya's pet) as well. 'I know this is brutal but on the other hand maybe it's the finger of fate pointing and I don't need to tell you which direction it's pointing in,' wrote Maya.

Sophie stumbled out and couldn't help exclaiming – 'I've lost my job.'

Vinetta said, 'Darling I know lots of job openings in Bangalore.' It turned out that as a result of the large number of cousins and friends and acquaintances and nieces of Vinetta's that had moved to Bangalore, she carried a version of naukri.com in her head. Even though Sophie was still trying to digest this piece of brutality and nowhere near ready to set out job-hunting, it was oddly comforting to sit there below the red balloons and the fluttering streamers and let Vinetta convince her (even as she kept the Dylan discussion going with the spiky-haired boy) that the least terrible thing that could happen to anyone in Bangalore was losing a job.

I Must Unpack My Heart with Words

Sophie found herself walking urgently towards Ribor's shop as if it were a shrine to which she must return every time there was trouble. This time Ribor himself looked troubled.

'There was a reporter here,' he said. 'He just left. They think I have some kind of hotline to Dylan and can check the facts with him. Some big-shot politician from the Rooster party is claiming he paid fifty lakh rupees to the event management company organizing the show so that he and his colleagues could use Dylan's name in their campaign. The company is saying – sorry, Dylan's agent has said a categorical no, his name or image is not to be used in any way in the elections. And they're denying having taken any money. The politician can't produce a signed contract. He says he gave it in good faith. It's probably black money. The politician could have handed it over to them in some seedy bar.'

'Why do the newspaper guys think you know anything about it?'

Ribor looked at her for a long moment, then said, 'Let's get out of here. They might come back and I can't go on pretending that I've never heard of Bob Dylan's plan to take Shillong by storm. Do you want to come to my place?'

Two hours later, her eyes shut, her left ear listening to Ribor's calm heartbeat, her right ear cold from the draught that came through the open window over which a blue-checked curtain had been drawn, Sophie started to lapse into the same dream of peace and happy endings she'd been dreaming the last few mornings. But this was afternoon, a small, private afternoon they'd created, enclosed within the larger one. And this was an adult love, even though Sophie felt like a child allowed into a fantasy. She knew it wasn't the same for Ribor, that his hard embrace was driven by some other need. Her own need was purely dramatic – she could be someone else in this room, she could enter the story of someone else's life. And it didn't matter to Sophie what Ribor was thinking; she was absorbed in the breathtaking symmetry of wanting. If they talked they'd say different things and express different problems (Max and Maya, Shillong and Bangalore), but lying together like this there was no discordance, and for once Sophie felt like a complete thing, free of the anxiety over the usual missing bits.

Ribor moved away and put a disc in the CD player, then returned to the same position, his right arm around her shoulders. His shirt smelt of sunshine. Occasionally, a breeze lifted the curtain revealing nothing but distant sounds – the honking of cars, the rumble of buses, the small, indeterminate noises a city makes in the afternoon.

Ribor sat up again. 'Tea,' he said.

She felt abandoned when he moved away. From the bed one could look into the small kitchen – a neat row of glass jars, a hotplate, Ribor setting out two matching mugs that could have belonged to a married couple.

'It's like your shop, this house,' Sophie said but wasn't able to explain how. It had something to do with its child-like smallness, the way it looked down onto the streets, like a peephole from the sky. Ribor appeared to live an orderly life in his one room hideout. A small couch in the corner. A pile of magazines. Two pairs of boots by the wall, carefully aligned with each other. A dresser of dark wood.

The sounds of a spoon tinkling against a cup and a crow

cawing nearby had a pristine clarity to them. She stored them away like she stored the patterns of checks on the curtain, the words of the song that was playing, the smell of Ribor's shirt. Maybe that's why people need each other, she thought as he came in with the tea: to satisfy nostalgia. The memory will never be good enough and we'll come back even if only to find out whether the memory was true or if it lied. She pulled her jeans back on under the blanket.

'I have to tell you something,' said Ribor, handing her a mug but not looking at her.

The future, the future, prayed Sophie. An escape plan, a tunnel burrowed through reality which takes you to the other side.

'This Dylan thing is a joke.' He looked her in the eye finally and said, 'He's not coming, you know.'

The story began five years ago when Ribor was occasionally playing guitar at Uncle Rock's gigs. For a while, Uncle Rock managed to get together a bunch of musicians who sounded good, so Ribor suggested they write some lyrics and maybe cut an album. Uncle Rock agreed and they worked on this for some months, trying out some of the material during their live shows and talking to a producer in Bombay who seemed interested. Just as they were going to sign a recording contract, Uncle Rock decided he didn't want to do it. He said something about how they needed to do more work before they were really ready to record. But he probably started to feel things were getting too cosy, said Ribor.

'He didn't want to be in a band, it would diminish him. But he wanted me to continue being his session's man which was bloody selfish so I quit. Some of the other guys also drifted away and started up their own bands, so he got a new bunch of people together and they'd actually play the stuff we'd all worked on together. He still does it and passes it off as his own. Anyway, I don't give a damn really. I just don't want to deal with him. A few weeks ago he buttonholed me on the street and he said – I'm going to write to Dylan's manager. So many people have been trying to get him to come, but I'm the one who's going to do it. Just wait and see.

'That evening there's a party at a friend's place and my

brother Max is there. He's another guy I cross the street when I see. We're all joking about Uncle Rock, and I say – I'm going to send him an email saying, this is God, otherwise known as Dylan. I hear you've been talking to my manager. Let's jam together in Shillong man, what are you waiting for? I'd been drinking for a couple of hours, I was just letting myself talk shit. And Max gets all excited and says – do it. Give him what he wants. I forget about that party till I hear the rumours. I just ignore them. Max is having some fun and everything will die down by itself. As usual I've underestimated my brother. That's why I was horrified when Mama Jo said, they're fighting over him for the elections. So I call Max and he says that after sending an email in Dylan's name to Uncle Rock, he went to him and said – let my company, Big Orange, handle everything. So he starts selling tickets, he makes T-shirts, he brings in sponsors, he suggests to the politicians that Dylan might be interested in the elections because he used to sing political songs in the sixties. He's created a whole fucking circus around this and it's going to blow up in someone's face soon.'

Sophie laughed out loud in amazement. 'What a hell of a scam!'

'And the bastard's been using my shop as an office address. So now a reporter turns up there asking me why Dylan is no longer interested in campaigning for the elections and where has the politician's money gone? It's gone into Max's pockets, that's where it's gone.'

'What'll Max do on the night of the concert when people want their money back?'

'He'll probably be on a flight to Delhi, ride out the heat, spend the money partying. He's been to prison once, he has no scruples. Sophie, do you think we could escape to Bangalore till this dies down?'

Bangalore again. Sophie considered it for a moment – she and Ribor alone in her place, the world shut out the way it always was the moment she met him. But in Bangalore, she was afraid Bangalore would intrude upon them, that Ribor's magic would not be able to hold it at bay. She told him about the murder, the news that she'd just been fired, the fact that if she turned up with Ribor, her landlord would promptly turn her out of the house. She was surprised, then, at the extent of her own troubles and how faded they seemed in this room that love had made vivid. Would he believe that anyone could be in such fantastic shit?

But all Ribor said, with the politeness of a stranger, was: 'Sorry, I really didn't know you had so much to deal with' as if he hadn't kissed her on the stairs, as if she hadn't followed him to a place where it was okay to have your shirt unbuttoned with one hand and your hair stroked with the other.

'Tell me about your art,' said Sophie, lighting a cigarette.

'Yeah, right. I was going to be this big-time artist. When I was eight years old, a teacher put one of my drawings on the bulletin board and after that I thought it was my God-given right that my doodling be admired. Every year I would wait for the art teacher to put my work up. Most of the teachers didn't care for that kind of thing – being nice to just one or two kids. But then I won an inter-school drawing competition and my work went up on the board again. After waiting breathlessly for, like, five years.' He smiled.

'What did you draw?'

'My mother. She's sitting at the table and drinking tea and looking out of the window. It was a pencil sketch. She used to get up very early in the morning. And I would wake up with her and sit at the table and be the artist. When I was in college, she was sick for a week and I would go to hospital every day after classes. She couldn't eat, so they put her on a drip but then she got a little better. I would go and help her eat lunch every afternoon. When they told me she's dead, I just lost my head for a while. I remember trying to feed her, asking her to open her mouth, begging her to eat. It's strange what happens to you when a person dies. Afterwards I made copies of her picture and gave one to everyone in the family.'

Sophie stubbed her cigarette in a saucer. So they were not alone in the world, after all. This room was not a private heaven.

'I didn't draw after that.'

And that poem she had invented – Sophie and Ribor, Ribor and Sophie – was a theme running in her head and no one else's.

'You look too serious,' said Ribor, laughing. That old Shillong laugh that could disguise so much. That quick Shillong kiss that promised nothing.

~

What had Killer Queen meant by saying that it would end on the last page? The view from the parapet was in some ways like it had always been – a man with a paunch and sagging jeans picking the remains of a Chinese lunch from his teeth, the mottled shadow of the weeping willow on the cobblestone path sloping down to the little kindergarten run by the ancient Mrs Hill, the overcrowded buses leaning to one side as they puffed round the bend, the paan shop where Jagjivan Ram sat cross-legged all day, occasionally flicking water from a paan leaf, stacks of which he kept floating in a steel bucket so that they stayed fresh. The paunchy man would stand there for a while ogling at passing girls; then, overcome with restlessness at their unattainability, he'd drop his toothpick and saunter off. In the afternoon, Mrs Hill's long-haired daughter would unlatch the gate with a wicker basket on her arm and go shopping. And the tinted glass front of Laboratory Aids would remain as inscrutable as it had been in her childhood.

Perhaps Killer Queen meant there was no use trying to resist the inevitable, thought Sophie, as she returned to the porch and slumped back into her easy chair. Her sister was painting purple whorls onto dirty canvas shoes. Every winter, when they were growing up, Sophie and Muku would take up separate positions in the small porch where the sun shone brightest at 11 o'clock, the wavy shadow of the tin roof high up on the face of the house. This was a common wintertime pursuit – sunning oneself, slowly going brown in a heat that was as intense as it was short-lived. Sophie had been sitting there for hours, meditating on Ribor and the still-attractive possibility of running away with him, till his name became a sweet stupefaction that shut out all other thoughts. Maya's emails seemed like minor distractions, being unemployed had become a half-remembered embarrassment, and even Muku was tolerable as long as she was absorbed in something – destroying a perfectly good pair of shoes, making extraordinary faces at herself in a pocket mirror, or going across the street to call Pavan and returning with news of every random thought that passed through his largely empty brain. Sophie yawned and stretched her legs, accidentally kicking the breakfast plate she'd left there that morning. Mrs Das had made aloo parathas whose sizzling, crisp surfaces, golden with mustard oil, she'd seared with ghee. Sophie ate two, delighting in the exquisite glut of grease, but by the third one had begun feeling disgusted at herself. This heavy food seemed to only emphasize her state of dissolution. Once she had cancelled her return ticket to Bangalore and lied to her family about having called office and taken sick leave because she still felt burnt-out, all Sophie had done for days was eat – pulaos with raisins swollen to a grape-like fatness, gravies dark with the juice of well-browned onions, meat carved into precise shapes as if it was not just going to be chomped down like everything else. All of them continued to eat as if nothing were the matter. Listening through the open door to the tinkling sounds of her mother's preparations for lunch, she wondered if it were not the reverse: as long as they continued to eat like always, they could pretend nothing *was* the matter.

As always, Mr Das (his self-imposed exile notwithstanding) put on his old jacket to go shopping for groceries, as always Mrs Das asked right after breakfast what she should cook for lunch, as always Muku was put to the task of chopping the vegetables and Sophie to making chappatis, as always cooking fulfilled some primitive routine. Sophie, fresh from a year of eating instant noodles and aware of how heroic it is possible to feel after turning out a chicken curry (actually wresting something coherent out of raw meat and haphazardly chopped onions and random amounts of spice powder), still felt there was something oppressive about this search for familial harmony through food.

'Have you talked to them?' asked Muku finally.

Sophie said nothing, concentrating on the rafters supporting the porch roof, which were the colour of toffee. She was going to join Ribor in the slow-moving song that was his life. She would spend a lifetime of winters noticing small things like the kind of shadows weeping willows make in the afternoon and how rafters can sometimes look edible. The very things about Shillong that had once seemed stultifying now seemed poetic. But Muku had run out of things to do before she slipped away for her evening date with Pavan, the leather overcoat absurdly and ineffectively hidden from her parents in a bulging plastic bag. And silence always started up dangerous trains of thought in her mind.

'Did you tell them that you met Pavan and he's fine? That he's not a junkie or anything.'

Sophie refused to consider her sister.

'Just because you're not saying anything it doesn't mean you're any better.'

When her father gave up and bought the television Sophie used to ache for, she had relinquished her childhood fantasy of having been adopted from parents infinitely more glamorous than her provisional ones. She'd invented another narrative for herself – the long-running story of being Muku's sole parent. Mr and Mrs Das never noticed, but Sophie and Muku were lodgers in their house. Sophie had to work hard to pay the rent and she liked to come back home from work and take her one-year-old daughter out for an evening stroll – a middle-aged woman balancing on her high heels, her long-strapped bag slipping off her shoulder, her unruly hair hiding half her face. It wasn't in the least bit strange that the man and woman who lived in that house, and occasionally watched from the doorway, never carried Muku or put her to sleep or combed her hair. Does she remember? wondered Sophie. For the first time that afternoon she sneaked a look at her sister. How could she possibly have forgotten? Muku caught her looking and for a few moments the sisters stared nakedly at each other.

'I'm going to ask Baba if we can all have lunch together. So that for once we talk,' said Sophie.

'About everything?'

Sophie nodded.

'Just two years more,' said Muku with a genuine note of pleading in her voice and Sophie found herself actually feeling sorry for her sister, for the fact that she had lived for so long with people who'd grown colder and colder till they had nothing left to say to each other.

Mr Das agreed to eat lunch with the rest of his family as if this were the most natural thing to do. They heaped their plates from the massive pot of biriyani in the kitchen and everyone except Mr Das drifted towards the sitting room.

'Can we switch it off?' asked Sophie of the television.

'No, it's time for one of my weekly serials,' said Mrs Das. 'I can't miss that.'

'But I want to talk,' said Sophie.

'Talk, talk. No one's stopping you.'

Sophie took a deep breath, then suddenly realized that she didn't know the words in which this was done – accosting one's parents, holding them responsible, compelling them to explain. It was exactly what Maya had said – one has lost the language. She started to pick on her rice, frustration making it hard to swallow.

'There's nothing to talk about really,' said Mr Das from the dining room. 'Everyone has their own priorities here. Some people can't function unless they watch television, others find it hard to stay in the house for two hours at a stretch.'

'I only watch three serials a week. They're the only thing I look forward to,' said Mrs Das.

'I want to ...' started Sophie.

'It's all been decided in your absence, Sophie. You have every right to ask,' said Mrs Das, her eyes trained on the screen.

'Sophie, it's very simple. I'm going to Shantiniketan, I've had enough,' said her father. Sophie stood up and, clutching her plate, moved from one corner of the room to another, till she found a spot from where she could see both parents at once.

'Even if it means breaking down the family?' she asked.

'I don't want to go to Bangalore,' chipped in Muku, riding on her sister's boldness.

'Mukulika, what you want is not in question,' said her father.

The latest episode of Mrs Das's favourite serial involved a heavily made-up woman who was in love with one man but forced to marry another. Her lover had turned up, Batman-like, on the balcony of the hotel room where the reluctant couple was honeymooning. The woman confessed to being torn between karma and dharma. Should she follow the logic of her own desires or should she heed the demands of duty? Mrs Das, while absorbed in the unfolding of this moral dilemma, was able to keep one ear open to the awkward discussion Sophie was trying to conduct.

'You're only thinking of yourselves,' said Sophie. They were the strongest words she had ever used with her parents and she wanted to run out of the room. Even Muku went silent at this – the betrayal by the favourite child.

Mrs Das said, 'Who thinks of anyone else? I asked Muku to be in the house the day you came, but does she care?'

'I had basketball practice,' said Muku.

No one responded, so she pushed the envelope. 'As if Sophie's the prime minister that we all have to stand in a line to receive her.'

'You think I don't know what you're up to? I'm going to put an end to it soon, just wait and see,' said her mother, her eyes suddenly ablaze.

Mrs Das always spoke in Hindi when she was angry, as if alongside berating her children or husband, she was also mocking at the English in which they argued with her.

Mr Das said, with steel in his voice, 'There's nothing left for us in Shillong.'

He'd used the word 'us' seemingly after years. He was saying – you and your sister were just interludes and now we're going back to where we came from. Sophie realized she was right as a child, when she'd slung Muku on her hip and thought coldly as she marched on the lawn about the man and woman who lived in the house. That man and that woman, those people.

And yet ... and yet: wasn't it her father who had stamped his angularities on her by giving her this name. Sophie Das. What kind of a name was that? She'd spent her whole childhood trying to explain (no, she wasn't Christian, Anglo-Indian, half-Khasi, or hiding her real name – Sophie Das was just what she was called). Eventually she had stopped explaining and decided to remain the oddity implied by her name. Hadn't she been faithful to her father just by staying Sophie Das?

'So why did you come here at all then?' she asked, trying to keep her voice reasonable yet feeling a raging determination to burn down one bridge after another. From the TV a crescendo of drums heralded yet another dramatic turn in the life of the woman with dyed blonde hair and a turquoise blue sari. Then a commercial break intervened and her mother snapped out of her hypnosis.

'Sophie, you went to Bangalore – it's the same thing. People move, we moved here, now we're moving out.'

'No, it's not the same thing.'

'You don't understand. I don't want to stand in that kitchen any more. I don't want to go to school and see the same faces. One is supposed to meditate on where one is going next. People have been doing it for centuries. You don't know about these things because you've grown up cut off from the real world.'

Sophie wanted her parents to acknowledge their troubles with each other but it seemed like this was not part of the official reason for their wanting to go away.

'Sophie, there are some things that must remain mysterious, you have to learn that. Like Hamlet says, 'I have that within which passes show, these but the trappings and the suits of woe',' said her father from the dining table where he sat eating his meal with old-fashioned decorum – a glass of water, a salt shaker, a few dwarf green chillies and a bowl of sliced onion doused in lemon juice arranged neatly around his plate. The sight of her father eating alone there was oddly moving and like always he had Hamlet on his side. He had literature on his side while Sophie had nothing except Ribor who was a secret and a very new secret at that.

'Can't you wait for just two more years?' asked Muku in a last ditch effort, seeing her fate was close to being sealed.

'What will change in two years?' asked her mother, suddenly suspicious. Then the serial resumed and she instantly lost interest in her own question.

Sophie asked: 'Why can't all three of you move to Shantiniketan ... or Benaras?'

'Your mother doesn't want to come with me. And Mukulika will be with you, that's where she belongs.'

'But what if Bangalore doesn't work for me? What if I want to come back?'

'Has something gone wrong?' asked her mother.

Sophie nodded in the negative with her head bent, regretting now that she had said this.

'Whatever happens, you're not coming back here, Sophie. You've moved on,' said her father, dismissing two-and-a-half decades of their lives with the wave of a hand in which he held a half-eaten chilli.

Mrs Das aimed the remote at the television and lowered the

volume. She started to catalogue the good things in Sophie's life. 'You have your own flat, which you always wanted, you can afford to come and meet us whenever you want, you have a well-paying job.'

Sophie caught Muku's eye and saw the fight go out of her. Her blackmail was irrelevant now. Even if she told her parents that Sophie had made up her job, would they care? Would they care if Sophie told them she had just been fired from her real job or that she was in love with someone who ran a shop ten minutes down the road?

Meanwhile, the father of the woman in the serial had learnt about his daughter's waywardness and his conscience was now delivering a monologue for the benefit of the viewers – how on earth could he have fathered a child so duplicitous? How would he face his son-in-law's parents? In response to these hard questions, the curtains in his room fluttered wildly and outside a storm raged.

A wave of determination rose in Sophie. She was going to stay on in Shillong and find a way to make a life with Ribor.

'Okay. I won't question what you do and you don't question me. Ever.'

'Sophie!' said her mother, while her father stared at her with an intensity that could have been either affection or its opposite.

Sophie marched off to the kitchen. She tried to fight down panic by scraping the food from her plate into the bin, something she had never done before because it was considered sacrilege in the Das household – however angry the tears, however bad the fights, food was never wasted.

As she went out into the garden, her mother said to Muku in a low voice, 'We'll find you a hostel in Bangalore. You don't have to stay with her if that's what the problem is.'

They've got it completely wrong, thought Sophie, slumping down under an orange tree and lighting a cigarette. She just hadn't been able to make them see. She listened to the completely normal sounds coming through the open door – her father's fork scraping against his plate, the undecided woman tearfully begging her lover to forgive her, an incorrigible Muku asking if she could go out and play basketball, her mother silent, lost in television.

Each member of a family is the clear mirror in which the

others see themselves – unflattering, familiar, comforting pictures of themselves. As she had grown older, Sophie had understood it – the delicate balance between resentment and affection, bitterness and fellow feeling. It was the work they did together behind the walls – her father insisting he could not take another day of adolescent brainlessness and then going out half an hour later, in keeping with tradition, to get the fish. Her mother swearing that in this good-for-nothing town Sophie and Muku had, insofar as culture was concerned, learnt not the first letters of the alphabet, yet content to just stuff them with biriyani as if that could fill the vacuum that culture had left unfilled. Overnight, it seemed, no one needed this arduous give and take anymore. They didn't need her either – standing between them as if on the axis of a scale and tipping in whichever direction was necessary to provide balance. She was alone from now on. She was her own context.

~

Sophie had her already short hair cropped so that it was plastered to her head like a pixie's. She stood in the parking lot outside the sports arena, awkward and alone, enclosed by the hectic sounds of people coming into their element – mothers yelling affectionate warnings to their straying toddlers, sons standing by cars and helping – with many shouts and gestures – their fathers reverse park them, friends calling to each other in voices of delighted recognition, voices that affirmed their right to be in this place at this time. There was a smell in the air to match these sounds, the electrifying smell of affluence – of perfume, pressed silk, shoe polish, car interiors. Sophie felt shorn in her new haircut. Then Ribor appeared and everything turned as soft as rain.

The previous day they'd visited Mama Jo's shack again and like the last time his knife had flown in the air between the onions and he'd whistled along with the blues on the player.

Ribor said, 'It's all my fault – I should have never opened my big mouth at that party and put this idiotic idea in Max's smack-fuddled brain.'

Mama Jo smiled a consoling smile. 'Shit happens but on the other hand miracles are born. Everyday.'

'Do you know how he's planning to get out of this mess? By

leaving me to deal with twenty thousand disappointed fans.'

'Relax, brother, relax,' said Mama Jo, handing him a steaming hotdog. 'Dylan moves in mysterious ways. And Max is not going to call off the concert in advance. Because that'll give the fans a chance to go berserk. He'll pretend everything is normal. I was chatting with Max and suggested that just before Bah Bob is to come on, Max announce that Bah Bob got his nose broken in a pub brawl and missed the flight.'

'Who'll believe that?' asked Sophie.

'But he'll refund everyone's tickets. No one will be mad at Max. And he understands – it was fun while it lasted but he's got to give people their money back.'

'And what about the money he took from the Rooster party? In return for letting them use Dylan's name in their campaign speeches?' asked Ribor.

'It wasn't him. Haven't you read today's paper?' asked Mama Jo. He wiped his hands and unfurled the paper. (This appeared to be one of his self-appointed functions – to read out the newspaper while the hotdogs fried or the water boiled for coffee; in another place and time he might have been the town crier, the king's messenger.)

As per the report, two members of a new and small political party (an ex-army captain and his sidekick) had been caught in a hotel room with a huge amount of cash on their hands. The newspaper described this as a 'sensational seizure' and spokespersons of other parties decried the 'money power' that was distorting the elections.

Where had the money come from and why was it under the bed on which candidates of this relatively minor party (known by its election symbol – Betel Nut – rather than by its name) sat drinking Royal Stag? They couldn't have got rich businessmen to sponsor them because rich businessmen were busy sponsoring the guys who were likely to win the elections. According to the paper it was a bribe. Someone in the Rooster party – the largest in the state – had been doing some thinking and figured that there was very little chance it would come to power on its own. On the other hand, it was bound to win a decent number of seats. It was crucial therefore to buy up as many parties as possible before the election results were declared and the horse-trading started in earnest.

'Don't you see?' asked Mama Jo.

Neither Ribor nor Sophie could, so Mama Jo explained. Rooster had bribed Betel Nut. Rooster also claimed they'd given Big Orange fifty lakh rupees as payment for appropriating Dylan. Big Orange swore it was a lie. So? The Dylan business was a red herring. The Rooster politician who had put out the claim probably needed to explain to someone (A nosy colleague? A businessman who had donated him black money?) where that money had gone and he'd concocted the Dylan-related story.

'Perhaps the Rooster guy also wanted to take revenge on Max for something that might have happened in the past,' said Mama Jo with a look Sophie was learning to recognize, a look that suggested he knew much more than he revealed.

'There are lots of people waiting to take revenge on Max,' said Ribor.

Mama Jo proceeded to read out the editorial. It had not picked up the connection he had just made, but nevertheless stated that something murky was going on in which, inadvertently perhaps but not without a degree of culpability, Dylan had a hand. The singer clearly knew what a minefield the Meghalaya elections were and was it not his responsibility, given that he was coming here during election time, to issue a clear statement about his position, instead of letting speculation run rife and giving people the licence to claim that money had changed hands in his name?

Dylan, said the editorial, had 'failed the litmus test' by turning out to be just a showman like the rest of them and not taking a position on Meghalaya politics. Within the Rooster, 'the left hand did not know what the right one was doing' even though both seemed to be working overtime, trying to 'sell refrigerators to Eskimos' and 'turning a blind eye' to the fact that their electorate was fed up of them. With the news of this huge bribe 'the die had been cast' and it was up to the voters now, over whom 'hung the Damocles sword' of coalition politics.

Sophie started daydreaming (as Mama Jo rambled on) about living in Shillong with Ribor and writing newspaper editorials like this one, building up a marvellous stock of idioms with which to decorate problems rather than analyse them – resonant phrases such as 'all shambolic icing, no substantive cake' or 'defying the current like a trout rather than clamping up like an oyster'.

Now Sophie and Ribor were at the concert, anxious to see how the fiction of Bob Dylan would resolve itself; perhaps they even wished in some childish corner of their hearts that he would actually appear, that Max's scam would, through the sheer force of its perversity, overtake him and manage to upturn his lies.

First came the opening acts. A leading composer had put to music a tribute in verse to Dylan written by a leading Khasi poet. This was sung by a choir of uniformly gorgeous girls in silk jainsems accompanied by two boys on guitars. The astonishing range of harmonies produced by the girls and the grand gesticulations of the composer, a big, thickset man with something approaching a leer on his face, his baton an ecstatic blur and his thin long hair whipping about his face, made the song appear sublime. Then a tiny, emaciated man with outsized glasses – chosen as if to contrast with the composer – came on and read out an English translation of the poem in a whisper and the song deflated into merely corny – '... you say you've gone alone but what about the countless songs that always thrill ... you say you've lost direction but no! you've made your way to these eastern hills ...' An ex-politician traced the Dylan-induced awakening of his youth – moved by 'Don't Think Twice' he had, in opposition to his dear mother's wishes, become a potato farmer and rejected the 'fansy-pansy IAS officer career'. It was a long journey from the potato farm to the legislative assembly; his rambling speech was enlivened only by his tendency to suffix every second word with 't'. Ribor started mimicking him in an undertone, but Sophie, her hand growing warm in his, heard nothing. She dreamt on indiscriminately. She imagined marriage – a long-running, always light-hearted conversation. She imagined living in rooms like peepholes in the sky.

A band from Delhi now appeared on the giant screens that relayed the action. It was led by a fantastically thin, womanish creature with a wild shock of frizzy hair who introduced himself simply as Pandey and bounced about the stage signing Dylan songs to the accompaniment of screeching electric guitars till he was cut short by representatives of the May 24th Committee which organized solemn birthday concerts in honour of the singer. Their leader made a speech recounting the more rousing of these annual events, appealed for contributions and bowed low before Dylan, anointing him a 'fairy light in a hostile world'. A tribal musician in a short sarong and a black shawl draped cross-wise around one shoulder, sang liltingly in his own secret language – his songs appeared to have passed through Dylan and come out sweeter on the other side.

Ribor said, 'I thought once of calling you after you'd left town, but in the end I didn't want to mess with the life you were leading there.'

'But I want to move back here,' said Sophie and told him about her parents separating, now that they had spurned her reconciliation efforts. 'I want to stay in my childhood home till I die.'

He said nothing but kissed her furtively, and she tried to be pleased because he was the very opposite of Swami – Swami thrived on the romance of the long-term; Ribor shrunk from it.

Two hours after they'd started, the opening acts continued unabated.

The legendary Shillong musician – Bah Lou – who had, all those decades ago, inaugurated the Dylan mania, appeared in his flowing grey hair to rapturous applause and blessed the proceedings by singing 'The Times are A-Changing'.

Old-time preachers spoke about their nostalgia for Dylan's religious phase; ethereal-voiced women were granted seven minutes each for 'Sara' and 'Girl from the North Country'; schoolchildren stood in a row and inappropriately sang 'I Want You'.

Finally, Uncle Rock came on. He staggered on his matchstick-thin legs to the mike. It was possible he was drunk.

'Ladies and gentlemen,' he shouted.

Where was Max with the vital announcement? Ribor started to shift worriedly in his seat.

'There are only two things that are absolutely true today. One is that I am forty years old, wish me happy birthday, and the other … the other …'

He embarked on a do-or-die tribute to Dylan without completing his sentence. He really believed all it took was a simple twist of fate, that being like a rolling stone got you tangled up in blue, that you needed to keep an ear out for the chimes of freedom, that after braving buckets of rain, you reached the gates of Eden, knocked on heaven's door, took shelter from the storm and stayed forever young. He played out the lines with such passion and flair, such a doggone faith in the lines, that the shy man Sophie had seen on the Bangalore stage seemed pretended. Here, prancing about drunkenly as the crowd cheered him on, or singing sad ballads that hushed the stadium to silence, Uncle Rock was at home. Directly below the stage, a small army of boys were dancing in a jerky, robotic fashion. Sophie, to whom all time before the late eighties was indistinct, thought of how there must have been a year, a month when all this was new – when Shillong witnessed a Dylan concert for the first time, when there were people to whom the words of 'Desolation Row' sounded like the words of a newly-minted poem. There was pleasure in newness and pleasure in familiarity, she thought, and ringing through the stadium were shouts of joy connected with both.

As Uncle Rock got wilder, Sophie sensed Ribor's sarcasm quietening down. He continued to hold her hand, told her that one day he would drive her out of town to his favourite places and looked at her with a thoughtfulness that could have been love. Meanwhile Uncle Rock, who was dressed, unreally, in a fluorescent green jumpsuit, danced in a sideways shuffle across the width of the stage, occasionally leaping into the air or marching in circles, booming thunderously into his hand-held mike. Then he sprinted down the steps and began dancing with the boys, singing – baby, let me follow you down – a chorus he'd detached from the rest of the song and was repeating so often it began to sound absurd. Sophie could see on the screens how sweat poured off his happy face and drenched to a thinness his big head of hair, and still he said – baby, let me follow you down. Some of the dancing boys were lying flat on their backs now and waving their legs in the air like drowning ants. Uncle Rock ran up to the stage, returned the chorus to its song and the band played out its final notes.

Instinct told Sophie he would never play these songs again, that this was his resounding goodbye to Dylan.

'And now ... and now ... and now,' said Uncle Rock, his

panting booming through the air as the cheering died down.

'My friends, I have news for you. There is a time and a place for everything. We had believed that today would be the day, we had prayed for it and made all the necessary arrangements, but God had other plans. Listen to me, listen to me ...' he shouted, as a tentative booing started in the stands. 'I just learnt that Dylan will not be able to join us. He sends his deepest regrets and he is thinking of us. I have an email from him [he waved a sheet of paper] and I swear to you these are his exact words. But have patience, have patience ...' he said, as the booing grew louder. 'There is a very good reason why he could not come. He dictated this email from a hospital bed. His nose is broken, three of his ribs are broken, his left wrist is broken. Some force of evil has turned against him and the devil's trident has pierced our hearts along with his. I do not know the details, but you'll be able to read it in the papers soon. All I want to say is that I, you, all of us are as shattered as Mr Bob. Personally I feel like dying, but as Mr Bob said – just remember, death is not the end. So we have to carry on, we have to keep the faith. And how else to keep the faith expect by keeping the song alive? So I'm going to sing one last number now and I want all of you to join me. The least we can do ...' Here Uncle Rock's voice cracked and the band struck up 'I Threw it all Away' to cover up his weeping.

A minute into the song, all hell broke loose and a sea of roaring people surged forward. Soon the stage was overrun and the last Sophie saw of Uncle Rock he had his hands raised, messiah-like.

Ribor said, 'Max has fucking screwed it.'

He ran towards the riot and Sophie unthinkingly followed.

~

How it was that an hour later she and Ribor found themselves not just alive but part of Uncle Rock's birthday party, drinking the punch that Aunty Rock was handing out in little white teacups, Sophie could not entirely understand. Aunty Rock was a female version of her husband. Like him, she was small, smiling and confident, with the same slightly mocking look in her eyes. Her husband had retreated to a corner of the living room and was strumming on a guitar. Soon a crowd gathered around him.

Ribor had a darkening purple bruise on his jaw – the result of a blow delivered to him by a disappointed Dylan fan he'd tried to restrain. Sophie had red scratches on her hands which she examined ruefully – someone had tried to snatch her bag in the melee and she had fought with all her might, later realizing that there was nothing of value in that bag except the email address and phone number Ribor had written down for her more than a year ago on a scrap of cigarette carton. They'd looked for Max backstage but he wasn't there. Ribor tried phoning him but couldn't hear anything in the pandemonium. Then the heavy bamboo poles holding up the stage started collapsing and everywhere little fires were starting, while in the distance Sophie could see that the rest of the audience had turned upon itself – beer bottles were being waved about and stones whizzed through the air. Uncle Rock had appeared before them, looking strangely calm, and told them to follow a boy wearing one of the 'Bah Bob is Coming Home' T-shirts. The boy, perhaps on the basis of a complete misunderstanding, drove them to Uncle Rock's house, where Uncle Rock and his musicians had, surprisingly, already reached and the front room was stuffy with the atmosphere of men and guitars. Someone informed them that the police had been called out and the riot was under control – none dead but many wounded.

Sophie and Ribor went up to Uncle Rock to wish him happy birthday. He stood up and wiped his sweaty, gleaming face with another of the Bob Dylan T-shirts, at the same time swigging beer from a bottle.

'Best concert ever, moh,' he said to Ribor.

Ribor shrugged with an eloquence that could mean anything. It could mean – of course; it could mean – of course not.

'If you'd played with me it would have been a good concert – isn't that what you're thinking?' said Uncle Rock.

'I don't play anymore. You know that.'

Sophie and Ribor retreated to a corner of the room to smoke a joint. Ribor said, 'I've got to find Max.'

A journalist from a Kolkata paper was interviewing Uncle Rock.

'So do you think Mr Dylan knows about this? That you and your friends in this town have been singing his songs for so many years?'

'I've told him all about it. We do it for the people. We do what we enjoy doing. He thanked me in an email and even suggested we cut an album together sometime.'

'Why do you only sing Bob Dylan songs?'

'If you've listened to Dylan you wouldn't be asking that question. His music is the book that has all the answers.'

'Who is responsible for what has taken place today?'

'No one's responsible – people are just very disappointed. Do you understand disappointment? Waiting for years for something to happen? But Dylan has his reasons. He has a broken nose, I have a broken heart.'

The interviewer surged on, barely waiting for answers to his stock questions. 'What did you feel when you first heard Dylan?', 'What do you think of his later albums?', 'Why is it that people are so musically-oriented in Shillong?' Finally he said, 'Okay. Now we need a picture.'

People shifted to make room for the photographer.

Ribor and Sophie surreptitiously made for the door but were stopped in their tracks by Uncle Rock booming out, 'Ribor! Come here, come here.'

He was introducing all his musicians to the interviewer.

'And this is Ribor ... ex-guitarist.'

'Do you have anything to say about Bob Dylan?' asked the interviewer. He was not interested in people's biographies, only in sound bites for his story.

'Dylan said – just because you like my stuff, doesn't mean I owe you anything,' said Ribor.

'Meaning?'

'Well, just because I'm an artist doesn't mean I have a message for you, you know ...'

The journalist scribbled furiously. Uncle Rock looked as if he were trying to work out if there was a hidden insult in this.

Then he said, 'Ribor's not a Bob Dylan fan, moh? That's okay. Not everyone's a fan of everyone.'

'I *am* a fan,' said Ribor quietly. 'I just don't want to make a big thing about it.'

Uncle Rock paused.

'See, that's the problem. I didn't ask you to leave the band. You left of your own accord. And now it hurts you. Everything I do hurts you now.'

'That's what you always say. You don't get it. It's not about me. It's about you. You and your mountain-sized ego.'

'Come again?' said Uncle Rock. The buzz of the party died down and Aunty Rock, still handing out the punch, glanced coolly at her husband. Sophie noticed the journalist scurrying out, while the photographer clicked furiously, anxious to get out as well. They clearly didn't want to witness anything that contradicted their story of the charming Dylan-soaked town in the hills.

'Let's all be sad together because Dylan didn't come. I mean, did you really believe that?' asked Ribor and laughed a dramatic, bitter laugh. 'You really believed the guy would turn up? It was a joke, my friend. Ask Max. He'll tell you.'

Sophie saw how the light slowly dawned on Uncle Rock's face. 'Have you and Max been pulling my leg?' he asked in an awed voice. 'Are you responsible for all the tears and all the bruises, for so many innocent people getting hurt?'

Ribor and he launched into a rapid-fire Khasi that made no sense to Sophie.

'They're fighting over Dylan. This is absurd,' she said to no one in particular.

'They're not fighting over Dylan, they're fighting over a girl,' said Aunty Rock disdainfully, at her elbow.

'A girl?' Sophie felt her face go hot. *She*? She was a bone of contention?

She stepped forward to ask some questions but just then Ribor punched Uncle Rock squarely in the middle of his face.

Shadows are Falling

They were frozen in a semi-circle around Muku. She cowered on the sofa, her legs drawn up, her head hidden in the circle of her arms, whimpering like a wounded animal. Then Mrs Das collapsed on her wicker chair as Mr Das began to circle the dining table. Sophie's eyes prickled as she stared, unblinkingly, at Muku, then at her parents, then at Muku again. No one spoke for a whole minute.

Mr Das stopped pacing and came back scowling. 'Take her to a doctor,' he said.

Mrs Das replied with remarkable resignation, 'For twenty-five years we've been working, trying to build up a name, trying to lead respectable lives. How will we ever show our faces to anyone in this town?'

'*Take her to a doctor,*' said Mr Das.

'You raise them, you feed them and this is what they do to you in return.'

Sophie felt this was a warning to them all – not what her mother was saying (which somehow implicated Sophie in her sister's crime), but the crime itself. It was a warning to those who decided to make up their own rules. Sophie had made up her own rules with regard to Ribor and he'd punched Uncle Rock in the face, he'd been shoved out of the house by the bass player and the drummer, old friends who had decided to throw in their lot with Uncle Rock when it came to the crunch. And it had come to the crunch, hadn't it? They'd been fighting over her and she didn't even know why.

She continued staring at her sister, a sister rendered unrecognizable by the fact that she was pregnant. Sophie was hardly able to say the word to herself – a word she associated with middle-aged women, long years of marriage, domesticity, all the things Muku had absolutely nothing to do with. Sophie did not dare dwell on what Muku was herself thinking, what horrifying new perceptions of herself she was grappling with. All she seemed to project, lying huddled and shrunken on the sofa, was the greatest self-pity. There was neither remorse nor embarrassment in her crying.

Sophie's long-standing anger at her sister started to thaw when she realized it might as well have been her, cringing on that sofa. Mrs Das's attention had, in the meanwhile, shifted to Pavan.

'Let him come anywhere near here and I'll spit in his face. I'm going to call his parents, what do these people think of themselves? She's only sixteen years old, what right do they have? Okay, fine, she has no brains, any boy who looks at her she'll throw herself at him. But what about that bastard? I'm going to call his mother right now. Give me his number.'

Muku remained the way she was. It seemed impossible that she would ever sit up, talk, walk – do anything that implied normalcy.

'Sophie, get the number from her.'

But Sophie found it hard to confront her sister. 'Muku ...' she said, hesitantly.

Muku's whimpering suddenly turned to howling and hearing this, a great rush of rage propelled Mrs Das towards her. She pounded her fists into her, yelling at her to shut up and bring out the phone number. For a few moments, Mr Das and Sophie were only able to watch, both of them shocked by this transformation. Then Sophie tried to pull her mother away. Mrs Das elbowed her away, but Sophie persisted and the recognition of what her life had come to – trying to prevent one family member from killing another – made her say 'Stop,' in a voice she had never used before.

Her mother looked into her eyes and stopped. She sat down again and said, 'What should I do, dear god, what should I do?'

'Don't just sit there saying "What should I do?"' said Mr Das, livid with impatience. '*Do* something.'

'She's destroyed herself.'

'Don't theorize,' said Mr Das. 'Take her to a doctor. How many times do I have to say it?'

'Of course I will. I'm the one who'll have to take on the whole burden of this. What can anyone else in this family do? You're useless, the whole lot of you.'

Mr Das went into his room and slammed the door shut. Sophie, in order to bring back something of the everyday into this horrible situation, said, 'I'll make tea.'

She went into the kitchen, filled the kettle and quickly lit a cigarette. A few days ago she had stood in exactly the same spot, throwing away her lunch, trying to steel herself against her family's betrayals. But they weren't done yet. This was Muku's big revenge. And in true Muku fashion, the most effective revenge was the one which resulted in Muku herself suffering the greatest hurt.

The year Muku was born her father sat in his chair day after day, teaching Sophie English grammar in the evenings or trying, clumsily, to help with the house work which only irritated his already-irritated wife. Muku, when she came, became another troublesome thing in addition to all other troublesome things. She cried too much. She was frail and sickly. She demanded attention when her parents' attention was on staying afloat. And afterwards it was too late. Afterwards, she became someone who needed to be reined in because she was always in danger of going too far. That had given her parents a function – they were the people who were going to keep Muku from straying. And even in that they've failed, thought Sophie angrily, spooning more tea leaves than necessary into the hot water. And what about me? Didn't I run away to Bangalore, didn't I come running back because of Ribor? It all felt contrived now. All the secrets and lies, all the dirty work around desire. Muku had brought it out into the open now. She was going to crucify herself for the sake of it.

Sophie poured the tea, then carried the tray out; her hands were shaking so hard the cups rattled. Her father emerged from his room and asked in an ominously low voice, 'Who's to blame for this?'

The eternal Das question. Sophie opened her mouth but no sound came.

'We … all of us,' said her mother.

'I don't take any responsibility for this,' said Mr Das, continuing to address Sophie. 'I used to tell her once: Mukulika mend your ways. I've given up.'

'The problem doesn't disappear by giving up. The problem remains,' said his wife.

'Who was hitting her just now – she or me?' Mr Das asked Sophie.

They were returning to Sophie the role she had played all her life – an adjutant trapped between parents who couldn't bear looking each other in the eye.

'I was hitting her because she needs to understand that she's taking us to hell with her,' Mrs Das said in the voice of the entirely rational person she wasn't.

'She was hitting her because she feels guilty,' said Mr Das, while Sophie tried to maintain neutrality by handing out the tea.

Muku had stopped crying and opened a small vent in her arms to look out at the proceedings.

'That's better than feeling nothing. Seeing your daughter destroyed and feeling nothing,' said her mother.

'I will not be judged by you,' said Mr Das, directly addressing his wife at last. He had raised his voice. Soon, as Sophie knew from experience, he would shout.

'I'm taking an appointment,' Sophie said putting the shaking tray down. 'Be quiet. I'm calling the clinic right now.'

~

The following afternoon, Sophie went in a taxi with her father to the hospital. Her mother and sister came down the stairs slowly, looking pale and diminished. The foetus was three weeks old,

Mrs Das told her elder daughter in a whisper and Sophie, thinking back, realized it could be traced to the evening Muku had not returned home and her mother had called her in Bangalore to tearfully report on this. Mrs Das had known without actually knowing.

No one spoke on the way back. Sophie watched the town sliding past the window – painted election banners, the traffic policeman with enormous white moustache who'd been helping schoolchildren cross the road since Sophie was a child, Sarak Singh, the aloo-muri wallah, posters of Bob Dylan still in the windows of restaurants and beauty parlours, the grey Presbyterian Church which she always associated with the feeling of marital cosiness because as a child she'd once attended a beautiful wedding there. Everything was utterly familiar and at the same time elusive. Perhaps if I spend my whole life here I'll find the heart of this town, she thought, but did not allow herself to move on to the related thought, which was Ribor. This was her own small private chastisement – trying not to think about him.

The morning sun continued to be as brilliant as it was on the day the truth about Muku was revealed, quite by chance, by a doctor her mother took her to see because Muku had been feeling nauseous for some weeks. Ten days went by since the operation and all Muku did was lie back in bed and stare at the ceiling. Her mother cooked khichri and made big mugs of Bournvita and bought the kind of biscuits Muku liked and Sophie urged her sister to sit up and eat, fixing the pillows behind her back.

Whenever anyone tried speaking to Muku, she would shut her eyes, but when they left her alone she would open them and continue staring. Sophie had never known her sister to be this quiet; she'd always resented quietness. Now she looked set to never speak again. Once, while Muku was bathing, Sophie had quickly lifted up the mattress on her sister's bed, looking anxiously for the strips of Ibuprofen she had once found there. Instead she found a hoard of what were clearly gifts from Pavan – CDs, T-shirts, a pair of gold earrings, a small bottle of perfume. Sophie had let the mattress drop without touching anything. The heavy metal inspired signs of 'Kill, Kill, Kill' and the black skulls and crossbones that were painted all over

Muku's bed and desk contrasted oddly with the femininity of those hidden gifts.

Her mother would come into the bedroom from time to time to ask Muku if she'd like to drink tomato soup, or her father would bring her a magazine with an article in it on attractive career choices for young people. Muku would nod vehemently in response to every question, her eyes shut tight. No one could breach this wall; her silence infected the whole house. Mr Das's habitual reserve grew more profound, while Sophie took to sitting in the kitchen in the evenings as her mother cooked, the two of them talking in low voices. And even the cooking was affected by this state of mourning. Her mother slowly gave up making the food that implied a state of permanent celebration, those kofta curries and kebabs and mutton chops dripping with fat, those oversweet mithais and oily vegetable mixes. If Muku ate something, the whole family grew relieved and ate the same thing, even if it was bland and made them feel like invalids.

Sophie had, at her mother's insistence, called Muku's friend, Priya and got Pavan's number from her but before she could call him, he called.

'I haven't heard from Muku for a while, I'd like to speak to her,' he said, and Sophie was struck by how much like an adult he sounded, how much in control. Where do people get that sort of confidence from, she wondered. Was it money, was it blood, was it upbringing? Her mother was gesticulating wildly at Sophie, urging her to inform Pavan that he was a monster. Sophie would have liked to break the boy's coolness, shout on the phone and make him stutter. She wanted him to take responsibility for some of the world's sordidness, not fuck her sister and remain untouched, insulated by his swimming pool and his CD player from Singapore and whatever else it was that gave his voice its note of entitlement. But she couldn't bring herself to do it, so she told Pavan that Muku was sick and couldn't see him and then hung up before he could say anything else. He called every afternoon and eventually Sophie started hanging up at the sound of his voice, tired of telling him to stop calling because Muku was not going to come to the phone.

So unless he guessed, Pavan remained ignorant of the pregnancy, which was just as well because that way the shame could remain confined to the house and not seep out and ruin the Das reputation as Mrs Das had feared. Sophie could see the shame in the angle of her mother's head as she bent over her chopping or kneading or peeling, and in the way her father cleared his throat when he emerged from his room to take a plate of food back into it. The shame had made them stop talking about going away. Instead, Mrs Das said how grateful she was to God that she'd been able to organize a timely abortion and Mr Das said he was confident Muku could pass her exams if she managed to do a little bit of study over the next few weeks.

And then Mr and Mrs Das slowly stopped referring to this shared shame, even obliquely, and became protective of Muku. Their manner took on an unusual gravitas whenever they approached the hushed room where she lay all day. Only Sophie remained unawed by the new Muku and read to her from the tattered *Jane Eyre* and *Little Women* of their childhood or told her stories about life in Bangalore – the landlord, the friends, the parties, the music, the murder, Maya. Muku was still dazed and the stories were only diversions for her; as soon as Sophie stopped talking she would lapse back into her dream state, thinking thoughts Sophie didn't especially want to probe.

~

Once life in the Das household settled into its lugubrious rhythm, thoughts of Ribor crept back into Sophie's mind and she started to wonder why he didn't call till she remembered that he had never called. It had always been her, running to his shop, breaking into his life. After he'd been thrown out of Uncle Rock's house and hustled into a taxi (which was a good thing because if he'd hung around there, the enraged Uncle Rock, held back by the party guests, would have punched him back), Sophie had walked back alone. But Uncle Rock knew where to find Ribor, she realized now. What if he'd come to the shop and attacked him? The thought made her stand up one afternoon, mumble something about needing a walk to her mother (who was expounding on the lessons the *Bhagavad Gita* held for all those who cared to receive them), and head towards Ribor's shop. It was shut. She tried calling him, he didn't answer. Not sure she'd be able to locate his house in the network of allies where it lay, she went to Mama Jo's joint.

Mama Jo hummed along with the music wafting from the stereo (*'I'm going out of my mind, ohhhh with a pain that stops and starts'*) and tore out bits of lettuce while Sophie sat and waited.

'Do you know anything?' she asked finally.

'You're a hardworking girl. You should go back. To Bangalore,' he said.

'Do you know where Ribor is?'

'He's ... busy. He told me to tell you if I saw you that he's not going to be around. For a few days.'

'Has he gone out of town?'

'No, no. He's gone. Underground. Have a hotdog.'

'Has Max been troubling him? Or is it Uncle Rock? What happened, where is he?'

'Things are getting messy around here. You might be better off in Bangalore. None of the people got their money back, did you get your money back? No you didn't. There's a police case on. Max will have to cough up the dough. Sooner or later.'

'I don't care about the money. I just want to talk to Ribor.'

'Ribor should have given you. The whole picture.'

'But you have the whole picture too. You have to tell me.'

'I usually mind my own business. But I remember the woman Ribor used to hang out with because she's always leaving her umbrella behind.'

Madonna! The parasol woman.

'If you ask for my opinion she talked too much. Then one day she goes off with Uncle Rock. And Ribor's so mad. First because she never even discussed it with him. Why she was leaving him. And second because she knows that he can't stand Uncle Rock. It's like she did it on purpose. And Uncle Rock lured her away on purpose. They both did it to spite Ribor.'

Sophie took a deep breath.

'I think he wanted to marry her. Anyway, from what I heard, the other evening, on Uncle Rock's birthday, Uncle Rock started taunting Ribor about the girl and Ribor couldn't take it any more so he hit him. She came running to me, asking – what happened, what happened, I heard they had a fight? I told her what I knew. And she feels horribly guilty now, she says she was an idiot to even think about Uncle Rock, he's not the person for her. Besides, Aunty Rock will murder her. And I don't think Uncle Rock was serious. He was just playing with her for a while, he was just doing it like a joke on Ribor because Ribor had left the band. You know that story, don't you? This is all so messy, too messy for you. You're young. You should go back.'

But Sophie couldn't go anywhere, she was nailed to the bench with shame. The shame of having a sister who had suddenly turned into a pregnant woman was nothing compared to this, the shame of not knowing, of being horribly out of joint.

'And there's more, there's always more,' said Mama Jo grimly, chomping on one of his own hotdogs.

'Uncle Rock really believed that Bob Dylan got into a fight in a pub and broke half his bones so he cancelled at the last minute. That's what the email said and he was sad but he accepted it. Then Ribor spoils everything by telling him it was a joke. So then Uncle Rock starts believing Ribor and Max planned this together to pay him back. For stealing Ribor's girlfriend. You see? So what does Uncle Rock do? They've rubbed his face in the mud, moh. Everybody will get to know that Uncle Rock, being the sucker for Dylan that he is, happily allowed these brothers to take him for a ride. He must take revenge. So he goes straight to the police and tells them the brothers have cheated people of thousands of rupees and are responsible for starting a riot. He shows them the tickets that Max printed. A case is registered. There's a warrant out for them both. Max should have told the police Ribor had nothing to do with it, but he's a selfish man.'

'What was it all for?' asked Sophie

'Haven't you seen the papers? The election results are out. The Rooster won only 19 seats out of 60. Why is that? Because of corruption. Everybody read about the bribe given to the Betel Nut. Everyone knew they were playing a dirty game. And it was exactly like I had thought. The claim they gave money to Max for using Dylan's name in the campaign was a lie. The newspapers caught on to it only recently.'

Sophie looked out at the street, expecting Ribor to walk in any minute.

'Dylan moves in mysterious ways,' said Mama Jo. 'Did you

hear about the success of the Fourth Time Around party? They had innocently called themselves. That. Because they have not won a single seat in the last three elections. So when they decided to contest one last time, they changed their name to Fourth Time Around, just for fun. And then! Someone discovered the Blonde on Blonde song with that name. So lots of young people from Laitumkhrah and Lachumiere and Nongthymmai started voting for this party, because one guy wrote about it on his blog, made a whole big thing out of it, like it was a sign from Dylan himself.'

But of course Ribor wasn't going to walk in. He had gone underground. Sophie tried to think of the places where he might be, but how could she guess, what did she know about his life?

'And now Rooster has to buy up Fourth Time Around if they want to form a government! FTA got the most votes out of all the small parties. But FTA won't be bought. They refuse. To be bought. Dylan made a difference without even coming here. Dylan always makes a difference. Dylan ...' Mama Jo continued on his staccato expounding on Dylan's long-distance genius, on which combination of corrupt and incorruptible parties was likely to form the next government, on how Sophie should get away from all this and return to Bangalore.

Sophie stood up and backed away. She was going to walk till it hurt, till she was as far away from all of them physically as she was in every other sense – from Ribor, Mama Jo, the umbrella girl, Uncle Rock. They lived in a different town from the one in which she had lain awake dreaming of a life without a history, made up of just the glances and words between two people.

The last thing she heard Mama Jo say as she walked out was, 'Two's a company. Three's a crowd, moh.'

In the Spring Time

Sophie stood in the garden smoking yet another cigarette, thinking – but how do I know a shred of what Mama Jo is saying is true?

Her mother opened a window and called out – 'Some Swami on the phone for you' and for a fraction of a second Sophie truly did not know who it was. Leave me, she thought then. *Leave me alone.*

She dragged herself inside.

'I've been trying to call you for days. I emailed you twice.'

As if it were a scene from a movie about someone else's life, Sophie remembered seeing Swami's name in her inbox.

'My cellphone's out of range here,' replied Sophie tersely.

'I spoke to your office and got your home number. So how did you sprain your ankle?'

'My ankle?' Sophie asked, puzzled, then remembered this was the hastily-concocted lie she'd emailed Anu as a reason for extending her stay. 'I didn't.'

'Then?'

'Swami, why have you called?'

'I'm at your place. You need to come back. Anu and Shiva have messed up things and your landlord wants you to vacate.'

'What did they do?'

'They had a barbecue going and fed Mani some sausages.'

'Are they out of their bloody ...?'

'Mani went home with a sausage stuffed in his mouth and before they knew it, Mr Bhatt came here and flung the burning hot barbecue across the balcony.'

Sophie groaned.

'Anu says she didn't realize the family was vegetarian.'

'Did she and Shiva take him and Mrs Bhatt to see Baba Sampige?'

'They'd been planning to. But Anu is too frightened to bring it up now. She just ran off. And so did Shiva. And now Bhatt's saying he's going to throw you out. He has to do pujas for Mani and pujas on your balcony to get rid of the polluting effects of the sausages.'

'I thought he'd calm down after knowing Ringo is off his back and he doesn't have to worry about his damn loans for some time.'

'He was delighted. He started to come over and chat with Anu and Shiva.'

It was only when she'd spoken his name that Sophie actually focused on Ringo. Swami told her what was going on. It would take a while for the case to come up for hearing. Meanwhile, Ringo was talking to his lawyer and waiting patiently in jail.

'Sophie, I think I should keep your stuff in my place till you come back. Let me know quickly, this guy's going berserk.'

The eagerness in his voice made Sophie close her eyes tight and turn her face away like Muku did several times a day.

'I don't know when I'm coming back ...'

'Have you got a job there? You didn't really sprain your ankle, no?'

'I can't explain it all on the phone.'

'But you haven't explained anything. You haven't replied to my mails.'

Sophie wondered, fleetingly, about what had happened to the car loan, the land loan, the promotion he was sure he would get. I used to know this guy, she thought.

'Swami, can you please just get my stuff together and drop it off at Anu's place?'

There was a long moment of hurt. 'Okay, okay,' said Swami then, sullenly. 'Whatever you say, man. Don't speak to me unless you feel like.'

Sophie went back to her smoking and waiting. Through the open window she could hear the murmur of her parents talking. Her father spent less time by himself now and had taken to working in the sitting room with his hardback, yellow-paged copy of *Hamlet* and his sheaves of foolscap paper with more lines of close-set Bengali writing on them crossed out than not. His translation project seemed to be going very slowly. Every time Sophie looked, he appeared to be on the same page, the thickness of the book's untranslated pages on the right contrasting sadly with the thinness of the translated pages on the left. She felt daunted by the mountainous nature of the task he had set himself and she didn't entirely understand what it was for.

A couple of mornings ago her mother had tried to explain to her the delicate intersection of karma and dharma, which held the key to life. 'Everyone has a duty in life,' she said, as the steam from the tea she was pouring rose in a cloud and misted the reading glasses perched on her nose. 'Like it says in the *Bhagavad Gita,* sometimes you may think your duty is taking you on the wrong path, but even then you have to do your duty first and think of the consequences afterwards. My parents only did their duty. I didn't marry the man they wanted so they cut me off. It's not their fault. You can't have everything. You can't be happy all the time, but you can do your duty. But what one tends to forget in this blind pursuit of dharma is that all the time your karma is also building up. What about that? Muku is in this state because of our bad karma – his and mine. My God! I really thought my duty to my family is over. I was thinking about the straight line of dharma and I forgot about the crooked line of karma.'

Sophie had never imagined her mother to possess the capacity for self-correction, but she had managed for some time now to scrupulously avoid all mention of Pavan and his family and focus all her attention on Muku. She tried to get Muku to read a few lines from her geography textbook, do a few maths problems, because the exam, the all-important exam, was approaching. Or maybe she only brought out Muku's schoolbooks because that would restore a sense of normalcy, just as Mr Das, returning as always to Shakespeare, talked to Muku about the wonderfulness of *As You Like It* to remind her that the essential things remained the same.

They were talking to each other too, her mother and her father, awkward sentences about practical things (Should we make some tea? Is it time for the news?) all within earshot of Muku. If Muku responded to these shifts she did not show it. Talking was still very far away. But she moved, sat up and stared at pages in books as if they were alien but not unfriendly things. And Sophie stood at the parapet and waited, smoking till even ordinary air tasted of tobacco, till a small thing with dry fingers constantly tickled her throat, till she could see in her mother's eyes that she knew that something was devouring her daughter's heart.

~

Ribor and Sophie. Sophie and Ribor. Two people sitting by a lake, holding hands as if they loved each other. For the longest time they just sat in silence, watching the cold lake before them and the little red and yellow boats that couples pedalled with their feet. On the far side, under a giant oak tree, sat a family that from this distance at least, presented the very image of happiness. A man smoking contentedly with his knees drawn up and the tips of his shoes pointing heavenwards, while a toddler tried to climb onto his back, and next to them a woman slowly packing the remains of their picnic lunch, shaking out crumbs from a red-checked table cloth. Sophie hoped, with a sudden vehemence, that on closer inspection there would appear a frown on the woman's face and disenchantment on the man's and that her own unhappiness would find a reflection in theirs. Then she realized that to them, she and Ribor must suggest as powerful an image of contentment – two people sitting hand-in-hand with so perfect an understanding of each other that they didn't need to speak.

Finally Ribor said, 'So you want to know where I've been? Hiding in my shop with the shutters down. I've just been lying low, trying to think things through. Yesterday Max was bailed out by some rich businessman. It turns out this guy has just bought up that whole block where my shop is. He wants to tear down all the shops and make that 1000 square foot all-American store that Max has been planning. I can't understand why he thinks Max is worth putting his money on, but he does.'

Sophie was silent.

'I asked Max, so what should I do – work as a chowkidar for your store? He said, join a call centre, man. It's reasonable money. He's always been a real bastard. But the one decent thing he did was to clear my name. He told the police that I had nothing to do with the Dylan scam. And he doesn't seem worried about the charges against him. Some fat bribes will probably make their way into the right pockets.'

Sophie said, 'Remember what you told me a year ago? You have the right to stay. I can't unless you let me. It's up to you.'

'What do you want me to say, Sophie? Marry me? Do you know how old I am? Do you know what my family is like? I don't even have the shop anymore. I feel like nothing.'

'We should have left town that time when you wanted to escape. Everything would have been different then,' said Sophie.

Ribor shrugged. 'Don't blame yourself,' he said but didn't look at her.

'I blew my only chance. And now it's too late,' she said in the voice of someone pleading silently to be contradicted.

'By the time one has figured out what to do it's always too late. That's the way life is. But maybe I couldn't handle being anywhere else. However fed up I get, maybe this is the only place for me.'

They looked at the painted sky and the water and for a moment Sophie felt such a strong rush of love that it became a pure, objective thing sans connection with past or future. Ribor was more vivid to her than any other person she had ever known. All the time they'd spent together had a separate existence inside her and maybe it was enough to live on. But soon her hurt came clamouring back.

Ribor said, 'I have nothing to give you but I still want to see you every time you come back.'

They had gone back to being strangers and it was so intolerable, Sophie said angrily, 'I'm not coming back.'

It was impossible to imagine – a lifetime of regret, thinking of Shillong and not being able to associate it with anything except this afternoon by a lake.

'Everyone does,' said Ribor, ignoring the tears in her voice.

He put his arm around her and then they just sat there, in the uncertain light of evening, the light that wavered between night and day. The unanswered question, the unfulfilled hope remained as the scene grew dark, not all at once, but in a mysteriously selective way – the little curved bridge over the lake from which children had earlier flung popcorn to orange-lipped fishes, the rows of cypresses, the sloping grassy bank that led to the water, the geometric, crayon-coloured flower beds, people lolling on the grass in twos and threes – all of it was slowly and sporadically blotted out till eventually the only light that remained was the cold grey wash of a twilight sky.

It was only then that Sophie actually understood the dharma-karma thing her mother had been talking about. All of her life had been like an equation and having Ribor love her would upset the equation: it would mean that life was giving her far more than it took away.

She went home, already steeled against Ribor's final embrace in the back of the taxi, already turning her face away from him.

In the house, everything was as quiet as it had been for the past few weeks. She went and sat by her sister, who was lying with her back to the world, and shook her by the shoulder.

'I'm going back to Bangalore to look for a new job and find a new place. Do you want to come and stay with me?' she asked Muku.

I'm So Tired of You, America

'I wasn't having a party Sophie,' said Anu for the umpteenth time. 'How can I have a party so soon after Rukshana died? Mia got a portable barbecue from her colleagues as a farewell gift before she left for England and we thought – let's try it out in Sophie's place because after all that happened, this place (she gestured at her dusty, roach-filled apartment) just depresses me.'

Rukshana's death had resulted in a slow exodus and now there was only Anu left in the once crammed apartment. Soon she'd have to move out too; it was too expensive for her. Sophie had been back for forty-eight hours and done nothing but lain on a couch and watched Hollywood films sideways, the same line from the same song constantly running through her head – 'I'm so tired of America … I'm so tired of you, America.' The fans that constantly whirred overhead did little to dispense the dry late February heat. She'd let Anu talk on, comforted by the sound of her voice and letting it obliterate the dialogues of films she would never subtitle again.

Anu described how when Mr Bhatt learnt of the sausage defilement, he had, after lifting the barbecue with one hand and delivering it to the empty lot behind Sophie's flat, stormed inside and flung out a pair of her shoes to inaugurate her eviction. Swami, coming up the stairs, had caught the worn-out sneakers before they could hit him in the face.

'You remove all her things or I will call the police,' Bhatt had declared, reluctant, after that initial show of bravado, to handle any other object in that den of vice.

Shiva and Anu had got their things together and fled with Mia in tow, leaving behind lots of empty Kingfisher bottles, the smell of weed combined with the smell of burning meat, and a brave Swami trying to calm Bhatt down. In the end, he had called a taxi and stuffed it with Sophie's things.

'He's a marvel,' said Anu.

The doorbell rang before Sophie could answer and Shiva lumbered in.

The tenor of all conversation inevitably changed when Shiva entered a room. People grew embarrassed at the pettiness of their personal problems. Shiva reminded them of larger, much more grotesque and unresolved horrors – how could one pretend, in the face of Shiva's onslaught, that romantic entanglements and money worries were of the least consequence.

Now he ran, without much of a preamble, through the news of the previous week – a politician's son who'd been drinking all night drove his Audi onto the pavement and mowed down four pensioners out on their morning walk; a twenty-one-year-old member of a south Bangalore gang was hacked to death in the early afternoon on a crowded pavement by members of a rival gang; a man had bought a can of acid, forced his wife to drink half of it and splashed the other half onto her face.

But Anu was growing increasingly impatient with Shiva's public-mindedness and she cut him short with, 'When will you get us that appointment with Baba Sampige?'

Shiva said he had spoken with his cousin. She'd invited him and his friends to drop in at the ashram for half an hour any time that week.

Anu produced a tattered map of Bangalore and they tried to locate Baba Sampige's ashram. Shiva, as he pored over the map, said, 'Do you realize what a huge brown cancer of a city this is?'

He tried to get the girls to grasp Bangalore – the twin centres at its heart arranged on either side of the tiny patch of nineteenth century mint-green that was Cubbon Park, and its mad radiation from those centres in every possible direction. Sophie looked at the map with suspicion. How could this be Bangalore? Where was the messiness, the noise, the shops, the people? Even the slums were marked out by neat little fawn-coloured boxes. She squinted at Cubbon Park and tried to picture them separated by it – Sophie and her friends on the right half of this centre, drinking cold coffee in styrofoam cups, and Shanthi's mother and great-grandmother on the left half, selling breakfast to lewd lorry drivers. As he talked to them, Shiva worked his way out from this divided heart in concentric circles – the first circle encompassed Malleswaram on the left, its grid of streets designed by British engineers; on top was the grand Indian Institute of Science with its own irregular camouflage of green; on the right, Indira Nagar with a ring of pleasure to its name – its high street crammed with glitzy shops, its dozens of restaurants, and Anil's apartment where they'd partied that long-ago night; below, Lal Bagh fell well within the circle – this older cousin of Cubbon Park. Then Shiva drew a wider circle moving clockwise again from the left, including Bangalore University at the south-west, pulling in the industrial suburbs of Peenya and Yesvantpur where Baba Sampige's ashram was, the lake in the north (where, said Shiva, cormorants and egrets lived), travelling down to Banaswadi with its desultory railway station, closing in on the abandoned airport in the east and coming to rest in the south, right on top of the Indian Institute of Management.

As he started to draw the final circle, Shiva growled in self-admiration, for there was no doubt that he had created this city and it was his hand that would decide what could fall into its widest ambit. He still had his thumb firmly planted on Cubbon Park and now stretched his hand out and rested his little finger on the far edges of the city – places made mysterious by distance. At the farthest western corner, Magadi Road ran to the edge of the map and fell off it; in the far north, a straight road raced on to the new airport; on the right were the international technology parks and brave new mini-cities of the future; and at the bottom of the map was the zoo.

Sophie took the map from Shiva once he had completed his cartography; she looked at her enormous, churning city made humble by a picture and for the first time felt something like love for it.

Shiva had located the ashram on the map but was still certain that going to see Baba Sampige was a ridiculous idea. He and Anu started arguing about it and soon their argument segued into one about Australia.

'Shiva, I'm giving you one last chance to apply for that bloody passport.'

'If I hear the word 'Australia' one more time, I'll puke.'

As their fight grew more virulent, Sophie thought – Killer Queen was wrong, it doesn't end on the last page. It just goes on and on and on.

Sophie insisted that Anu go to the Bhatts' place that very evening, apologize about the sausages and invite them to visit Baba Sampige.

'I've got to get the flat back. I'm not giving up,' said Sophie.

Anu went swearing to Sophie she would be arrested. She came back laughing.

When Anu arrived, the Bhatts' house was, a good one week after her unspeakable crime, still ringing with the sound of Vedic chants. She saw Mani through the open door, pinned between two priests, his forehead smeared with differently-coloured pastes and a large-eyed look of chastisement on his small face. Anu had never paid attention to this miniscule creature before; she was one of those people who do not really notice children. But at that moment, she was sorry for being the cause of Mani's suffering as he struggled, while his grandfather lectured him, with the distinctions between wrong and right, virtue and vice, vegetarianism and barbarism.

'What are you doing here?' asked Mr Bhatt sternly from the floor where he was seated with the priests, poring ghee into a fire.

Anu had managed to get Mr Bhatt to the door by mentioning Baba Sampige. She told him in a subdued voice about the darshan. Bhatt looked from the priests to Anu and then back to the priests, as if trying to work out how they had engineered a divine intervention so speedily.

'Will you come with us to the ashram, Sophie? It might do you good,' said Anu now, aware that her friend had broken down over something. She assumed it was the separation from Swami and the near-simultaneous loss of both her job and house.

~

The ashram was a fat slab of strawberry and chocolate confectionary with a riot of stucco work on its façade. Gods, sages, musicians, cattle, apsaras, elaborately coiled snakes, peacocks, doormen with swords, parrots, angels and scores of other unidentifiable creatures of plaster greeted visitors. Once the group entered, however, they discovered that this structure was not the ashram itself but more like the gopuram of a temple – meant to impress the visitor from the outside and serving to hide from view what lay inside. Baba Sampige's ashram, once one was properly in it, was no different from the campus of a software company, with anonymous glass-plated buildings connected with tidy red-brick lined walks. Entering the largest of these buildings, the group were surprised again, for it was just a huge empty hall with columns, halfway up which was a gallery with rooms running all around it.

On the far side of this vast hall lay Baba Sampige's inner sanctum. Sophie, Mr and Mrs Bhatt, Shiva, Anu, Anand and Anandi were met at the door and asked to take off their shoes by Miss Priya – Shiva's cousin, the young software yuppie who had renounced the material world to serve the Baba and run his website from which weekly spiritual bulletins were sent out to far corners of the world bearing enigmatic subject lines such as 'God Will Not Send You a Message' and 'The World Does Not Care What You Are Inside'. She welcomed them in a whisper, smiled at everyone, gave each a marigold and a flyer with a grainy picture of a Baba Sampige sans his moustache, looking like Shah Rukh Khan, and asked them to walk in a single file towards the room where Baba was waiting. Priya reminded them that they were to wind up the interview as soon as she returned to collect them. Baba led the meditation session at 5 o'clock every Saturday evening and they were not to linger beyond five minutes to five though they could, of course, join the mediation.

Shiva said, 'And we must make sure he doesn't miss his flight to Rotterdam. From where he will go to St Petersburg. From where he will go to Costa Rica. From where he will ...'

He was interrupted by Mr Bhatt, who roughly elbowed Shiva aside in his haste to be the first one to lay his eyes on his beloved Baba. 'Make a queue, make a queue,' he said bossily to cover up his just having broken the existing queue. He didn't look at Sophie; he pretended he didn't know her.

Anand was explaining to Sophie his growing belief – derived from his recent reading of spiritual magazines – that his son would be reborn any day now. He just needed to find out from Baba Sampige how to read the signs correctly so that he would be there to receive his child when the time came. Sophie tried to gauge from Anandi's expression what she thought of this extraordinary belief, but all Anandi had to offer was an impenetrable wall of blankness. Sophie didn't know which was more unsettling – Anand's growing excitement over the concept of rebirth or Anandi's empty eyes.

Shiva tried to provoke his cousin by asking if it was true what he had heard – Baba Sampige managed to be in so many places at the same time because he didn't actually exist – there were just several unemployed actors playing Baba Sampige, a fictional character invented by some witty college dropout who was now controlling the Sampige spiritual empire from behind the scenes.

Miss Priya's smile was like a slide down which everything rolled unhindered and she ignored both Shiva's sarcasm and Mr Bhatt's rudeness. Neither did she seem disturbed by the fact that one of her cousin's friends was a murderer. When Anu brought up the subject, explained what had happened, and asked if Baba Sampige could do anything for Ringo, Miss Priya said – we can pray for him, we can pray for everyone – and the unwavering smile remained in place. That's the problem with brain dead people, thought Sophie. They assume everyone else is brain dead too. Mr and Mrs Bhatt were meanwhile arguing over whether her hernia was an appropriate subject to bring to the Baba's attention.

They were admitted by another soft-speaking aide into Baba's room and found him seated – not on a throne as they had all in their different ways imagined, with a halo around his head, but at a plush desk, tapping at a laptop.

'Sit down, sit down,' he said with a wave, his eyes on the screen, and since there were no chairs, the seven visitors dropped to the carpet on the floor and sat cross-legged, waiting, like children, for further instructions from a teacher.

'I'm addicted to online chess. Helps to clear the mind, you know. But it takes too much time. And you don't move your limbs. Better play tennis, I tell my followers, even though I don't practice what I preach.' He cackled. His devotees remained silent.

While the aide stood by respectfully and the visitors fidgeted, Baba Sampige finished his game.

'I won, I won,' he said jubilantly and the group was reminded that he was, after all, only thirty years old – a mere child where godmen were concerned. Then his expression turned serious and he joined them on the floor, fixing them all with a stare.

'How can we be sure you won?' asked Shiva but Baba appeared not to have heard. Or recognized his childhood friend.

'You're crying inside,' he said to Anandi in a conversational tone. 'Bring it out, bring it out – don't sit on it.'

Anu tried to explain about the tragedy but Baba raised an authoritative hand, commanding her to silence, and continued addressing Anandi.

'You are suffering because you imagine these are two different things – you and your suffering. You think it's like someone bringing a flame to your skin – two different things – your body and the flame, you and the cause of your suffering. But there is no such thing, ma. It is just a combination of different atoms moving about all the time – this person you think is you. Combine them one way and you become someone who suffers, combine them another way and you are a joyful person. You understand? Choose the combination.'

'Baba, nan hushaar illa,' Mrs Bhatt interjected impatiently but as soon as Baba turned his attention to her she forgot about her illness and blushed with embarrassment under his gaze. She wriggled on her ample behind to a spot where she was shielded by her husband and could not be seen by Baba.

Baba pointed at Bhatt. 'You speak.'

Bhatt began on a long disquisition in Kannada about his

many woes – the loans which he certainly meant to repay – it was just that people had been harassing him and he had no one to turn to, how his grandson had been forcibly fed meat, his bad stars, the rising costs of everything, the fact that their colony received insufficient water even though they had bribed the crooks at the water supply office so often that bribery had now become counter-productive.

'And she …?' asked Baba Sampige, referring to Mrs Bhatt.

Bhatt tried to convince the Baba that his wife and he were a unit and that his troubles were by definition her troubles.

Baba wagged a finger admonishingly. 'This is the first mistake we Indian men make. Always imagining we are talking on behalf of our wives.'

So Mrs Bhatt wriggled out again and announced, 'Hernia.'

Baba raised a hand to indicate that he had heard and taken in her suffering along with everyone else's. His manner seemed to suggest that he had an infinite capacity for other people's troubles.

'You have come with them?' he asked Sophie, who nodded. 'So what do you think? What advice do you have to offer this troubled family?'

'I used to be … err … their tenant but they had problems with me …'

Anu butted in confidently and ensured this time that she got the chance to explain things. She wound up by saying: 'Some things have happened that shouldn't have happened, but Sophie is not a bad girl. And she really cares about their grandchild.'

'Sophie?' asked Baba Sampige.

Shiva spoke up. 'Anu, don't give him our names. He's a fraud … he collects information about people so he can pretend he knows about their lives.'

Baba Sampige, not a muscle twitching, turned to consider Shiva with the same calm, detached interest with which he considered everyone.

'Your name?'

'Don't act, man. You know my name. You know me just as I know you.'

'Ahahaha …' exclaimed Sampige appreciatively. 'There is a hymn like that. You know me and I know you.' He hummed tunelessly with a briefly vacant look, then asked Anand suddenly, 'Do you pray?'

Anand nodded ambiguously.

'If you pray deeply you will find that it all becomes so light. All ...' his gesture seemed to include the whole group, '... the world.'

Anand was rapt.

'Go deep, go deep. There is a place where it all becomes one.'

'Where should I look for him?' asked Anand.

Baba Sampige suddenly looked cagey. 'I make no promises. I am not here to bring you the future. But, on the other hand, the future is so clear. We only have to look. We only have to look. We run an ashram in Kerala. Very lovely place. You can book rooms online by credit card.'

Sophie felt sleepy. Was he hypnotizing them?

Anand's face was radiant with yearning. The hope that Superman would return to him in Kerala was the slender thread by which he now hung. Even Baba Sampige could not ignore that look.

'You have lost someone ... your child. If you have faith, he will come back ...' He took Anandi's hand and joined it with Anand's. 'He will come back.'

He seemed to be praying over the couple and then went into a trance suddenly, his hands clasping theirs. A convulsion passed through his body and he mumbled incoherently with just the whites of his eyes visible. Bhatt looked ready to faint with reverence. 'Baba!' he shouted in ecstasy. Everyone else remained silent and Baba took his own time coming to.

'Wrong focus,' he said, eventually to Bhatt.

'Wrong focus?'

'Howdu ... wrong focus. Start repaying your loans. Let the girl stay. These are small things ... don't make big things out of small things. Take your wife for an operation. For everything there is a time. Learn this. At your age, you should be spending more time in the temple, singing bhajans, thinking of the next stage, contemplating the future.'

Bhatt bowed before Baba with folded hands. He was not going to try and question his guru.

Shiva, who had been squirming impatiently, now stood up.

'Ai Raghavan,' he said. 'Listen to me carefully. I've had enough. I'm going to the press and I'll give them every petty detail about you – all the money you made off small children, all the scams you ran. Not everyone will believe me, but it's enough if some people do. Enough to burn a bit of a hole in this posh estate you have, huh? What do you think? It'll be funny, no?'

Baba Sampige did seem to think it would be funny. He laughed uproariously while the others looked ashamed. Then Mr Bhatt, thinking it would be disrespectful not to join in, let out a small giggle. The others cautiously joined him. Soon the hall was echoing with laughter.

Shiva came closer and lowered his face so that it was level with Baba's. 'I'm tired of seeing your mug everywhere. What do you think you know? I've been listening to the crap you've been spewing for the last half an hour. What do you think you know?'

Baba Sampige didn't look at Shiva. Instead he turned to his devotees and said with a chuckle, 'Take this man away.'

At this command from God, Mr and Mrs Bhatt, Anand, Anandi and Anu simultaneously fell upon Shiva, while Sophie watched in horror. Still laughing, they started to drag him away, with the aide holding the door open for them. Baba clapped his hands in glee. Shiva was so surprised that he didn't resist; then seeing how their ecstatic laughter bared their teeth, and feeling the clawing hardness of their hands on his arms and shoulders, he understood that they had turned robotic, and he tried to break free, run back to Raghavan alias Baba Sampige, and fight.

But he was overpowered and dragged away, shouting: 'Why don't you just tell the misled people who come to you that there's no such thing as a godman running the lives of those he doesn't give a shit about. Why don't you just let people think for themselves? This city is full of greedy, demented capitalists, and you know what you're doing? You're pumping them up. You're telling them – you guys are okay. You guys are good. You can suck this city dry and kick your servants in the face as long as you sing birthday songs to me and repay your loans. I want you to stop this fucking charade. You don't have the truth. You want to know what the truth is ...'

Alone on the floor, Baba Sampige continued laughing.

~

Sophie woke up one Monday in her own flat and tried to shake off the numbness of the past weeks. She spent the morning scanning websites for job openings. Muku would join her in a week's time. She needed to find a job.

In the afternoon, she went to Star Titles to collect her pending salary cheque. The staff was polite – every week people left or were thrown out; they were used to it. When she was done with her work, Sophie headed to the balcony for a quick smoke. Maya was there, puffing nonchalantly.

'You're here!' exclaimed Sophie before she could stop herself and express her shock more politely. She had blanked Maya out but that did not mean that Maya had ceased to exist.

'I got two months' notice. What did you think ... that I'd just be dropped in the garbage can after all I've done for this company?'

'I didn't tell Naomi Picks a thing,' said Sophie defensively, thinking back to the accusation in Maya's email.

Maya kept looking at Sophie, trying to size her up. 'It doesn't matter. I owe you an apology too. He wouldn't have kicked you out if it weren't for me.'

'Not true. I was asking to be kicked out.'

Maya shrugged. 'Well ... maybe. You always messed up the fight sequences.'

'I hated fight sequences.'

'And I wouldn't have been there to shield you so it was inevitable that sooner or later you'd go.'

'It's okay, I'll get another job.'

Maya smiled indulgently at her and Sophie slowly edged away, took a deep breath and said, 'Got to go and write out job applications.'

Maya looked away and said, 'Smoke your cigarette at least.'

Eventually they went to Sophie's favourite pub, after Maya announced that she was going to vanish and the least Sophie could do was buy her a farewell drink. They sat on the upper floor and talked, awkwardly at first. The same jugs of piss-coloured beer, the same boys in dimly-lit corners cracking crude jokes, the same sanguine waiters.

Shanthi Gowda's mother had committed suicide. Maya had run into Shanthi – now a well-paid teacher in a coaching centre – who'd described the tragedy in graphic detail right there on the roadside.

'She went the old Indian way – hung herself with a sari from a ceiling fan wearing all of that heavy gold jewellery that had driven her mad. She'd been getting better, that's why she killed herself, Shanthi said. I guess when you're totally cracked you're somehow beyond the pain, but when you start to see things a little more clearly you get desperate,' said Maya.

Some Hamlet memory stirred in Sophie at this analysis of madness. Something about one who in suffering all, suffers nothing. How had she believed that it would be easy to get rid of Hamlet-Shamlet? Perhaps her father was right – *Hamlet* was the book that contained all the answers, just as Uncle Rock believed about Dylan.

'Listening to Shanthi talk in that absolutely natural way about her mother going made me think of my own mum. I try not to, it just starts up too many painful things, but maybe I will go and talk to her before I go. And to him. Weirdly, that chat with Shanthi calmed me down. Of all people! I've been wondering why she even stopped to talk to me. She knew I could never stand her when she was in Star Titles,' said Maya.

'She has nothing to do with you now, that's why. Now you can be civil to each other.'

Just as Sophie and Maya were being civil to each other. Sophie took a large gulp of beer. She wasn't saying much, anxious not to trigger anything in Maya that could not be stemmed. It was difficult to have those clear eyes boring into hers.

The waiter replaced their empty jug with a fresh, foaming one.

'So what have you lost?' Maya asked Sophie, pouring beer for her, and Sophie looked up startled, then laughed. *God, how can she always tell*?

'It's not Swami for sure, so what is it?'

'Madame Bovary,' said Sophie, even though Maya didn't read. 'Do you know what the best scene in the novel is?'

'Tell me.'

'Emma Bovary arrives in the village with her husband. It's a wet, cold night and they come into an inn where there's a fire going and a bored clerk is having his dinner. Emma doesn't see him. She goes to the fireplace, starts drying her clothes and the light plays on her skin. Leon is transfixed but Emma hasn't noticed that she's being watched. That scene is at the heart of the whole book. Everything will be destroyed, every last thing will be eaten by worms, but that moment will stay unchanged – Emma innocently drying herself and Leon looking at her. And no one's against anyone else, no one's hurt anyone, no one's disappointed – everyone and everything is innocence.'

'So how bad was it?' asked Maya.

Sophie nodded with her eyes closed, trying to make the subject disappear. Her grief was mysterious even to Maya who could always tell – what made people cry, when they were lying, how to manipulate them. Maya leaned over, took Sophie's chin in her hand and forced her face up.

'You okay?'

Sophie nodded. 'My sister's moving here.'

'And you?' she added.

'Going,' said Maya.

They considered each other in silence.

Sophie lit a cigarette. I'm so tired of you, America.

The Rest is Silence

Sophie stood next to a man sitting on a ladies seat. The front half of the bus was for ladies; if men happened to be sitting there, they were meant to get up – hurriedly, respectfully – and make way. But this man hadn't, not even after Sophie tapped him on the shoulder. So she'd just kept standing there, hoping to shame him into standing up at some point on her slow, long journey into town. A man behind her said, 'Madam, that is ladies seat.'

'I know but he won't get up.'

'Saar,' called out Sophie's benefactor. 'Idu ladies seat, saar.'

The seated man seemed not to hear.

Other men got into the act. Everyone was unanimous in their view that the seat rightfully belonged to Sophie.

But a large man with a large red tilak on his forehead disagreed. It's not a ladies seat, he said. He pointed at the image of a woman's face painted above the window. Everyone scrutinized it. The image was one of a row of identical faces, and meant to mark the last of the ladies seats. But which row exactly did it pertain to – the one on which the man was sitting, or the one before it? It was painted in between the two rows – there was room for confusion here.

An appeal was made to the conductor, but the conductor, shoving people aside in order to get to the front of the bus for his fares, could not be bothered. The complaints died down and the man remained sitting.

Sophie's benefactor said, 'Leave it, Madam. You please go to the front. There you might get some seat later. *These* people will not listen.'

Another crowded bus, another weekday morning, the same manic city whizzing past the window. It seemed to Sophie that Bangalore's buses got more crowded every day. Every time the bus came to a halt before yet another stop to let yet another bunch of eager people squeeze in, it allowed itself a tiny pause – just after it stopped and just before the first, still unsullied, person hoisted herself onto it, there hung a moment. And in that moment, when the people inside clung on even more tenaciously to their tiny patches of space and the people outside resolutely prepared to displace them, Sophie sensed a tremendous impossibility. Sometimes the bus yielded to this impossibility and would sail past upturned, expectant faces without stopping. Sophie would look out at them and say silently – see, I told you. It's not going to work. It's going to break down, all of it.

But here and there amidst the brutal chaos, like soldiers of some guerrilla army, were Bangalore's angels – the man who had tried to wrest a seat on the bus for her, the bakery-wallah who gave her his freshest loaves, the withered grannies at the grocer's who'd warn her if he tried to short-change her, the girl who'd share her rickshaw with Sophie if Sophie was going the same way and there wasn't, on some particularly bad morning, a chance in hell that she'd get a rickshaw to take her the two kilometres from the bus-stop to her office.

When she got to work, Sophie sank into her chair with the sigh she sighed every morning – an expression of relief at having got there and a recognition that the hassle of getting there was not worth what she actually did. Which was to read page after page of jargon-ridden prose from the world of business studies – essays and research papers on subjects like the stock preferences and investment behaviour of stock managers in Belgium, the efficacy of the generalisability theory in studying cross-nation business practices, the relationship between the goal orientation and performance of Taiwanese employees – and check them for consistency with the grammar book and style manual maintained by the particular journal in which they were to be published.

These were journals published in the UK and USA. Sophie was one of a hundred language editors hired by the journals via Opus, the publishing giant, which had started out with the books that Sophie had read as a child, but which now made big money collaborating with publishers abroad and outsourcing to India anything in the publishing field that could be outsourced. On the floor above Sophie's were a hundred copy editors, who had higher degrees in business management or economics, and on the floor above them another hundred people working on graphics and design. Sophie had been surrounded by fifty people in her earlier job and felt dwarfed, but now she was truly a cog in a machine, an ant among other stupidly industrious ants who just carried on tapping on their keyboards without a clue as to their impending fates. She earned less here than in her previous job and had to work harder. Ninety pages of text a day was the minimum requirement; one got an incentive of three rupees per page if one could pack in more.

Sophie had treated her soundtrack transcription job with amused cynicism but here the industrial scale of the operations and the dead seriousness of her colleagues – mostly women who in another era would have been housewives – gave her no scope to fool herself. Everyone here was a Shanthi Gowda, and you either had to keep your eyes trained on the computer nine hours a day (with a thirty-minute break for lunch) so you could collect your salary at the end of the month, or quit. But Sophie knew what it would be like to quit. It would be exactly like it was now; she would find some other job that was different from this one only in the details, and she'd be back to where she'd been in the first place. So instead she allowed herself to grow mesmerised by the boredom of her job. She shut out all thoughts and scanned page after page, pushing herself past the ninety-page barrier.

Today, she worked all morning and then skipped lunch and continued working. She had found a way of reading text that enabled her to ignore its meaning but notice a missing comma, an error in the way a book was referenced, an inconsistency in the naming of a business firm. Words became solid, three-dimensional objects whereas images were slithery and flat. Sometimes she lifted her eyes to look outside the open window, two consoles away, on her right, but all she could see was the office building across the road, its reflector glass walls hiding all evidence of what went on inside. On sunny days it captured the sky and Sophie would gaze at this inverted, shiny sky for some moments, her mind empty as a Buddha's, before returning to work.

At 6 o'clock that evening she shut down her computer, said goodbye to all the Shanthis around her, and headed for the door. She felt hollow with hunger and fatigue, but the fact that she'd been able to finish off 120 pages gave her a minor sense of victory.

The sound of a bus's brakes screeching violently made her stop and turn back. Two girls were gazing out in that still, concentrated way that meant something was going on in the street below.

'Accident,' one of them called out, her face towards the window. Everyone surged forward. And there, down on the street, was the thing that Sophie dreaded seeing every time – the man sprawled out with half his face crushed, the bicycle flung to one side, the bus frozen at an odd angle in the centre of the road, the crowd pressing down, and over everything an aura of shocking inevitability. Sophie forced herself to keep her eyes on the dead man. *Look at him, look at him,* she said to herself. He died so that you can live.

She pushed her colleagues aside, took the elevator down and walked out, ignoring the people jostling her, trying to get a glimpse of the accident victim. She felt fine. Nothing frightened her anymore – not walking into a shop in a plush mall, trying on clothes and then buying nothing. Not waking up in the middle of the night and being unable to go back to sleep. Not seeing a man crushed to death on the street.

~

Muku came towards her, swinging her bag, her hair in disarray from the rickshaw ride. They were in a swanky new nightclub.

'A pint gone already?' she asked.

'I didn't even notice,' replied Sophie, grimacing.

Her phone rang. It was the real estate broker, Sarath, who was on a perpetual mission to get Sophie a new house.

Bhatt's first few months of Baba Sampige-induced goodwill had worn off and he was starting to become the old Bhatt all over again – objecting to the smoking and reporting on how his neighbour Chinnappa was bad-mouthing Sophie. Even though Sophie had paid her thousand-rupee fine and delivered a written apology to the Resident's Welfare Association over the choultry incident, Chinnappa continued to see her as a direct threat to his moral principles. It remained to be seen how long Bhatt could resist the pressure of Chinnappa's voice in his ear.

Muku was convinced that they needed to move to a place where they could live in peace, so Sophie had contacted Sarath – the same broker who had found her the Bhatt house. Sarath kept phoning her with suggestions, but Sophie kept rejecting his offers because all the rents were out of her reach. Sarath had been a software engineer till he noticed that brokers made more money for less work. He seemed to be of Sophie's age and his arms and legs were of normal size but beneath his T-shirt great masses of fat wriggled as if he had stuffed cushions in there in a childish imitation of fat. He drove his car very fast and was never without his Ray Bans. Sarath disdained the idea of looking for apartments that suited Sophie's modest budget, and spent much phone time trying to convince her that she needed to shell out more to live in an even halfway decent place. 'Bill Gates ...' he'd say on the phone, with the air of someone who knows the man intimately. 'Bill is opening a new Microsoft centre in town and creating three thousand new jobs. Why do you think rents have gone up like this?'

Sarath made two per cent off every house he sold and got the equivalent of a month's rent for every house he arranged to have rented out. Swami had once calculated that Sarath, even if he sold a house a month and rented out two houses a month, must make at least twice what Sophie and Swami earned put together. 'But that's if we think of the minimum,' Swami had said, his eyes alight. 'His phone is ringing all the time, you try calling him ... it's always engaged. So it's possible that he's actually cracking a rental deal a week, and as for selling houses …' Sophie had switched off like she always did when the talk got too arithmetical.

Now Sarath was telling Sophie about two fantastic apartments she needed to check out right away. 'You see them first, we'll talk about rents later,' he said. 'Good location, two minutes from the main road, respectable neighbourhood, brand new building, good quality fittings, owners live in the States so they're not here to hassle you.' Sophie stayed quiet. He caught the hint. 'See, just last year I got you a great place for your budget. But things have changed. Bill Gates …'

Sophie tuned out and watched her sister order a drink, seventeen years old and trying to pass off as twenty-two. She looked fine, despite the city's foul air, the makeshift meals they ate, the packets of cigarettes they smoked sitting on the balcony in the evenings and talking about everything but the past, or playing with Mani who had fallen in love with Muku with a spontaneity that would make Sophie cry out loud with jealously.

Mani was now three years old and something had changed in him too. He no longer resisted his grandparents as much as he used to, instead spending long hours inside the locked gate, his face pressed between the bars, repeating the calls of the itinerant men and women who passed through the lane starting from the crack of dawn – the sellers of tender coconuts, gunny sacks full of puffed or beaten rice, orangey roses, brilliant rangoli powders, assorted greens, starched petticoats and cotton nighties, small river fish, packets of popcorn, apples and mosambis, potted plants, ice-cream from a red ice-cream van, cucumbers, brooms, seedless papayas, the knife-grinders and sofa repairers and silver jewellery polishers, the buyers of old newspapers and the travelling mendicants blowing piercingly into their horns. Once in a while, he would reveal a little of his former spirit, break out of his prison, come upstairs to Sophie's flat and raid her fridge when she wasn't looking.

But the girls had a maid to clean up when Mani messed the floor or when they spilled tea. It was the woman Sophie had spotted on the construction site, tying her toddler to a block of granite, the woman with the ready smile, whose husband beat her. Sophie had seen her being beaten again, taken the woman home and invented a cleaning job for her, even though she had always resisted the idea of having a maid. It was hard to tell whether Priya preferred the life of being Sophie and Muku's maid to the life of carrying cement up scaffoldings, just as it had been hard to gauge the feelings of the rickshaw driver who'd been beaten up by the Punjabi men on the day Sophie missed her flight. The enduring mystery of other people's feelings.

When Sarath eventually hung up, Sophie asked Muku, 'What have you done to your face?'

'Tried eyeliner.'

'You look like me.'

'No way.'

'You look exactly like me,' Sophie said, smiling at her discovery.

Muku didn't argue; she just swirled her mango daiquiri and said, 'College sucks. I'm getting a job as soon as I can.'

~

'I *can* survive another year and a half. But college just doesn't seem connected to anything. Everyone feels that way. They all want to get out and start making money.'

They had spent an hour on the subject and got nowhere.

'Start by asking yourself what your purpose in life is,' said Sophie.

'How come Anu looks so tall?'

Anu was standing by the entrance, squinting in the dark. The sisters waved to her and she wobbled over in the high heels she had recently taken to wearing.

Anu unpacked her shopping for them to see – all of it boxes upon boxes of shoes. She had developed a shoe fetish since Anil proposed to her – Anil, the birthday party boy whom Sophie associated with that night when it was so late things started to curdle and Ringo put a knife in Rukshana. Anu and Shiva had split after Shiva's attack on Baba Sampige; their arguments had turned so bitter that there was no going back.

In two weeks' time Anu would marry Anil, though she'd only really got to know him since the night of the murder. They were going to honeymoon in Maldives. They were going to move to

Australia. Muku's eyes widened as Anu lined them up on the table – sparkling, sequined sandals, sleek stilettos, studded slip-ons, soft sneakers, satin slippers. Muku caressed them, held them to her cheek, counted them, and asked Anu how much each had cost. Anu had already forgotten. She'd gone silly with happiness.

Then Anil came with his shades on and he dandily hugged all three women one by one. Seeing Muku's delight at the shoes, he said, 'Let's go and get you a pair for the wedding.'

And Anu said, 'Yes and clothes too. They haven't even started thinking about what they're going to wear for the wedding.'

Muku cast Sophie the tiniest of glances, seeking some subtle sign of big sister approval.

'Don't be ridiculous,' said Sophie. 'Let her get a job first before you start putting ideas in her head.'

'Sophie, we're just heading out to do some more shopping. Do you mind if we give your sister a birthday present? Do we have your permission?' said Anil.

'It's not my birthday,' said Muku.

'It will be some time,' said Anil. 'Consider it an advance gift. Or a belated one.'

'She's only seventeen,' said Sophie.

'Make some effort on behalf of my wedding, Sophie please. Anand and Anandi are coming all the way from their ashram in Kerala – breaking out of God knows what kind of half-starved lifestyle to spend that one day with us,' said Anu.

Swami arrived, talking on his cellphone, with Shiva in tow. He had begged Sophie to meet him one last time and she could not think of a reason to refuse.

'I love the idea of you getting married, Anu,' said Sophie soothingly, inadvertently catching Shiva's eye. He was still friends with everyone, despite Anu's betrayal. Yet like Mani, Shiva had in some sense given up the fight.

'This city is going to the dumps,' he said.

'And?' asked Sophie cautiously, expecting a peroration, a lecture, a rant.

'Laugh. That was a joke,' he said. They all laughed dutifully. This was possibly the first joke Shiva had cracked in his life.

'Ringo Saar got his sentence,' Swami announced and they

all went quiet. 'Fifteen years. The fact that he had the knife in his car looked bad on him. Otherwise he might have got away with less.'

Sophie looked at her friends. She knew they were thinking of life fifteen years from now, and she knew that it seemed to them exactly the same as the present. Their own apartments, their own cars, jobs that made them money which they could leave for jobs that made them more money, freedom to sit in any bar and drink anything they wanted, to holiday in the Maldives, to buy eight pairs of shoes at once. Ringo Saar would come back and find them in their forties, unchanged.

'Let's go, Sophie,' said Swami.

'You got it?' screeched Anu.

Swami had finally got it – his car – a sleek, bright, cherry-red, luxuriously elongated, new-smelling, upholstered in black leather, and, to Sophie, no-name car. He'd brought it right up to the door of the club.

Sophie followed him out and Swami opened the passenger door for her. He waited for her to express shock and delight but all she said was, 'Did it have to be so big?' They took off, honking imperiously at the rickshaws trying to manoeuvre their way through the usual chaos, and the suicidal cyclists.

They were going to see Ringo Saar before he started on his sentence the following day. Rukshana was already a memory and all that remained was the fate of Ringo Saar. Sophie had held off till it seemed cruel to hold off any longer. Outside the Central Jail, waiting for the gates to open, were people wearing the look that one saw on the faces of visitors to hospitals, that refugees of war and famine wore, the expression that was stamped on the audience of the accident Sophie had seen a few hours ago – a stone-faced look of utter resignation.

When they entered and found Ringo Saar, she saw, from across the mesh, that he had grown thinner.

'So what are you going to do about it?' he asked, shrugging at his own question. All three of them laughed hollow laughs, Sophie unable to ask Ringo the question that recurred in all her nightmares about him – why didn't you let her live? Why had he found nothing in himself to stop him, why had he not searched harder?

She saw the bones sticking out from his cheeks and neck

and she realized how wrong she'd been to think that she had a role to play in this tragedy. Ringo had scripted this himself and she had no right to claim a share of it. She ought to have just stood to one side and respected his suffering, the way her other friends did. Around them people shouted as if an ocean instead of a wall of wire separated them from those on the other side.

Sophie had brought Ringo a present – her childhood copy of *Vivekananda: Awakener of Modern India*. The guard standing on watch flipped through it slowly, then opened a hatch to pass it on to Ringo. Ringo looked at her with a fleeting expression of surprise, then said, 'What Sophie, I didn't know you're into spreading the word and all that,' and they laughed again. Everything was potentially funny.

Ringo read out the epigraph to the book – 'The older I grow, the more everything seems to me to lie in manliness. This is my new gospel.' He nodded as if he understood perfectly and slipped the small book into the pocket of his ill-fitting prison uniform.

Sophie wanted to ask Ringo what his parents felt – his cheerful, chocolate making mother and his alcoholic, prawn millionaire father. She wanted to know what he dreamt of and which dreams recurred. She wanted to know what Rukshana had said when she knew he was killing her. She wanted to know what he would do over the next fifteen years instead of drumming, what would he do with his hands when they itched?

But Ringo, she realized, was not going to reflect on these larger questions. He was not going to sit there and lament the loss of his future. For it was his life disappearing along with Rukshana's – baby, let me follow you down, as Uncle Rock would have put it. But no big themes. Instead, Ringo started describing with a poetry that Sophie didn't think him capable of, the meals in the Andhra restaurant near his house – the one thing, he said, he would miss the most, when Swami asked him.

He described, as if these were miracles, the steel tumblers, the banana leaves you ate on which matched the green banana leaf shaped menu, the chutney pudi holder with four kinds of fieriness in its four compartments, the taste of just rice and ghee before you tipped the sambar into it. He explained the fine differences between the many chicken dishes – Gongura, Guntur, Kakinada – the waiters with their pails of vegetables, the superiority of the biriyanis, the greatness of the salt lassi, the unsurpassable perfection of the rasam, the regular lunch timers who always sat at their appointed places, said a single word – 'Meals' – and then never made a sound till the burp accompanying the bill-paying. Sophie, who didn't care for that kind of food, to whom only burgers and noodles and fizzy drinks were exotic, decided that this is what she would do every week for the next fifteen years – go to the Andhra restaurant Ringo loved and get him packets of as much food as he could eat. She looked mournfully at his thinness again and then it was time to go.

Back in the car, sitting in her oversized seat, the noise and smells and jolts cut out, the air-conditioning on, the music on the stereo conjuring up its own images, the pot-holes and road humps distant, gentle occurrences, Sophie felt like they were sliding in a silk cocoon through Bangalore. She nestled deeper into her seat and started to think. First – as Swami explained to her the beauties of his car (its suspension, its steering, its seats, its stereo) – she thought about him. He'd been promoted. It had been noticed – the seriousness with which he treated the clients, the concern he felt for them and their credit card machines, the effort he made to understand and be understood. He'd become a trainer now. He and his trainer colleagues taught newcomers in batches of forty, six weeks at a time. He no longer needed to work nights. He looked like he had arrived at the destination of that endless journey he'd been on. He'd told her on the phone that at his present salary, he'd be able to pay off the loan on the car in three years.

Sophie thought about Muku, moving from one shop window to another now, trying to decide and knowing that any decision would be a compromise. Is that what she would replace the rebellions of old with? Shopping? She thought of her mother who wanted to live in a bare room in a dharamshala in Benaras with her *Bhagavad Gita*, and her father who wanted to live in a bare room in Shantiniketan with his *Hamlet*. Now they were in the only place Sophie had ever known them to be – the Shillong cottage.

Sophie tried to think back to the map that Shiva had drawn for them, but she had no clue where they were heading and Swami was silent now, lulled by the sleek movement of his velvet beast. Sophie thought of how benign Bangalore looked on the other side of those thick windows – the people waiting for buses no longer seemed desperate to her and the lights of a hospital they passed were like beacons of kindness. She thought of the chance encounters that the city had, with an almost human intelligence, granted her.

'Ring Road,' said Swami, as they zoomed down it, a beautifully smooth, gently curving highway. Sophie thought he might be drawing a circle around the city too – laying claim to it with his car.

The old man was singing about pain – there's not even room enough to be anywhere, it's not dark yet but it's getting there. It was the Dylan album Ribor had given her when she was leaving Shillong the first time, even though she didn't care about Dylan. Half an hour later, they were in Marathahalli. The evening crush of people on those sandy, potholed, garbage-strewn, once-pavements, seemed to Sophie, from this side of the window, to belong to some savage past and she watched it numb with distance. Between the multiplexes and shopping malls and the narrow road over which cars impatiently spilled, were squeezed an impossible number of perpetually in motion men and women – shopping couples, chaat-wallahs manoeuvring their pushcarts, men trying to park their bikes, sellers of tinselly windmills, groups of teenagers, and even, right there on the road-side and seemingly oblivious to the possibility of being trampled upon, women selling ear-buds and toothpicks from small squares of plastic spread on the ground. Every few minutes, Sophie spotted another one of them. They were so dark they could have been confused with the night but their bright blue bits of plastic gave them away.

Eventually they reached the sprawling information technology campuses on the outskirts of the city, those gleaming, self-contained, futuristic worlds that showed it was possible to do away with the things that the rest of the imperfect city was still saddled with – bazaars, temples, itinerant hawkers, religious mendicants, cows, vendors of fried food and fruit juice, blaring loudspeakers, roadside shrines, slums, pavement bookshops, flower-sellers, film posters. They drove further and came up against looming corporate offices and giant apartment blocks, which looked as if they'd arisen overnight on those desert lots, nothing but dust between them. Swami pulled up, killed the engine and stretched his arms over his head.

'Hey, I read the book,' he said casually.

Sophie turned her whole body to look at him. She had agreed to go on this one drive with him as a kind of farewell. But he was referring now to some long ago pact, some unspoken deal.

Other cars roared past and then all was quiet again; in the apartments before them, lights came on and went off in a pattern that could not be decoded.

Swami had read *Swami and Friends* and was still himself! Where was the expected transformation? Sophie looked out at the cars. Up to the point when they had actually passed by, it seemed inevitable that they should crash into them.

Swami cleared his throat. 'It was okay.'

Sophie said, 'Let's keep driving.'

The traffic had thinned and Swami drove with a speed that could have been joy. The car, with its twinkling dials, turned into a spaceship – below them lay Bangalore and they were flying over open-mouthed, late night shops and trudging daily wage workers and smashed stray dogs.

I don't want to feel the knife edge of anything ever pressing into me again, thought Sophie. Whitefield Road became Old Madras Road became Swami Vivekananda Road.

When they came up to Trinity Circle and joined the cars swarming excitedly in every direction, freed of traffic signals at this hour of the night, Swami turned to Sophie and said, 'The only problem we'll have in life from now on is the problem of where to find parking space.'

Acknowledgements

Many thanks to: Gordon Wise, my always morale-boosting agent; Priya Kapoor and Nandita Bhardwaj for putting their weight behind this novel; the Charles Wallace India Trust which funded my stint as writer-in-residence at the University of Kent, Canterbury and Richard Alford of CWIT for his generosity; all staff at the University's Department of English, particularly Caroline Rooney, Lucy Ellman and Todd McEwen for the conversations and the wine; Arul Mani, Chiki Sarkar, Stellan Wahlström, Judy Das, Sumana Chandrashekar for their many enthusiasms and suggestions; Amitav Ghosh for believing; all the Hasans for various Hasan reasons; and Zac as always: for dreaming up *Neti, Neti* with me, for patiently reading several drafts, and for everything in between.